ALICE & JEAN

ALICE & JEAN

LILY HAMMOND

sapphicabooks

Always for you, my darling Valerie

CHAPTER 1

Alice switched off the radio and listened to the birds instead. They piped their songs in through the open window, telling her about spring and how the sunshine slanted across the branches where they perched in the apple tree. Alice wondered if she'd ever noticed any of this before and found that perhaps she'd missed a lot of it.

She'd been getting the children's breakfast ready. The porridge warmed on the old coal range and she blew an errant hair from her eyes before smoothing it back and checking the clock.

It was almost time. She had butterflies in her stomach and cocking her head, she listened again. There it was – the cheerful shout of voices out on the street. Fumbling with the ties, Alice tore off the worn and dirty apron she'd put on to light the unruly range and tugged on the one she'd made the week before. It was a pretty red and white pattern that made her feel cheerful just to see it, but did nothing to settle her stomach.

'Milk's here, Mama!' Tilly shouted from the other room,

and Alice heard the sound of the front door being tugged open by the small child.

'Tilly,' she called. 'Don't you go out onto the road!' She bustled down the hallway after her daughter, ready to catch the child's skirts.

'Morning Tilly,' a voice outside said and Alice felt her heart pound faster, and she pressed a hand against her chest, feeling the heat of her flesh through the fabric of dress and apron.

It was a warm, rich voice and she hurried toward it, hands flying from stomach to skirt to hair. She stood on the doorstep at last, flustered despite herself, and hoping that she hadn't accidently chewed off her lipstick during the morning's wait.

'Hullo Alice,' the same voice said, accompanied by a smile that reached cocoa-coloured eyes dancing in a sun-golden face. 'One pint of our finest, and a bottle of cream – what's the cream for, Alice my love? Are you baking me a cake?' The voice was full of laughter and seeped in under Alice's pale skin and warmed her from the inside out.

Tilly turned to her. 'Can we bake a cake, Mama? Please?'

It took a moment for Alice to answer the child. All the words were backed up in her throat, coating it like she'd swallowed a mouthful of honey.

Then she shook herself out of her fancies. She was being silly. Her hand patted Tilly's shoulder.

'We are going to bake a cake, Tilly,' she said. 'That's exactly what the cream is for. We're going to make a nice Victoria sponge.' To her ears, her voice sounded clogged with cream already.

Tilly looked up at her. 'Can Jean come help us eat it?'

Jean grinned at her, pushing the small bottle of cream into her hands. 'Victoria sponge is my favourite,' she said to the child, and looking at the mother.

Tilly piped up. 'Come for afternoon tea. It's Mama's birthday!'

Those milk chocolate eyes warmed another degree and Alice shifted under their gaze, skin prickling against the soft cotton she wore.

'Happy birthday, Alice,' Jean said, her voice low, a whisper Alice imagined she could almost feel against her ear. She wanted to fan herself, suddenly hot, and then blushed deeper, alarmed at the way her body was responding. It wasn't right. Jean was, well, Jean. A woman.

She opened her mouth. 'Thank you,' she said. 'Please come.'

The eyes blinked at her.

'For cake.' She cleared her throat. 'This afternoon.'

The driver of the milk truck shouted. 'Oi Jean, we don't got all day. Tell Alice she's looking right pretty today.' Laughing, he dropped an empty crate in the back of the small truck and climbed behind the wheel with a wave and a wink.

'You're looking very pretty today, Alice,' Jean said with a grin. 'I'd be honoured to share your birthday cake with you.'

'And me,' Tilly butted in.

Jean smiled down at the three-year-old and swept her cap off in a sudden bow, backing away from their doorstep.

'And you, Tilly, my lass,' she said, laughing again.

With a wave, she was gone, sliding into the truck with Tim Fry, and rollicking off down the potholed road.

'Let me carry the cream,' Tilly said, little hands reaching

up, grasping at the bottle and breaking Alice from her reverie.

She looked down at her daughter. 'Only if you're very careful,' she said, arranging the child's two small hands around it so it wouldn't slip.

'I'm careful,' Tilly said, little pink tongue poking out from between her lips in concentration.

'Yes, you are,' Alice agreed, straining for a last glance at the road, then turning into the house, following her daughter into the dimness and wondering what on earth she'd just done, inviting Jean around for cake. She arrived back in the kitchen and stood there for a moment, just blinking, her mind blank.

Tilly put the cream bottle on the table and climbed up onto a chair to look at it. 'Look Jack,' she said when her brother came in the room. 'We got cream!'

Jack's eyes widened. 'Can we have some with our porridge, Mum?'

She came back to herself, standing in the kitchen feeling their two pairs of eyes on her. Her hands were cold from holding the pint of milk. She licked her lips.

'Okay,' she said. 'Just a little though.'

'The rest is for the cake,' Tilly said in a confidential manner to her brother. 'Mama's birthday cake. It's Mama's birthday today.'

Jack turned his gaze on Alice and she looked at him, his eyes a grey-blue under sandy hair so like his father's.

'Happy birthday, Mum,' he said, all the seriousness of his eight years behind the words. 'Let me make you a cup of tea.' He took the milk bottle from her and put it in the cold store, then led her to the table where she sat automatically.

'The porridge,' she said.

He nodded and took three bowls down from the shelf, setting them on the table then going back to the range.

'Get the spoons, Tilly,' he said.

The little girl slid off the bench and scuttled over to the cutlery drawer. Alice watched both of them in bemusement.

A moment later, the porridge was divided between the three bowls, and Jack was struggling to make tea with the heavy kettle. He wouldn't let her help him, though and in a moment, her teapot was filled, cup and saucer ready. He stood back to check his handiwork and Alice leaned over and kissed his cheek.

'You're a wonder, Jack,' she said. 'Best son ever.'

He beamed under her attention, then took his place at the head of the table. It had been his father's seat, until they'd had word from the army that Terry Holden had died under the hot sun somewhere in the Pacific in 1944, fighting the Japanese. The day after they'd had the news, young Jack had taken his father's chair at the table. Afterwards, Alice had gone into her bedroom and wept for both father and son.

'What sort of cake are you going to make, Mum?' he asked, spooning porridge into his mouth, the unruly cowlick on his head bobbing with the movement.

'Oh,' Alice said. 'I was thinking a nice Victoria sponge, for something special. Mrs Reuben will let us have some eggs.' The Reuben's' had a small farm just out of town, and Mrs Reuben, round and jolly, had taken a shining to Tilly and Jack. Her own three sons were long grown, though only one had made it back from the war.

'Jean is coming to help us eat it,' Tilly said, unable to keep any news under her blonde curls.

The boy looked startled for a moment, his eyes going to his mother. She stilled the commotion under her breast and simply gave him a smile.

'Tilly invited her,' she said.

Tilly pouted in her porridge. 'No I didn't,' she said. 'You did, Mama.'

Alice pushed away the bowl and took a sip of her tea, hand trembling minutely. Had she invited Jean? She didn't look at the children.

Had she really?

CHAPTER 2

It was too warm to wear a coat. Alice took off her apron and put on a cardigan instead, tucking her hair under a scarf. She captured Tilly and popped the squirming child into the pram.

'Hold still, Tilly,' she scolded. 'You'll wiggle your way right out.'

'But where we going, Mama? I wanted to play with Prudence. We're going to have a tea party.'

'Well, your doll will have to come for a ride with us instead. We need some eggs.'

The girl wiggled in her seat, her dolly under her arm as she held onto the sides of the pram. They bumped down over the step and down the short path to the road.

'For the cake!' she crowed.

'For the cake,' Alice agreed. 'But we have to go see Grandma, first.'

Tilly stopped her wiggling and clapped her hands over her eyes. She sat there blind for a long moment before dropping her plump little fingers and looking at her mother in dismay.

'I know, sweetheart,' Alice consoled her. 'But she is my mother, and your grandmother, and she likes to see us.' She forced a smile on her face. 'It's a special day for her too, after all.'

A tiny frown burrowed between Tilly's eyebrows. 'Why?' she asked.

'It's kind of a birthday for her too, don't you think? When I was born, she became a mother. That's special.'

Tilly thought about it, then lay herself back on the pillow in the pram, staring up at her mother as they walked alongside the road.

'So you get kinda birthdays when Jack and me have them?'

Alice nodded.

'You don't get any presents,' Tilly said.

'I don't need to. I got you two, and those were the best presents ever.' Alice smiled at her daughter, and they trundled from one side of the town to the other, to the shady street where her mother's house sat back from the road, white and lovely. She opened her mouth to say something, then closed it again. Tilly was too young to understand. It wouldn't be fair to ask her not to say anything about Jean coming for afternoon tea.

'Ready?' she said, speaking more to herself than Tilly. On a deep breath, she bounced the pram down the path and parked it outside the door. Gathering Tilly in her arms, she knocked and waited to say hello to her mother.

'There you are,' her mother said when she came to the door, lips pursed. When she turned her head for a kiss, Alice touched her lips dutifully to the powdered cheek.

'How are you, Mother?' she asked.

'Can't complain,' the older woman said, although Alice knew that before long she would indeed be complaining.

'It's Mama's birthday,' Tilly said, set down on the floor and twining in and out of Alice's legs, peering up at her grandmother.

'Yes, it is. Come this way, Alice. I have a pot of tea made.' The stiff back was implacable. 'And a gift for you, of course.'

'Mother,' Alice said, stifling her sigh. 'You needn't have.' She stepped inside and followed her mother into the dim depths of the old villa. The floorboards creaked under her steps and she listened to them echo about the house, as though no one had ever stepped foot there before and it was alarmed at the intrusion.

More fancies. She shook her head. Seemed she was full of them, lately. Maybe it was the spring that had blossomed outside, pushing the bright faces of daffodils and crocus up from the soil.

'I needn't have,' her mother said, and it took a moment for Alice to remember what they'd been talking about. 'But you are my daughter, and there is an obligation to look after you.' She cast an iron glance back at Alice. 'Lord knows, someone needs to. You're not doing a good job of it yourself.'

'Please, Mother,' Alice said, Tilly silently holding her hand. 'Please don't start.'

They arrived in the drawing room, and Geraldine Thomas gestured at the small table set for morning tea beneath the window. There were three chairs and Alice winced at the sight of them, knowing the next half an hour would be torture as she made Tilly sit still upon the chair set for her.

'I've put a cushion on the chair for the child,' her mother said. 'And you know I must start, as you say it, Alice. Someone has to say things, and it's my duty as your mother, since you no longer have a husband.'

Alice looked down at her hands, clasped white-knuckled around Tilly's waist. It took an effort of will to place the little girl on the chair and sink into the one next to it.

Her mother gave her a smile and poured hot tea from the flowered china pot sitting on the white table cloth. 'There's a little cordial for the child,' she said.

Alice poured some of the orange drink in a glass. 'Her name is Tilly, Mother. You can say it.'

Geraldine looked surprised. 'I'm aware of what my own granddaughter is named, Alice, there's no need to be rude.'

It was a waste of time. Biting down on a sigh, Alice picked up her cup and gave Tilly a side-long smile. They'd stay for the lecture, then be on their way. Outside the sun was shining, and she had a nice little spectacles case she'd sewn that Mrs Reuben would be pleased to have in exchange for some eggs and a little butter.

Her heart lifted on a cresting wave, the season's lightness coursing suddenly through her body.

'Your colour is high today, Alice,' her mother said. 'Are you coming down with something?'

She shook her head. 'Not at all, Mother,' she answered. 'I've never felt better. It's a beautiful day.'

Her mother nodded heavily. 'Yes, I must get out in the garden today and see what needs tending to.' She said it as if it would be a chore. Her thin lips pressed against the delicate china of the cup.

'I was thinking this really can't go on, you know,' she said suddenly, putting the cup back on the saucer with a determined, clinking sound.

Alice drew breath, glanced at Tilly who was staring outside at a black bird on the lawn. 'You know how I feel about it, Mother,' she said. 'We have a home.'

The snort in response was quick in coming. 'Alice, your home is a house barely standing. A grimy four rooms. I'm surprised it has running water. It should be demolished.'

'Nonetheless, it is our home. We are comfortable there.' Alice's shoulders tightened, and she despised the defensiveness that crept into her voice.

'You are to move in here,' Geraldine declared. 'You and the children.' She waved a hand at the room. 'It is gross stupidity for you to stay there when you could quite easily come back home.' She blinked at her daughter, the lines of her face set. 'Until you marry again, it makes complete sense for you to live here. Your father would have wanted it.'

'My father is not here.'

'God rest his soul. He would be furious to see where you are living. How you get by, I've no idea!'

Alice looked away, eyes sweeping over the furniture in the sitting room, all the occasional tables, the plant stands, the knick-knacks everywhere. Her mother had been thirty-five when Alice had been born, and still lived as though in a different era.

It was not a place for children. Alice knew that from experience. And her mother was wrong about how her father would have felt. He would have wanted Alice to be happy.

'We will stay where we are,' she said. 'It might not be

much, but it is our home, and it is where we lived as a family. If you want to help, there are better ways to do it.'

Her mother shook her head, the grey hair pulled tightly back against the skull in a harsh bun. 'It is not even your own home,' she said, ignoring Alice's last statement. 'Your husband did not even own it.'

Alice tried to ignore the sneering way her mother said the word husband. Neither had liked the other. This issue of her house was dangerous territory. The fact that she did not own the house she and her children lived in was a cross Alice found it difficult to bear. Because of the woman sitting across the small table from her. She lived in fear that her mother would take her landlord aside and order him to evict Alice and her children.

She closed her eyes for a moment, breathing in through her nose, trying to stay calm. Luckily, Bob Forrester was a good man, and had no liking himself for Alice's mother. He wouldn't turn her out onto the street.

Not as long as Alice could pay the rent every month, that was. In her lap, her hands twisted together.

'Let's talk about something nice, Mother,' she said. 'How is the good Mrs McMurtry?'

Rowena McMurtry was her mother's closest ally. That was the only way to put it.

'We're having cake today, Grandma,' Tilly said, unable to hold in the news any longer. She twisted on her chair and got up to sit on her knees, leaning over the table.

Her grandmother frowned at her. 'Sit down properly, child,' she said.

Tilly paid no attention, and Alice put a restraining hand on her, but it was too late.

'Mrs Reuben is giving us eggs and butter and Mama and me going to make cake and then Jean is going to come help us eat it!' A quick pause for breath in the rigid silence of the room. 'She's coming for afternoon tea!'

Geraldine Thomas sat stiffly in her chair for a full minute after this pronouncement, then turned her gaze onto her daughter. Her eyes were a washed-out and faded blue, but they could still convey considerable disapproval.

'This wouldn't be Jean Reardon, would it, Alice? Who worked for Jim Dempsey until he had to fire her? I only know of that one Jean.'

From thick with honey earlier in the day, Alice's throat now was dry with sand. She swallowed, and it made a rasping sound.

'She's really very nice, Mother,' Alice said. 'And she's only coming for afternoon tea.'

Her mother blinked at her. 'You are a respectable woman, Alice. A woman like that shouldn't be setting foot anywhere near your house.'

Alice licked her lips. 'A woman like exactly what, Mother?' she said.

The eyes gazed at her with contempt. 'I'm sure you're aware of the reputation Jean Reardon has, Alice. Do not play the stupid innocent with me.'

'But I am innocent, Mother. Whatever you want to accuse me of by seeking Jean's simple friendship is beyond me.' The words fell limply from her mouth and she hoped her mother wouldn't notice.

Because when it came to Jean, she didn't feel innocent at all. She didn't even want to. The dancing brown eyes came to mind again, and she felt faint under their gaze.

Her mother was watching her. 'It is entirely inappropriate, Alice, and I forbid the relationship.'

'There is no relationship!'

'She's gonna eat cake with us,' Tilly said, and her bottom lip trembled even while she did not understand the conversation.

'The woman enjoyed the war too much,' Geraldine said. 'The men being away. She is entirely unsuitable, and hearing this has made up my mind completely.'

Alice stared at her.

'You and the children will move in here. I will organise everything.' She turned away to the window, her back decided. 'Your gift is on the hall table. Take it on the way out.' She spoke without looking at Alice. 'I will contact you with some help to move your things. You won't need anything but clothes and personal items.'

Alice stared at her mother, speechless. She tried to think of something to say, but a queasy knot of terror and fury tied itself in her tongue and no words came. After a blank moment, she stood, plucked up Tilly and turned on her heel, stalking out of the room on unsteady legs. She closed the door to the drawing room, blotting out the picture on her mother's intractable back.

'Mama?' Tilly said, a small finger touching Alice's cheek and coming away wet.

'Never mind, Tilly,' she said. 'Everything's okay.' She sniffed and wiped a hand across her face, then walked down the hallway back to the front door.

Her birthday present sat on the small table beside the door, a small white envelope. Alice knew without looking what it contained. Swallowing, she stared at it for a long moment, then left it where it was and went out the door.

She couldn't bring herself to take her mother's money, no matter how much she needed it.

CHAPTER 3

Jean walked back down the hallway in the boarding house towards her room. She'd scrubbed herself clean, looking at the big cast iron tub and wishing she had time for a bath too. But a glance at her wristwatch told her that if she wanted to get there on time, a quick dunk in the basin was all she could afford.

There was a pounding under her breastbone she was trying to ignore. Invited for cake by Alice Holden! She shook her damp hair, not quite certain how it had all happened.

A quick stop in her room and she picked up the bunch of flowers she'd splurged on for the birthday girl. Usually when she was out and about, she would just pick some of the prettiest blooms from the fields, but not this time. She'd taken herself into the florist's shop in town and stood itching with self-consciousness under the lady's gaze as she ordered the prettiest posy there.

But Alice Holden deserved it. A smile hovered around Jean's lips. Alice had been making an appearance in the mornings more and more often, and Jean had flirted with her as a matter of course. It was what she did. Just a cheeky, harmless bit of flirtation. It made her laugh. Made everyone laugh. Mostly. Some of the old biddies were a bit stern, but in general, everyone had a good time. It was all a bit of fun.

But Alice, with her kaleidoscope eyes, hazel, some mornings brown, sometimes green, and her waving honey-coloured hair – what a picture she was. Jean blinked, hand tightening on the posy. She'd have to step carefully here. This might mean something.

Outside and it was a perfect day. In the distance Mount Egmont sat on the horizon wearing perfect robes of snow. Closer, the breeze rattled cheerfully about, bringing with it the sharp salt tang of the sea. Breathing deep, Jean turned her feet towards the little street on the edge of town, where Alice and her two children lived in a ramshackle little place that she still kept spit-polished to a happy shine.

The school bell sounded, and Jean was overtaken in a rush of children spilling out of the building. She laughed at their rough and tumble as they surrounded her, then moved on, leaving her high and dry on the footpath like a piece of flotsam.

One kid, however, she found dawdling behind her, heavy boots kicking at a stone and his hands dug deep in the pockets of his shorts.

'Jack?'

He nodded shyly at her from under sandy brown hair. She smiled at him, thinking how much he looked like his dad.

'I reckon we're going the same way,' she said. 'What do you say – can I walk with you?'

Another nod, the eyes downcast to the dusty footpath, but

he kicked the stone into the gutter and caught silently up with her.

'So,' she said, not looking at him anymore, but gazing up at the blue sky. 'Good day for cake, huh?'

'It's Mum's birthday,' the boy blurted out.

Jean nodded. 'Yeah. It is.'

Walking next to her, Jack seemed to be chewing over some fathomless problem. Jean stuck her hands in her own pockets and hummed a song she'd heard on the radio. She didn't know what it was called, but it was cheerful enough for the tune to stick in her mind.

The boy made his move at last, pulling a hand from the depths of his pocket and holding something out in the palm of his hand. Jean bent over to look as they walked.

'I got something for Mum,' he said. 'Won it specially for her on the playground.' He rubbed his fingers over the glass marble. It sparkled sapphire blue in the sunlight.

'It's a real beauty,' Jean said, nodding in approval.

'The boy I won it from got it from an American soldier.' There was a touch of wonder in his voice.

'Bet he played hard to keep it then,' Jean said. 'You did good.'

He looked up at her with a fierce expression. 'I wanted it to give it to Mum. Blue is her favourite colour.'

That was a handy piece of information. Jean filed it away for future reference.

They passed Alan Farmer stacking oranges outside his grocery shop and Jean gave him a wave.

'You know him?' Jack asked.

'Alan? Yes, he's a good guy.'

Alice's son nodded, then dropped his head again. Jean watched him for a moment, then cleared her throat.

'She's going to love it, you know,' she said, nodding at the marble still clenched in his fist.

He nodded, sniffed, then sent her an anguished glance that reminded her the kid was only seven or eight. Still a child.

'I haven't anything to wrap it in.'

Ah, so that was the problem. She tilted her head, pretending to ponder the question. A smile bloomed on her face and she pointed over the road. The kid's gaze followed her finger.

'The drapers?' he asked.

'You got it.' Jean nodded sagely. 'Come with me.' She stepped onto the road, looking both ways for traffic to set a good example, then strode out for the other side. Jack trotted along at her ankles.

'What's in there?' he asked, worry threading through his voice.

'Something we want,' Jean said and opened the door to the silver tinkling of a bell. She ushered Jack into the dimness and stood there a moment, waiting for her eyes to adjust, then led him to the great wooden counter, scanning the displays of cloth, hats, artificial flowers, and jewellery.

'Hi Jean,' the voluptuous blonde smiling behind the counter said. 'What can I do for you today?'

Jean pulled the boy in front of her. 'Susan,' she said. 'This young man needs something.'

Susan blinked her big cow eyes at her.

'It's his mum's birthday, and he's gone and won her the biggest, most beautiful marble in the school yard.' She leaned forward over the counter, judiciously keeping the bunch of flowers knee-height out of sight. 'All's he needs now is some pretty tissue paper to wrap it in.' She gave Susan a winning smile and lifted her eyebrows in entreaty.

Susan looked at her dubiously for a moment, then shifted her gaze to the boy and softened. With a smile back at Jean, she glanced out the door behind the shop, then leaned her curves over the counter and peered down at Jack.

'Something special, is it?' she said.

The boy nodded, face flushed but solemn. He lifted up his hand and spread his fingers wide. The marble gleamed there in the low light in all its glory.

Jean gave a low whistle. 'It's a real corker, all right. What do you say, Suzy? His mum's going to love it.'

'Sure she is,' Susan said. 'It's the nicest marble I've ever seen.'

The boy's eyes went from Jean to Susan. They were almost as big as the marble.

'So, what do you reckon? A pretty little piece of tissue paper to wrap it in?'

Another glance at the door to the draper's office, then a conspiratorial smile.

'I don't think Mr McDougal will mind,' she said. 'It will only take a little piece.' She straightened and opened a draw set into the heavy counter. 'We have pink or white.'

Jean nudged the kid. 'What will it be, sport? You heard the lady – pink or white?'

He didn't hesitate. 'Pink, please.'

'Good choice.' Jean gave Susan a wink.

A pink square of tissue paper made an appearance and Susan held out a soft palm into which Jack dropped the gleaming blue marble. She held it up to the light for a moment and they all looked admiringly at it.

'It looks like the ocean on a summer's day,' Susan said.

'It looks like a precious jewel,' Jack added.

Jean grinned. 'You did well, lad, winning this gem.' She leaned towards Susan. 'Came from some Yank soldier, that one did. A real piece of treasure.'

Susan dropped her hand and deftly twisted the marble into a piece of tissue, working some magic sleight-of-hand so that it almost looked like a pink flower when she was done with it. A chrysanthemum, perhaps. Jean lowered the posy she'd bought even further.

Jack took the little package back in a hand that was almost trembling with excitement. He looked at it in awe then lifted his gaze to Susan.

'Thanks,' he whispered. 'It's beautiful.'

Susan leaned back on her heels and waved a hand at him. 'Think nothing of it,' she said. 'I hope your mum has a real nice birthday.'

Jack couldn't tear his eyes off the gift for his mother. Jean blew Susan a kiss across the counter and turned to herd the boy back out the door. She was almost out the door when Susan's voice slowed her.

'Nice flowers, Jean,' she said.

Holding the door open, Jack slipping out under her arm, Jean looked back across the shop at the woman standing against the counter, a wry look on her face.

Jean grinned at her, lifted her shoulders in a helpless shrug, and followed the boy out the door.

CHAPTER 4

*A*lice found her heart stuttering at the sudden commotion at the door. She'd been trying not to look at the clock on the wall, but all she'd been able to hear for the last half an hour was the minute hand counting off the time until Jack was home from school and Jean was due for afternoon tea.

She smoothed her hands over her hips, straightening her dress. She'd changed into her nicest dress while the cake was baking in the range, and now she felt vaguely silly, self-conscious. Nervousness threaded through her body until she thought she'd start shaking where she stood.

Tilly was squealing in the hallway, and from her spot rooted in the kitchen, Alice heard Jack's voice, and another, deeper, richer, with something so warm about it, things inside her were threatening to melt.

She pulled herself straighter with an effort, glancing at the cake on the counter and wondering if she should move it to the centre of the clean and polished table. Again. She'd already set it there, then picked it back up and put it on the kitchen counter. She didn't want to make it look like such a big fuss. Already a deep blush was spreading down from the roots of her hair, across her cheeks and darkening her neck. Lifting a hand, she paddled desperately at the air in front of her face to cool herself down, but her embarrassment was just making things worse.

At least the cake looked nice. Mrs Reuben had been happy to hand over eggs and butter, especially when Tilly had piped up and told her all about her mother's birthday. Bless her heart, the child couldn't keep anything to herself.

But it had earned Alice a warm, motherly hug, and a basket full of eggs, and butter freshly churned that morning by Mrs Reuben's own meaty arms.

On the way home, she and Tilly had stopped in at the grocer's and bought an orange. It was thinly sliced, the rind removed, decorating the top of the Victoria sponge. Even to Alice, it looked beautiful. She closed her eyes and took a deep breath.

'Hullo,' she said, stepping out of the kitchen. 'What's all this hullabaloo, then?'

Tilly giggled louder, Alice astonished to find her perched in the air on a strong pair of shoulders, hanging over a grinning face.

'Mum!' It was Jack, coming full-tilt towards her down the narrow hallway, clasping something in his hand. She had a glimpse of pink, then he was on her, wrapping his arms around her waist. 'Happy birthday! Look what I got you!'

'Goodness me,' Alice laughed. 'A present for me?'

Jack pressed it into her hand and turned toward the advancing figures. 'Jean helped me get it wrapped,' he said, then lifted his eyes to her. 'But I won it for you, fair and square, Mum, honest.'

She dragged her gaze away from Jean's face and looked down at her son. Ruffling his hair, she assured him she completely believed him.

Jack ducked past her into the kitchen and tugged on her skirt for her to follow.

'Hullo Alice,' Jean said, suddenly right in front of her. With one easy, fluid movement, she swung Tilly down off her shoulders and held out something.

Alice felt Tilly swing around her legs and into the kitchen, and she heard her say something, but she was helpless to focus on anything but Jean in front of her. The cocoa-coloured eyes were close enough for her to see flecks of gold around the irises, and she discovered with surprise that the eyelashes surrounding them were beautiful, thick and dark.

Underneath the extraordinary eyes, a slow smile dawned. 'Happy birthday, Alice,' it whispered. Alice dragged her gaze away, remembering to breathe, and looked down to see strong brown hands holding a bunch of flowers.

'Oh,' she said. 'They're exquisite.'

'Not more so than you,' Jean said, and for a moment it seemed like her breath was so close that Alice could feel it warm against her cheek and she tilted her head and closed her eyes.

'Mama!' Tilly yelled. 'We want some cake!'

Alice snapped her eyes open in time to see Jean's smile widen into a grin. She stood swaying slightly, then made an effort to gather her wits about her.

What was this thing happening to her?

Jean pressed the flowers into her hand and stepped backwards, and Alice filled her lungs with air. 'Thank you,' she said, and her voice only wavered slightly.

'You're welcome.' The smile turned lazy, like some sort of invitation, and Alice felt herself flush again. With an effort, she drew herself up, half-turned away.

'Would you like some tea?' she asked, then dropped her head. 'I'm afraid it's all I have. Or you could have a little of the children's lemonade. I made it myself.'

Jean tipped her head to the side and Alice made herself slide her eyes away and step into the kitchen. Being close to Jean was doing ridiculous things to her insides. Turning them upside down and inside out. And warming her all over. She'd never felt so warm. She licked her lips.

'A nice hot cup of tea would be perfect, Alice,' Jean said and took another step back, making Alice realise they'd been standing jammed together in the doorway. She blinked and looked into the kitchen. Both children were silent, staring at her.

She looked down at her hands, the flowers in one, Jack's gift in the other. Then she pulled herself together and put on a wide smile.

'How lucky am I?' she said. 'Beautiful flowers, and a special surprise gift.'

'Open it up, Mama,' Tilly demanded. 'Me wanna see what it is.'

'I want to.' Alice said.

'So do it!' the child said.

'No, Tilly, I meant it's not me wanna, it's I want to.'

Her daughter looked at her in supreme confusion and Alice ended up shaking her head, laughing.

'I'll make the tea,' Jean said. 'You open your gift.'

Grateful, Alice sank down at the table next to Jack and put an arm around his shoulders. 'Thank you for my present,' she whispered to him.

'You haven't opened it yet,' he answered.

'I know it's something special. Look how prettily it's wrapped.' She watched her son look up and catch Jean's eye, get a wink from her. Then she lowered her gaze and plucked at the pink tissue paper, unwrapping it gently so that it didn't tear.

'Oh Jack,' she said when the marble lay in her hand. 'It's beautiful, it truly is.' She held it up to the light and it glittered like a piece of night sky. Closing her fingers around it, she kissed Jack on the temples, then rubbed the smear of lipstick off with a laugh while he groaned.

'Do you really like it, Mum?' he asked.

'I really do, sweetheart. It's lovely.'

He nodded. 'One day I'll get you a real sapphire.'

'This is the one I'll treasure always.'

Jack leaned against her, his sharp shoulders bird-like against her. 'I won it fair and square,' he repeated happily. Sitting up he waved his hands in the air. 'You should have seen the game, Mum, it was magnificent! We played for hours, Jimmy and me. He didn't want to lose it because it was his best marble, but I wanted to win it for you.' He settled back down in his seat. 'It's all the way from America,' he said on a happy sigh.

'America, huh?'

'Yeah.'

'Wow.'

'I know.'

Tilly clambered half onto the table and held out a hand. 'I

wanna see it,' she said.

'Sit down properly and you can,' Alice said, passing over the marble when Tilly had her bottom back on the chair. She goggled at it and only reluctantly handed it back, Jack's eyes like a hawk's on her.

'Here's your tea, Alice,' Jean said, laying a cup and saucer in front of her and sitting down across from her at the table. 'Cheers to the birthday girl, what do you say, kids?'

Jack held up his glass of lemonade. 'Hip hip hooray!' he whooped and they all laughed.

'Cake?' That was from Tilly, who had been hanging around the cake the whole time Alice had been making it, like a little alley cat over a fishbone.

The cake appeared on the table in front of Alice with a flourish. 'Best looking cake I've ever seen,' Jean said. She stood back with her hands on the leather belt at her hips and everyone looked up at her. 'Only needs one thing, let me see.'

Hemming and hawing, Jean made a production of digging in her pockets, then emerged triumphantly a moment later with a handful of little birthday candles. Tilly squealed at the sight of them.

Jean plugged them into the cream on top of the cake with hands Alice found surprisingly delicate. They were thin and strong, the skin rough from carting milk crates every morning, but they moved with an ease that Alice discovered was hypnotic.

She found herself wondering what they would feel like to touch.

Or what sensations they would tease out of her, if they were to brush against her skin. It was difficult to find enough breath to blow out the candles.

CHAPTER 5

It was Saturday morning, and outside the window, Alice could hear the sounds of the world stirring. It stretched and rustled, finding its voices in the shouts of children, and the deeper calls of men, the fluted greetings of women.

She rolled over in the bed, sheets crumpled about her, and turned her head from the brightening window. Certainly it was past time to get up. The children had already been in to see her, Tilly clambering up onto the bed to kneel next to Alice, peering at her like a small, concerned bird. Alice told them she was having a lie-in, and Jack could make them their breakfast.

There'd been no going back to sleep. Instead, she lay on her back in the bed, tracing the meandering crack in the ceiling, turning the spreading stain of damp there into some resemblance of a face, and feeling how heavy her limbs were.

It should be impossible, she thought, to feel at once so heavy, and so light, to oscillate between one and the other so that it felt like there was electricity roaming through the veins in her body. They no longer carried blood, her veins, but a humming, buzzing energy, that made her want to lie still at the same time she wanted to jump up, rush about, do something, anything, move, spin, dance.

Even turned away from the window, she heard the familiar sounds of the milk truck. Down the road it trundled toward her doorstep, just like it did six out of every seven mornings. Her muscles galvanised, wanting to jump up at the sound, rush her from the bed out into the hallway, tug open the front door that sometimes got stuck on days when the sky overhead was grey and damp, and plant herself on the doorstep quivering, straining for a glimpse, for a sight, for a sound.

Of Jean. She squeezed her eyes shut.

That was what she wanted, and it confused her, made her lie in the bed far past time to rise, the children talking and knocking about in the next room while she lay on sheets tangled around her legs, and still was unsatisfied.

There was the clatter of milk crates outside her little front gate, which screeched whenever you pulled it open, the once-white paint flaking off onto your fingers. She heard it screech now, heard the children suddenly thumping down the hallway outside her room and the front door opening.

Alice kept her eyes shut. Bottles clinked and there were the piping voices of her children, Jack who would one day sound like his father, and little Tilly, whose chatter always made Alice think of a shallow stream burbling over brightly-coloured stones. There'd be no bottle of cream today. Just the one pint of milk.

Tilly laughed at the deep voice speaking to her, and then there were footsteps down the hall again. A moment later,

Tilly appeared like a cat around the door to her room to launch herself onto her mother's bed.

'Mama, we got the milk!'

Alice dragged herself up to sit against the pillows, automatically smoothing the blankets over her knees. A breeze strayed in through the open door and whispered around her hot skin. She closed her eyes for just a moment, feeling its breath on her cheeks in a way that made something in her heart want to burst open.

Tilly hadn't finished. She pouted at her mother. 'It wasn't Jean though,' she said, leaning forward and tucking herself into the warm spot under her mother's arm and looking up at her through a tangle of blonde curls. 'Why wasn't it Jean, Mama? She delivers the milk.'

Alice stroked her daughter's cheek and gave her a kiss on the top of her head. 'Go and get your hairbrush, love. We need to do your hair.'

Tilly just looked at her, and Alice smiled. 'It's Saturday, Tilly,' she said. 'I think Jean gets Saturday off work.'

'Oh.' Tilly spread her hands over the candlewick bedspread and stroked the little tufts of cotton. Then beamed at her mother. 'That means she can come and play instead.'

'I don't know what she has planned,' Alice said. 'She probably has things to do. I don't think she'll be coming over to play.' They hadn't made any plans after the little birthday party.

Alice cursed herself under her breath. Jean probably thought she was a complete idiot.

It had been the birthday candles that had done it. That casual production of them, drawn from the depths of a pocket with a flick of a wrist that was tanned and sinewy.

How Alice longed to reach out a shy finger and feel the hard flicker of a pulse there, trace the tendons in that wrist, follow them up under the edge of the shirt Jean had been wearing until she reached the smooth, thin skin in the crease of her arm.

She'd had to swallow, blow out the candles, laugh and smile with the children, all the while inside there was a great, rising cloud of confusion, of something that felt distressingly like desire, welling up in her from deep within her belly.

It had made her fumble and blush, unable to look Jean in the eyes, too awkward to do anything more than busy her unsteady hands sharing out portions of the cake, not tasting a single mouthful of her own. It had been glue, not cream, she'd taken between her lips, sealing them so that she could do little more than mumble over the rim of her teacup for the rest of the hour that Jean spent with them. It had been almost a relief when the woman had left.

Alice's hand went to a spot high on her cheek, where Jean had leaned down and kissed her, pressing her lips to Alice's flushed skin, making it heat all the more, the little pulse in her temple jumping under the skin as the sensation of lips lingered even when Jean straightened and took herself off down the hallway and into the late afternoon.

Jean had probably left thinking Alice was a bumbling fool. Burning fingertips pressed to the spot where the ghost of the kiss was still felt, Alice swallowed down the dry lump in her throat. The kiss had been a pleasantry, that had been all. Jean had not meant for it to burn deep down into Alice's soul. She was just being nice. Making her feel better for getting all tongue-tied and embarrassed, for making a complete idiot of herself.

She wouldn't be back. Alice blinked away sudden hot tears, alarmed at the way her body had taken over her woozy mind, feeling things it had no right to.

Jean wouldn't be back. She'd deliver the milk with a cheery greeting and wave, but that would be the end of it.

If only, Alice thought, it had been the extent of the beginning of it as well.

She shook herself, forcing herself back to the real world. It laid heavy against her skin, pressing against her like a damp cloth. The thought of not seeing Jean again drained the morning sun from the day and turned it foggy in her mind.

'Here Mum,' Jack said, coming in the open door balancing a cup and saucer in his hands, little face frowning in concentration. 'I made you a cup of tea.' He looked at his sister. 'Get down from there, Tilly, so Mum can have her tea without spilling it.'

Tilly tumbled from the bed, but not without poking an impudent tongue out at her brother. She bounced over to the dressing table instead and wiggled her little bottom onto the stool in front of the mirrors, leaning forward to sift through the few tawdry treasures Alice kept there.

The tea was good, and Alice gave her son a warm smile. 'Jack,' she said. 'You're a marvel. This is perfect.'

The boy warmed under her praise and stuck his hands in his pockets. He looked at her, sudden anxiety replacing the smile.

'Are you sick, Mum?'

She shook her head. 'No, not even a little bit.' She gave a self-conscious laugh. 'I guess I'm just feeling lazy this morning.' A make-believe slyness in her glance. 'After all, I've reached a very advanced age now. I get to be lazy on occasional Saturday mornings.'

Tilly spun around on her stool, a string of coral beads in her fist. 'Are you very old, Mama?' she said. 'Who will look after us if you die?'

Alice widened her eyes in astonishment, then discovered Jack was looking at her intently. He lifted his shoulders in a painful shrug. She saw his throat move.

'Who would look after us, Mum?' he asked.

She cast around for an answer, completely blindsided by the question.

'Daddy died,' Tilly said. 'He never came home. He died in the war.' She blinked owlish blue eyes at her.

'The war's over,' Alice spluttered.

'Yeah. But you could still die of something else,' Jack said.

Alice put down her cup of tea on the bedside table and spread her arms wide. 'Oh, come here you two! I'm not going to die!'

Tilly slid straight off her stool and climbed up into her mother's lap.

'You too, young man,' Alice said. Jack moved forward and leaned into her embrace. She kissed him soundly. Then another for Tilly.

'I'm not going to die anytime soon,' Alice said. 'By the time I die, you'll both be grown up with your own families, and you'll be perfectly okay.'

She felt Jack shake his head. 'What's the matter?' she asked.

It was a choked moment before he answered. 'You can't know that.'

No. It was true. She couldn't know that. And there was

just her. Their father was dead. They had no one else. Not really.

She sighed. 'You're right, Jack,' she said. 'I can't be absolutely, completely sure of that. But I can be mostly absolutely sure of it.' It was all she could give them.

But her son was stubborn. 'Who would take care of us?'

She really hadn't wanted to say. None of them, she knew, would like the answer, but there really wasn't anyone else.

'Grandma would,' she said. 'If something were to happen while you were still young.'

Tilly leaned back and looked at her with wide, appalled eyes. 'But Grandma doesn't like us!'

She patted the small girl. 'She does, really. It's just that... Grandma's a bit stuck in her ways. When she was young, children were expected to be meek and quiet. That's all.'

'What does meek mean?' Jack looked just as horrified as his sister. How did they get here, Alice wondered? She'd been mooning lovesick over Jean just minutes before and now she was talking about her own death as though it was imminent. A hand reached inside her chest and grabbed her heart, squeezed it. What had she just said? Mooning lovesick?

Lovesick?

Love?

With an effort she pulled herself together, feeling almost as though she had to gather up a great many pieces of herself and sew them back together.

She tried to remember Jack's question. 'Um, meek. Well, it means obedient, I guess. Not answering back, doing what you're told, and not arguing about it.'

Jack's lip was stiff. He pulled into himself, out of her grip.

She reached for him, held him against her side, keeping him there until she felt him relaxing a fraction.

'You'd survive it,' she said, and added a wry smile. 'I did. But honestly you two, I'm healthy as a horse. Nothing's going to happen to me.'

Tilly's curls were shaking from side to side in an emphatic negative. 'You're never gonna die, Mama,' she said. 'I'm not gonna live with Grandma.' Her face was terribly serious. 'Never.'

'Me neither,' Jack said, mutinous. 'I'd run away first.'

'I'd come with you,' Tilly said. 'Wouldn't I, Jack?'

He nodded his head vigorously and Alice had to laugh.

'You two,' she said. 'Enough of this. We're all going to be fine. I'm going to live a very long time, and you both are going to grow up and be marvellous.'

There was a commotion at the front door, then a loud knocking.

'Oh no,' Alice said. 'Quickly Jack, see who's at the door. I'm not even out of bed!'

'Hullo?' a voice called. Then footsteps. A head appeared around the doorway. 'The door was open,' Jean said, voice apologetic, eyes dancing, taking in the view of Alice sitting up in the bed. 'You look like the lady Madonna,' she said. 'Sitting there with your children.'

Alice clutched Tilly closer, using the little girl to cover the fact that she was sitting there in her cotton nightdress, not even a dressing gown to cover her. Tilly squirmed out of her arms and hurtled herself towards the intruder.

'Jean!' she squealed. 'You came back!'

'You bet I did,' Jean did, helping herself into the room and planting herself on the end of the bed, Tilly now hanging off her neck. 'Hey Jack, how ya doing this fine Saturday?'

'I brought Mum a cup of tea,' he said. 'She's having a lie in.'

Jean turned her eyes to Alice, and all the air inside Alice's lungs evaporated. All she could hear was the rush of blood in her ears.

'I can see that,' Jean said. Her lips twitched in a smile.

Tugging the sheet over her breasts, Alice searched for something to say. 'I didn't know you were Catholic,' she said, then immediately felt stupid.

'Lapsed, I'm afraid,' Jean said in a tone of confession. 'Completely. I'm a lost cause when it comes to all the saints.' She tickled Tilly. 'Much happier being a sinner.'

'We only go to church because Grandma makes us,' Jack said.

'Is that right?'

'We go to Saint Thomas's. It's the Anglican one.' He pulled a face, then brightened. 'Afterwards in the summer though they have free apples and sometimes you even get cake.'

Jean nodded, her face serious. 'Cake would be a decent reason to go.'

He shrugged. 'I mean, it makes it a bit better. But I hate having to sit still.' His eyes widened in indignation. 'On a Sunday. It's the weekend.' He spoke with an aggrieved disbelief that made Jean laugh.

'The things you gotta do, kid.'

Jack was looking at her in sudden admiration. 'Did you really quit?' he asked.

She raised her eyebrows. 'Quit?'

'Going to church?'

Jean relaxed into a grin. 'Sure did.' She flicked a glance at

Alice still pressed against the headboard. 'Wasn't really my sort of place.'

Jack nodded sagely. 'It's not really mine, either.'

But Jean had her gaze on Jack's mother, and Alice felt it as though it was a thing with weight and form, touching first her face, eyes, cheekbones, grazing her chin, then down the heated length of her neck to her hands clasped like knots around the sheet. They were both silent, looking at each other, and Alice was acutely aware of her body beneath the thin cotton, noticing it in a way she'd never quite done before, as it melted under Jean's eyes, then started a slow burn that brought bright spots to her cheeks. She cleared her throat and closed her eyes, wanting to fan herself suddenly. But that would require untangling her hand from the sheet, and now she was confused, light-headed.

'Well,' Jean breathed, then seemed to catch herself. She stood up, still dangling Tilly. She looked around the room, blowing out a small puff of air.

'I…ah…got my car going for the day,' she said. 'Been having some trouble with it, but it's going well enough for a trip. I thought you lot might want to go for a picnic at the seaside.' She quirked a smile at Alice. 'If you can get yourself out of bed, that is.'

CHAPTER 6

*J*ean looked over at the woman in the passenger's seat. 'Penny for them,' she said.

Alice turned green-brown eyes on her, wide open and dazed. For a moment, their expression made Jean's heart stutter in her chest, wondering what the hell she was doing in this car with this woman.

'I'm sorry,' Alice said. 'What did you say?'

What the hell. In for a penny, in for a pound, decided Jean. And it was already too late anyway. Whether it was a good idea or not, here she was in this car, driving this woman and her two children to the beach for the day. She even had a picnic packed in a basket on the back seat, and her landlady had dug out a pair of kiddie's buckets and spades, shaking her head and tsk tsking as she did so.

'Mind you don't go getting in serious trouble,' Mrs Boone said.

Jean had tried her usual trick. She placed a dramatic hand on her chest and opened her eyes wide. 'Who?' she asked. 'Me?'

Mrs Boone, her landlady, had shaken her head. 'I'm not joking around this time, lass,' she said. 'Alice Holden might not have much, since her hubby didn't make it home from the war, but she is Geraldine Thomas' daughter, and that should raise a bright red warning flag.'

That had Jean rolling her eyes. 'Alice is not her mother and I can't believe you're judging her on her parents.'

Mrs Boone had straightened her bulk from the cupboard and handed Jean red and blue buckets. 'I'm not judging Alice on any such thing. But it doesn't change the fact of who her mother is, so mind yourself nonetheless, Jean. Isn't anything more dangerous than a sour old woman who thinks she's important, and that is Geraldine Thomas to a T.' The land-lady waggled a finger in Jean's face. 'There's no way she's going to even come close to accepting you anywhere near her daughter.'

They were next to the doorway leading out onto the boarding house's veranda. Jean stepped outside and looked up at the clear sky. It was the perfect day for a picnic at the beach. She'd already spit-polished her old jalopy. She was all set. Well, except for asking Alice out. Nerves tickled her from the inside out. Alice would say yes though, surely?

She reached into her pocket and took out a crumpled packet of cigarettes. Damned habit. She was trying to quit. But a moment later one was lit between her lips and she inhaled the smoke gratefully. Mrs Boone stood in the door-way, filling it almost from one side to the other, and she was staring at her like she wanted to start waggling that formidable finger again.

Jean sniffed, tipped her head on the side. 'Tell me, Mrs B.'

Her landlady's eye narrowed. 'Tell you what?'

A diffident shrug. 'Why you don't have a problem with… well, you know.'

A deliberately raised eyebrow. 'I had a friend once,' she said. 'When I was a girl.'

It was hard to imagine Mrs B ever being anything other than the sixty-something year old woman she currently was. Jean squinted at her.

The woman's voice turned sad, but not before she'd done a quick scan of their immediate vicinity. They were alone except for a pair of squawking starlings on the roof of the house next door.

'I was at school,' she said. 'Her name was Hermione and I remember she had the most beautiful hair.'

Jean was grinning.

Mrs B rolled her eyes at her. 'Hermione fell in love with one of the teachers, I can't remember her name, but she taught literature.' For a moment her eyes had a faraway look again. Then she shook her head and spoke in a soft voice that belied her bulk. 'I just think it's natural for some, that's all. And it doesn't do any harm. Not really. I think friendships between women can be precious.'

The grin widened. 'Does that mean I can have guests in my room?'

Mrs B swatted a beefy hand at her. 'It certainly does not, and don't you even go thinking of it!'

Jean held up her own hands in mock surrender. 'No worries, Mrs B. I'll stick to house rules.' She couldn't help but give the landlady a wide smile. 'What about you, Mrs B? I know there wasn't actually a Mr B, so what's your story?' she asked.

'That is not your business, Jean Reardon. Except that I am

in a decided position to warn you against nudging up against Geraldine Thomas in any way whatsoever.' The finger did come out again, the hand attached to it heavy with gold rings. 'You watch yourself with Alice Holden, my girl.' She heaved a sigh and put her hand away. 'Couldn't you have chosen someone else? She doesn't mean anything to you, does she? Why do you want to play with fire like this?' A decided shake of the head. 'You'll regret it, you mark my words. Geraldine Thomas will see to that. She's good at that.'

Jean took another puff of her cigarette and tried to smile through the smoke, but this time it came off a little crooked.

Why was she so taken with Alice? She'd been getting along just fine the way she was. Good job, good mates, evenings down at the pub with the men she worked with, nice blokes every one of them. There'd been the odd woman to keep company on a lonely night, but always it had been a passing thing.

Until Alice. With her soulful eyes and her soft breasts, and her pretty little hands. Hands that Jean wanted every time she saw them to take in her own, to press her lips to, and to press the palm against her skin.

The cigarette was almost burnt down. She bent and stubbed it out in the can of sand placed on the veranda for that express purpose. Standing back up, she stretched, then sighed.

'I can't help it, Mrs Boone,' she admitted. 'This one's different, that's all I can say.'

Her landlady shook her head but said no more. Simply patted Jean on the shoulder and turned, disappearing into the house.

Jean gazed at the twin buckets and spades, then picked them up and carried them out to the car.

Now here she was, looking across the seat at Alice, wondering what the woman was thinking, wanting to peer into her mind and read all her thoughts, wanting while she did it to lean close to that pretty shell of an ear and put her lips to it, whisper sweet things. She shook herself.

'I was wondering what you were thinking,' she said, glad she wasn't one to blush easily under her tan.

Alice, on the other hand, had the sort of fair complexion that turned pink at the drop of a hat. It was doing that right now, and Jean felt a warm gladness at the sight of it. If the woman was blushing just from being asked what she was thinking – well, that was a mighty intriguing sign.

The little pulse in Alice's throat jumped and it took all Jean's power to turn her head back to the road and not lean across to touch her lips to it. She wiped a sweaty hand on her trousers and concentrated on the road.

'I was thinking…what a lovely day it is for a picnic,' Alice said, and Jean was completely sure, if she hadn't been a moment ago, that Alice had not been thinking that at all.

On impulse, she reached out a hand and laid it on Alice's. 'Tell me what you were really thinking,' she said, and her voice was low, husky from the sudden energy she could feel jolt between them.

Her foot on the accelerator lessened its pressure, and the car slowed to a walking pace. Jean stared at Alice's face, watching the expressions pass over it.

The lips parted under her gaze, showing small white teeth. 'I…I was thinking how much I wanted to do this,' Alice said, and twisted her hand around under Jean's until their fingers were entwined.

Jean sat back, turning to look where they were going again, and pushing their speed back up. She couldn't answer. Any words she might have thought of were backed up in her throat.

She squeezed Alice's hand instead, and drew it over to sit on her thigh, aware of everything suddenly, the fresh warmth of the breeze outside the car window, the press of the seat against her back, the low mutterings and murmuring of the children in the back seat, the thrumming of the tyres against the dirt road, even, in the distance, the great rush and break of the waves against the beach.

Most of all, she was aware of the hand in hers, the delicate bones clasped in warm, smooth skin, and how it wrapped around her own, holding on to her just as tightly as she held onto it.

CHAPTER 7

*A*lice sat under the shade of her hat casting sidelong glances at the woman sprawled out on the blanket beside her. Jean's eyes were closed, her face relaxed as it faced the sun, the skin clear, tanned to a deep gold. Alice wanted to reach out and touch a fingertip to Jean's skin, feel how warm it was.

Jean's lips, pleasantly full under a narrow nose, quirked in a smile.

'I can feel you looking at me, you know,' she said.

Quickly, Alice closed her eyes, as if that would change the fact that she'd been staring. Then she forced herself to open them again.

'I'm sorry,' she said.

One eye opened, looked sideways at her, then closed again. 'I didn't say I was complaining.'

Alice licked her lips, looked out at the waves whispering back and forth along the sand, stared up at the sky, a billowing blue umbrella, then turned at last back to Jean. 'Is it okay to be feeling this way?' she asked.

Both eyes opened this time to regard her steadily. The smiled under them turned to pursed lips. 'How are you feeling, Alice? Jean asked.

Alice blew out a deeply held breath and looked back out over the beach. There were things going on inside her. She groped for understanding of what they were and couldn't deny it.

'I…want to touch you,' she said.

Jean rolled over onto her side and held her head up with a hand while she regarded Alice.

'I want to do…something,' Alice said, trying again.

'What sort of something, precisely?' Jean's lips twitched.

Alice narrowed her eyes at her. 'You're teasing me.'

A nonchalant shrug. 'Maybe a little.' A smile bloomed and inside Alice's body, everything melted into liquid gold.

Before she could stop herself, she leaned across and brushed her lips, across the sun-heated skin, across Jean's high cheekbone. Then she sat back, astonishment making the hair on the back of her neck stand up.

'I'm sorry,' she said. 'I don't know what came over me.'

Jean's eyes widened, their cocoa and gold depths bright against her lashes. She moved her lips but was silent.

Alice felt tears sting at the corners of her eyes. She'd just been so stupid! What did she think she was doing? Turning her head, she looked away out over the water, wishing she could just curl up and climb into a shell like a crab, and not have to come out ever again.

There was movement beside her, but she was too embarrassed to see what Jean was doing.

For goodness sakes, she'd just kissed the woman's cheek!

'Alice.'

She shook her head.

Jean made an odd, growling noise from beside her, and then there were hands on her arms, turning her. And there were fingers in her hair, stroking it back from her face, and earnest eyes searched her face.

Lastly, there were lips on hers. Barely more than a whisper of breath at first, then the gentlest of touches, a light brushing, and then something firmer. Soft in a way that a kiss had never been before, Alice registered everything about it in the same moment that all her senses filled to overflowing. She closed her eyes and held onto the kiss, a hand sneaking out to slide up the hard muscle of Jean's arm, feeling the warm kid leather of her skin and all the while there was a kiss, soft lips, the slight down of an upper lip, an indrawn breath. She didn't want it to end.

Jean drew back, lashes shaded darkly over hooded, dazed eyes. Alice looked into them and saw herself reflected, lips parted, wanting more.

She wanted more. Her fingers tightened on Jean's arm and she swayed forward slightly, looking for more, moving instinctively towards more, every particle in her body alight with glowing, humming energy.

'Are you kissing?' The young voice was curious, excited.

Alice leapt back, hand going back to cover her lips, and she stared at her daughter for a moment, mute at the sight of the little girl in her swimsuit, sand coating her legs, a red spade slung over one plump shoulder. The yellow curls jiggled as Tilly looked from her mother to Jean.

'Yes,' Jean said, and to Alice's ears, her voice sounded unbelievably normal. Low and rich and warm, and unperturbed. 'That's exactly what we were doing.'

Jack joined the crowd of one, gazing curiously at his mum. 'Don't be silly,' he said. 'It's only boys supposed to kiss girls.'

Alice felt Jean's shrug, rather than saw it. 'Well, I don't know about that. I've met plenty of girls that like to kiss other girls.' She sat forward and linked her hands around her knees.

'But two ladies can't have babies,' Jack said.

'No, they can't. But sometimes they love each other anyway.'

That met with silence, and Alice could hear her heart pounding with the tide. She wanted to get up, say something, herd the children away from the subject, but she was frozen to the spot.

Jack stared at them. 'Does that mean you love my Mum?'

Now Jean cast a glance in Alice's direction. Alice opened her mouth to say something, to defuse the situation, but only the tiniest squeaks came out.

'Well,' Jean said slowly.

Alice found her voice. 'You don't have to answer that, Jean,' she said and turned to her son. 'Of course not.'

Jean looked at Alice again, dark eyes regarding her, before dropping an unexpected wink. 'Actually, I think I will,' she said. 'Jack asked a very sensible question. I reckon he deserves to know the answer.'

This was more than Alice could bear. She got up onto her knees, started blindly poking at the picnic things. Then stilled when Jean spoke again to Jack.

'It's true, Jack,' she said. 'I do love your mum. She's pretty damned wonderful, don't you think?'

Alice dropped the fork she was holding.

Jack seemed to think about it.

'I think she's wunnerful,' Tilly said decisively and plumped down onto the blanket between them. 'I'm hungry.'

It was hard for Alice to make herself look at her son, or Jean. Jack seemed to be considering the matter deeply.

'Does that mean you're going to keep kissing her?' he asked.

A shrug from Jean. 'I guess so. But probably not in public, how's that?'

'You were doing it in public just then.'

Jean tipped her head to one side in silent concession. 'I don't think we'll make a habit of it.'

Alice's eight-year-old boy scratched his head. 'I don't know,' he said. 'I've never heard of girls kissing girls.'

'All sorts of things happen in the world, buddy. This is just one that nobody talks too much about.' Jean shifted slightly on the blanket. 'Now, are you too ready for some lunch? I'm starving.'

She shot Alice a wry look and unpacked the picnic basket. 'Looks like we have some sandwiches, and wait for it...yes, cake – we have ourselves an absolute feast.'

Jack dropped down onto his knees on the blanket, face lighting up. Alice passed round some plates, trying not to let her hands shake too much, but the kids were both chattering now, and neither were talking about anything but beach and sand and sandwiches and cake.

They weren't giving the kiss any thought.

But it still burned there on Alice's lips, and when no one was watching, she pressed her fingers to her mouth and found herself wanting Jean's lips on hers again.

The sun was tipping towards the horizon when they finally convinced the children it was time to pack up and head home. She and Jean had dangled Tilly in the tideline between them, both of them laughing at her high-pitched squeals of delight, while Jack had gone further out, lost in a game of his own devising and perfectly content.

Later, Alice had sat on the sand, feeling it warm under her from the heat of the sun, and watching as Jean and the two children meticulously shovelled and piled and patted until they had a sandcastle of impressive proportions. Alice watched them, wishing she had a camera. The children were having so much fun. Jean too, seemed to be enjoying herself, whooping and hollering with the kids, sleeves and trouser legs rolled up, damp from splashing in the tide.

There'd been no more awkward conversations, except for a moment over lettuce sandwiches when Jack had asked why Jean wore trousers. She'd looked down at her legs and frowned.

'Suits me better, I guess, Jacky boy. That's all there is to it.'

'Mama always wears dresses,' Tilly piped up to say.

'And she's pretty as a picture in them.' Jean smiled at her, and Alice found herself returning it.

'I worked on a farm during the war,' Jean said. 'I guess I just got used to wearing them. Much easier to chase those cows around when you're wearing pants.'

That had made both children giggle and the three of them spent the next five minutes talking about cows while Alice simply watched and listened, marvelling at how much at ease Jean was. She itched to find out if Jean had any nieces and nephews, because she was a natural with the children.

But now those children were folded into the back seat of the old Ford, and Alice had slipped back into the passenger's seat beside Jean.

'I had a wonderful day,' she said softly, looking at Jean's profile in the dimming light. Jean's hair was short, tucked behind an ear and skimmed the top of her neck in a no-nonsense style that looked a little like she'd taken the shears to it herself. Alice wanted to reach out and touch the vulnerable skin of Jean's neck.

'Bugger,' Jean said a little later, hands tight around the steering wheel.

'What's the matter?' Alice sat forward in alarm, realising that she'd been a million miles away and that the car was drifting soundlessly to a stop at the side of the road. 'Where are we?'

'Not far from home,' said Jean. 'But the bloody car's broken down.'

Alice blinked at the gathering dusk. 'What do we do?'

But Jean was already opening her door and swinging out onto the road. She poked her head back in and grinned.

'Don't worry about a thing,' she said. 'I've fixed this old piece of junk more times that I've had hot meals. I'll have it going again in no time.'

With that, she disappeared out of view, and Alice opened her own door and climbed out. Wrapping her arms around herself, she shivered. It was cool outside.

Jean was rummaging around in the back of the vehicle. She emerged with a metal toolbox, which she lugged around to the front of the car and set on the ground with a soft grunt.

'You're going to repair the car?' Alice asked.

'I sure am,' Jean answered. 'Though I'd rather be taking you home and having a nice cup of tea to end a perfect day.' She looked up and smiled across at Alice. 'Hey now. Don't worry – I really do know how to get this thing going again. Done it a hundred times already.' Another reassuring smile, then she bent to the bonnet, lifting it up, securing it, and bending over the engine, humming to herself. Tinkering sounds started moments later.

Alice checked on the children, but both of them, worn out by sun and sand and fresh air, had fallen asleep on the back seat in an untidy tumble of limbs.

'They okay?' Jean asked.

'Asleep.'

Jean wiped her hands on a rag then tucked it into the toolbox. 'Come here,' she said.

Alice picked her way around the car. It was still only spring, and the sun was almost done with the day, settling itself down for the night.

'Pretty out, isn't it?' Jean said, holding out a hand and

taking Alice's. She drew her close and tucked an arm around Alice's waist. 'The sunset is beautiful.'

Alice looked out west, nodding, feeling the warmth of Jean's body pressed up against her. It was soft and lean at the same time and Alice stared at the streaks of red clouds for a moment then closed her eyes, soaking up the sensation of Jean's arm around her.

It felt good. She tipped her head to the side and moved slightly to rest it on Jean's shoulder. That felt even better. She felt Jean's chest rise and fall against hers, their breasts touching, Jean's soft breath tickling the hair by her ear.

'This is good,' Jean said, and her voice was low, hoarse. Alice opened her eyes and looked at her.

'Yes,' she whispered. 'It is.' Her breath came faster, and she reached up a hand to touch Jean's shadowed cheek, her fingertips drifting over the skin until they grazed against lips. The sharp intake of breath made her knees weak.

She thought of asking Jean to kiss her again, but there was no time, no need, because Jean's lips were on hers already, soft, tasting hers, lingering there. Alice's fingers slid around to stroke the back of Jean's neck, the same spot she'd looked longingly at earlier, and the woman made a sound deep in her throat that touched something inside Alice, that warmed her belly, spreading and settling all through her.

It was a revelation, and a moment longer, she could think of nothing more than Jean's lips on hers, the pointed press of her hip in Alice's belly, the lean length of a thigh against her own, and still those lips on hers, the kiss deepening, making her sway, making her want to wrap herself around the woman, forget all thought except the demand her body was making to be closer, to touch, to be touched.

They broke away panting, staring at each other, then stumbled back another pace when twin headlamps pierced the road behind them. Alice looked at Jean in the oncoming light, and saw her face dark and dazed, and thought that her own must look much the same.

'Everything okay here?' The car slowed to a stop beside them, the window wound down. The voice was accompanied by a man who examined Jean for a long, painful moment, then turned his attention to Alice standing there beside the car, the bonnet still in the air, the toolbox at her feet.

'Alice Holden.' He said it slow, and she recognised him.

'Jim,' she said. She wasn't going to call him Big Jim like his friends did.

But his eyes were on Jean again, looking her up and down, taking in the boots, trousers, white shirt with the sleeves rolled up to the elbows. When he got to her head, he stared at her, and Alice could feel Jean tense, so that Alice put out a hand to Jean's arm, silently wondering what was passing between them in that long examination, and asking her to stay still.

'We've been to the beach, Jim,' she said. 'The children had a lovely time.' Her voice was slightly too high, and she licked her lips, tried again. 'It was a beautiful day.'

He turned to look at her only when she fell silent.

'We had some car trouble, but it's fixed now. My friend is about to drop me off at home. The children are in the back seat.' She had to make an effort to breathe, stop herself from babbling.

'Perhaps I should give you a ride home, Alice,' he said. 'That would be a better idea.'

She shook her head, felt the swish of her hair against her

cheeks. A little too emphatic. 'No, please Jim, we got the car going again, and the little ones, they're asleep. I wouldn't want to wake them.'

He was looking at Jean again, as though she were some exotic species of bug. When he spoke, it was to her, ignoring Alice.

'Well, well. Jean Reardon.'

'Yes,' Jean said. 'That would very well be me.' Alice had dropped her hand, but they were still standing close enough that she could feel Jean vibrating where she stood, like a wire fence in the wind. She bit at her lip. 'Like Alice said,' Jean continued, 'the vehicle's running again, so we can be on our way.' Her voice had a slight lilt to it, the remnant of a family's Irish accent.

Big Jim ignored her. 'Why are you taking Alice here to the beach.'

Jean blinked at him. 'I am taking her *home from* the beach.'

'You know perfectly well what I'm asking.'

Head tilted to one side, Jean regarded the man in the car steadily. 'I do,' she said. 'But I don't know what business it is of yours.'

Breaking her gaze, Big Jim reached across and took a packet of cigarettes from the dashboard. He took his time shaking one out of the packet and putting it in his mouth. Lighting it was equally leisurely.

Then suddenly he was looking back at Alice, blowing a thin stream of smoke from his nose.

'Does your mother know what you're up to, Alice?'

'I'm not a child, Jim,' she answered him, drawing herself up to her full height. 'My mother does not get to weigh in on my every activity.'

He inclined his head to the right and took another puff of his cigarette, this time blowing out the smoke so that it clouded in Jean's face.

'That's right,' he said. 'You're a respectable widow now, aren't you? So, tell me then, what are you doing running around the countryside with this?'

It took her a moment to figure out that he was referring to Jean, and the understanding rooted her to the spot for a long second, before fury turned her blood to white phosphorescence.

'Come on, Jean,' she said, catching hold of Jean's shirt at the elbow and tugging on it. 'Let's get home. We've got better things to do than stand here.' She turned and picked up the toolbox, the weight of it surprising her, but determined not to show it, she carted it around the side of the car and dropped it into the footwell in front of her seat, sliding in after it and slamming her door.

She watched Jean fold down the bonnet, securing it, then cranking the car to start it. Alice clamped her eyes shut, praying that the engine would catch.

It did, with a spluttering cough, and Jean was at the door, grinning, her lips pulled too wide in her own fury. They both heard the barked laughter from the other vehicle and then it was pulling away from them, red taillights mocking. Jean pulled out onto the road behind it, reached out a hand, groping around for Alice's. She took it in her own and held onto it, pressing it against the thin cotton of her dress.

Neither of them said anything the rest of the way into town.

The street was deserted when Jean parked the car in front of Alice's small house, but she noticed Alice doing the same as she did – scanning the street, seeing who was peering out from behind the curtains at them. She swore she saw the green ones in the house next door twitch from an invisible hand.

'Well,' she said, hand still in Alice's. 'We're here.'

Alice looked at her and even in the dim light, she looked beautiful, like some sort of angel, a cloud of dark honey hair tousled like a child's around her head, and eyes wide in the dusk. They were staring at her.

'It's going to be all right, you know,' Jean said, suddenly uncomfortable. Damn Big Jim Dempsey for showing up and spoiling things. 'We only went to the beach. People do it every day.'

Alice's lips parted, and Jean wanted to lay a finger across them, so that she couldn't say the words that were suddenly rolling around inside her head like a couple loose ball bearings. *Not people like us.* She should help Alice take the children inside, then come back out, climb into her old car and drive away.

And she shouldn't come back.

Alice was a respectable widow.

What was Jean? She straightened in her seat, hating the way she was feeling. It wasn't like her. She was Jean Reardon. Unapologetic, was what she was. Worked hard, enjoyed life.

And was falling for this woman beside her in the car.

Alice smiled, small neat teeth white in the dimness. 'I had a wonderful day,' she said fiercely. 'The best day ever.'

Jean wanted to kiss her again, but the thought of that twitching green curtain stopped her. Already they'd sat in the car too long. She squeezed Alice's lovely fingers.

'Come on. Let's get these sleeping babes inside.'

A groggy voice answered them from the back seat. 'I'm not sleeping.' A pause. 'I'm not a baby either.'

Jean laughed. 'You're right, Jack,' she said. 'Which means I'll only have to carry your little sister. You can go under your own steam.'

A vigorous nodding from the back seat, and the boy was grappling the door open. Jean looked across at Alice and bit down on the urge to kiss those ripe lips again and smiled instead. 'Ready, sweetheart?' she asked.

Alice's eyes widened momentarily at the endearment, then she nodded and turned to her own door.

'All right, kids,' Alice said, pulling a sleepy Tilly out of the back seat before Jean could do it for her. 'Time for your supper and bath!'

'But I bathed in the sea,' Tilly said over Alice's shoulder, rubbing her eyes and looking at Jean as they trooped up the short path to the front door. 'Didn't I, Jean? I got clean in the sea.'

'You got salty in the sea,' Alice corrected her.

'All pickled in brine,' Jean agreed. They arrived in the kitchen and Jack was turning lights on, looking around blinking.

'What's for supper, Mum?' he asked.

Jean watched Alice look over at the cupboards, a slight frown marring her face as she took inventory. 'We'll boil some eggs,' she said. 'You can have toast soldiers with them.' She looked at Jean. 'Will you stay?' she asked. 'I'd love a cup of tea.'

Jack was already pulling a pot from a shelf and taking it to the tap to fill. Tilly had slithered from her mother's arms to stand on a chair, stretching theatrically. Alice herself looked crumpled but beautifully radiant in the homely domestic setting.

She shook her head. 'I'd best be off,' Jean said, wincing a little at Alice's crestfallen expression. She lowered her voice. 'It would be best,' she said.

The expression became mutinous, but surprisingly, Alice nodded. 'Okay,' she said. 'I'll walk you out.' She turned. 'Kids, say goodbye to Jean, and thank you for our wonderful day.'

Tilly waved from her chair. 'Bye bye Jean! Thank you for the beach!'

There was a scoffing sound from Jack, who was putting his pot of water on the stove. 'She didn't give us the beach, you silly goose,' he said. 'She took us to the beach.'

'Jack,' his mother said, warningly.

'Sorry Tilly,' he said automatically, then turned to Jean. 'Bye Jean, it was a smashing day.'

'It sure was, kids,' she said. 'I'll see you later.' Turning for the hallway and the front door, she felt Alice right behind her.

It was Alice who spoke first, jammed up in the tiny hallway before the front door.

'I want you to stay,' she said.

Jean shook her head. 'The neighbours will be talking already.'

'Let them talk!'

'No, Alice. We can't be silly about this. We had a fantastic day.'

Round, serious eyes looked at her. 'Are you saying you don't want to see me again, Jean?' Alice asked. 'Because I thought you told my son you were falling in love with me.' Pink spots appeared on Alice's fair cheeks. Jean reached out and stroked a thumb over one of them.

'I'm not saying that, Alice,' she said. 'Although maybe I should.'

Alice shook her head. 'No. Don't you dare. I don't want you to.'

'I don't want to either,' Jean said, and it was true. She didn't even want to leave. She wanted to go back into the bare little kitchen and help cook eggs and toast. She wanted to sit Alice down at the table and bring her a cup of tea, made exactly the way she liked it with two teaspoons of sugar and a dollop of milk. She wanted to argue with little Tilly about whether a dip in the sea counted as a bath.

'What?' Alice asked, searching her face. 'What is it?'

Jean shook her head, all the words and wants crowding up inside her. Instead of speaking, she leaned forward and sought Alice's lips, finding them, and closing her eyes at the touch, the softness, the incredible softness that made her unsteady on her feet right there in the darkening hallway.

'I want you to stay,' Alice said, and her words brushed against Jean's lips in a whisper that made her heart pound.

'I can't,' she answered, swallowing. 'I want to, Alice, but I can't.' She fought to clear her head. It was difficult. 'It really is a bad idea with the neighbours.'

'I don't care about the neighbours!' Alice hissed, her breath hot against Jean's cheek, while the rest of her leaned close against her, curves touching in a way that had Jean's hands prickling with the need to touch them, to smooth her hand over Alice's waist, hips. She shook her head again.

'I can come back,' she said. Giving up.

Giving in.

Alice stood immediately straighter. 'Promise?' she said. 'We can...talk,' she said, and Jean knew she was feeling suddenly shy again. But then Alice rested a cheek against hers and knew the shyness would come – and go.

'I promise,' Jean said, the words scratchy with desire. 'I'll come back, after the children are in bed, when the neighbours are all tucked up too.' She moved her head, stroking her cheek against Alice's.

Alice moved, and her lips pressed themselves against Jean's cheek instead. 'I'll be waiting up for you,' she said, and her smile in the hallway was shy again, but brilliant.

It took almost everything Jean had to get herself outside the door, down the path, through the gate, and climbing in behind the wheel. Then she realised she'd forgotten to crank the car started, and she heaved herself out into the chill of the evening again, cursing, aware that it was the turn of the curtains on the other side of Alice's house to flutter at an invisible touch. She felt the sting of watchful eyes and turned her back on them, bending to the crank, getting the bloody car going, and sliding back at last into the driver's seat.

It was impossible to think straight. Her thoughts wandered down their own paths, all of which led back to Alice, with her soft hair, her warm lips, and her eyes, the way they darted to and from Jean's face, then settled there to gaze at her in a way Jean didn't think she'd ever been seen before.

A deep breath and she clamped her hands on the steering wheel, focused on making the right turns, and parked outside her boarding house. She'd go home, drop off the picnic gear, and the little red and blue buckets and spades, then take a good long soak in the tub.

In cold water.

CHAPTER 10

Alice gave into Tilly's argument that she'd already bathed, the salt water at the beach being a good enough scrub for once. Tilly stared at her for a moment after the capitulation, her little rosebud mouth open in amazement, then she clapped her hands in delight.

'Silly Tilly,' Alice told her, scooping her up from her chair and suddenly, wildly, dancing around the kitchen with the child. 'It just means going to bed earlier!'

His sister squealing in delight, Jack jumped up and went over to his father's old radio, switching the dial on. It wheezed a little, then belted out the Glen Miller Band playing In The Mood. Alice swung Tilly around again, then propped her on a hip, hanging onto her with one arm while the girl promptly flung herself backwards and hung with arms and hair trailing towards the floor. Laughing, Alice flipped her upright and held out a hand to her son. Jack gave a mock bow, and took her hand, and the three of them waltzed around the little kitchen until the song ended and they collapsed giggling onto chairs.

'Did you have a good day, kids?' Alice asked, looking at their shining faces and swaying to the next song. It was something slower and made her feel warm and melancholic at the same time.

Tilly squirmed on Alice's lap. 'I had a great day!' she shouted.

'What about you, Jack?' Alice asked, looking at her son.

He nodded. 'I like going to the beach,' he said.

'It's been a long time since we got to go,' Alice agreed.

'Grandma took us last time,' Jack said, and he looked unimpressed at the memory.

'I like Jean better than Grandma,' Tilly said, resting her head on Alice's breast and looking up at her mother with earnest blue eyes.

'So do I,' Jack said, and with eight-year-old matter of fact-ness added, 'she's a good egg.'

A golden glow of contentment spread upwards from Alice's belly. She basked in it a moment, feeling like there could never again be anything wrong with the world. Looking from one child to the other, she took in their round, happy faces, and thought that maybe she'd never quite had as perfect a moment as this before.

Especially as it came with the promise of more of them.

The memory of Big Jim's hard stare wormed its way into her mind, but she stamped on it. She'd had nothing to do with him for over a year. Hadn't even seen him for almost as long. He had nothing to do with anything.

'Right, you two,' she said. 'Finish up your cocoa, and let's get you to bed. It's been a long day, and you need your beauty sleep.'

There were groans and half-hearted complaints, but she

got them herded into the bathroom, supervised the washing of faces and teeth, then tucked them into their narrow beds, giving each a sound kiss goodnight.

It was only when she stood in the kitchen, suddenly alone for the first time since that morning, that everything hit her in a wave that had her shaking.

Putting out a hand, she steadied herself on a kitchen chair, gazed around the room with its clean but peeling paint, not seeing any of it, remembering instead the hot sand and sun of the beach, back there again, Jean's lips on hers.

She felt it again, as if it was still happening, as if it was such a momentous thing that somewhere in the universe it was still going on, Jean's lips were still on hers, she was still leaning into the kiss, eyes half-closed, breath caught in her throat, her whole existence changed forever.

It was impossible not to touch her fingertips to her lips, then to her cheek, feeling the ghost of Jean's caresses still upon the skin. Then she moved her palm to her chest, press it there, trying to steady herself, trying to slow the beating of her heart.

The kitchen swam back into view and Alice breathed deep, willing herself to be calm again, feeling the nervous excitement humming under her skin. Her eyes sought the clock, stared at it for a moment unable to translate the time from its face, then dismay coursed through her when she realised it would likely be at least an hour or two before Jean returned.

Well. She cast her gaze around the room. The tea kettle stood in its place on the stove. There, she would have a cup of tea. That would use up some minutes.

In her mind though, Jean's arm was around her waist,

holding her with a strength and certainty Alice wanted to feel again. The cup and saucer clattered in her fumbling grasp, but she was dreaming and didn't notice. She was leaning into Jean's body again, feeling it warm and real against her own.

Her eyes flew open and she put down the box of tea and the spoon she'd dipped into the leaves. The kettle was taken off the boil, and Alice flew down the hallway to her room.

She needed something to wear. She needed to bathe.

CHAPTER 11

Alice had been waiting for the rattle at the back door, but when it came, she was still startled, her mouth drying as though she'd drunk some of the sand from the beach earlier, and when she opened the door, it was with trembling hands.

Jean appeared there in the door frame, materialising out of the darkness, and Alice looked across at her face, unable suddenly to think of a thing to say.

'Is this okay?' Jean whispered.

Alice just stared, her mind a flood of disjointed words, pictures, feelings.

'Coming here, I mean,' Jean said. 'You haven't changed your mind?' She gestured back out into the darkness. 'I can go, if you like.'

That roused Alice to her senses. She reached out and tugged Jean inside, looking at her curiously.

'What's wrong?' Jean asked.

Alice shook her head. 'You look nervous,' she said, and there was wonder in mind. She felt like a cat on a hot tin roof, but not for a moment had she expected Jean to be the same way.

Jean glanced back outside, then closed the door. 'I've never done this before,' she said. 'Sneaked into a woman's house like this.'

'It's not sneaking, is it, when you're invited? And you could have come to the front door.'

A sad shaking of the head. 'You know as well as I do, Alice, that you couldn't have let me in the front door.'

She did. Nodding her head in agreement, she knew she'd been stupid to say otherwise. Still, she tilted her chin defiantly.

'I'm not afraid.'

That made Jean laugh. Still standing by the door, she tugged Alice into her arms and Alice breathed in the chill night air that clung to her coat. 'You're a very pretty liar,' Jean said. 'And I admire you for it.'

Alice fingered a button. 'I am apprehensive,' she admitted. 'But not about what other people will think.' She paused. 'Not right at the moment, anyway.'

A hand stroked Alice's hair back from her forehead, and gentle lips pressed there. 'What are you nervous about?'

Jean's eyes were hooded, the pupils dark, dilated. Alice leaned back and examined them, finding them beautiful. She wanted to kiss the delicate skin of Jean's eyelids. She pecked a kiss onto lips instead. 'This,' she said. 'I've never...done this before.'

Jean winced, and for a moment, Alice thought she'd said the wrong thing, hurt her. Then Jean shook her head.

'Nor have I.'

Alice's hand flattened against the coat Jean was still wearing. 'Oh, I thought...' She petered out. 'I don't know what I thought, actually.'

'Well, you know. I've kissed a woman before.' A shrug that said there might have been more than one. 'But...not like this.'

Alice leaned back on her heels, hearing something that made her suddenly light-hearted, flirtatious. How could one woman make her feel so many things? The hesitancy disappearing for a moment, she gave a feline smile.

'Not like this?' she purred.

A shake of the head, dark eyes riveted on her.

'What is different about this?' Alice's hand slipped under the coat and felt the warmth of Jean's skin through the cotton shirt she wore. She splayed her fingers against it.

Jean caught her hand, pressed her own against it so that it lay trapped under hers. 'You,' she said. 'You're different.' The eyes blinked slowly.

It was impossible to keep up the teasing tone. Alice swallowed. 'I'm different?'

A considering nod. 'I flirt,' Jean said. 'A lot. It's just what I do. It entertains me.' A humorous smile. 'Only gets me in trouble a fraction of the time.' She paused, seemed to be thinking what to say. 'But it's all pretty meaningless.'

Alice interrupted. 'You flirted with me.'

A smile. 'Yes, I did, and it started out just being a bit of harmless fun with a pretty girl.'

'You think I'm pretty?'

That got a laugh and a quick kiss. 'Extremely pretty, and now I can't remember what I was saying.'

'You were talking about how you flirted with me.' Alice

stopped. 'No, actually you were telling me why you're nervous.'

It took a moment for Jean to speak. 'Because while I was bringing you your milk every day, I was falling in love with you.'

Alice stared at her, mind tumbling over the words.

'I was dismayed about it, to tell the truth.' Jean shifted, took Alice's hand from her chest and led them over to the chairs, sat Alice down and pulled another chair close so she could sit down with her knees pressing against Alice's. She took her hands again.

'Sorry I don't have a sofa,' Alice whispered.

'It's okay,' Jean said. 'I understand.'

'Were you really falling in love with me?' There was wonder in the thought.

'I was.' Strong fingers squeezed hers. 'I didn't want to. Tried to make myself believe it wasn't happening. That every morning when we pulled into your street, the churning in my stomach wasn't at the thought of seeing you, but because I hadn't eaten enough breakfast.' She wrinkled her nose. 'Except I've always had a decent appetite and a full meal in my stomach.'

Alice giggled. 'I didn't know,' she said.

That made Jean groan. 'I know!' she said. 'You were oblivious for so long. You'd just smile whenever you saw me and wish me a good day.' She lowered her face to Alice's hands and kissed the fingers. It sent tremors through her.

'And then I did,' Alice said, sobering. 'I found myself looking forward to seeing you each morning, without quite knowing why. You just brightened my day. I liked seeing you.'

'I thought about quitting the milk run,' Jean blurted out.

'What? Why?'

Her fingers were being stroked now, and the firm but gentle touch quickened her breath.

'I didn't know how it could ever work between us,' Jean said. 'I still don't, but I thought about going away, starting somewhere new in another town. I never thought feeling this way would ever work out.'

That made Alice turn her hands over and grip Jean's while she considered what the other woman had said.

'Let's not think about it too much,' she said at last. 'Not right now, anyway. Let's just enjoy the moment.' Alice smiled. 'We don't know what's possible.' She wanted to kiss Jean again. 'All I know is that now I realise how I feel about you, I don't want to let it go, I want to find out more about it. I want to find out more about you – everything about you – and I want to discover what I can be like with you.' She stopped suddenly, abashed at her outburst.

Jean was staring at her, and those lovely cocoa-coloured eyes were wet.

'You are the loveliest thing I've ever met,' she said.

Alice felt the smile spread across her face. 'You make me feel things I've never felt before. I want to sit here like this forever – I want this moment to never end; I want you to tell me all about yourself, every single detail!' She reached up and touched Jean's face, wiping away a single trail of dampness and touching her lips to her tear-stained fingertips. 'Tell me all about yourself, Jean Reardon. Please.'

The kitchen was dim at the back of the narrow house, but outside Alice could hear the birds singing brightly in the trees, and she leaned over the sink to see if she could spot them, wishing the window would open, but the wood was old and swollen shut.

Still, it was going to be another beautiful day, the sun already letting loose its shining skirts over the lawn and trees outside. Both the children were outside, and Alice turned her gaze on them, smiling at them hunched over the little pond there, stirring the dirty water with twigs, looking for tadpoles.

Everything was perfect. The children were happy, absorbed in their task, the birds were twittering, even the breeze through the open back door seemed to taste of delight. Alice picked up her cup of tea and spun around where she stood, knowing there was a silly smile on her face and not caring.

Jean had stayed late the evening before, well into the darkest hours of the night, and when they finally did say goodbye, an owl hooted peevishly at them from the trees, and the moon sailed between the clouds high above it. Alice noticed everything. The whole world had come to life around her, brushing up against her in a swirl of colour, sound, texture.

Now, she glanced at the two chairs where they'd sat, knees touching, hands entwined, lips coming together every now and then in a type of punctuation as they spoke.

And how they'd talked! Endlessly. Openly. About everything. It had been, Alice decided now, standing in the middle of her poor little kitchen, one of the most intimate evenings of her life.

No, she corrected. It had been the best night of her life. She'd never felt closer to anyone than she had to Jean, just sitting on a hard kitchen chair talking.

A warm blush spread across her cheeks and she felt it there and didn't care. It was a beautiful day and she was happy.

'Alice?' There were steps in the hallway and Alice's mother appeared in the room, making it seem immediately too small. She was wrinkling her nose as if there was a bad smell, her eyes giving the room a once-over before settling on her daughter. 'Why aren't you ready?'

Frozen to the spot, Alice gaped at her mother. 'What?'

'It's Sunday, Alice.' She peered behind her daughter and out the back door. 'What on earth are those children doing? Really Alice, this is too much. Get those children inside and ready.'

'Ready?' Alice said.

'Close your mouth, Alice, it's rude and you'll catch flies in it.' Geraldine leaned closer. 'It's Sunday. The third Sunday of the month. The third Sunday in September to be precise.'

Alice snapped her mouth shut with an audible click. 'I'm sorry!' she said. 'I forgot.'

'Is it that hard to keep track of the days, Alice?'

She shook her head automatically. 'Of course not, Mother. I just forgot.'

Geraldine sniffed as if Alice was the source of the unpleasant smell. 'You've offended me, Alice. Now we shall be late for the service, and you know how I dislike being late.'

Indeed she knew. Very well. Punctuality had been drilled into her from an early age. Such a relief it had been when Alice had escaped from her mother's clutches.

'Perhaps we should make it another day, Mother,' she said, trying to keep the hopefulness out of her voice. The last thing she felt like doing today was sitting in the airless church beside her mother, trying to keep the children from squirming throughout the service as if they had a plague of ants in their pants.

'Certainly not,' her mother said, bursting the bubble. 'It is the third Sunday of the month, and as it is all my ungrateful daughter allows me to spend with her and my grandchildren, I refuse to cancel it.'

'I said postpone, Mother, not cancel. We can make it next week instead.'

Her mother was intractable. 'I am here. Mrs McMurtry and her daughter are waiting outside in the car, and I am not leaving this house without you and the children.' She shuddered as if that would be a terrible humiliation, and Alice drooped in defeat.

'Children,' she called, going to the door. 'You must come inside and get ready for church.'

They groaned at her announcement but stood up a moment later and dragged themselves into the house.

'Hullo Grandma,' Jack said, dutifully kissing her on the thickly powdered cheek she turned toward him. Alice touched hands to his shoulders.

'Go and quickly change into your Sunday clothes, Jack,' she said.

Tilly had trailed into the house behind her brother. 'Hullo Grandma,' she said, misery warring with mutiny in her voice and winning.

'Child,' Geraldine said. And sniffed again.

Alice picked Tilly up and gave her a squeeze. 'Come on sweetheart,' she said. 'Let's get you looking clean and pretty.'

'Has the child not even had a bath, Alice?'

'She is perfectly fine, Mother,' Alice said, hoping her daughter wouldn't spill the beans about not having a bath before bedtime the night before. Or, for that matter, about their trip to the beach.

Tilly stuck her fingers in her mouth and said nothing.

'Take her hand out of her mouth, for goodness sakes, Alice,' Geraldine said. 'Bring me her clothes and I will dress the child myself while you make yourself presentable. You are completely dishevelled.'

There was nothing for it but to obey her mother, standing Tilly on a chair and fetching her dress and shoes, handing them over to her mother while Tilly stared at Alice with suffering in her blue eyes. Then, feeling guilty, she hurried to her own bedroom and buttoned herself into her own Sunday best.

They made a sombre procession out the gate to the car, where Sally, Mrs McMurtry's daughter blinked at them from behind thick glasses and waited for them all to get into the back seat before grinding the clutch and lurching them down the road toward the church. Mrs McMurtry twisted around in her seat to peer over at Alice.

'So nice to see you again, Alice,' she tittered. 'And aren't the children getting big?'

'Hello Mrs McMurtry,' Alice said, putting her arms protectively around Tilly beside her.

'Your mother tells me you and the children will be moving back in with her shortly. Such wonderful news.'

Alice stiffened in her seat. She put a warning hand on Jack's shoulder and pulled Tilly even closer.

'I'm afraid that hasn't been decided yet at all,' she said, the words falling coldly out of her mouth.

'Oh?' The older woman's eyes grew owlishly round. 'I understood it to be all settled except for the exact date.'

Shooting her mother a venomous look, at which the woman merely blinked unperturbed and certain of eventually getting her way, Alice spoke through gritted teeth.

'We are perfectly fine in our little house.' She tried a smile. 'Safe and snug. We've no need to move.'

'But it's really not much of a house, is it, Alice?' Mrs McMurtry placed a melodramatic and wrinkled hand on a padded bosom. 'Every time we come to pick you up for church I practically fear for my life.'

'You exaggerate,' Alice said. 'My neighbours are as respectable as yours.'

'But think of the children! All the advantages your mother can offer them!'

'My children have everything they need already.'

Her mother finally broke in, her voice exasperated. 'Come now, Alice, you're being a fool. Your children have everything they need? You live in a filthy little hovel with barely tuppence to rub together. Your husband left you nothing but debts. Not even your own home.'

'I've paid the debts,' Alice said. 'And I have his war pension.' She was too furious at the ambush to look her mother in the eye. 'We get along,' she said.

'Hah, now you are lying, to myself and Mrs McMurtry, as well as yourself, you silly girl. You know perfectly well that without my continued and generous support you would not survive the next week.' She shifted her bulk on the seat and delved into her navy leather handbag. A white envelope appeared in her hand.

'It also appears that you forgot to pick up your birthday present the other day when we had tea together, Alice.' She reached over and held the envelope suspended in the air in front of Alice. 'It could hardly be that you would snub your own mother by being petty enough to refuse your own birthday gift? From the woman who birthed you?'

Alice stared at the envelope, her anger making her inarticulate.

'Stop being such a child, Alice,' her mother said, and the envelope waggled up and down. 'I'm entitled to give my only daughter a gift. Just take it. We're almost there, and I was hoping to speak to the vicar before going in.'

There was the familiar feeling of being cornered. Alice took the envelope and let her hand fall to her lap.

'Thank you,' Geraldine said, with the air of a smug cat.

'That wasn't difficult at all, was it now? You're twenty-five years old now, Alice. It's time to act your age.'

Alice turned to stare out the window although nothing outside the thoughts in her own head registered. Acting her age was exactly what she'd been doing when she'd left the money in the envelope on the small table by her mother's front door. She was tired of being manipulated, and yet, as always, somehow her mother too often got her own way.

She and the children were not moving in with her, however. She drew the line at that. Thank goodness for her own little house. It might not be much, but it was home. She'd sewn the curtains at the windows, and made the counterpanes for the children's beds, and out the back she and Jack had laboured to dig a garden, and there was even a small flower bed that meant she could cheer up the place with cut flowers looking bright and pretty in a milk bottle.

The thought of the milk bottle brought Jean rushing back to her mind. She leaned her tired head against the car window and closed her eyes, willing herself back to the kitchen the night before, sitting with Jean, feeling shy and excited, bold and brave, all at once. How much she had loved watching Jean's face while she talked – the way her eyes lit up when she was talking about the work she'd done during the war and how much she wanted to work on a farm again, maybe even one day own a few acres of her own, have a cow and a few sheep, some chickens, a tractor...

Alice imagined herself in that very picture, her and Tilly feeding the chickens, a fat barn cat watching them from its favourite spot in the sun, while in a distant paddock, Jean sweated over her tractor, turning the fresh black soil over behind the plough, a flock of hungry birds following along every furrow she made.

'Alice!' Her mother's voice knocked her head against the glass. 'Were you asleep? We're here. Get out of the car and straighten up the children.'

Alice let herself out of the car and took the children's hands, looking down at their scrubbed faces and combed hair. She squeezed their little fingers.

'Don't worry, kids,' she whispered. 'It's only one day a month, right?' She smiled at them. 'We can do that.'

Tilly looked up at her with a gaze that said it counted every time she was called *that child* and stuck her fingers back in her mouth. It was a habit that only reappeared every third Sunday of the month. The sight of it made Alice's insides ache.

'Don't worry, Mum,' Jack said, and his hand returned the squeeze. 'She's only an ugly old woman. We get to go home after this, she's stuck with herself all the time.'

Alice looked at her son in surprise. 'Gosh Jack,' she said.

He shrugged and looked around at the people crowding into the stone church. All of them were carefully pressed and ironed into respectability, with not a hair out of place. The women wore gloves and hats, and carried small purses and expressions ranging from bored to beatific.

'It's true, though, isn't it?' he said.

Tilly popped her fingers out of her mouth. 'She's mean,' she whispered.

Alice looked over at Mrs McMurtry's daughter who was helping her mother fuss with her hat. Sally was about the same age as she was, but she'd never left home, and Alice was sure that was the cause of the washed-out and vaguely hopeless expression on the poor thing's face. The girl was completely hen-pecked.

Alice suddenly smiled to herself. If Jean was here, she'd say something funny, tickle Tilly until the girl was all curls and giggles and shining brighter than the very sun. Hugging the secret of Jean to herself, Alice lifted her face to the warm rays of spring sunshine.

'What are you smiling about, Mum?' Jack asked.

'You,' Alice said. 'Because you're right. We do get to go home after this, and it might not be much, but it's ours and we're happy there.' She opened her eyes and looked at her two children. 'It's only church,' she said. 'Then lunch, then we get to go home again, and be our own happy selves, while Grandmother will spend the afternoon on her own being miserable, because that's the way she likes it.'

Tilly tugged on her hand. 'Can we go to the beach again?' she asked. 'Can Jean come and get us in the car and take us to the beach again?'

Alice bent down and kissed her daughter on the cheek. 'Probably not today, sweetheart. But maybe soon. Would that be nice?'

Tilly nodded her head, looked a little happier. Alice looked over at Jack, at the little frown playing over his forehead. 'What about you, Jack?' she asked.

He gave a shrug, then straightened and nodded. 'Yeah,' he said, and Alice didn't even bother to make him say the word properly. 'Yeah, that would be neat.' He blinked. 'Maybe we could even go other places as well.'

'Now that would be lovely,' Alice agreed, her heart lifting. 'But we'd better go and take our seats. Grandmother will be waiting.'

Jean tipped her hat down further over her eyes, seeking the shade and sitting deeper in her saddle.

'Jean!' A shouted greeting from the back of an energetic chestnut. Horse and rider danced over to her. The rider grinned at her. 'Tell me you're back to order us all around again.'

She laughed and shook her head. 'Nope, just an ordinary grunt like you these days.' She gazed out over the group of men getting ready for the day's mustering.

'Aw, come on, you can't say you don't miss it.'

It was true. She did. Terribly. She shrugged, leaned forward to give Thistle, her horse for the day, a pat. 'You know how it is, Jamie. It was only a temporary job.'

Jamie spat his disgust onto the grass. 'Maybe, but things were better back then.' The skin around his eyes creased with his smile. 'Except for the cooking. You were shit at rustling up the bacon and the beans.'

Another laugh. 'Just not one of my talents, I guess. How

are you anyway, you old coot? Still going strong, by the looks of you.'

Jamie Jones flexed a stringy sixty-year-old bicep and leered at her. 'Good as the day the good lord made me,' he told her.

Jean nodded. 'Not bad at all, old man,' she said, then turned to scan the yard. 'So how are things here?' she asked.

'Not as bloody well as they were when you were in charge, that's for sure.'

'I wasn't in charge.'

Jamie scoffed at that. 'You and me, we bloody well ran the place, what with all the young fellas off getting themselves blown up.' He blinked watery eyes at her. 'Wasn't no one else to do it, and we did it fine, if I do say so myself.' His horse stilled, and he leaned confidentially toward her in his saddle. 'Was a crying shame what happened to you. I told the boss – I told him he'd rue the day he let you go.'

Jean shook her head. 'Will Dempsey didn't have any choice, and we both know it. Once Jim came home from the war, of course he had to have back the running of the place.' She blinked in the shade of her hat. 'I was okay – what with getting the job at the dairy.'

'Bollocks to that, Jean, and s'cuse my French and all that.' He scraped a hand across the whiskers on his face and dug into a pocket, pulling out a battered hip flask Jean recognised well. Unscrewing the cap, he took a contemplative swallow, then passed it to her. 'Will would have kept you on, if it hadn't been for Jim. Big Jim.' He shook his head. 'That man can kiss my hairy white arse if he thinks he does half the job you did.'

The whisky burned its way down Jean's throat then

exploded into her stomach. She leaned over, gasping. 'What sort of gut-rot is this, Jamie?'

'All I can bloody well afford these days, girl.'

She handed the flask back, squeezing her watery eyes shut. 'Remind me to donate something that doesn't taste like turpentine.'

The old man laughed, his phlegmy chest rattling. 'I'll hold you to that, count on it.'

They ambled over to the man organising things. He was trying to make himself heard over the bluster of dogs.

'Oi, Boyd,' Jamie shouted. 'Jean and me'll take the Millar's Burn block.'

That got a tick of the finger in return, and they wheeled their horses around, Jamie giving a sharp whistle that peeled two dogs off from the pack.

'Nice easy block, whaddya reckon? My bones are getting old enough for this jaunt.' He slid her a sideways glance. 'And your rump hasn't even seen a saddle for a good while, I'm thinking.'

'You're thinking right there, Jamie,' Jean said, gazing up at the day. Another perfect day, sun warming the greening grass, breeze fresh from the sea, a hawk a high smudge in the sky riding the air currents. 'Good to be out here, though.'

'Miss it, do ya?'

She sighed. 'Yeah.'

The old man shook his head. 'You oughta speak to the boss man. You were a good worker. Woman or not.'

They were through the gates and heading out into the open land, the station spreading out around them. Jean sucked in the fresh air and adjusted her seat to the horse's rolling gait.

'Big Jim's the boss here these days, Jamie.' The hawk spotted something and brought its wings together in an arcing dive. 'And you know how he feels about me.'

'Ain't how the rest of us feel, but.' The flask reappeared. 'Big Jim, my arse. That man ain't nothing but an overgrown playground bully. And his daddy knows it.'

'Maybe so, but Jim is his son, and he made it home from the war, and he gets to run the farm. That's just the way it is.'

Jamie's gnarled hand passed the flask. 'Gets to tasting better the more you have,' he said. Jean rolled her eyes but took it anyway. 'Well,' Jamie said on a heaving sigh. 'You and me, we made a bloody good job of running this place.' He shot her a sidelong glance, waggled a mossy eyebrow. 'My brains, your brawn.'

Jean snorted in laughter, coughing up the mouthful of whisky. 'Yeah, old man,' she said. 'That's just how it was.'

'My story and I'm sticking to it.'

The day smelled of grass and horse and whisky. It made Jean nostalgic and she rode on in silence for a while. She'd missed this for sure.

'So,' Jamie said, unable as ever to keep silent for long. 'What's the gossip down in town then?'

'I wouldn't know,' Jean said. 'Gossip's for old women eating sandwiches after church.'

That got a chortle far louder than it deserved. 'That's a good one. Those fat old women should get out here once in a while, see what life's really about.' He sniffed appreciatively and whistled at his heading dog. 'June!' he called. 'Get your hairy arse back here!' The black and white dog zigzagged in front of them, tongue lolling, grinning comically.

'So,' Jamie said. 'You got yourself someone to take care of hearth and home, yet?'

Jean shifted in her saddle, eyeing the old man, then looking away. She didn't answer.

He leered at her. 'So that's a yes, then, girl? Come on, out with it. You can tell old Uncle Jamie.'

When still no answer came, he gave her a longer look, eyes narrowing under their tufted brows. 'You haven't found yourself some trouble, have you Jean?'

She looked off up the sloping river valley in front of them. couldn't think how to answer.

'I'm serious, Jean. Tell me about her.'

'How do you know there's a her,' Jean answered, sidestepping the question.

His brow beetled under his sweat-stained old hat. 'Listen, Jean. You know me. You and me – we go back a ways now. I ain't gonna judge you like some.' His face broke into a sunny grin. 'Hell, I know all about fancying a pretty woman.'

There was no helping the laugh at that. Jamie Jones was a confirmed bachelor. 'What do you know about women, Jamie?' she teased. 'When was the last time you even saw one besides me?'

He wrinkled his nose and pretended to think about it. '1914,' he said. 'Just as the Great War was starting. 'She said she'd marry me if I made it back, and it was the thought of her that kept me going.' He shook his head, surprisingly serious. His eyes were faraway, peering back into a past Jean had had no idea of.

'Kitty, her name was, and she was cute as a damned kitten too. The biggest grey eyes you ever seen, and hair that came all the way down her back. Could sit on it when it were loose.'

'She sounds lovely,' Jean murmured.

'She was at that. The loveliest woman in Greymouth.' He glanced at her. 'That's where I grew up, you know.'

Jean reached out and laid a hand on Jamie's sleeve for a moment. 'What happened, Jamie?'

He wiped a hand under his nose. Gave another sniff. 'I bloody well avoided getting shelled in the trenches, made it all the way back home from France, only to hear that she'd died just weeks before the ship brought me back to home shores again.' He took out the flask, helped himself to a healthy dose. 'Flu it was. There was an epidemic in 1918, you know. As if the German's hadn't done enough damage.' His head shook slowly, drooping on its neck. 'The bloody flu.'

The flask came her way again, and Jean gulped a mouthful from it. 'I'm real sorry, Jamie.'

He shrugged under his shirt. 'Was a long time ago now. I moved on.'

'But never found anyone else?'

'Not for me, girl. Kitty was the only one for me, and one day soon, I'll get to see her again.'

Jean fell silent. The horses picked their way along the riverbank in the surefooted certainty of long habit.

'So tell old Jamie about the woman who's got you all in a tangle.' He shot her a look of sudden alarm. 'It isn't a man, is it? Because you know if you ever decided to go that way, I was to be first in line?' His mouth split into a grin, but his eyes were serious under the wide brim of his hat.

'Not a man,' Jean said.

'Never been one, for you, has it girl?'

'Not for me, no.' A sigh.

'And now?' He was prompting her, and she gave in at last, simply collapsed into his listening ear, knowing she'd find no judgement.

'Her name is Alice,' Jean said, staring up at the fringe of white clouds bunching up over the horizon. The weather would change. Late afternoon, she guessed.

'I didn't mean to fall for her,' she said. 'I meant to stay clear.' A long, sad breath. 'What future could we have together, after all?'

Jamie whistled under his breath. 'I don't know. This is a small town, but you got an awful lot of friends. Friends who don't much care what you do between the sheets, long as you ain't doing it in front of them. I reckon it's not hopeless.'

That made Jean laugh. 'You're just an old romantic, Jamie, that's what you are.'

The old man pretended to look offended, then laughed, grew serious again. 'What I said is true, Jean. Friends who might be happy for you, if you found someone to keep house with.'

She shook her head. 'We'd have to pretend we were only friends.'

'Friends set up house together. And no one knows for sure what you get up to when the door is closed and the fire bedded down for the night.' He glanced at her. 'Tell me about Alice.'

Jean listened to the stream burbling away to itself beside them, and the cheerful squabbling of birds in the trees.

'She is the most beautiful woman I've ever met,' she said.

CHAPTER 14

Alice climbed out of the car in front of her mother's house and braced herself for the next part of the third-Sunday-of-the-month ordeal. The children came reluctantly after her and for a moment all three of them stood looking at the house in a fug of gloom.

'Come on, kids,' Alice said. 'At least we'll have a nice lunch. Some roast beef, perhaps. Potatoes, parsnips.'

'I don't like parsnips,' Tilly said, trying to hide herself in Alice's skirt.

'But you'll like the pudding afterwards. Ice cream, probably. Some fruit salad? That will be nice, won't it?'

The little girl nodded her head, but still look unconvinced. Jack took her hand.

'Listen,' he whispered. 'I'll eat your parsnips when Grandma isn't looking, how about that? Then you'll still get your pudding.'

Tilly gazed up at her big brother and a hopeful smile bloomed across her face. 'Promise?'

'Pinkie promise,' he said, and they twisted their little

fingers together in some sort of esoteric binding process Alice didn't understand but which seemed to satisfy everyone.

Her mother tapped her on the shoulder. 'Inside, Alice. Children. I've a surprise for you. And luncheon will be on the table shortly.' She stalked towards the house. 'Freshen up and I'll pour the tea.'

Alice looked at her mother's retreating back, then forced her legs to move into the house after her. What did she mean, a surprise?

'What does she mean a surprise?' Jack asked, looking as dubious as Alice felt.

'I don't like Grandma's surprises,' Tilly added.

Alice couldn't make herself say something reassuring. The fine old house seemed to swallow them up as they stepped inside, and she paused on the doorstep for a moment, feeling the same sense of claustrophobia that had her running away at sixteen to get married. She would have done almost anything to escape the place.

It hadn't been too bad a plan, as far as they went. She'd got the children out of it, after all, and her husband Terry had been a good, if unimaginative man. He'd held down a job, even if it hadn't brought much meat to the table, and he'd always been decent enough to her. Until the end.

Alice's mind wandered to Jean. Her thoughts went in a never-ending loop, always back to Jean. Now, she thought, if she'd been more like Jean, had simply left home and got a job, been independent, what would life look like now?

She shook her head. It was silly to ask herself that. She wouldn't swap her children for any life of daring adventure.

Not that it would have been an adventure, of course. Jean

had worked here and there until the war, which had seen her doing quite well on a farm hereabouts – and then the men came home from war and she found a job at the dairy company. Which brought a smile to Alice's face. If Jean hadn't been delivering the milk, would they even have met?

Alice's mother appeared again. 'What on earth are you three doing? Alice, stop wool-gathering and go get washed up.' She lifted her eyes to the ceiling. 'Your combs and things will be in your new bedrooms.' Her eyes blinked at them. 'Although of course, I've put you in your old room, Alice. Tilly has the nursery, and Jack the blue room.' She rubbed her hands together. 'There is plenty of room for all of us, just like I said there would be.'

It was impossible that Geraldine Thomas had just said the words Alice thought she'd heard. Her grip on the children's hands tightened, and she stood staring at her mother. Then, picking up Tilly, she turned and ran up the stairs, heels clacking on the wood.

'Mind my stairs, Alice,' her mother called. 'There's no need to run.'

No. It was impossible. Of course it was. There was no way her mother could have done what it sounded like. Alice made her way to the room that had been hers for too many years. She hesitated in front of the door, suddenly afraid of what she would see if she pushed it open.

She'd not taken her mother seriously when the old woman had told her she was arranging for everyone to move back in with her. Why would she? Alice was a grown woman, widowed, for heaven's sakes. She couldn't be forced to move back home.

She couldn't.

The door swung open and there was Alice's heavy old bedstead from childhood, the furniture that had probably been in the room since her mother was a child, and planted there on the rug beside the bed were two suitcases.

A wail of distress escaped Alice's mouth, and she clapped one of her hands over it.

'What is it, Mum?' Jack asked.

Alice could only shake her head. Venturing into the room, her knees shook, and when she let Tilly slide down onto the bed and reached for the first of the suitcases, her hands were trembling too.

The suitcase on the bed, she lifted the lid, drawing it back slowly, frightened to see what her mother might have done.

'Are those your things, Mum?' Jack asked, and there was a dawning horror in his voice.

She was shaking her head, but of course the clothes in the suitcase were hers. The second case was placed next to the first and opened.

'Jack,' she said. 'Go into the blue room and see if your things are in there.'

His eyes stared at her for a moment, wide and shocked, then he spun around and disappeared into the hallway. Alice looked down at the second suitcase.

'It's your hairbrush, Mama,' Tilly said. 'And all your make-up.' She sifted a small hand through the contents. 'Where's the perfume Daddy gave you?' The perfume was all gone now, but Alice kept the bottle on her dresser anyway. Tilly liked to play with it and it was just about all she had to remind her of Terry. When she swallowed, her throat made a clicking sound. Everything else was there, powder, lipsticks, but no perfume bottle.

Jack came back into the room, dragging two more cases with him. 'My things,' he said, putting one down. 'Tilly's things.' The second was placed beside the other.

There was silence in the room that stretched out for a long moment. Tilly stared up at her mother.

'Are we going to live here now, Mama?'

Alice looked at her daughter, felt her son's eyes on her, then in an abrupt movement, she slammed down the tops of both cases on the bed and snapped them closed. She gathered them both up.

'Jack, can you manage both of those ones down the stairs?'

He nodded.

'Good. Then pick them up, and let's go.'

Tilly climbed down from the bed. 'Where are we going?'

'We're going home, Tilly, that's where we're going.' She made for the doorway, anger flooding through her body like coal-fired steam. 'And when we get there, children,' she added, 'we're never coming back here.'

Between them, Alice and Jack humped the four suitcases down the stairs.

'Is Prudence in there?' Alice heard Tilly whisper to her brother. His voice was harder than it should be for eight years old when he answered.

'No.'

Prudence was Tilly's favourite dolly and Alice's blood boiled at the thought that whoever had done her mother's evil bidding and packed up their things while they were at church hadn't even thought to pack a little girl's favourite dolly.

Her mother appeared in the doorway to the dining room when they reached the bottom stair.

'Ah, there you are. Come along now, Mrs. Birch has luncheon on the table. We don't want it to get cold.'

Alice put her cases on the floor and turned to Jack.

'Please take Tilly outside and wait for me.' She summoned a smile for the children. 'I won't be long.'

'Come on, Tilly,' Jack said, and Alice watched them step out into the sunshine. They'd be fine there for the few minutes this was going to take. And then they'd go home.

'We won't be staying for lunch, Mother,' Alice said, drawing herself up to meet her mother's gaze.

Geraldine shook her head. 'What do you mean you won't be staying for lunch? It's on the table as we speak. It's going cold while you dither there at the bottom of the stairs.'

It was impossible to believe. Even with all the years' experience Alice had with her mother, it was still beyond belief.

'I'm confused, Mother,' she said, fury turning her voice to ice. 'Tell me what made you think you had any right whatsoever to send someone to my house – send a stranger to my house! – and get them to pack my belongings and those of my children and bring them back here.' She shook her head. 'You'd best tell me, because even for you, this is beyond anything acceptable.'

Geraldine took a few steps closer, her face gaining a pinched, righteous look that Alice had seen too many times before.

'I have been telling you and telling you,' her mother said. 'With your no-good husband dead, there is only one suitable place for you and the children, and that is here with me. I will look after you. Here, you will have everything you need.'

'You could easily make sure we have everything we need without us moving in here! You've more than enough money to make sure the children don't have to wear second hand clothing and eat eggs and toast for their dinner more often than not.' She shook her head, her temper finally lost.

'And at what cost would we live here, Mother!' Alice continued, every muscle in her body clenched tight. 'You cannot even call Tilly by her name, and you wouldn't know how to treat a child nicely if it came up and sat on your knee – which no child would ever do without being coerced, because there isn't a single child in the world who would like a witch like you!'

She paused for breath, panting. When she spoke again, her voice was low. 'I left home and got married simply to get away from you, Mother, and there isn't enough money in the world to make me come back here. You're manipulative, and completely deluded. Not to mention just plain mean.' She waved a hand at the door. 'You think you're something because Father was a banker, but he's long in the grave, and probably pleased to be there, out from under your tongue. Now you play on your big house and your money and trail weak little women like Mrs McMurtry and her daughter around just to make yourself feel good. You gossip and plot and plan and make others completely miserable just to make yourself feel good, and I will not be part of it.'

Her mother opened her mouth to respond but Alice ploughed on. 'I haven't finished, Mother.' She barked a laugh. 'Hell, I haven't even barely got started, but I'm not going to waste the rest of my day on this, so I'll condense everything into just this one thing.'

Her mother's eyes hardened into glass balls of obsidian.

'I am a grown woman, Mother, and I will not ever step foot in your house again, except to take your dead body to its grave.' She opened her hand bag and took out the white envelope and waved it at her mother before putting it back on the console table by the door. 'I don't want, and I don't need your money. You cannot buy me anymore.'

Her mother snorted. 'You cannot afford to live without my continued support.'

'I can, and I absolutely will. I have skills, and good sense, and I can support myself. I can sew curtains and furnishings for people.' Yes, Alice decided. She could do exactly that, and she and the children would be fine. She could open her own little business doing alterations as well. She was a fine sewer.

'I had my man take your machine to the dump,' Geraldine said, triumph in her voice. 'Along with every other piece of rubbish in that nasty house of yours.' She sniffed, and advanced another few steps, thin lips stretching into a smile. 'So, you see, Alice. You need me. You can't manage on your own with those two children without my help.' Her arms folded across her chest. 'And I refuse to help you unless you come home where you belong.'

Her things had been taken to the dump? Her sewing machine? Her sewing machine was gone?

'How dare you, Mother?' she asked, dazed at the lengths her mother had been prepared to go to. Her head shook from side to side in disbelief and she turned for the door before glancing back at the figure of the mother she'd been trying to get along with all her life. 'You are a terrible person, Mother,' she said. 'The most terrible person I've ever met.' The sun shone on the world outside the house with her mother in it and Alice knew in a moment she would step out into it and leave her old life completely behind.

'Don't try to contact me, Mother,' she said. 'I'm no longer your daughter.'

The sun reached out and wrapped its arms around her, gathering her up and propelling her down the path where her two children waited for her by the open gate. Jack picked up the two suitcases and led Tilly out onto the footpath, turning towards the long walk home.

Alice fell in beside them.

CHAPTER 15

'Mama, I'm tired,' Tilly said. 'I'm tired of walkin'. Where'd Grandma put my pram?'

Alice gritted her teeth. That was a very good question. She hadn't seen it anywhere at her mother's big white house and wasn't surprised by its absence. Her mother had said more than once that the thing was an eyesore and that the child was too old to need one.

Which was fine, if you didn't do as much walking as Alice and Tilly did. She felt the anger burn in her chest again and damped it down with a quick hand.

'We'll stop here, Tilly, and have a sit down for a while.' Jack's heels were starting to drag too, though the boy hadn't once complained, even though the suitcases would have been getting heavier by the step.

The Egmont Tea Rooms were open on Sunday afternoons, despite the dire frowns of people like her mother, and Alice pushed the door open with a grateful heart, ushering the children in and over to a table. The suitcases were lined up neatly out of the way and both children sat down and drooped over the scarred table top.

Alice calculated the number of coins in her purse, turning her mind resolutely away from the white envelope. There was no way she would ever take anything from her mother again.

'I'll get you an orange drink,' she said. 'And I'm parched for a cup of tea.'

'I'm hungry too, Mama,' Tilly said.

The coins again. Then Alice decided she had nothing to lose. 'Right. Something to eat as well. We could all do with some lunch.' She had a terrible suspicion that when they regained their home, all the food would have been taken away along with most everything else she owned. It would be just like her mother to instruct that everything be taken and gotten rid of.

So they may as well eat now, because there wouldn't be anything at home.

Up at the counter Raylene was wiping down the surface with a checked rag. 'Alice,' she said. 'You and the kids look all done in.' She glanced back at the table where Jack and Tilly were sitting uncharacteristically silent. 'You lot leaving town?'

'What?' Alice blinked. 'Oh. The suitcases.' She shook her head and took out her purse. 'No, just the opposite actually. We're on our way home.'

Raylene, who had been at school with Alice, frowned. 'You been on holiday, Alice? I hadn't heard.'

Alice looked over the counter at Raylene, her friendly face with its wide, generous lips that smiled so easily, and couldn't help herself. The truth spilled out.

'My mother decided to move the children and I into her house with her.' Raylene's eyes widened. 'She sent someone around to my house to pack up our personal things.' Tears of fury and fatigue sprang to Alice's eyes. She blinked them back, mortified.

'Anyway,' she said. 'We're going back home.' A bitter laugh. 'Although she said that everything not in those cases went to the dump. She took my sewing machine to the dump.'

Raylene's mouth had fallen open into a wide, disbelieving O. 'Hey Donny,' she called back to the kitchen. 'Come here a minute.'

'Oh no, Raylene. I didn't mean to make a fuss about it. I'm just tired and the children are hungry. Can we have some cordial and a small pot of tea, please?'

But Raylene was shaking her head and her husband, who did all the cooking, appeared in the doorway, face red from the heat of the stoves.

'Donny,' Raylene said. 'Alice's mother has lost her marbles at last. It's official.'

Donny blinked at his wife, then took in Alice, who wilted under his gaze. 'What?' he asked.

'She tried to force Alice and the young ones to move back in with her. As if anyone in their right mind would want to live with that domineering old cow – no offence, Alice.' Alice didn't take any offence. 'So now they're all walking home with suitcases, and most of their things gone when they get there.' Her black hair whipped across her face as she shook her head.

Donny's gaze came to rest on Alice. 'You'll all be needing lunch then,' he said. 'If you've not eaten already.'

'They haven't, Donny,' Raylene chipped in. 'You cook them up a good feed and then we'll see about getting them home.'

A nod from Donny, then he disappeared into the kitchen again, the sound of his wooden leg tapping across the floor. Alice looked at her old school friend.

'Really,' she said. 'I only wanted a cup of tea and some cordial for the children. And perhaps some sandwiches.' Her hands whitened on her coin purse.

Leaning across the counter, Raylene patted Alice's arm. 'Don't you worry yourself, Alice. Donny'll take care of you, and it's on the house.' She gave Alice a brilliant smile. 'Good on you for sticking to your guns!' A confidential whisper. 'You couldn't pay me to live with your mother, Alice. I don't know how you stood it all those years, I honestly don't.'

'My father,' Alice said. 'He was a good man, and a good father.' She shrugged. 'He's the only thing that got me through.'

'I sure wish he was still around then.' Raylene gave her a wink. 'Now you go and sit yourself down, and I'll bring you a nice cuppa, and how about a pair of Coca Colas for the kids? Something special? Don't you worry about a thing.' Another pat on the arm. 'We'll see you home. I'll drive you myself, if you don't mind going in the delivery van.'

At this point, Alice would have travelled happily in the back of a truck piled high with chickens, if it meant that she could be in her own home again, putting everything back to rights.

'Right now, Raylene,' she said. 'I'll take whatever I can get. The children are exhausted. Thank you.'

The drinks arrived within minutes, served with jokes for the children, and a squeeze of the shoulder for Alice. They'd barely taken a sip when three plates arrived, delivered personally by Donny, piled high with sausages, eggs, and toast. It was a feast.

The hospitality didn't end there. With plates cleared, cups and glasses emptied, Raylene arrived dangling a key from her hand.

'Ready to go, kids?' she asked, and picked up two of the suitcases. 'Let's get you guys back where you belong.'

They followed her out of the building and piled into the van, Tilly sitting on Alice's knee and Jack squeezed in between the women.

'Do you know where the boarding house is?' Alice asked. 'I think there's only the one in town.'

Raylene shook her head. 'There are two. Mrs Boone runs one, over in Hay Street, and The Cotton's run the other. Theirs is a strict establishment.' A look of merry glee transformed Raylene's face. 'You'll definitely want to try to get rooms at Mrs Boone's.'

Alice shook her head. 'No, I've a friend lives there, that's all. I wondered if we could stop so I could leave her a message. I don't have a telephone.'

'Do you want me to drop you off there?'

'I don't know. I don't know if she will be home.'

Raylene turned several corners and the van rumbled to a halt in front of a large weatherboard house, the white paint peeling over the veranda. 'Who's your friend?'

There was a moment's hesitation before Alice answered, opening the door and sliding out of the van, leaving Tilly on her seat. 'It's Jean Reardon,' she said. 'I promise I won't be a moment.'

A wide-eyed gaze followed her as she stepped up onto the footpath and walked down an overgrown path to knock on the front door.

She had to lean in to knock, the door open to a hallway that dipped and swayed on uneven floorboards. A door opened to the left and Alice stepped back, startled.

'Yes?' A large woman in a print cotton dress bustled out to the doorway, a worn pinny apron stretched over her bosom and talking as she moved. 'How can I help you, love? We don't have any rooms available at the moment.'

'No.' Alice shook her head. 'I mean, I'm not here for a room.' She tripped over the words, sudden nervousness flooding through her like static electricity.

'All right then. What can I do for you?'

Alice bit at her lip. 'Is Jean Reardon here? I think she has a room here. I was wondering if I could talk to her.'

The woman, Mrs Boone, Alice guessed, glancing back down the path at Raylene watching her from the van, stared at her for a moment that went on too long to be comfortable.

'What do you want with Jean?' she asked at last.

Her tone had Alice frowning. 'We're friends,' she said.

'Wait a minute, love.' Mrs Boone considered her more closely. 'I recognise you. You wouldn't happen to be Alice Holden, by chance, would you?'

She blushed. She felt it spread warm hands across her throat, and up over her cheeks until her entire face was burning. 'Yes,' she said, then cleared her throat so the rest of her answer wouldn't come out a squeak. 'How do you know?'

Mrs Boone settled her bulk against the doorframe as

though she needed support to stand while she sniffed at Alice. 'Because yesterday morning I was digging around for two children's spades and buckets for Jean to take to the beach. I believe you have two children?'

A dumbfounded nod. 'Yes. A girl and a boy.'

'Ah, yes. Jean did say.' The eyes, bright as buttons in a face of dough, squinted at her. 'I must say, you're as pretty as she said you were.'

The blush deepened, and Alice put a hand to her cheek hoping to cool it. 'Is she here? Jean, I mean. Is she here?' Another glance down at the road where Raylene had gotten out of the van and was standing on the grass verge smoking. She caught Alice's eye and waved. Alice's hand hovered in the air in return, then fell to her side. 'I really need to speak to her.'

The landlady straightened and turned serious. 'Why?' she asked. 'What's going on? You're not going to do something stupid, are you?'

Confusion had Alice blinking at the big woman. 'I don't know what you mean. Another quick look at the children. They were sitting in the van, peering out at her. She turned back to the woman in front of her. 'Please, if Jean isn't here, can I leave a message for her?'

Another considering look, then finally an answer that Alice could understand. 'She isn't here. She's helping out with mustering for the day.'

Well, Alice had thought she'd be able to understand it. 'Mustering?'

A shrug of heavy shoulders. 'Yep, out on old Dempsey's farm. Where she used to work?'

The news had Alice taking a step backwards. 'She used to

work for Big Jim?'

The landlady barked a laugh. 'That'll be the day. She worked for his old man, during the war. Practically managed the place.'

'But she delivers milk now.'

'Yes, she does. Because Jim Dempsey – I refuse to call that human piece of rubbish Big Jim – didn't like a woman doing his job better than him when he came back from the war. And he especially didn't like that woman being Jean. And you can guarantee he's not out there on a horse bringing in the stock today. She wouldn't go there if he was.'

Alice was confused. 'She told me she'd worked on a farm during the war…'

'But not the whole sorry story? She won't tell much of it. A decent sort is Jean. And happy enough with her job now. Won't complain, that's for certain. Still, it was ugly for a while then.'

With a sigh, Alice turned and stared out over the starved front yard. 'There's so much I don't know about her yet,' she murmured.

'Ah well, Jean can't afford to go around telling everyone everything, can she?'

Alice thought about that one for a moment. She hadn't considered what Jean's life had been like, not really. Not in practical ways. She itched to find Jean and beg her to trust her with everything.

But trust had to be deserved. Standing taller, she smiled at the woman in the doorway. 'Thank you. It's Mrs Boone, isn't it?' At the woman's nod, she continued. 'I'd be very grateful if you could tell Jean I was here on the off-chance she was home. And that I'll see her tomorrow.'

She smiled and hurried off down the path to the van where Raylene was stubbing out her cigarette.

Mrs Boone stood on the path and watched her as Alice climbed into the van and she could feel the considering gaze all the way down the street.

CHAPTER 16

Jean dragged her sorry behind out of the car and stood in the cooling breeze, groaning and rubbing at her rump. It had been too long since she'd been on a horse. Damn things took practiced muscles and she was out of shape.

Still, she thought, closing the car door and heading down the path to a hot cup of tea and a soft bed, she wouldn't have missed the day for all the world. Talking with old Jamie had been a treat, and all that fresh air, the mountain in the distance overseeing everything, the back and forth of the dogs, good old Thistle snorting under her – Jean missed it all more than she cared to admit,

Mrs B pounced on her as soon as she had the front door open. Bloody thing squealed on its hinges and the landlady never would let her squirt a bit of oil in it to quiet it. Jean reckoned the landlady used it as an early warning system.

'Good day?'

'The best,' Jean replied. 'But my arse begs to differ.'

Mrs Boone gave a shrug as though she didn't give a fig for

the state of Jean's backside. 'Had a visitor while you were out playing cowboy.'

'Yeah?' Jean waited.

'Yeah.'

She counted to three. 'You going to tell me, or I gotta crowbar it out of you?' She put a hand on the bannister to go upstairs to her room. Wash, cup of tea, soft bed.

'Pretty young thing name of Alice Holden came by to see if you were home.'

Jean dropped her hand and swivelled slowly on her heels. 'What did you say? Alice came here?'

'She did, sure as I'm standing here.'

'What did she want?'

'Did not say. But she looked mighty flustered and upset when she came tearing down that path to find you.' Mrs Boone lifted her chin. 'Seemed to go back to her pal feeling considerably better, however.'

Jean blinked in the yellow light from the single bulb above them. 'What do you mean?'

'Well, I don't rightly know. I told her you were out mustering for Old Man Dempsey, said what a crying shame it was that shit Big Jim did you out of your rightful job...'

'Mrs B. for the hundredth time, it wasn't my rightful job. I was only filling in while he was over in the Pacific. And what on earth were you telling Alice that for?'

'Secret is it? Bad way to start relationships, with secrets.'

Jean dragged a hand through her hair. 'You know perfectly well it's no secret. We haven't got to telling each other every little thing, is all.' She looked up the stairs, then back at the door. 'There isn't even a real relationship. What did she want? How did she even get here?'

'Not a real relationship yet, Jean. I see the way you feel about the girl.' Mrs Boone looked at her, then obviously decided to answer the question.

'I don't know what she wanted, said only to tell you she stopped in on the off-chance that you were here.' The landlady paused. 'Which wasn't my impression. I think she'd had a bad day and her first impulse was to come find you.' A shorter pause, just for a breath. 'Came in the van belonging to Donny and Raylene.' She saw Jean's uncomprehending look. 'They run the Egmont Tea Rooms. Alice probably went to school with them.' Mrs Boone squinted at Jean. 'Where did you grow up, again?'

'Little place outside Wellington,' Jean said tersely. Something had obviously happened to Alice. She couldn't think of any other reason for Alice to come round here to find her. Another glance up the stairs, thinking of the bathroom, a much-needed wash. She turned for the door.

'Where are you going? You've just got in. I've kept some dinner warming for you. Thought you might be glad of it after a long day in the saddle.'

'Thanks, Mrs B, but I need to go find out what Alice wanted.' She opened the door and stepped out into the evening, the landlady trailing after her.

'Guess I'll eat it myself,' Mrs Boone said. 'Go on with you then. Just make sure you don't lose your head over this one, Jean Reardon. Tread carefully. Isn't no one in town doesn't step light around that girl's mother.'

Jean gave her a perfunctory wave and walked back to the car, pulling out her cigarettes and lighting one as she did, breathing in the smoke and calming down a fraction.

If anything had happened to Alice...she opened the door

and climbed back in, unable to bite down on the whimper of discomfort that was her aching muscles. What day was it? Hadn't Alice said something about the third Sunday of each month? She did a quick calculation. That was today.

Which meant that Geraldine Thomas was likely involved in whatever had upset her daughter. Jean didn't let the thought slow her down and she was there by the time she was putting out her cigarette and wishing she had a breath mint or something.

Not that she was counting on Alice being in a kissing frame of mind.

From the front door, it didn't look like there were any lights on in the house, but Jean tapped on the door anyway, then did it again, louder, turning on the doorstep and looking left and right down the street while she waited to see if Alice and the children were home.

But where else would they be, at this time of night? She scuffed her boots nervously, wishing she didn't smell quite so much like horse and dog and cow, but it was too late now to go back home for a quick bath. At least the fatigue was gone. She was as wide awake as she'd ever been.

A black cat stalked along the top of the fence, its eyes like yellow headlamps. It sat down on its haunches, lowering its head and staring at Jean.

'You look like you know what's going on,' Jean said to it. 'You wanna let me in on it?'

'In on what?' The door behind her was open, Alice standing silhouetted in dim light from the end of the hallway. She looked slim, pale, and tired. Jean had never seen her looking more beautiful.

'I was talking to the cat,' Jean said, wanting to lean

forward and breathe in the subtle spice of Alice's skin. She stuck her hands in her pockets instead and stood up straighter. 'Mrs B told me you'd been around to the boarding house?'

The tired face relaxed and broke into a smile. 'You came around here because of that?'

'I thought there might be something wrong.'

The smile broadened, and suddenly there were arms around Jean's neck, and a soft body pressed against her. Her own arms, of their own volition, encircled the slim waist.

'What are you doing?' she managed to whisper. 'We're on your front door step.'

'I don't care,' Alice said, but she stood back on her own feet again, her face warm and flushed now. 'I've had the most dreadful day, and I was missing you so much, and here you are, like some miracle, on my doorstep!'

'Not so much of a miracle,' Jean said, although she was enjoying the smile. 'You came around to see me, remember.'

'Yes, but I wasn't expecting you to turn up here because of that.'

Jean reached out and stroked Alice's cheek, before catching herself. 'Can I come inside? Or are we going to give that cat and the rest of the street something of a show?'

'Definitely come inside. I am so glad to see you.'

Jean wanted to ask about the bad day, and she was going to, just as soon as she'd got something else out of the way, now that there was no one to see them. The door closed behind them and Jean was acutely aware of Alice right next to her in the narrow passageway.

'I'm glad to see you too,' she breathed, one hand going to

seek the warm length of Alice's neck, drawing her lovely face nearer, looking for her lips.

She found them against her own, and for a moment she forgot herself in their exquisite softness, the whispering breath between them, and the deepening kiss reverberated downwards to nest deep in her belly, spreading out a warm glow that had her humming under her breath before she pulled back and gazed at Alice, looking silently into her eyes for a long moment, neither of them speaking.

She sought Alice's hand, the cool fingers entwining around her own. Wanting to focus on Alice's lips again, Jean cleared her throat and forced herself to speak instead.

'I'm sorry about the way I must smell,' she said, and gave a shamefaced laugh. 'I didn't stop for a bath.'

Alice broke into a beaming smile. 'You do smell rather of horses. Your landlady – who by the way seems rather formidable – told me you were out mustering.' She narrowed her eyes. 'She also told me some things you neglected to mention the other night when we were talking.'

Jean couldn't help the sigh that escaped her. 'I didn't want to turn our conversation to unpleasant details.' She touched the silky skin of Alice's cheek again. 'We were having such a nice time.'

'I told you all of my secrets!' The most delicate of shrugs. 'Or all the interesting ones, anyway.' Her smile was full of humour.

Jean nudged her down the hallway. 'Well,' she said. 'How about we put the kettle on and you can tell me all about your terrible day? Then if you have any questions for me about anything, I promise to tell you the whole truth of it all.' She opened her mouth to say more, paused, then went ahead. 'I was worried silly all the way here that something terrible had happened between you and your mother.'

They landed in the kitchen, and Jean looked about, frowning slightly. Something was different about the room, but she couldn't properly place what.

'Something did happen between my mother and I,' Alice said, going to the coal range and lifting the kettle onto the burner. 'That it did indeed.'

'You've got a new kettle,' Jean said, finally hitting on one of the incongruities.

'Well, that's part of the story,' Alice said, turning to pick up two mismatched cups from the draining board. 'New kettle, new cups, two new breakfast bowls, and two whole sets of new cutlery.' She placed the cups on the table. 'Also, a new teapot.' That went onto the table too, and Jean sat down, looking up at Alice in silence. There was an edge to Alice's voice that told Jean the story was going to be an impressive one. She felt her internal temperature rise at the thought of anything going wrong for Alice. There were enough pressures in Alice's life already.

'Are the children all right?' she broke in to ask.

'Yes, they're fine. They're asleep, thank goodness.' She shook her head. 'I ought to start at the beginning, because otherwise I'll lose my temper all over again, and it will just be a big jumble.'

There were two spots of high colour on Alice's cheeks, and Jean found herself admiring them. Alice wound up was quite the sight. She blinked the thought away and told herself off for thinking with her goddamned hormones.

'Tell me what happened,' she said.

Jean spent the next half an hour in a state of growing disbelief. 'She did what?'

'Took all our possessions to the dump,' Alice said. She cocked her head to one side over her teacup. 'All, that is, that didn't fit in four small suitcases.'

Aware that her mouth was hanging open, Jean couldn't seem to get it otherwise.

'We're drinking tea kindly donated by Marjorie next door. It's her teapot, and cups as well. Angela on the other side gave me the kettle and the blankets the children are sleeping under and the set of sheets on my bed. That's all I have to sleep under tonight – a sheet, thanks to my mother.' Her eyes hardened to green flints. 'Mother had the beds completely stripped and all my linen thrown out. We're lucky the beds themselves were still here.' Alice looked around the bare kitchen. 'Any of the furniture for that matter. Particularly as it came with the house and doesn't belong to me at all. I don't know how I would explain that one to Bob Forrester, my landlord. He would not have been at all pleased.'

Jean took Alice's hand and held it in her own. 'I'm so sorry,' she said.

Alice shook her head, although there was a film of moisture in her eyes that she couldn't hide from Jean.

'The worst thing is the loss of my sewing machine,' Alice said. 'I will miss all the pretty little things I'd managed to find over the years, but without my sewing machine, I don't know how I'm going to support us.' Her shoulders slumped. 'I'll have to look for work, but I don't know who will give me a job. I'm not qualified for anything. I never stayed at school long enough, and never paid much attention when I was there.' Her fingers went limp in Jean's hand.

Jean was shaking her head. 'There's only one thing for it,' she said.

'What's that?'

'We have to get your things back.'

Round eyes stared up at her. Jean nodded. 'Tomorrow, we'll take a trip to the dump and retrieve your things. We'd have done it today if I'd known what was going on.' She winced. 'I'm sorry,' she said. 'I feel as though I've let you down.'

The already round eyes widened. 'How on earth have you let me down? It wasn't your fault this happened.'

'No,' Jean squeezed the fingers in her hand. 'It wasn't of course, but…'

'But what?'

'I guess I feel that if I hadn't been out on the muster, I would have been around to help sooner.'

Alice's hand twisted in her grasp and held onto hers. 'I was all right,' she said. 'Well, I managed, put it that way. I would have loved it if you had been here, but the kids and I – we're used to coping on our own.'

A sharp pain dug in under Jean's rib cage.

'Is something wrong?' Alice asked, alarmed.

'No.' Jean rubbed a hand across her face and winced. 'It's just that…I want to say things to you that I have no right to, and it hurts me.'

There was a brief silence, then Alice put her cup down and leaned towards Jean. 'What things?' she asked. 'Tell me anyway.'

A shake of the head. It was an impossible situation, Jean realised.

'Please?' Alice edged her chair closer, until their heads

were touching. Jean could feel her breath on the side of her face. Alice's slim fingers squeezed hers.

When Jean lifted her head, Alice's eyes, back to their warm hazel, were looking seriously at her. A lump pressed against her throat. 'You are so beautiful,' she croaked.

Alice lifted her other hand and stroked Jean's forehead and down her cheek, until her fingertips grazed the edge of Jean's mouth. A look of revelation spread across Alice's face.

'I want you to make love to me,' Alice said. The hand against Jean's face shook and her voice had a tremble to it.

Jean couldn't speak.

'Please?' Large green-brown eyes looked at her, and the hand flattened until Alice's palm cupped Jean's cheek. 'You make me feel so many things, and I know what they mean.'

'What do they mean?' Jean's voice was strangled with her own feelings.

The pause before Alice answered was so long that Jean thought she'd changed her mind. But then Alice was moving, sliding from her chair onto Jean's lap, arms wrapping around her neck, thick hair tickling Jean's face. Alice lowered her lips to Jean's ear and the warm breath against it had Jean closing her eyes against light-headedness.

'They're telling me about love, Jean. That's what all my nerve-endings are screaming about. Every time I'm near you I want to be held by you, hold you to me. I want to spend an hour just gazing into your eyes, I want to put my face next to yours and just breathe in the scent of your skin. You make me dizzy just by looking my way, you make me feel faint just with the way you smile at me. You make me want to take you in my arms and kiss you wildly, and you make me want you to hold me and love me and not just with words and looks, but with everything you are.' She lifted her head and Jean gazed up at her, all words and thoughts falling from her mind.

'I think it's called love, Jean,' she said, a furrowed little frown appearing on her brow. She looked momentarily young and vulnerable.

Jean was overwhelmed, flooded with feeling like it was a physical thing. She tightened her grip on Alice, pulling her closer, sliding a hand up her back and pulling her head down so their lips could touch. There had never been a kiss that tasted sweeter.

CHAPTER 17

*A*lice tapped on the bathroom door, the towel her neighbour had given her folded tightly in her arms.

'Come in.'

She had to swallow before opening the door. Even then, she pushed it open slowly, tentatively.

'It's all right,' Jean said. 'I'm not going to jump on you and drag you into the bath with me.' She was leaning forward and Alice could see the water droplets running down between her shoulder blades.

'I'm not entirely sure I'd mind if you did,' Alice said, coming two steps into the small room and staring at the constellations of freckles on Jean's shoulders. One of them looked just like the Southern Cross.

Unable to stop herself, she crossed to the bath and traced a finger over the damp, freckled stars. Jean stilled under her touch.

'You have such wonderful skin,' Alice murmured, fingertips moving to follow the curve of shoulder up to where it met spine. She smiled at the knobs of backbone under the skin. 'You're too thin, though.'

'I prefer to think of it as wiry,' Jean said. 'Full of understated strength.'

A giggle welled up inside Alice and escaped. She sat on the edge of the old tub and found the soap. Dipping it into the hot water, she ran it over Jean's back, leaving a trail of white, soapy bubbles. Then she dropped it into the water and used her hand instead, smoothing it over the wet skin, feeling the contours of ribs, spine, the flesh prickling under her touch. Her lips parted slightly, and she bent down, pressed them to one golden shoulder. Jean held herself completely still under her touch and Alice sat back up, flustered at herself.

'I'm sorry,' she said. 'I shouldn't have done that.' She went to get up, back out of the room, get her breath back.

But Jean grabbed her hand. 'Don't go,' she said. Alice sat where she was and looked at her. Jean closed her eyes and laid Alice's hand against her breastbone, pressing it there at the base of her throat. Alice felt the rise and fall of Jean's chest, looked down at where her hand was held, hot bare skin beneath it. An unruly lock of hair shadowed Jean's face.

Slowly, barely moving, wondering if she was dreaming, Alice slid her hand down Jean's damp skin, feeling skin and bone give way to something softer as she touched Jean's breast.

A sound escaped her, not any word, just an exhalation of surprise. And pleasure. She moved her hand more, until she was cupping the heavy softness of Jean's breast.

'It feels good,' she said, barely able to breathe, to form the words. 'You feel so good.'

Jean's eyes came open, looking up at her, holding her

gaze. Her lips moved but Alice didn't make out any words. She didn't know if Jean had spoken out loud. The nipple under her hand hardened and Alice let go, brushed her palm across it, wondering at the way Jean's eyes widened, their gaze still holding steady on hers. Alice slid off the side of the tub onto her knees and leaned over the edge, feeling the steam from the water settle on her skin in a caress of its own.

'I want to kiss you,' she said, her lips only an inch away from Jean's.

Those cocoa-coloured eyes, with their close-up flecks of gold, looked at her without blinking, and there was a hand in her hair, drawing her that last inch closer until there wasn't any distance at all, they were touching, and to Alice, it felt like they were sharing the very same breath, the very same soul.

She was gasping when the kiss ended, and Jean's face had turned a dusky glow under her tan.

'I need to get out,' Jean said. 'I need to get out of this bath, or else I'll prove myself a liar and pull you in here with me after all.'

Alice could feel Jean's heart beat against her ribs. She took her hand from Jean's breast and pressed it to her own, feeling the rapid beating as she nodded. Then smiled.

'Let me wash the soap off your back first,' she said, and standing up again, she dipped her hand into the water that felt cool now compared to the heat that had built inside her and splashed it gently over the curve of Jean's back as she leaned forward in the bath again. Alice's hand slowed, washing off the soap, feeling the slick skin under her palm, enjoying the sensation of touching another adult, another woman.

Then she laughed, realising she was slipping into some sort of trance, entranced, delighting in Jean's body beneath her hand.

She stood, picking up the towel and unfolding it, holding it out.

Jean stood up without taking her eyes from Alice, the water rushing from her body. Alice held her gaze, then unable to help herself, let it wander down over the curves and angles of Jean's nude body.

When she stepped out of the bath, Alice wrapped the towel around her, and then her arms, resting her forehead for a moment on Jean's damp shoulder and just breathing in the warm, clean scent of her, knowing that there was more to come, if she wanted it. And she wanted it. She wanted to feel Jean's skin against her own. She wanted to lose herself in that gaze, feel those strong hands against her flesh, and open herself up to this woman standing in front of her.

She trembled where she stood, and Jean kissed her temple, moved her gently, took her to the door, and together they walked through the kitchen, past the door to the room where her children slept, and into her bedroom where she thought, stepping across the threshold, that finally her life was beginning.

'Is it always like that?' Alice asked, lying on her back in the bed, staring up at Jean with eyes that were bright and wet in the light shining in from the street.

Jean, on her side, resting her head on one hand, looked down at the woman beside her, the woman she'd just made love to. With. She had to swallow before she could speak. Alice's skin was cooling under her hand, and she drew up the sheet with regret. A moment later, she swept it back down over Alice's thighs again, not wanting to take her eyes off the curves and hollows of Alice's body.

'Has it ever been like that for you?' Alice asked before Jean had managed an answer to the first question. She put her hand over Jean's and smoothed it over her skin, cupping the fingers around a breast for a moment, them stroking Jean's hand down over the swell of belly to slip it between her thighs where she was still damp.

Jean shook her head. 'Never,' she said.

Alice laughed, rolled over onto her side to face Jean, trapping her hand as she did so. 'Good,' she said, then sobered and traced a fingertip over the contours of Jean's face. Jean closed her eyes. The touch felt like the whisper of butterfly wings. 'I want that to have been special between us.' Her eyes gleamed in the shadows of her face and her fingers pressed against Jean's lips. 'Your body against mine, your lips on my skin,' she whispered, and Jean could feel her warm breath. 'Your touch inside me – right deep inside me – your murmured words in my ear, your legs wrapped around me, all of it was so beautiful I could cry.' She licked her lips but there were no sign of tears, only a mouth curved in a smile.

Which Jean kissed, shifting her hand from its warm trap and smoothing it over the round hip, down the pale thigh, and hooking the knee up over her own leg. She shifted slightly, until Alice was tucked up close against her, coming willingly, moving closer so that Jean could feel the heat of her against her leg, and then unable to help herself, she was rolling them both over on the bed so that Alice was looking up at her, lips parted, hair spread in a rich halo around her head.

Another kiss on those lips, Jean closing her eyes and losing herself in it, so that when the tip of Alice's tongue touched her own, she couldn't help the groan, the tightening of need inside her again, every part of her alive and wanting Alice.

There were so many places to press her lips to. The line of Alice's jaw, the delicate hollow under her ear, a trail of kisses down the neck, Alice gasping, whispering something Jean couldn't hear, but arching up against her, pressing her breasts into hers.

The shoulder and back again to Alice's throat, the skin tasting sweet and salty, and moving down, the hard knot of a nipple against Jean's lips, Alice's cry in her ears as she took it into her mouth.

'Shh,' she said. 'You'll wake the children.'

Alice's reply was a strangled moan, and Jean moved on, dipping her head between Alice's legs, tasting her with her tongue and Alice was sweet, tasting somehow golden, and Jean felt dizzy with pleasure. Here was her secret dream, made flesh.

The hands in her hair stilled, Alice's whole body stiffening in surprised sensation. Jean ran her tongue over her swollen nub again, and the fingers tangled in her hair moved, tugging at her, then shifting away to grip at the sheet underneath them. Jean closed her eyes and surrendered herself to the exquisite feeling of Alice's letting go, the way she moved against Jean, crying out as her pleasure built higher, towards a great, shuddering, flooding climax.

And somewhere deep inside her, Jean let go as well, of all the fear, all the frustrated desire she'd felt her whole life, and she gave herself over, crying out at the same time that Alice did, knowing that as she too surrendered, she was gaining everything she'd ever wanted.

The morning came too swiftly, the early hour when Jean had to ease herself out from under the warm drapery that was the sleeping Alice. How she wanted to stay. How much she wanted to lie there and watch the dawn light the room, sending its golden touch stealing over Alice, lighting up her skin to a molten glow. How much more she wanted to wake Alice with her hands, her lips, her mouth, feel her turn sleepily towards her, eyes opening, lips parting in a smile brighter than any sun, and arms that reached for Jean, drawing her into an embrace she never wanted to leave, wanted instead always to feel around her.

But reality intruded, pressing its mundane demands upon Jean, demanding that she slide from the bed and into the cool pre-dawn air, and get ready for work.

She stood beside the bed in the light from the street and gazed down at Alice before drawing the sheet back up over Alice's beautiful body. Perfect, so perfect. Jean looked at her and a dazzling happiness spread throughout her, a physical thing that made her tremble as she tucked the sheet in around Alice's shoulders, dropping a kiss as light as dandelion fuzz on the warm skin as she did.

There was only the towel there for her to put on. With a smile, she realised all her clothes were still back in the bathroom where she'd left them the night before. Hours ago. A lifetime ago. The towel was damp against her bed-warmed skin when she wrapped it around herself and crept to the door.

In the bathroom, she closed the door and switched on the light, standing there blinking for a moment before her eyes adjusted and making a running assessment of the way she felt.

Like she'd been riding a horse all day and making love all night. It was, she decided, the best feeling in the world. She stretched, went searching for her watch.

'Shit.' Just enough time to dress, go back home and get changed, then turn up for work. Monday morning and milk to deliver. She bent for her clothes.

In the kitchen she stopped for a drink of water, searching for a glass before she remembered that Alice's mother had sent some goon to clear the place of everything Alice owned, food included. A tea cup had to do instead, Jean burning with anger over it, and wishing she could go storming over to Geraldine Thomas' fancy house and shake the woman out of bed…

'What are you doing here?' Tilly stood beside the table rubbing at her eyes. 'Did you sleep here?'

Jean put the cup down and crouched down in front of the child. 'I did,' she said. 'I fell asleep. What are you doing up, sweetheart? It's much too early.'

A soft little frown. 'You're up.'

The kid's logic was unassailable. 'I have to go to work.'

That got a smile. 'You have to bring us our milk.' The look turned sly. 'Can we have cream too?'

Jean laughed. Even at four in the morning the girl was an opportunist. 'We'll see, shall we? Now, how about getting you back to bed?'

'I'm thirsty.'

'All right. One drink coming up.' She refilled the tea cup and passed it to Tilly, watching the child slurping down the water.

'I gotta go to the toilet now,' Tilly said, passing the cup back and disappearing into the bathroom.

'Okay,' Jean said. 'That's good.'

The child was back a few minutes later and looked up at Jean still standing there. 'Will you tuck me back in?'

She nodded her head, no words appearing on the sudden welling of feeling. Tilly took her hand and led the way, looked up at Jean as she lay back in bed.

'Night Jean,' she said. 'Don't forget the cream.' She closed her eyes.

'Night kid,' Jean whispered, then hesitated a moment before bending to plant a kiss on Tilly's forehead.

A smile appeared on Tilly's rosebud mouth. 'You gonna help us, aren't you Jean?' Her eyes were still closed.

Jean breathed deep and backed out of the room. 'Sure am, Tilly,' she said. She faced the front door and the world outside, her car which had been parked in front of the house bold as brass all night long, and took another breath.

'Sure hope so.'

im Fry kept shooting her sidelong glances as they loaded the milk crates into the back of the delivery truck. Jean straightened, finally, hands on her back, stretching.

'What is it for god's sakes, Tim? You've been looking at me like I turned green over the weekend.' Her muscles ached, and other parts of her as well were very pleasantly fatigued.

'You've been humming,' Tim said.

Jean raised an eyebrow.

'Sometimes actually breaking into song.'

The other eyebrow joined the first.

'And when you're not humming and singing, you're whistling.'

She blinked at him and he shrugged.

'Look. I'm not saying there's anything wrong with any of those things. Or even anything especially unusual…'

She picked up the last crate and heaved it into place, a smile curving her lips. 'Then what are you saying, Tim?'

Her work partner scuffed his shoe on the gravel in front of the loading doors to the dairy, then grinned at her.

'Only time I get to feeling that much like singing is when the wife's been extra nice to me, if you get my drift.' He cocked a crooked smile at her.

Jean shook her head. 'I do not want to hear about you and Rosie.'

The smile widened into a grin and Tim swung into the driver's seat. 'Well I sure want to hear about whoever put you into such a good mood.'

Jean took her place in the seat next to him. 'I don't kiss and tell, Tim, you ought to know that.' She leaned back in the seat and turned her face to the rising sun, closing her eyes.

'Not going to fall asleep on me, are you? Didn't happen to stay up all night getting lucky, did you?' He turned out onto the road and headed for the first street on their route.

'Staying awake will not be a problem, I promise.' Jean stretched again, luxuriously this time, then caught Tim's eyes on her and laughed. He was right. She was feeling pretty bloody incredible.

'Aw, come on, Jean. Spill the beans.'

She shook her head. 'You don't really think I'm going to, do you?'

Tim pretended to concentrate on the road. 'So just the one thing, then.' A quick glance at her then back to the road. Jean looked at him, wondering what was coming. Or rather, she had a fair idea what was coming, she was just wondering the exact format she'd hear it in.

'So what...' He cleared his throat. Rubbed at his nose. Leaned forward closer to the windscreen as though driving this particular stretch of perfectly straight empty road took extra concentration.

'So what?' Jean prompted. She liked Tim. And she was feeling good. Nothing Tim said could erase the memories of Alice's kisses upon her skin. She shivered, remembering.

Tim cleared his throat again. 'So what do you do?' he asked. 'You know.' His face bloomed bright red. 'In bed. Two Sheilas, like.' A pause. 'I know that's how you are.'

'You do?'

'It's ah, kinda obvious. Bit of a ladies' man.' His face got even brighter. 'Ladies' lady. Or whatever you'd call it.'

Jean tipped her head back and looked out at the brightening sky. 'I don't know. Ladies' man – I rather like that.'

He risked a look at her. 'So, what's it like then?'

She shrugged. 'I don't know, Tim. What's it like with you and Rosie?'

'What do you mean? You ain't got the same equipment I got, if you get my meaning. You can't tell me it's the same.'

'No, I haven't got quite the equipment, as you say.' She grinned. 'Although there's a shop in the big city that would sell me certain, ah, attachments, if I so desired.'

Wide, shocked eyes turned to her.

'Watch it, Tim, you're going to go into the ditch.'

He swung his head back to the front and the truck veered back onto the road, the milk bottles rattling in the back.

'Take it easy, Timmy, we'll lose the lot if you're not careful.'

He was shaking his head. 'Tell me it ain't true.'

It was hard to admit, but she was enjoying herself. 'Can't say that, my friend.'

The eyes were on her again, mouth hanging open under them. 'How do…do you..?' His brain hit overload.

'The road, Tim,' Jean said, and he looked automatically back in front of them.

'A kind of belt, Tim.' She stifled the laugh. The poor guy wasn't ever going to be the same. His innocence was lying somewhere back there on the dirt road behind them, dead as a squashed possum. 'You wear it belted on.' She whistled a tune for a moment. 'They've been around a very long time, you know.'

Again with the amazed glance. 'How long?'

She shrugged. 'No real idea. Hundreds of years?'

He shook his head in disbelief. Opened his mouth. Nothing came out. Opened it again. Squeaked out a question.

'Do you..?'

She took pity on him and didn't pretend she didn't know what he was asking. A shake of the head. 'No,' she said. 'Never had the call to use one, to tell the truth.' The sun was spreading its wings above the horizon now, feathers of orange and yellow reaching into the sky. It would hopefully be another nice day. She had a lot she wanted to do.

Tim was blinking rapidly, as though he had something caught in his eyes. 'So what do you do then?' he blurted.

'Same as you, Timmy Boy. Same as you when you want Rosie to have a good time.'

She missed Alice, she realised. Physically missed her. Wanted to feel the silk of Alice's skin against her. Wanted to trace lips and fingers over that skin, memorising every dip and curve, all the sweet spots that made Alice moan, arch towards her.

She let out a breath.

'Lickin' and flickin', you're telling me?'

She closed her eyes in a wince. 'Well, that's a crude way of putting it, but I suppose so.' Opening her eyes, she gave Tim a sly look. 'I'm impressed, Tim,' she said. 'Sounds like you take good care of Rosie.'

He sniffed, nodded, some of the hectic colour gone from his cheeks now. 'Rosie, she likes it, see?' He shook his head. 'Now Sarah, my first wife, much as I loved her, she wasn't, well, as keen as I might have liked in the bedroom, see?' He heaved a sigh at the memory obviously playing out inside his head. 'Always in the dark, under the covers, nightdress on. Don't even know if I ever got a decent look at her.'

Jean didn't say anything, too amused at the turn of the conversation. She knew she'd never probably have one like it again, but it tickled her that Tim, ten years older than her, was talking to her about the subject in the first place, let alone warming to it.

'Rosie, though,' he said on a contented sigh. 'She's the sort what makes your poor heart sing.' He sniffed again, but not from embarrassment this time. 'And other parts of you, if you get my drift.'

She did. She didn't have his exact parts, but her own were still humming away very happily.

'She don't mind what time of the day it is either, Rosie don't. Middle of the day suits her just fine.' He turned suddenly, charmingly shy. 'And she lets me touch her, you know? I always dreamed of having a woman let me touch her.' Another sigh. 'Women are the most beautiful creatures on earth.'

They both sat silent on that thought a moment, Jean almost with tears springing to her eyes over the touchingly simple sentiment. Yes, she thought. Women were indeed the most beautiful creatures. Alice Holden especially.

'You love her?' Tim asked suddenly, breaking the silence.

Jean only paused a moment. 'Yes,' she said. 'Yes, I really think I do.'

He nodded in the driver's seat next to her. 'That's good, then.'

They took the long slow curve into town in silence, then Tim took to whistling a tune and Jean looked out the window, simply enjoying the moment.

'Tim, stop at the grocer's, will you?' she asked, seeing the shop coming up on their right.

'What for?' He looked at her. 'Boss wouldn't like it.'

Jean rolled her eyes. 'We have to deliver their goddamned milk anyway. I just want to pop in a get a couple things. Won't take a minute, honest. Just park in front.'

'Okay,' he said. 'Keep your hair on. We'll do the street first, then you can nip in.' He pulled over and applied the hand brake, scratched his head. 'Maybe I'll pop in to the bakery at that, get me one of Ruthie's custard squares. No one makes them near as good as she does, and I was running a bit late on breakfast this morning.' He winked at her. 'Slept a bit late, if you get my drift.'

Jean laughed, shaking her head. 'Yeah Tim,' she said. 'I get your drift.'

CHAPTER 20

Alice woke when the front door closed, lying there in the dark of the morning listening to Jean's footsteps going down the short path and out the gate. She lay on her back, staring up at the ceiling, waiting for the sound of the car starting. Pressing her cheek against the sheet – she had no pillow, it had gone the way of the rest of her possessions – she realised Jean's car had been parked outside her house since the evening before. And she was only just thinking about it now.

Still. No one would know what the two of them had done here inside the house, in this bed. They would never guess at the things Alice now knew. She ran a hand down her body, skimming it over her breast, hip, belly, until it touched between her legs. She was wet there still, and the memory of Jean's lips on her, tongue on her, had Alice hugging herself, rolling over onto her side and squeezing her eyes shut.

Thoughts tumbled around in her head, jostling with remembered sensations, and she cried out, a soft whimper, her body still fresh from Jean's touch.

Already Alice missed her. Wanted her back, stretched out in the bed beside her, body pressing against the length of her own, all skin and bones and muscles – and softness too. Alice rolled back over and stared at the ceiling again. She wanted Jean back beside her, she wanted to smooth her own hands over the lightly-freckled skin, feel the strength of Jean's muscles under her palm, and she wanted to find Jean's own secret places, the ones that would make her cry out, fingers digging into Alice's flesh.

She wanted Jean's weight on top of her. Wanted to wrap her legs around the slim waist and feel the tickle of Jean's panting breath against her ear as she moved slowly against her.

Her skin prickled with all the wanting and she swallowed in the dimness, feeling herself fill with all the colours of the rainbow, all the colours she associated with happiness, the swirling blue of a clear sky, the tumbling red and orange of a passionate dawn. She closed her eyes and felt herself alight, alive, melted like honey onto the sheet, and smiling, joy in every humming nerve, and one word repeating over and over in her mind. Jean. Jean was the real world now. The things they had done, the things they had shared – that was real, and everything else paled in comparison.

She would see her again later, after Jean had finished work. She would see her before that, when she brought the milk to the door. Flushing at the thought, Alice imagined it, seeing Jean again for the first time in the light of day since… since they had lain together, shared themselves with each other, tasted the sweet musk of each other's skin.

Alice swung her legs out of bed and sat up. She had to get up or she would go crazy, lying there remembering everything, going over and over it, wanting it all again. Her hand went to the end of the bed, expecting to find her dressing gown there like every morning, and came only upon empty air. Her things were still in the suitcase.

Nude, Alice slipped from the bed and padded across the floor, smiling at the memory of wrapping a towel around Jean in the bathroom, and which with shaking hands, she'd peeled from her damp skin in the bedroom, letting it fall to the floor. It was no longer there, and Alice went to her suitcase and in the light from the street and pulled out clothes to wear. It was early, but she'd make herself a cup of tea, draw a bath, wash herself, the warm water a poor substitute for Jean's arms, but as much as she didn't like the thought, she needed to freshen up. The scent of lovemaking was heavy on her skin.

Tilly and Jack were up as she let the water out of the tub, drying herself and dressing. She listened to their young voices in the kitchen and remembered that she had nothing to give them for their breakfast. There was only tea, and perhaps a crust of bread from their donated supper the night before.

'Mum,' Jack said as she came out of the bathroom, trying to dry her hair with the same towel she'd given to Jean the night before, the only one they had.

'Morning Jack,' she said. 'Hi Tilly.' She gave the girl a kiss on the top of her head. 'Did you two sleep okay?' It was hard not to wince at the question. What if the children complained of the noises they'd heard last night from her bedroom? They'd tried to be quiet, but Alice knew well she'd not been able to stifle every delirious sound.

'There's nothing for breakfast,' Jack said, ignoring the

question altogether. 'I have school this morning. What are we going to eat?'

Alice cast her mind towards her purse again. She still had a little, on account of Raylene not letting them pay for the meal Donny had cooked them. Biting her lip, she chastised herself for not going out to the shop the afternoon before. But the state of their house – the sheer emptiness of it – had upset them all, and she'd stayed with the exhausted children, and her neighbours, who had seen them through the evening.

But now it was morning and breakfast was a pressing concern. She glanced at the wall, gave a start when she saw again that her little wall clock was gone.

'What time is it, Jack?' she asked.

'I don't know, Mum. There's no way to tell the time.' He looked around the kitchen. 'The clock's gone. Dad's radio is gone.' He stared at her. 'Everything is gone.'

'Well we will get everything back,' she said. 'This afternoon.'

'How are we going to do that?'

'Yeah,' Tilly said from the chair at the table. 'How we gonna do that?' Her eyes threatened to fill with tears. 'I want Prudence.'

Alice sat down and pulled Tilly into her lap. 'It's all right, sweetheart,' she said. 'We're going to get Prudence back.'

Startlingly blue eyes gazed up at her.

'We're going to get all our things back,' Alice said.

'How're we going to do that?' Jack asked. 'They're gone.'

Alice sucked in a deep breath. 'This afternoon, Jean is going to pick up us and take us to the dump where Grandma had all our things taken.' She looked at the children. 'We should be able to find them there.'

Jack wasn't convinced. 'What if we can't?'

'Then we'll find a way to replace what we need.'

Tilly rested her little head against Alice. 'I still want Prudence,' she said, fingers inching towards her mouth, then falling to her lap as she looked at her mother again. 'Jean will help me find Prudence! She said she would help us.'

Alice raised an eyebrow. 'Did she, sweetheart?'

The little girl nodded and rested back against her mother. 'Yes she did. I saw her when I got up to go to the toilet. She slept here the night.' Blue eyes on Alice again. 'Did you know that, Mama?'

Alice tried to smile over the shock racing through her body. She nodded. 'Yes, I did.'

Tilly nodded. 'She's gonna bring us cream for another cake.'

There was a moment's silence, and Alice didn't know how to fill it. She risked a glance at Jack, but he was looking down at the floor, frowning.

'What are we going to do about breakfast?' he asked. 'If you give me some money I can run down to the shop and get some bread and jam. I'll go real fast.'

Alice stood up, popping Tilly back on the seat. 'That's a good idea, Jack. I'll get my purse.'

She heard him grumbling as she left the room and wished she could wave a magic wand and make everything better. Unfortunately, that would involve exorcising her mother from the world, and the best she could do was remove her from their lives.

Tilly raced past her in the hallway and tugged on the front door, grappling with the handle which was low enough for her to pull open.

'Jean's here!' the girl crowed.

'Are you sure?' Alice asked, a hand fluttering to her chest where her heart was suddenly pounding loud enough to break through.

'I heared her,' Tilly shouted, finally getting the door open, and charging out onto the step. 'Jean!' she squealed.

Alice stepped out behind her, mouth dry.

'Tilly!' Jean said. 'Did you sleep well?'

Tilly's curls bounced up and down as she nodded her head. 'You tucked me in real good,' she whispered loudly. 'But I still miss Prudence.'

'Who's Prudence when she's at home?' Jean asked.

'She's my dolly.'

Jean straightened from talking to Tilly and her eyes met Alice's.

'Alice,' she said. 'How did you sleep?' Her voice was low, words falling on Alice's ears like caresses.

'Well,' she said. She wanted to step down onto the path and place her hands on Jean's face, draw their lips together, see what Jean's mouth tasted like the morning after it had kissed her all over.

They stared at each other, neither moving, talking. Alice could feel her though, even from a few steps away, could feel the way they were drawn together, could read in Jean's eyes the desire to step closer, bend her head slightly, and capture her breath in her own. She gasped.

'What's in the box, Jean?' Tilly asked.

The spell broke and the morning resumed its normal run. Alice could hear the birds again, sitting on the power lines that ran from the street to her house. She could feel the breeze cooling her cheeks, and her mouth widened in an easy, graceful smile that Jean returned before looking to Tilly who was straining to look into the box Jean carried.

'I brought some things from the grocer's,' Jean said, dipping the box down to let Tilly see. She glanced at Alice. 'I know you hadn't had time to get to the shops yesterday, and this little tiger here would be hungry come morning.'

Jack had joined them on the step, crowding around with Tilly to look into the box. 'There's bread,' he said. 'And porridge. Thanks, Jean!' He looked up, frowning again. 'Do you know what time it is? All our clocks are gone.'

Jean shook her head, and Alice could tell it was in frustration, rather than an answer. 'That's terrible,' she said. 'Here, take the box, Jack.' She slid the box into the boy's arms and reached under her sleeve. A moment later a wristwatch dangled from her hand. 'Take this as well,' she said.

'You can't do that,' Alice said. 'I mean, won't you need it?'

Jean shrugged, smiled. 'I'm sure Tim will let me know when it's knocking off time. And I can get it back when we have all your own things back again.' She looked at Jack. 'It's seven o'clock now. Plenty of time to cook up some breakfast and get to school on time, what do you reckon?'

Jack watched wide-eyed as she put the watch in the box. He looked at his mother. 'It's not even a ladies one,' he said, then turned back to Jean. 'Can I wear it?'

Alice was about to protest, but Jean got in first. 'Sure you can, Jacky boy,' she said. 'Now how about taking that stuff inside for me?'

Jack nodded and vanished into the house, Tilly running after him. Jean turned to look at Alice.

'Hi,' she said softly. 'Sorry I had to run out on you. I tried not to wake you. You looked so beautiful.' She smiled, but her hands were in her pockets and she didn't move closer.

Alice too stayed where she was, but she returned the smile. 'I missed you when I woke up,' she said. 'I liked it better with you there.' She spoke low enough so that even the birds wouldn't hear her.

'I liked it better there too,' Jean said, then broke their gaze to look back at the milk truck. 'I can't stay,' she said.

'Work calls,' Alice said, and Jean nodded.

'But I'll see you later. As soon as I'm done here.' She looked like she wanted more than anything to come closer.

'I'll be here,' Alice said. She frowned. 'But I'll have Tilly with me.'

'Good,' Jean replied. 'She can help us find Prudence.'

Alice laughed. Quietened. 'I love you,' she whispered.

Jean gazed at her, eyes deep and serious. 'I love you too,' she whispered back, then smiled, turning to go. At the gate, she stopped.

'Tell Tilly I remembered the cream.' With a wink, she walked to the milk truck and climbed in.

CHAPTER 21

*M*rs B was there to meet her, as though she'd been lurking out on the rocker on the veranda just lying in wait, an ungainly tiger of a woman.

'Afternoon,' Jean said, stepping up onto the grey boards and slipping her hat off, wiping her forehead. The day was heating up. If this was a foretaste of summer, they were in for a real corker.

'A certain someone didn't make it home to her bed last night.' Mrs B's eyes roamed around the neighbourhood then zeroed in on Jean.

'A certain someone pays too much attention to the comings and goings of certain other people.' Jean rummaged in her pocket and drew out the pack of cigarettes, lighting one and inhaling on a smile.

'It's my duty to ensure a decent house is kept.' The land-lady sniffed and shifted her bulk in the chair. 'This place is only as good as my reputation, you know.' A strangely feline smile that struck Jean for the first time as holding secrets she knew nothing of. 'And my reputation is only as good as yours reflects on it.'

Jean leaned against the tree growing up out of the ground beside the veranda. She looked at Mrs Boone and kept on smoking.

'Fine, have it your way,' the landlady said. 'But don't say I didn't warn you.'

'You're not really worried about your reputation,' Jean said and looked up at the tall building where her room was.

Mrs Boone shook her head. 'No.' She pointed a fat finger. 'You however; I have warned you.'

Jean shook her head. 'First you're sympathetic, now you're warning me off?'

'I admit – I am in two minds about this business.' She heaved a sigh. 'I just don't see how it can work out. And Alice Holden?'

'Don't you say a bad word about her, Cleo, or you will have a pair of attic rooms to rent out.' Jean looked at her.

'I've no bad words to say about Alice, so don't go getting all worked up. She seems a real sweetheart, and pretty as all get out too.' Mrs Boone shook her head. 'No, it's her mother who'll be your problem.'

'God, am I sick of Geraldine Thomas. I've never even met her and I can't stand the witch – do you know what she did to Alice?'

'I don't,' Mrs B said. 'But I doubt I'd have any trouble imagining.'

'She decided that Alice and the children should move back into her big ol' house with her, and so she had some goon pack their clothes and bring them round while she took Alice and Jack and Tilly to church.' Jean glowered out at the bright day, chest tight with anger. 'Then she had some goon take everything else Alice owned, including the little girl's doll, to the dump. Only things left in that house are the few scraps of furniture that came with it. Not even a sheet or towel or box of tea leaves.' She dropped her cigarette and ground out the butt under her heel like she wished it was Geraldine Thomas' face.

Mrs Boone sighed. 'She really did that?'

'She really did. Alice didn't put up with it, of course, but now she's there in her home again with nothing to her name but a few clothes.' Jean could feel her skin growing hot with indignation.

The landlady heaved herself up from her rocker. 'I'm going to go telephone old Sims.' She kept talking as Jean followed her inside. 'He's in charge of the dump. Drives the digger, buries it all.' She picked up the telephone receiver and waited for the operator to answer. 'He can tell us what's become of their things.'

Jean heard the bright voice of the operator come on, then the connecting clicks as the call went through. 'Ask him about her sewing machine,' she hissed.

Mrs B nodded and waved at her. 'Go get out of your uniform. We'll sort this out.'

Jean was back downstairs in record time, freshly changed, her face still damp from its scrubbing. She could have done with a proper bath, but a wash, she decided, was all she had time for. Her mind flashed to the scene in Alice's bathroom the night before.

'What are you all red about?' Mrs B boomed, looking at her. 'Get your head together, Jean Reardon, we've got a trip to the dump to make.'

'I said I'd pick up Alice and take her there.'

'Nope. You and I are going. I just spoke to old Simsy, among others, and he said a bunch of stuff came in yesterday – he ain't usually open on a Sunday he told me, but some geezer paid him good money to open up. He was just scratching his head over it this morning, wondering why someone was wanting to chuck out perfectly good stuff.'

Jean shook her head. 'Those have got to be Alice's things, then.'

'I reckon.'

'So I'll get Alice and take her.'

'You and me are doing this, Jean,' Mrs B said. 'Didn't I just tell you that?' She lumbered into her private sitting room and was back a moment later clutching an old blue leather handbag, digging in it and coming out with a set of keys. 'We'll take the truck.'

'But…'

'But nothing.' She went to the door and lowered herself down the steps. 'You can drive, you know how well enough, since it's you who keeps the damned thing going.' She stopped and looked back up at Jean. 'What's the problem, girl?'

'Why are you coming?'

'Because Sims is making too much noise about how everything that goes to the dump is then his, and he is looking to make a tidy profit on your Alice's bits and pieces.' A slow smile spread over her face. 'And I happen to know things about Michael Sims that he wouldn't want to become common knowledge.' She bared her teeth. 'Besides, we've a couple other stops to make.'

'But Alice…'

'Will be fine. We won't take long. Did you say precisely when you'd be there?'

'No, but...'

'But what? You miss her?'

Jean did, but she scowled at her landlady. 'You're being too bossy,' she said. 'What's going on?'

Mrs Boone threw her the keys to the truck. 'What's going on is that I've finally had enough of Geraldine Thomas thinking she has the right to do whatever she wants. I knew that woman when we were both young and we have some history, her and I. She was born mean, that woman, and that god she spends money on every week might forgive her all her sins, but me – I've kept score.' She grunted. 'Alice is a lovely woman and deserves much better.' A sidelong glance. 'Besides, if you're to have any chance whatsoever of this not blowing up in your face, you need a lot more people on your side.'

'I don't understand,' Jean said, but she was walking over to Mrs B's old truck.

Washed-out grey eyes regarded her over the cab. They may have faded in colour, but they were still sharp enough. 'This is the way it is, Jean,' Mrs B tapped a finger on the roof. 'You are fairly well liked around these parts, as far as that goes.'

'Well, thanks.'

A shrug. 'You're different, Jean, and different stands out. But you're also easy-going and hard-working, and people like that.' Jean got a squinting look. 'Some of the ladies might have liked you a little too much during the drought of the war years, but somehow, god knows how, you've got away with that, and even the blokes seem to think you're decent enough.'

Jean squirmed, uncomfortable. 'Is this going somewhere?'

Mrs B didn't seem to hear her. 'And Alice, now she is universally looked upon with pity.'

'That's not very nice!'

'But true. Being her mother's daughter. Her own husband not coming home. The poor thing's had the worst luck. Her father was an angel though, so most feel kindly towards her because of that. He cared about this town, him and his bank financed a lot of blokes where others of a different ilk wouldn't have gone.' The fingers tapped on the warm metal roof again. 'And she's got her own little reputation. She sews beautifully, she's generous, helpful, and she loves those kids of hers to bits – anyone can see that, and things like that go a long way.'

Jean was shaking her head. 'I still don't see where you're going with this.'

Mrs B sniffed. 'Get behind the wheel, Jean, and we'll go get these things back.'

Jean did as she was told, but even though she was behind the wheel, she had the feeling that it was Mrs B driving this one.

CHAPTER 22

Jack went off to school with a full stomach and Alice watched his sandy head all the way down the road. He was a good boy, and she was lucky to have him.

'Mama?' asked Tilly, and Alice looked down at the small child by her side. She was lucky to have her too, despite the bad time it had been during Terry's last and only leave home from the war.

'Mama?' Tilly pulled on her dress, bringing her back to the present. 'What you smiling about?'

Alice scooped her daughter into her arms and went back inside. 'About how lucky I am, that's what I'm smiling about.' She turned into the house. 'Now, what shall we do this morning?'

'Get Prudence!'

'No, sweetheart. We have to wait until Jean can give us a ride in her car. It's too far to walk.'

The little girl's face fell. 'An' I don't have my pram.'

No. That was another thing conspicuously missing. It

hadn't been new when Alice had got it for Jack when he was a baby, but it still had enough wear left in it for the loss of it to really hurt. Without a car, Alice relied on it for carting both Tilly and groceries.

'We might be able to get that back too,' Alice said, unable to stay gloomy about anything. She thought about the way Jean had looked at her that morning, keeping her distance, hands in pockets, but still her lovely eyes had glowed rich and deep with feeling when she'd looked at Alice.

'You're smiling again, Mama,' Tilly said.

'That's because I'm happy.'

Tilly looked at her, wriggled down from her arms and climbed up onto a chair like a little monkey and began rooting through the box Jean had delivered.

And she'd given Jack her watch, Jean had, Alice remembered. Right off her wrist. Without being asked or anything, she'd just given it to him as though such a thing was completely normal. Alice wrapped her arms around her waist and hugged herself, wishing she had a watch herself so that she could see how many hours it was until Jean finished work and they could see each other again.

But her wristwatch was with the jewellers, its band being replaced. It had been there for two weeks, waiting for Alice to have enough money to pay the bill for it. She touched her wrist where it should have been, a gift from her father for the last birthday she'd had with him before he'd had a heart attack and died before the doctor could even reach him.

Alice sucked in a deep breath. She still missed her father, but it was with a sweet, sorrowful longing now. The pain had faded with the years. He would have liked Jean though, she was sure of it, even if he wouldn't have understood or approved of their bond.

'Mama!' Tilly squealed, pulling out a small paper bag. 'Lollies!'

'What?' Alice took the small sack and looked inside. Two peppermint sticks, and a handful of caramels nested inside the bag. She passed it back to Tilly. 'Aren't you a lucky girl?' she said, a lump forming in her throat. Not only had Jean thought about breakfast for them, but she'd included a treat for the children.

If Jean was a man, Alice would want to marry her.

She flushed at the thought. Jean was a woman though, and no one would understand what they'd done together the night before, or how they felt about each other.

She blinked, staring out the window, lost in thought. It didn't matter, she decided. They would act as friends. No one would have to know what else they were.

She wasn't going to give it up. She'd live from moment to moment and enjoy whatever she could have with Jean. That was all there was to it.

'What are you doing, Tilly?' she asked, coming back to the kitchen.

The little girl had tipped the lollies onto the table. 'I sortin' them out, Mama.' She pointed to one peppermint stick. 'That one's for me.' The other peppermint stick was with a small pile of caramels three inches away. 'And those ones are for Jack.'

Alice smiled and bent to kiss her daughter. 'You're a dear child,' she said. 'You eat your lollies, since you've had your breakfast, and I'm going to unpack our suitcases. Then we can decide what we're going to do after that.'

Tilly nodded, little mouth pursed in concentration as she dropped her brother's share of the lollies back in the bag. Alice headed off to the bedrooms to put their few things back away and tidy up, keeping herself busy until Jean arrived.

It wasn't Jean who turned up after their lunch, however, knocking on the door, then calling out a cheery hullo.

'Alice, isn't it?' the woman at the door said when Alice went to see who it was.

'Yes,' she said, bewildered.

'I'm Margaret Wilson,' the stranger said. 'Goodness me, it's turning warm today, isn't it?'

'Ah, would you like to come in, Mrs Wilson? How can I help you?'

'Please, call me Margaret. And yes, some shade would be lovely for a moment. Is this your daughter? Isn't she a delight?'

Tilly peered at the woman from behind Alice's skirts.

The woman was giving Tilly a considering look. She nodded. 'Yes, I think the clothes should fit.' She picked up a box from the front step beside her and entered the house. Alice, not knowing what to say, showed her down to the kitchen. The box joined Jean's on the table.

'I'm sorry,' Alice said, springing forward to move the box of food. 'I haven't quite put the groceries away yet.' She blinked. 'Would you like a cup of tea?'

The woman laughed. 'You're very gracious, seeing as how you don't know me from Adam.' She smiled, showing very white, even teeth. 'A glass of water would do very well, I think.'

Alice went to the tap and filled a cup with water. 'I'm

afraid I don't have any glasses at the moment.' She looked around. 'They…ah…broke, I'm sorry.'

Margaret Wilson took the cup and sat down at the table, reaching out a hand which she placed lightly on Alice's arm.

'I know what happened to your things,' she said. 'That's why I'm here.'

Alice stared at her, then glanced at the door to the passageway. Tilly sidled away to climb onto a chair, a look of avid interest on her face. She pressed a hand onto the box then tucked it quickly back under the table. Alice gave her a distracted smile.

'I don't understand,' Alice said.

'Of course you don't,' Margaret agreed, then drained the cup and stood up. 'Thank you – I really was getting hot out there, and I've still several errands to run today.' She smiled at Alice and set the cup on the table, then pointed at the box. 'I was having a clear out of clothes my Mary has grown out of. She's a year or so older than your little sweetie, I would think. I was hoping you could make use of them?'

'Of what?' Alice said, unable to process what was happening.

The hand went back to her arm, and Margaret leaned forward slightly. 'Your mother,' she said. 'I'm afraid it's around the whole town what happened, and well, there are a lot of us who want to help.' The hand fell to her side and she shrugged gracefully. 'The clothes are for your daughter, if you want them. If you don't, then it's the annual Rural Woman's jumble sale soon – you can pass along anything you don't need to go into that. We're holding it at the fair in two weeks.' She patted Alice's arm and turned to go, giving Tilly a little wave.

'Bye bye for now. I do hope we'll see each other again soon. I can see myself out.'

But Alice followed her to the front door, still bewildered. 'How did you…' she started. 'I mean…'

The tall woman turned and smiled at Alice before stepping outside. 'You have friends, Alice, that's all.'

Alice had barely watched her leave when another woman came huffing and puffing up to her door straining under the weight of another box.

'Food for you dear,' she said. 'Mrs Boone said you could do with it, and here it is!' Lively eyes danced under a pert little hat. 'You look after those lovely children of yours.' She was turned and gone before Alice could even stammer out her thanks.

Back in the kitchen, Alice sat down at the table and stared with Tilly at the two boxes. She didn't know what to say.

'Can I open them, Mama?' Tilly said at last.

A nod, and she helped the small girl pry the cartons open. Food spilled out of one, bags of flour, jars of homemade jams and pickles, a veritable feast of things to replenish the cupboards. Alice looked at it in amazement, tears in her eyes, then watched Tilly, wide-eyed with wonder, pull out dress after dress from the other box.

'Take me home, Jean,' Mrs Boone commanded, wiping perspiration from her forehead. 'You can take it from here, I think.'

'Of course,' Jean said. She pulled into the driveway beside the boarding house and watched a puffing Mrs B get out of the truck. 'Thanks!' she called and got a wave in return before she backed out onto the road again.

Jean went to check the time and stared for a moment at the bare skin of her wrist before remembering that she'd given the timepiece to Jack to wear. The kid had seemed absurdly pleased with it too. With a smile on her face, Jean drove the truck through town to park outside Alice's house. She sat for a moment, thinking of the night before when she'd parked in the same place, and hoped Alice hadn't had any neighbours commenting on it. Pressing her lips together, she winced.

The thing was, she wanted to park out there every night.

A deep breath and she got out of the truck, looking around at the street. The houses were small, but the road was tidy, and in most of the windows were hung cheap but cheerful curtains that made Jean smile despite her fear of who might be peering out from behind them.

There were two other cars parked in the road and Jean raised an eyebrow at them as she walked around to the back of the truck and pulled a pretty dark-haired dolly out of the box there. She'd deliver it first, then come back for everything else.

Voices came from the kitchen, the varied sounds of women laughing. Jean slowed her pace, edging forward down the hallway.

'Jean!' A little blonde bullet hurled itself at her. Laughing, Jean swung Tilly into her arms and grinned at her.

'Guess what?' she said.

'What? Tilly was gazing at her face, hands linking around Jean's neck.

'I have someone who's been missing you,' Jean said, watching Tilly's eyes widen as she brought the doll out from behind her back.

'Prudence!' Tilly opened her arms and took the dolly, hugging it. 'I missed her,' she said on a soft, satisfied sigh.

Jean looked up finally, the smile dying on her face, realising the room had gone silent. Three pairs of eyes stared at her from the kitchen table.

Alice got up from the table, high pink spots shining in her cheeks. 'Jean,' she said. 'Thank you so much! I can't believe you found Prudence!' She dropped a kiss on the top of Tilly's head, smiling into Jean's eyes, so that Jean couldn't help but feel like the kiss was meant for her. She swallowed, mouth suddenly dry.

'Jean,' said one of the women at the table, forcing her to

drag her attention away from Alice, who looked radiant, flushed with laughter and pleasure. She looked at the woman sitting with a cup of tea at Alice's table and almost dropped Tilly in shock.

'Martha,' she said. 'What on earth are you doing here?' She wanted to clap a hand over her mouth as soon as the words were out.

Martha looked at her with amusement in her face. 'I could well ask you the same.'

A slow burn that felt dangerously like embarrassment climbed up into Jean's face. She glanced at Alice, but that was no help. Alice looked only slightly confused.

Jean made a show of shrugging. 'I've got Alice's things back from the dump.'

'You have?' Alice stared at her with glowing eyes. 'That's wonderful!'

'Well, all except the food, and maybe a few other things. The guy who runs the dump seemed like he might have stashed a few items for his own gain.' Although personally, Jean thought, if it had been her on the other end of Mrs B's dressing down, she would have handed everything over and been thankful to do it.

'Fortunately,' Martha said with a wave of her hand, 'that's where we come in.'

Jean didn't understand.

'Your Mrs Boone said jump and we jumped.' Martha's face creased into a smile. 'Only stopping to ask how high.' She turned to Alice. 'And glad we are, to be able to help.'

The other woman at the table smiled and nodded. 'Yes indeed,' she said. 'And you must promise, Alice to let us know if there's anything else we can do for you.'

Alice burst abruptly into tears. 'Oh, I'm so sorry!' She jabbed at the tears, tugged a handkerchief out of a pocket and wiped at her eyes, then sobbed some more. 'You must think me such an idiot,' she said. 'It's just that you've all been so nice!'

The two women stood and gathered up their things. Martha patted Alice on the shoulder. 'It's really the least we can do,' she said. 'We're all happy to help, so dry your eyes. Remember to call into the office tomorrow, and I'll have your little ad all neatly typed up for you.' Another pat. 'You'll be on your feet again in no time.' A sidelong glance at Jean. 'And with new friends to boot.'

A moment later Martha was squeezing past Jean and out the door with her friend, but not before pressing a kiss to Jean's cheek. 'You look good with that child,' she said with a wink, then breezed out of the house on a cloud of lily of the valley perfume.

It took almost a minute for Jean to find her voice. 'What was all that about?' she asked.

Alice's tears had stopped flowing and she stood in the middle of the kitchen, the handkerchief knotted in one hand, chest heaving. Tilly, still on Jean's hip, hugged her dolly and stared at her mother too.

'I don't know,' Alice said softly. 'I really don't know.' Her eyes moved to several boxes on the floor round about the place. 'People just started turning up with things. Food, clothes, linens.' She blinked, shaking her head. 'They said they'd heard I needed some help.'

Jean narrowed her eyes, remembering what Martha had said. Before the kiss and the quip about the child. 'Mrs B,' she said.

'Who's Mrs B?'

Jean shook her head. 'Couldn't be, could it?' The boxes on the floor overflowed with food. She looked at Tilly. 'You look very pretty,' she said.

The little girl in her arms nodded and leaned back, flinging Prudence wide so Jean could see what she was wearing. 'I got a new dress. Lots of new dresses.' Her eyes grew wide in her face. 'One has duckies on it.' Looking down at what she was wearing, she pointed at the cotton print. 'This one has flutterbys.'

'Butterflies,' her mother corrected automatically.

'It's a lovely dress,' Jean said, and popped the child down onto a chair. She turned to Alice. 'Are you okay?'

Alice leaned against her. 'Yes,' she said. 'Just a bit over-whelmed.' They stood like that for a silent minute, Jean sliding an arm around her and breathing in the warm scent of her skin and hair. Alice looked at her. 'Who's Mrs B?' she asked. 'Mrs Boone? I'm sure I've heard that name before, but I don't remember where.' She paused. 'And why is she yours?'

Jean groaned. 'She's my landlady, and apparently has a lot more pull in the town than I ever supposed.' She narrowed her eyes, thinking about it. 'I should have known the crafty old witch had more going on than just the boarding house.'

Alice hugged her. 'I don't know what I've done to deserve this,' she said, then leaned forward and kissed Jean on the lips, lingering there a long moment before pulling away. 'Any of this.'

'I think that's my line,' Jean said, and went after those lips again, before realising Tilly was sitting at the table watching them. 'Sorry,' she said. 'I forgot about little eyes.'

Alice pulled back straight away. 'So did I,' she said, clearing her throat. 'Would you, um, like a cup of tea?'

Jean shook her head. 'I'd better unload your things.' She hesitated. 'I know I said I'd take you to the dump to get your things, but Mrs B, she insisted on going instead. Good thing too, actually, because she has a pretty handy line of black-mail.' She laughed, a short, amazed sound. 'I don't know if we would have got as many of your things back if she hadn't.'

Alice touched her arm. 'It's okay,' she said. 'Let's go see what we have, shall we?'

It didn't take long for everything to be brought inside. Jean set down the last box to find Alice standing over her retrieved things, knuckles pressed to her mouth. She looked up at Jean's entrance and gave her an anguished look.

'What's wrong?' Jean asked.

She saw Alice swallow, the hand going to her throat. 'My sewing machine,' Alice said. 'It's not here.'

Jean looked down at the array of things on the floor. Alice was right, she hadn't seen a sewing machine anywhere and was pretty sure those things would be hard to miss.

'I'm so sorry, Alice,' she said, reaching out to touch her.

Alice shook her head, taking Jean's hand and squeezing it. 'It's okay,' she said, then sighed. 'Martha, who you met just before, she is going to type up an ad for me to put in the window of the draper's. For sewing and alterations.' Another sigh. 'I guess I'll have to go along tomorrow and tell her not to bother. I can't do anything without my machine.' Her face hardened, jaw set. 'It's all my mother's fault. If she wasn't trying to control my every move, then none of this would have happened.'

Jean looked at her, ached to be able to make it all better. Somehow. 'We'll think of something,' she said.

Alice turned to look at her and her face softened. She leaned against her for a moment and Jean soaked up the feeling of her warm and soft beside her.

'You've done so much already,' she said. 'Can you stay for supper?' A hand waved at the boxes. 'Thanks to you, there's plenty to eat.'

Jean shook her head. 'I wish I could. I really do.' She brushed her lips against Alice's smooth forehead, glad Tilly had been popped down for a nap and Jack wasn't back from school yet. She could sneak a kiss. 'I have to take the truck back to Mrs B.' She stifled a sigh. 'Besides, we can't have me parked outside two nights in a row, can we?'

Alice was running her fingers down Jean's chest, making her shiver and close her eyes, catching the hand before it squeezed in between the buttons on her shirt.

'Thank Mrs Boone for me, please Jean? And then come back tonight? There must be a way you can sneak in…'

There was no way to say no, and Jean didn't want to. She wanted to spend another night lying beside Alice, wanted to feel the silk of her skin on her own, her warm sweet breath in her ear. She was getting light-headed just thinking about it.

'Say you will, please?' Alice said. 'I want to be with you.'

Jean nodded wordlessly, trying to breathe around the knot in her throat. 'I will,' she said, choking the words out.

'After the children are in bed.'

She'd already decided where to park the car. 'I'll come in through the back,' she said.

Alice kissed her. 'I'm looking forward to it already.'

So was Jean.

CHAPTER 24

A wind had sprung up from the east, carrying with it the smell of salt and waves and Alice lifted her head, breathing it in as she watched Jean walk back to the milk truck and lift her hand in a wave. The man behind the wheel did the same, baring surprisingly white teeth against his tanned face. She waved back to them both and suppressed the desire to run after Jean and kiss her.

Jean had untangled herself from Alice late the night before, dressing in the light from the street, neither of them suggesting they turn the bedroom light on. It was okay anyway, Alice lay on her side watching the light and shadows slide over the shape of Jean's body as she pulled her clothes on.

'What are you staring at?' Jean teased.

'You,' Alice said. 'You're beautiful.'

Jean laughed. 'You're the beautiful one. I'm too skinny, rough around the edges.'

She shook her head. 'You're not skinny,' she said. 'You're all lean and lithe, like a big cat or something.'

Jean laughed again, but Alice wasn't in the least offended. 'It's true,' Alice said. 'You're awfully strong.'

Leaning over the bed, Jean dropped a kiss on an upturned, naked breast and Alice closed her eyes a moment, her breath catching.

'It's all those milk crates I throw about each day,' Jean said, lifting her head, letting Alice breathe again. She reached out and pushed back a strand of Jean's hair, tucking it behind an ear.

'Do you ever miss working on a farm?' she asked.

'Every day,' Jean said. 'If I had a dream, it would be to have my own little place, a few animals, chickens, ducks, some sheep, a house cow…'

'And me,' Alice said.

'Of course.' Jean grinned. 'Someone has to milk the cow every morning.'

Alice laughed and tugged Jean's head down so she could kiss her. 'I'd do a great deal more than that for you,' she whispered and felt Jean shiver.

'Which reminds me,' Alice said, thinking of something.

Jean sat back on the bed. 'What?'

'Martha,' Alice said, and watched Jean's face in the light from a pair of prowling headlights from the road outside. 'She seemed to know you already.'

She couldn't hear any hesitation in the answer. 'She does,' Jean said. 'Or did, at least. It's been a fair while since I've seen Martha.'

Alice picked at a button on Jean's shirt, suddenly shy, not sure she ought to ask what she wanted to know. Or even if she really wanted to know it. She chewed on her lip. Jean took her hand and stroked the fingers.

'It's okay,' she said. 'I know what you want to ask.'

Alice looked up at her and wanted to tug the sheet up over her bare skin. 'You do?'

'You want to know if there was anything between Martha and I.'

'Was there?' It was out, the question hanging in the air between them.

Jean squeezed her fingers and Alice tightened them around hers. 'Yes,' she answered. 'A few years ago, near the beginning of the war, Martha was…let's say she was lonely, and I kept her company for a while.' The brown eyes looked steadily at Alice.

She thought about it for a moment. 'The way you and I…'

But Jean was shaking her head. 'Nothing like the way you and I are together,' she said. 'Martha was never serious about me, and I never had any deep feelings for her.' She blinked.

'Deep feelings?'

A shrug. 'I liked her, but nothing more than that.' She looked down at Alice. 'Nothing like the way I feel about you.'

Alice nodded, let it go, smiled, her heart lifting. 'And remind me how you feel about me?' she said.

'I love you.' The answer came straight away, and Alice sat up, touching Jean's face.

'I love you too,' she said.

She'd fallen back to sleep after Jean had left, one hand on the cooling sheet where Jean had lain next to her, and when she'd woken in the morning to the sound of the children's voices, it was with a smile on her face.

A car had pulled in behind the departing milk truck and the happiness Alice had been basking in withered and died like an autumn leaf. Briefly, she thought about turning around and walking into the house, closing the door behind her and ignoring the woman in the car.

But she straightened instead, knowing it was better to just get it over with. She saw Mrs McMurtry standing watching Jean drive away in the milk truck, and Alice winced at the considering look on the woman's face. A light sweat broke out on her skin, immediately cooled by the breeze. She met Sally McMurtry's eyes, but there was nothing in them, just sullen disinterest.

Mrs McMurtry stopped looking at the milk truck and turned her attention to Alice instead, walking across the footpath and through the gate to Alice's doorstep.

Alice waited for the woman to speak, glad the children were busy inside with their breakfast.

'Alice.'

'Mrs McMurtry.'

'I won't come in, I'm afraid, although I certainly won't make a public spectacle the way you just did with the woman who delivers your milk,' the other woman said.

Alice ignored the pointed reference to Jean. 'I'm afraid I wasn't going to invite you in,' Alice answered.

Her mother's handmaiden stared at her, taken aback. Alice shrugged and stood her ground.

'How very rude. It makes me sure I was right when I said to your dear mother that I thought she was wasting her time trying to deal so fairly with you.'

'What?' That was too much. 'Fairly?' Alice repeated. 'You think taking all my things – and my children's things – and throwing them away was fair?'

Edith McMurtry puffed herself up to her full height. 'You

could have everything you and the children could possibly need, right at your very fingertips.'

'Yes,' Alice said. 'If I lived back home with Mother.'

'It's your duty as a daughter to look after your mother.'

'It's my duty as a mother myself to make sure my children don't have to grow up in the same misery I did!'

Mrs McMurtry's eyes narrowed. 'Your parents were upstanding people.'

'My father was. He was a good man, and I would not be half the person I am today if it weren't for his good influence.' Alice stopped to draw breath. 'Because goodness knows, if it was just up to my mother I would be a nervous, miserable wreck.' She crossed her arms, glanced over at Sally McMurtry who was watching every move, and Alice was sure, listening to every word. Her attention went back to the woman in front of her. 'I take it you bring a message?'

'Your presence is requested at luncheon today.' Mrs McMurtry squirmed uncomfortably. 'You mother wishes to make amends between you both. She regrets the misunderstanding of Sunday.'

Alice's laugh was bitter, and she shook her head in disbelief. 'Tell Mother the misunderstanding was only on her side. I understood her intentions all too well, and I won't be coming to lunch, and I won't be moving in, and I won't, the way I feel right now, be seeing her ever again.'

'You cannot keep her grandchildren from her.'

'I can, and it would certainly be the best thing for them.'

They stared at each other, Alice unbudging.

'Very well then, if that's the way you feel,' Mrs McMurtry said.

'It is.'

The woman stared at her a moment longer, mouth opening then snapping shut, before she turned on her heel and stalked back to the car. Alice watched her go, then stepped into her house, carrying her daily bottle of milk, heart pounding.

The children looked up at her as she walked into the kitchen and put the milk on the table.

'Did ya see Jean?' Tilly asked.

'Did she want her watch back?' Jack asked, looking anxious. Alice ruffled his hair and dropped a kiss on Tilly's head.

'Yes, I saw Jean,' she said. 'And she didn't say a word about her watch, Jack, so you'd better look after it for another day, okay?'

He nodded, and she knew he was secretly happy to be able to wear it again. The truth was, both she and Jean had forgotten all about the watch, or she'd have insisted he give it back to Jean. But she also knew Jean wouldn't mind at all.

'Right, children,' she said. 'Jack, wash your face and brush your teeth then away to school with you.' She turned to Tilly. 'And you need a wash too, young lady.' She smiled, a warm glow of contentment seeping through her body, as though Jean's hands were still smoothing their way over her.

CHAPTER 25

'You're being very good,' Alice said, looking down at Tilly toiling along the footpath beside her.

Tilly nodded, then looked up at her mother. 'I'm thirsty,' she said.

They were on the main road, finally, shops and businesses spreading out to either side of them. 'We'll just go to the Post Office Bank,' Alice said. 'And then how about a nice sit-down and something to drink? You've been such a good girl walking all this way.'

Tilly nodded but her forehead was knotted in a frown. 'We gotta get a pram for me,' she said.

That had been another thing that hadn't turned back up. Her sewing machine and the pram for Tilly. She clenched her fists. Both things she couldn't easily replace.

Still, her widow's benefit would be in her bank account today, and with all the food they'd received the day before, they could afford a cup of tea, and after she'd been to speak to Martha about the job ad, she might go along to the second-hand goods shop and see what a pram might cost.

'Hullo Alice!' Raylene slung herself over the counter and kissed Alice on the cheek. 'Tell me you got everything sorted out!'

Alice picked up Tilly and sat her on a hip, smiling at her friend. 'I did, thank you Raylene. With a bit of help, that is.'

A nod. 'I heard there were some efforts going on to give you a bit of a hand.' She turned her head sideways and examined Alice. 'How'd you get Mrs Boone working for you?'

Alice raised her eyebrows. 'I don't know what you mean. I've only met Mrs Boone the once, that day you gave us a ride home.'

Raylene picked up a tray and arranged teacup and saucer on it, poured a glass of lemonade for Tilly. 'Well you must have made an impression, because quite a few telephone calls went out on your behalf, so I was told.'

Alice shook her head helplessly. 'I don't even know who she is, not really. She just owns the boarding house where...'

'Where what?'

'Where my friend lives, that's all.'

Raylene filled a teapot and put it on the tray where it steamed gently. 'Jean Reardon,' she said.

'Yes.'

'Tell me,' Raylene said. 'How did you two meet?'

Alice cleared her throat. 'Ah, she delivers our milk.'

Heavily plucked eyebrows raised. 'And you just got to chatting?'

'Actually,' Alice answered. 'That's exactly what we did.'

Raylene laughed, leaned forward and a speculative look crept into her eyes. 'There are rumours about her.'

But Alice shook her head. 'She's a good person, that's all Raylene. And she's helped out with a lot of things. The kids love her.' Snapping her mouth shut, she stared at her old school friend, feeling something close to dismay.

'Okay. Then I'm glad.' Raylene's voice was soft. 'Just watch yourself, okay? I hear a lot of things, standing behind this counter every day, and not all of it has been good, especially the last couple days.'

Alice frowned. 'I don't know what you mean.'

Drawing herself upright, Raylene fiddled with the things on the tray.

'Raylene, please,' Alice said. 'If there's something I should know…'

She watched Raylene draw in a deep breath. 'You remember Big Jim, of course,' she said.

Immediately wary, Alice glanced around the Egmont Tea Rooms as though Big Jim was going to stand up from one of the tables. 'What about him?' she asked nervously.

Raylene shook her head. 'You need to watch out for him, is all. He's still got a bee in his bonnet, I reckon, over you.'

'I had the right to turn him down. I'd only just buried Terry!'

'Hey, I'm with you there, kid,' Raylene said, and smiled down at Tilly who had her head tucked against her mother's shoulder. 'Listen, we shouldn't be talking about these things, not with the little one listening.'

'I'm not listening,' Tilly said. 'I'm waiting for my drink.'

'Course you are, sweetheart,' Raylene said. 'Let me carry your tray to a table for you.' She picked it up and came around in front, leading the way to a table and setting it down before turning to Alice.

'Look,' she said. 'I'm on your side, no matter what. But you gotta keep an eye out for Big Jim, okay? He's been prowling around and I'm not liking the mutters I'm hearing about him.'

'About me?' Alice asked.

Raylene nodded. 'Just keep safe, okay? The guy's a snake.' She touched Alice on the elbow, gave her a smile, then went back to the counter to serve her next customer. Alice sank down onto one of the chairs.

'What's goin' on, Mama?' Tilly said, looking up at her.

'Nothing, sweetheart,' Alice said. 'Just grown up stuff, nothing for you to worry about.' She forced a smile, then popped Tilly on the seat next to her and passed the child her drink.

CHAPTER 26

The old woman opened the door and let him in. Her eyes raked over him, but she led him down the hallway in silence. Big Jim followed her as she stalked through the house in front of him, back rigid, head held high as though all the world belonged to her.

Judging by the house, at least a substantial part of the world did belong to the old biddy. It was filled floor to ceiling with the sort of fussy things he'd noticed old women tended to like. Tables with no apparent reason for being, stands with large potted palms that you had to edge around, more tables, too small to hold anything but blue and white vases from some Asian country. He scowled at them and edged around them too, uncomfortable in the clutter.

The sitting room she led him to was no better. He looked at the chair she indicated he should sit in and his brows beetled lower over his eyes before he lowered himself onto it, hoping it wouldn't break under his weight.

'I realise this is most irregular,' the old woman said after she'd sat and begun fussing with a teapot. He didn't like tea, looked around wishing for something stronger.

She was waiting for some sort of reply, but he gave her nothing more than a look across the table, waiting to hear why he'd been summoned to the queen bee's lair. She smelt of something sweet and flowery and it made him want to sneeze.

An irritated look and she spoke again. 'You are, I believe, acquainted with my daughter?'

Big Jim looked across the table at Geraldine Thomas. 'Somewhat,' he said, cautious.

Her stare was shrewd. 'Somewhat more than you ought to be, and yet less than I gather you would like.'

He wished she'd speak plainer. They'd grown up speaking their minds in his house, simple words, clear meanings.

'What do you want?' he asked, deciding to bypass all her niceties, but interested despite himself. Alice Holden was something he coveted.

Alice's mother hesitated as if wondering how to tackle the conversation. He made as if to get up.

'No,' she said, holding out a hand to stop him. 'Please sit down Mr Dempsey. I've something of a proposition for you.'

Easing back onto the matchstick chair, he stared at her. 'What sort of a proposition?'

'It's rather delicate,' she said, moving her mouth as though chewing on the inside of her cheek, like a cow chewing her cud. He decided he didn't like her.

But he did, however, like Alice Holden. So, he waited.

'You expressed an interest in courting my daughter when you came back from the war.'

Staring at her, he scratched his chin and waved away the cup of tea. 'Was that a question?' he asked.

She cocked her head at him, all her wrinkles sliding to the lower side. 'No. It is common enough knowledge.'

Enough of the dillydallying. 'So, what's the proposition?'

'I would like to see you renew your interest in her.'

He laughed. 'She wasn't interested in me, Mrs.'

Her gaze was steady, as was the hand that reached for her cup and raised it to her lips. She sipped and replaced it on the saucer.

'Perhaps it would do to be a little more persuasive?' She blinked hooded eyes at him. 'A man of your standing in the community, with your responsibilities would do well with a wife. Alice would make you a fine one.'

'If she could be persuaded, perhaps. But she was clear she wasn't interested.'

'She was grieving. Her husband had not come back from the war.'

Big Jim stretched out his long legs into the room and thought about that. They'd fought in the same battalion, him and Jack Holden. They were mates. Which had only strengthened his case for consoling the pretty widow on his return. They already knew each other well.

The old woman leaned forward, a bird of carrion. 'She comes into money if she marries.'

'She's already been married,' Big Jim said. 'She's a widow.'

'I'm afraid that didn't count, for the purposes of her inheritance,' Geraldine Thomas said. 'It was a foolish liaison, made with all the stupid impetuosity of youth.' Her eyes never shifted their focus from his face. He sat up and leaned forward.

'How am I supposed to persuade her to marry me?' he asked.

'It's a lot of money,' she said.

He argued for the sake of being perverse, but already his mind was turning to the problem. 'I've money already, enough for my needs.'

Her look turned contemptuous. 'A man like you never has enough for his needs.'

'I'm not the one trying to sell my daughter here, so watch your tone with me, old lady.' He leaned forward over the table. 'Why are you trying to marry her off to me anyway? Last I heard, you were trying to get her to come home and look after mummy.'

Her eyes turned to twin flints. 'I've been forced to reconsider what is best, it is true.'

'And I'm what's best?'

'Of a bad bunch, yes.'

A smile touched his lips. Widened. 'Better me than Jean Reardon, is that right?'

The woman blinked at him. Ignored the comment. 'If my daughter will not come home to live with her mother, then a respectable marriage is the next best thing.'

He regarded her steadily. 'And there's money?'

'A lot yes. Enough for you to buy that neighbouring block of land I've heard you've been wanting.'

That was enough. He stood up.

'We have a deal, Mr Dempsey?'

He looked down at her sitting straight-backed in her chair, grey hair in an austere bun against her head, then saying nothing, he left the room, navigated the passageway to the front door.

'I'll expect to hear of your progress, Mr Dempsey,' her voice said, drifting out from the sitting room as he opened the door and stepped out into the gathering dusk. It followed him to his car as he slid into the driver's seat and got the engine going.

So there was money for the woman, then. Which would be his if he married her. For a minute he sat there behind the wheel, thinking of Alice Holden, her shining skin, her soft curves.

And then he thought about seeing her standing there on the side of the road, the Reardon woman beside her, and his hands tightened around the steering wheel. Jean Reardon. He had a bone to pick with her. Several, actually.

Backing out of the driveway, he looked up at the house where Geraldine Thomas spun her evil little webs. Would it be worth having that black widow for a mother in law?

Yes, he decided. If it meant Alice in his bed, money in his bank, new land for the farm, and Jean Reardon put in her place once and for all.

He let the car drift along the road in front of Alice Holden's house, scanning the road for a familiar vehicle. It had been stopped outside – bold as brass – all night long on Sunday.

All night long.

He'd parked across the street and down from it, sitting in the car smoking, a bottle of bourbon propped between his thighs, and he'd watched that car like a hawk. He'd also watched the bedroom window, imagining writhing shadows behind it.

Jean Reardon hadn't emerged from the house until four in

the morning, and it only took the one look at her to know what dirty things she'd been up to.

He drove to the end of the street, turned at the end of the block and made a loop, peering out at all the cars as he passed them, looking for one in particular. Then he spread out the search and tried the next parallel roads, head swivelling from side to side, a cigarette burning down between his fingers.

She wasn't there.

Yet.

He chose a good position and parked, winding down the window and breathing in the salty air. He would wait, see what there was to see.

It paid to know what you were up against.

That way, you could figure out what to do about it.

They hadn't spent the night together, and Alice missed Jean, wondered if Jean was as restless as she was. The ghost of Jean's hands still lay upon her skin, but it only made her want the real thing. A yearning nested deep inside her belly, distracting her as she made breakfast for herself and the children, one ear cocked for the sound of the milk truck.

When the low clinking clanking from outside heralded its arrival, she found two sets of eyes looking at her from the table.

'Jean's here!' Tilly said and made to drop her spoon into her bowl, clamber down from the table and rush the front door. Alice smiled at her and straightened her skirt, smoothed her hair. She looked at Jack.

'You all right?' she asked him.

He nodded and also got up from the table. 'I'd better give her watch back,' he said.

They made quite the procession to the front door. Alice thought about staying in the kitchen but couldn't bring herself to. She met Jean's grinning wink with a wide, helpless smile of her own.

'Well now,' Jean exclaimed. 'Haven't I just the welcoming committee?'

Tilly giggled and lifted her arms to be picked up, Jean obliging her and giving her a squeezing hug.

'When we gonna go to the beach again, Jean?'

Jean looked from Tilly to the sky, squinting at the clouds. 'How about this afternoon?' she asked. 'Looks like it's going to be a sunny day.'

'Yay!' Tilly yelled then turned to Alice. 'Mama, can we?'

Alice, looking straight into Jean's glowing, smiling eyes, wanted nothing more than to say yes. But she shook her head.

'I'm sorry,' she said. 'We have to go to the cemetery today.'

The smile instantly turned to concern on Jean's face. Alice put a hand on Jack's shoulder.

'It's the anniversary of Terry's death, and we're going to go put some flowers on his grave.' She looked down at her son, trying to make her voice light, easy. 'Aren't we, Jack?'

Tilly, who had never met her father, swung on her arms around Jean's neck. 'I wish you were my daddy,' she said.

There was a moment's stunned silence, then Jean burst out laughing. 'Wouldn't that be a fine thing?' she said. 'But you have a father, and I think it's lovely that you're going to go visit his grave.'

Tilly pouted. 'But he can't take us to the beach, and you can.'

'Tilly, be quiet,' Jack said, shaking his head at his little sister. 'Jean can't be our dad, don't be silly.'

Alice reached for the little girl and set her on the ground.

'How about you two take the milk inside before it gets warm. Can you do that? Jean has to get back to her rounds.'

'But what about the beach?' Tilly said.

'How about Saturday?' Jean said. 'We could spend the whole day.' She looked at Alice, and there was more than one question in her eyes.

'Saturday would be perfect,' Alice said, trying to tell Jean that everything was all right. 'We'd love that, wouldn't we kids?'

'Yup,' said Tilly. 'Sure would.' She gave Jean a big grin. 'See ya Jean, I gonna help take the milk in.'

Jean ruffled her curls. 'See you later, Tilly.'

'Just wait, Tilly. I'll carry it, so you don't break it.' Jack turned to Jean. 'Here's your watch,' he said, struggling with the buckle.

'Oh,' Jean said. 'Don't you need it anymore? I haven't missed it, so you can keep it if you like.'

Jack looked up at her with big eyes. 'Do you mean it?' he said.

She shrugged. 'It looks good on you. Seems to me a young man needs a watch. If you like that one, you can have it.'

The eyes got rounder. 'Gee, thanks Jean,' he said, and spun on his heel, picking up the milk bottle and running back into the house, probably before she could change her mind.

Jean looked at Alice, a shamefaced grin on her face. 'Sorry for blatantly trying to buy the affection of your children.'

Alice giggled, enjoying the relief of being with Jean, even for a few minutes. 'What did you pay for Tilly's?' she asked. 'That girl adores you.'

Jean made a show of preening herself. 'I bring her milk

every day, don't you know?' Her expression turned serious. 'I missed you last night.'

Alice glanced at the milk truck just down the road. Jean's partner was swapping out empties in the back. 'I missed you too,' she whispered. 'So very much.' She wanted desperately to touch the palm of her hand to the warm skin of Jean's bare arm. It was all she could do to stay where she was, hands to herself.

'Can we see each other tonight, do you think?' Jean looked around. 'Maybe I can take you all out for a drive, or something?' Her face turned anguished. 'It's so hard not to take you in my arms.' She heaved a sigh.

'Come around for dinner,' Alice said impetuously. 'Please?'

'I would love to,' Jean said, voice fervent and husky. It was her turn to look at the milk truck. 'I have to go, darling,' she said.

'I know.'

'I'll see you later?'

'Yes, please.'

A sudden look of consternation crossed Jean's face. 'But it's the anniversary of your husband's death.'

Alice shook her head. 'Come anyway.' She hesitated. 'I...I would like you to. I need your company.' A pleading smile. 'Especially today. Say you will.'

Jean looked like she was about to say more, but she just smiled instead. 'I'd like that very much. See you later, my love.'

'For dinner.'

'Promise.'

Watching her stride back out to the milk truck, Alice pressed a hand to her heart. It was thumping too fast behind the protective wall of her ribs. She could feel it, feel the very rush of blood in her veins, and all around her the world felt more real and beautiful than it had ever been before. She drifted back into the house on a cloud of arousing sensation.

'Mum?' Jack said when she walked into the kitchen. He was frowning.

'What is it, sweetheart?'

His frown deepened, and Alice put a hand to his brow, smoothing it out.

'Do you think Dad would mind, you know? That Jean gave me her watch?'

Alice stepped back and looked at him, thinking about what he'd asked. She gave him a gentle smile. 'I think your Dad would have wanted to give you your first watch himself,' she said, not knowing whether that would have been the truth or not. Certainly, perhaps, before he went to war. The war had changed him. 'He loved you very much. But I also think he'd be happy that someone else has been able to, since he can't.'

'Do you think he would have liked Jean?' Jack asked, looking down at the watch on his skinny wrist.

There was a pause while Alice tried to think how to answer that question. What would her husband have thought of Jean? He would be horrified that she was the person Alice had chosen to share her bed with, that was certain.

'I think he'd like her very much,' Alice said. 'I think he'd find her hard-working and funny, and kind. I think those are very good things for anyone to be, don't you?'

Jack nodded, then gave his mother a shy look. 'I like her, Mum. Do you think he'd mind that?'

'I like her too!' Tilly piped up.

'I like her as well,' Alice said and bent down to put her arms around both her children. 'I think your Dad would be happy that we have such a good friend.'

'She takes us to the beach,' Tilly said. 'She gave Jack her watch.'

'Jean likes us,' Alice said. 'And we like her.'

Jack was nodding slowly. 'Yeah,' he decided.

'Yeah,' Alice mimicked. 'Now finish your breakfast and get along to school. We'll meet you at the school gate afterwards and go along to see your father.'

'At the cemetery,' Tilly said.

'That's right. And we'll take him a big bunch of flowers.'

'And cake?' Tilly said hopefully, looking at her mother with her big blue eyes.

Alice laughed. 'Maybe cake,' she said, already deciding to make one. They could take half for a little picnic with Terry for the children, and the rest for desert after dinner with Jean.

She thought about that some more and decided that life was a very odd thing.

But love, she also thought, having finally found it, was worth everything.

CHAPTER 28

She was glad of the cake by the time they'd trekked to the cemetery. Without a pram for Tilly, it was slow going, and the afternoon had turned very warm, the air scented with a slight overlay of salt from the sea, and the perfume of daffodils and fresh green grass.

There were only two war graves in the small cemetery overlooking the Tasman Sea. Alice stood for a moment, a child on each side of her, looking down at Terry's headstone with its cross and silver fern engraved on it.

'You were a good man, Terry,' she said, for her son's sake, trying to remember Terry's grin, the way he had a seemingly endless supply of jokes to tell instead of the way he'd been the last time she'd seen him, slumped in a chair, hand clamped resolutely around a bottle of spirits, eyes lifeless as he watched his best friend pawing at her right in front of him. She breathed deeply, calming herself, pushing away the image of that last night.

Jack left her side and laid the bunch of flowers Alice had prepared against the headstone. He patted the top of the granite and stepped back again, looking at his mother. Alice smiled at him.

'Let's spread out the blanket, shall we?' she said. 'We'll have something to drink, and some cake, and your father will see how well we're doing, and how happy we are.'

Tilly was looking dubiously at the headstone. 'Is he really there, Mama?' she asked.

'His bones are,' said Jack.

'His bones?' The little girl's eyes were wide with disbelief. 'What about his skin?'

'The worms ate it.' Jack didn't blink. 'Along with every-thing else. Except the bones.'

'Jack,' Alice said. 'That's enough.'

The eight-year-old shrugged but grinned secretly at his sister. Alice pretended not to see it. Tilly clambered onto her lap. 'Where's the rest of him really, Mama?' she asked.

Alice sighed, shot Jack a pointed look. 'Our bodies return to the soil when we die, Tilly,' she said. 'That's the way it works because we don't need them anymore.' She reached to pour Tilly a drink. 'But our souls live on always.'

'In the ground with the bones?' asked Tilly, a confused look on her face.

'No silly,' said Jack. 'Our souls go to heaven.'

Tilly's face was puckered in concentration. 'So is our daddy in the ground or in heaven?'

'Heaven,' Alice said. 'Now here's a slice of cake for you, Tilly. Sit on the blanket to eat it.'

The girl slid off her knee and tucked into the cake, her questions thankfully forgotten.

'Who's that?' Jack asked, pointing toward the cemetery gates.

Alice turned to look and froze. She would recognise that stance anywhere.

'He's looking at us,' Jack said.

'Just ignore him, children,' Alice told them. 'He's probably here to pay his respects to a family member, just like we are.'

'We sharing cake with Daddy,' Tilly said, then looked worried. 'Can he have some cake when he's in heaven?'

Alice was trying not to look at the man standing at the gate. Jack was right, he was watching them. 'Never mind, Tilly,' she said. 'Daddy will be happy you're getting to eat cake, so that's all right.' The figure wasn't moving, just staring in their direction.

She sighed. 'Stay here you two, I'll be back in a minute.'

Jack straightened in alarm. 'But who is he, Mum? Do you know him?'

Looking at Jack, Alice found a smile for him. 'I do, Jack. It's all right. He's a friend from a long time ago.'

'Did he know Dad too?'

'Actually, he did. He was in the war with him.'

Jack turned his head to look back at the man, a new respect and interest on his face. Alice wanted to lean over, put her hands on his cheeks and force him to look away. But she simply got up instead and walked towards the gate and the man standing there.

'Big Jim,' she said as soon as she was close enough to be heard. 'What are you doing here?'

He took off his hat and nodded at her. 'Thought I'd come pay my respects,' he said. 'But when I saw you and the kiddies there, I didn't want to intrude.'

'We won't be long,' Alice said, staring at him. 'Perhaps you could come back later?'

But Big Jim, six-foot-tall and stocky with it, was shaking his head. 'Got work to do later, Alice. Maybe I can chat to the children as well.' He flicked a glance at them, then turned his attention back to her. 'Seeing as how I'm practically related to them and all.'

'You're not related to them,' Alice said. 'And I'd rather you didn't speak to them.'

'You're looking very fine, Alice,' Big Jim said, ignoring her words. 'Very fine indeed. That dress looks very pretty on you.'

Alice felt the blood drain from her cheeks, and if she could have covered herself with just her two hands, she would have. Big Jim's eyes travelled up and down her body and she wanted to cry out, knowing he was remembering what lay under the thin cotton.

'Big Jim,' she began.

He held his hands up. 'I know. We had this conversation a year ago. You're not interested.' He smiled, tilted his head to the side in an effort she gleaned that was supposed to make him look boyish and charming. 'But it's been a year now, Alice. A long, lonely year.'

She was shaking her head. 'The answer's still no.'

'You're not still sore over our little tussle now, are you? Come on, Alice, that was three years ago. Terry and I were home from the war, and it was terrible, the things we'd seen there. Just a little bit of comfort, that was all I wanted.' He blinked, gaze locked on her. 'Terry didn't mind. No one else knew.' He smiled at her. 'And after the war, when Terry was dead, well you certainly can't blame me for courting you. We already had a connection.' He moved forward a step and she turned her head away. 'Alice, my dearest. It's been long enough now, don't you agree? No one would think twice about you remarrying now.'

She looked out over at the sea, green and silver under the horizon. 'No,' she said.

He sighed. 'Think about it, Alice. That's all I ask.' Fingertips touched her cheek and she froze. 'That and perhaps spending a little time with me.' He flicked a look over at the children. 'Especially considering the little girl over there.'

She stared up at him in shock. 'No,' she said. 'No, no, no.'

He gave an easy shrug, held his hands up. 'Okay Alice, whatever you say.' He stepped back and gave a mock salute. 'I will be a complete gentleman, you have my word.'

There was no chance to respond because a moment later, he was striding past her, calling out hello to the children. Alice turned, then hurried after him.

'Hello kids,' he was saying when she caught up. 'I'm Big Jim Dempsey, and I was a good friend of your father's.' He turned his head and gave Alice a wide, white smile. 'And your mother too, of course. We had us some good times together, didn't we Alice?'

Jack stared up at the tall man. 'You knew my father?'

Big Jim nodded and squatted down on his haunches. 'Sure did. It's Jack, isn't it? You certainly have grown. Like a weed. Your Mama must feed you plenty of good oats and hay.'

Jack and Tilly both giggled. 'She doesn't give us oats and hay,' Jack said. 'That's for horses.'

'Is that right?' Big Jim said. 'Well fancy that. Shows how much I know about kids. Guess it's pig slops you're supposed to give 'em for their supper then, is that right?'

Tilly squealed and held up her cake. 'We don't eat pig slops!'

'What's that then?' Big Jim said, pointing to her hand.

'Cake!' Tilly examined the piece she held. 'Mama made it for us.'

Big Jim turned his head and looked at Alice standing beside the blanket. He was sitting down properly now, looking perfectly at ease.

'What a clever Mama you have,' he said.

Alice opened her mouth. 'We're disturbing you, Jim,' she said, then smiled reflexively at Jack and Tilly. 'Come along children. Let's gather up our things and head back home. It's getting late and we have to get supper on.' She forced herself to breathe.

'Nonsense,' Big Jim said, turning up the brightness on his smile. 'You're not bothering me at all, in fact it's me who's barging in on your little picnic.'

'Did you really know my father?' Jack asked.

Alice wanted to run around the edge of the blanket to her son, clap her hand across his mouth and then drag him away, gathering Tilly under her other arm while she did so. But she stood frozen, praying that Big Jim would just get up and leave if she gave him his five minutes attention. Her head pounded as she waited.

'I sure did, Jack, and I gotta say, you're the spitting image of him. His hair, his eyes. Your mother must be reminded of him every time she looks at you.' He turned to Alice again. 'Isn't that right, Alice? Doesn't the boy look exactly like his good old dad?'

She forced herself to nod. Big Jim gave her another radiant smile.

'Your dad was a terrific friend,' he said, looking back at Jack. 'He and I, well, we got up to all sorts of mischief.' He wagged a finger against his nose. 'I could tell you all sorts of stories, if you'd a mind to listen.'

Jack was nodding, sandy hair flapping in his face. It was time to get it cut again, Alice thought inanely, her mind jumping around like a stone skipped out over water. She had to get them away, take them back home, bolt the door, not let Big Jim in. She shook her head, felt the whip of her own hair against her face, but no one was looking, and there was no voice in her throat.

'I would like to hear some, sir,' Jack said, smiling shyly. 'If you have time, that is.'

Big Jim stretched out his legs and placed his hat on the blanket next to his bulk. 'I've all the time in the world for you, Jack.'

'No,' Alice said, digging up a splutter. 'We have to get going.' She went to Tilly and picked her up. 'It's very nice of you to want to talk to the children about their father, but we really must get going, I'm afraid. Jack will have homework to do, and I have to get dinner on.'

'I don't have any homework, Mum,' Jack said.

'See there, Alice – the boy doesn't have any homework.' To Alice's horror, Big Jim winked at her son. 'As for dinner, it's still early.' He made a show of checking the fancy watch he wore. 'Yup. Still early.'

Alice put Tilly down behind her and gathered up the plates and cake anyway. 'I'm sorry,' she said. 'But we have to go.'

There was a pause, then Big Jim stood up. 'Well, that's a shame,' he said. Out of the corner of her eye, Alice saw him make a production of looking around. 'How are you getting home, Alice?' he asked.

'Walking,' Jack said. 'We don't have a car. Heck, we don't even have a pram for Tilly anymore.'

'Jack,' Alice warned. 'We don't speak like that.'

Big Jim grinned and gave Jack a manly pat on the shoulder. 'It's all right, son,' he said. 'How about I give you a ride back into town?' He shrugged and pointed towards the road. 'My car's right there, plenty of room for all three of you.' He looked at Alice. 'You're looking a little peaky. Let me insist on giving you a ride home.'

She stared at him, throat working over all the words she couldn't say in front of the children. Instead, she simply shook her head, mute.

'Now, now. I'm not going to bite. Come on, kids. What do you say? Let your dad's old friend give you a ride home in his brand-new automobile.'

Jack's eyes widened, and he shaded his eyes, peering at the car. 'It's brand new?'

'Sure is. Rolled off the assembly line just a few months ago. Want to have a look?'

Jack nodded furiously, then took off at a jog towards the road. Big Jim plucked up his hat and sat it back on his head with a grin at Alice.

'Boys, huh? They need a man in their life, Alice.' He tickled Tilly under her chin. 'Come on cutie, let's go for a ride back into town, shall we? Save your little legs from all that walking?'

Tilly nodded, wide-eyed, and Alice found herself with no choice but to trail behind to the car parked outside the cemetery gates.

Her head was filled with static.

CHAPTER 29

'Where are we going?' Alice asked, looking out the window of Big Jim's car, alarmed. 'This isn't the right way.'

Jim Dempsey had his window down, elbow cocked casually outside, a cigarette burning between his fingers. He looked at her, smiling.

'Thought while I had the pleasure of your company, we'd go have ourselves a nice drink, maybe a meal.'

Alice shook her head. 'I need to go home and get dinner on. The children have to be fed.'

'Wasn't that exactly what I was suggesting?' His smile turned to a grin. 'Isn't that right, kids?' he said over the back of the seats. 'I ain't going to sling you out of the car on the side of the road! What's your mother thinking?' He looked slyly back at Alice. 'We'll have us all something to eat.' Back to the children again. 'You'd like that, wouldn't you, Jack? I could tell you some of the adventures your pa and I had. That'd be neat, huh?' All the time, his eyes didn't leave Alice's face.

'Yes, sir,' Jack said from the back seat. 'That'd be real neat.'

Big Jim reached over and touched Alice's cheek. 'What you looking daggers at me for, sweetheart? Your boy deserves to know more about his daddy.' He was speaking in a low voice so only she could hear him over the car engine. 'Hell, both your kids deserve a man in their lives. They been too long without one. Especially Jack. A lad needs a father-figure.' He looked complacently out the windscreen. 'And that's not even getting started on the little girl, who looks less and less like Terry the older she gets. If she ever did to begin with.'

'No,' Alice whispered.

'No, what, Alice? No, you don't want what's best for your children?'

'I already give them what's best for them,' she hissed, uncomfortable, outraged, and more than a little afraid. 'Don't go telling me what's best for my own children.'

He pulled in beside the local hotel. Leaned over the seat and opened Jack's door. 'Hop out, Jack,' he said. 'Take your sister and wait on the footpath a minute for us, will you?'

Alice was looking wildly around. 'We can't go here!'

'Of course we can,' Big Jim said, scooting the two children out of the vehicle. 'They have a dining room here, perfectly respectable.'

'For guests,' she said.

He shrugged. 'I often eat here. They know me.' He stared into the distance. 'I don't much like to cook.' Turning to look at Alice, his eyes were flat, glassy, cold blue wells.

She didn't want to look at him. She wanted to get out of the car, gather up the children, and go home. When she got home, she wanted to go into her kitchen where everything would be normal, calm, and she would give the children a glass of milk and a sandwich each, maybe even another slice of cake, and then she would decide what to cook for supper, because Jean was coming around, they'd organised to have supper together, all four of them, sitting at the table in her kitchen, the clock back on the wall, comfortably marking the evening together.

Her hand went to the door handle and the heavy mechanism clicked open.

'Oh no you don't.' Big Jim said, snatching her wrist up in his large hand. She stared down at his clamped fingers. 'I want to take you and your children for a simple, civilised meal. Your boy wants to hear about his father, and that's a boy's right. Now don't you go making a scene, or you will regret it.'

Alice stared at him, then shifted her gaze to the two children standing on the footpath in front of the hotel, looking at her. She tried to smile at them.

'How are you going to make me regret it, Jim?' she asked through her bared teeth. 'The same way you did before?'

He laughed, and the grip on her wrist loosened. 'Get out of the car, Alice. Let's not make a scene in public.'

She turned to him, sudden fury making her bold. 'I will certainly get out of your vehicle, Jim, and what's more, I will never get back in it. Neither will my children, no matter what you say to them, no matter what you try and make them think.'

His fingers tightened back around her wrist and she knew she would have a ring of bruises there again. Leaning towards her, his face loomed close, breath hot on her cheek.

'Alice, don't go trying my patience. I'm a big man in this

town, and I can ruin what precious little you have.' She stared at him, wanting to bolt from the car, run.

But he hadn't finished. Her hand was going numb and she couldn't stifle the whimper. 'I know I'm Tilly's father,' he whispered. 'And with just a few words from me, so will everyone else in town.'

'What?' she said, forcing the words out. 'You're going to tell everyone how you forced yourself on me?'

'No one will believe that.' His eyes narrowed. 'But they will believe in you throwing yourself at me.' A smile quirked his lips. 'Even better, perhaps, I'll tell 'em how you did both Terry and me when we were home on leave. Same night, both of us in your bed.'

'That's not true!'

'And I'll tell them what you're doing in your bedroom at night with the Reardon woman.' His lips split apart into a grin. 'Such unnatural acts. Imagine the whispers, Alice. Imagine the looks. Imagine what the children will say to Jack at school every day.'

Alice shook her head, trying to tug her wrist out of his grasp. 'You've no right, Jim,' she cried.

'That's up for debate,' he said, letting his hand loosen and sitting back up to look at her. 'Considering you're the mother of my child, and I even have your own mother's blessing on our union. I'd say I'm damned close to having every right.'

Staring at him, Alice was horrified. 'Tilly is not your child,' she said, knowing she could never afford to admit that. Her face creased. 'My mother?'

He opened his door and let her arm drop, getting out of the car and coming around to open her door for her, putting a hand under her elbow so that she had to slide out and stand on unsteady legs, confused, shocked, the street around her blurred through tears she tried desperately to blink away. She was aware of her children's worried looks.

'Come on, children,' she said. 'Let's go have some afternoon tea. Would you like that?'

They gave her wobbly nods and she took them each by the hand, gathering herself together as best as possible and standing there looking at Big Jim. 'We're ready,' she said.

He smiled, delighted. 'Let's go then,' he said, and ushered them into the dim mouth of the hotel. 'A nice drink, lemonade for the children, or Coca Cola, what do you say? And for us, something stronger, a shandy for you, Alice.' The hotel smelled of beer, but he steered them away from the public bar and found seats in another room.

'This isn't the dining room,' Alice said.

He shrugged. 'No, it's the lounge bar. They won't mind a nice little family like us stopping here to quench our thirst for an hour.'

'I have to get dinner on.'

He looked at her. 'And so you will, Alice dear. I'll have you home in no time.' His gaze went to the children instead. 'How about that lemonade, what do you say?' Eyes widening, he snapped his fingers. 'Hey – I've just had the greatest idea! Do you want to hear?'

He didn't wait for Jack or Tilly to nod. He did it for them. 'How about on Saturday we go to the cinema? What a fantastic idea, I bet you don't get to go there too often, do you?'

Jack shook his head.

'Never, I'll warrant,' Big Jim said. 'Saturday afternoon, it's a date. I'll pick you up and we can go see the latest Hollywood stars and eat enough popcorn to make us sick.'

Tilly giggled, and Alice sat in stony silence.

'Saturday afternoon,' Big Jim repeated, looking at her this time. 'It's a date.'

Jean didn't have a watch to check anymore, but she knew she was on time. Come for dinner, Alice had said, eyes luminous and irresistible.

Well, maybe she was a little early, after all. It had been hard not to rush straight over after work, her mind yammering to talk to Alice again, her body itching to be close to hers, in the same room, in the same breathing space. She just wanted to be near her, to enjoy Alice's light, flowery fragrance.

She was parked outside the house, knew it was possibly a stupid thing to do, set the neighbours gossiping, but here it was still full daytime, and they were friends. Jean didn't feel like hiding that.

Although really, she admitted, she didn't know how to deal with it. She'd never been in this position before. Always her affairs had been secret, dark meetings never spoken of, never acknowledged except in the furtive couplings between crumpled sheets.

Jean wanted it to be different with Alice. Although she knew they couldn't walk around openly as a couple, she wanted to be able to be friends. She wanted to do exactly this – pop around for dinner, and on Saturdays when the weather was nice, she wanted to load everyone in the car and go to the beach. She'd never kiss Alice in public again, but she wanted them to be free to come and go.

A sigh escaped her, and she passed a hand over her warm forehead, wishing things were more straightforward. Maybe one day they would be. Not that it was terrible here. She thought of how Mrs B had rallied everyone to Alice's aid and smiled. There were plenty of decent people in town.

Twisting around in the car, she decided it was ridiculous to stay sitting in the front seat waiting for Alice to come home where everyone could look out their front windows and see her.

They were having the most marvellous spring. Gaily-coloured flowers waved their heads at her from gardens all up and down the road, bobbing about in the breeze. She shaded her eyes and looked up at the sky. It would be good planting weather, if she had a field to plant.

The front door was unlocked, but Jean already knew no one was home, and she felt awkward about walking through the house when Alice wasn't there. She squeezed instead down the side of the house, shielding her face from the untrimmed hedge.

The backyard was empty, and she wondered again what was taking Alice and the children so long. She hoped there was nothing wrong.

Of course there was nothing wrong. They'd decided to

take a little longer at the cemetery, that was all. Jean wandered over to where part of the garden had been dug over. There was half of it still to do, and spotting a spade leaning against the house, she decided she'd do the rest while she waited for them to get home.

And if they weren't home by the time she was done, she'd get back in the car and leave, knowing that something had come up and Alice had been detained. And that they'd probably see each other the next day.

It was hard though, to make herself think like that. She wanted to know Alice was okay. That Jack and Tilly were. What if something had happened to the children? What if there had been an accident? She had no way of knowing. She dug faster, trying to keep the thoughts from her mind.

She'd give it until the garden was dug then get back in her car and go looking. In fact, standing up and leaning against the spade for a moment, maybe that was exactly what she should do now. Maybe they were walking back right now and would appreciate a ride. After all, Tilly didn't have a pram anymore. And that was another thing Jean meant to do – look for a new one for her.

She put that thought on the list for tomorrow's errands and returned the spade to its spot against the house, looking regretfully at the half-done garden. Maybe she'd come and finish that job tomorrow too. And trim the hedge. That needed doing.

But right now, Alice would be glad of the ride home. Jean dusted her hands on her trousers and walked back the way she'd come.

Alice was already home.

Jean stopped still, standing on the front path, aware she'd frozen to the spot but unable to do anything about it.

Alice hadn't seen her yet, she was standing beside a car – a fancy new car with a shiny paint job and a soft top neatly folded back, oh Jean recognised that car – and Alice was there looking up into the face of a man. A man Jean also recognised, and he was staring down at Alice, their faces close to each other. Jean couldn't hear what he was saying.

Then Alice was ducking away, turning to Tilly clambering out of the back seat, picking her up and setting her on a hip, taking a bag from Jack, and moving away from the man without another look. Her chin was tucked down, and she still hadn't seen Jean standing there dumbfounded, staring at her.

He had though. He had, sure enough. Turned around to watch Alice lead the children across the footpath to the house, Big Jim had seen her straight away, rooted to her spot on the path.

A slow smile spread across his face when he recognised her, and he lifted a finger and tilted his hat to her in an insolent greeting. Then he winked, turned, and slid back into his car, revving the engine and pulling out onto the road.

'Jean!' Tilly saw her. 'Jean, we went somewhere with the man!' She squirmed in her mother's arm and Alice looked up finally, saw Jean there staring at her, and stopped walking.

'Jean!' Tilly yelled again, and that got Jean moving, although she couldn't feel her legs as they walked her over to where Alice stood.

'Hi Jean,' Jack said. Tilly leaned out from her mother and waved her arms at Jean.

'Hi Jack,' Jean said, relieved her voice was working. 'How ya doing?'

'Good thanks,' the boy said, then turned to his mother. 'I'm going to go inside and play with my new cards, okay Mum?'

Alice nodded mutely, and Jack pushed between them and opened the front door. Jean took Tilly into her arms before the child did anymore contortionist's tricks.

'Hi Tilly,' she said.

'Hi Jean. How ya doing?' Tilly put her little hands either side of Jean's face and stared into her eyes, forcing Jean to take her gaze from Alice and look at her instead.

She smiled and kissed the little one on the tip of her nose. 'I'm okie dokie,' she said.

Tilly giggled. 'I'm okie dokie too.' She twisted around to look at her mother. 'Why we standin' outside, Mama? I wanna go play with Prudence.'

Alice managed to look at her daughter, turn on something that resembled a smile. 'You go and do that, sweetheart. We'll be right behind you.'

The squirming girl took off inside as soon as she hit the ground. She was wearing the dress with the ducks on it. Jean remembered being told about it the day before. She stood back up and looked at Alice.

They stared at each other in silence for a long moment and Jean had time to register the shadows under Alice's eyes, the faint lines of strain in the fine, fair skin.

'Sweetheart,' she said. 'Are you all right?'

Abruptly, as though she'd simply been holding it in all along, Alice burst into tears. She shook her head.

There was no helping herself. Jean had her arms around

her in two quick steps. She pressed her lips to Alice's hair, smelling soap and sunshine. Alice pressed a hand against Jean's shoulder, dug fingertips in, and cried harder.

'Here, love,' Jean said, turning her towards the house. 'Let's go inside, okay?' The head against her made a nodding movement, and Alice straightened, looking at Jean for a brief moment before her gaze slid away. She swallowed, allowed Jean to lead her inside.

The children were in their room, Jean could hear their voices, both of them engrossed in their games. She breathed a silent sigh of relief and debated which part of the house to take Alice into. She chose the kitchen. She could make tea, sit Alice down, let her dry her eyes, tell her what was wrong.

Which is exactly what she intended to do, except when they were there, Alice turned and clung to her again, and Jean simply put her arms around her and held her, listening to her cry, feeling Alice's back shake with her sobs, feeling her own shirt grow wet with tears, and not caring one bit. She held on, letting Alice get it all out, not asking anything yet, not even letting herself try to guess what had happened.

Although Big Jim's face kept wavering in her mind's eye. Tipping his hat to her, expression smug, like he'd finally got one up on her, got his own back, and then that wink...she wanted to punch him just thinking about it.

What had he done to Alice?

Just what had the lousy thug done?

Jean didn't know, but she was going to find out, and if she discovered that he'd hurt her, well she was going to pay him a visit, and she was going to hurt him.

Damn the consequences. Men like Jim – Big Jim, ha! –

they didn't deserve to walk around on the streets, not when they made someone like Alice cry like her heart was broken.

'I'm sorry,' Alice choked out against Jean's breastbone. 'I'm sorry.'

'Hush,' Jean said. 'It's all right. Whatever it is, I promise it's all right. She felt Alice shake her head.

'No, it's not. It's never going to be all right again, and I'm so, so sorry.'

Jean stepped backwards, holding Alice at arm's length so she could look at her. It was her turn to shake her head.

'I don't know what's happened,' she said. 'But I know one thing – there is nothing on this earth that could make me feel badly about you.'

'You don't know,' Alice said, and her eyes, red and wet, stared at Jean for a moment before dropping to the floor.

Jean cupped Alice's chin in her hand and tried to make her raise her eyes again. Alice shook her head and wouldn't, so Jean settled for stroking her cheek instead.

'I know that something has happened that makes you feel bad, that makes you not want to look at me, and I'm telling you my darling, that there isn't anything you could do that would make it so that you couldn't face me.'

Alice lifted her hand and placed it over her own eyes, gave a small moan. 'You don't know, Jean,' she said.

Placing a kiss on the hand that covered the eyes Jean loved so much, Jean shook her head. 'Let's sit you down and dry your tears,' she said. 'I'll make us a cup of tea, and then you can tell me what has happened.' Alice sat, like an obedient child, and Jean felt around in a pocket for her clean handkerchief, found it, and knelt in front of Alice, drying her tears.

'There,' she smiled. 'That's better. Although I don't know how you manage it,' she said.

'Manage what?' Alice asked, voice still full of misery.

'Looking beautiful even when you've been sobbing your heart out.' She blinked into the hazel gaze. 'I always look a shock when I've been bawling. Like a grizzled little monkey.'

The eyes widened, and Alice laughed, a small, startled sound, but a laugh nonetheless. Jean grinned at her.

'There,' she said. 'That's better.'

Alice sniffed, took the handkerchief, wiped her cheeks again with it. 'I can't imagine you crying,' she said. 'Let alone looking like a monkey. You're far too handsome.'

Now Jean laughed. 'Oh, I can cry all right,' she said. 'Like a baby. All scrunched up and screaming.'

Alice shook her head, amusement curling her mouth.

Jean looked at her with satisfaction. 'Right. A cup of tea will do us both good.' She got up from her knees and aimed for the kettle.

'I need to make supper,' Alice said suddenly.

Jean shook her head. 'The kids are fine for a moment. We can worry about that shortly. Right now, I want to sit at the table beside you and drink a cup of tea while holding your hand.'

There was a moment's silence then Alice whispered to her. 'You're the most amazing thing that's ever happened to me,' she said. 'Don't you even want to know why I was with Big Jim?'

'Oh yes,' Jean said. 'I very much want to know what dreadful things that man is up to, making you cry like that.' She didn't want to add her thoughts about what she may want to do to him afterwards.

'But...' Alice squeezed her eyes shut, then they sprang open again. Her expression pleaded with Jean.

'But nothing,' Jean said, putting the kettle on to boil and coming to sit next to Alice, taking her hand and stroking the soft skin. 'Just sit here and have a cup of tea with me, and I promise everything will turn out all right.'

The house settled down to a still preoccupation, the waiting like a slow drift of dust. Alice, moving to the bedroom window, parted the curtain just a sliver and peered out into the deepening dusk, shivering. Jean stood in the doorway, Alice feeling her eyes on her.

'He's out there, watching us,' she said, turning around. 'Parked in his big fancy car, watching the window here.'

'Then let's do this,' Jean said, snapping off the electric light and moving over to the bed. She sat down and patted the neatly made bed beside her. 'Come over here,' she said. 'Talk to me. I assume you are meaning Jim Dempsey?'

Alice shuddered, patting the curtain back into place. She'd only peeked between it, not enough for him to see her, surely? She shouldn't have looked at all, she should have…

A deep breath, and she blew it out slowly through pursed lips, trying to calm down.

'Alice?' Jean called her back to herself. 'You're shaking.'

She was, as though palsied. Wrapping her arms around herself she couldn't make it stop. The room was almost in darkness, the light from the kitchen making it a short way up the passage to creep around the doorway, enough to shroud everything in shadows.

Hands fell on her shoulders and she stared up into Jean's dark eyes. Even in the poor light, she could see the way those eyes looked at her.

'Come, my love,' Jean whispered. 'Come and sit with me and tell me the story.'

Numbly, Alice nodded. What else was there to do but lay herself bare? She closed her eyes, breathed in, then out, measured, opened her eyes again and nodded.

'Yes,' she said. 'I want to tell you – all of it. She turned her head away from those eyes a moment. 'My darkest secret,' she said, and the words tasted of bitter almonds.

The hands moved, an arm encircling her, the other hand reaching up to stroke her face, slide back an errant lock of hair. Warm lips kissed her forehead, and a strange peace settled on Alice and she leaned into the embrace, breathing in the spicy scent of Jean's warm skin, sliding fingers between buttons so that she could feel it too, the steady beating of Jean's heart.

'Come,' Jean said again, and Alice let her lead them to the bed and she sat down, curling up into Jean's side, pillows at their backs, Jean's arm around her, encircling her almost like she was a child, except she'd never been loved this well when she was a child.

'I got married so I could get away from my mother,' she said from behind the safety of closed eyes and the warm arms around her. Soft lips pressed a kiss to her head and she smoothed the palm of a hand against the rough twill of Jean's trousers.

'I was sixteen. My father had died two years before, and life with my mother was unbearable. Terry was a few years older than me, had a job, not a great one, but enough to keep us, and we were young, optimistic.' She paused to think and heard Jean's soft, even breathing.

'For a while I think I was even happy. Deliriously so, to have my own house, to not have my mother breathing down my neck every minute of the day.' She slowed to a stop again and concentrated on the sensation of Jean's hair against her cheek.

'He was not a bad husband,' she continued. 'Not until the war.' Alice opened her eyes against the memories. This part she would have to tell with her eyes wide open, focused on the present, on Jean's comforting warmth beside her, on her strong arms holding her close. She swallowed, carried on. 'The war changed him. It broke him. I could tell in the letters he wrote home. Some men aren't meant for war, Jean, and Terry was one of them. It did something to him, wormed its way inside him, sliced through all the soft places in him.'

Her mouth was dry, but she licked her lips, spoke. 'I only saw him once after he left to fight. Two weeks leave, he had, and somehow he managed to come back here.'

'But he wasn't the same,' Jean said, voice whisper-soft.

Alice shook her head. 'No. He started drinking as soon as he was in the door, and he didn't stop. He was drunk the entire two weeks.'

She could feel Jean, listening patiently, sympathetically, without judgement. Reaching up, she touched tentative fingertips to Jean's mouth. The lips moved, kissed her and she brought her fingers back to her own lips, pressed the kiss to them.

'He had a new friend when he came back,' she said. 'They came back on leave together, and they both stayed here in this house, most nights.'

'Jim Dempsey?' Jean guessed.

Alice nodded, then cleared her throat, fingers wandering to worry at a button on Jean's shirt.

'Yes. Jim Dempsey. I knew him of course – no one who grows up here, doesn't, but we'd never had anything to do with each other.' She shivered again, despite being tucked in beside Jean, whose arms automatically tightened around her.

'He encouraged Terry's drinking.' She fell silent, forced herself to continue. 'I think he took pleasure in watching Terry disintegrate.' She blinked as the room darkened further, the sun outside sunk below the horizon, leaving the world to the sometimes-harsh vagaries of the night.

'He would watch me,' she said, the words tumbling from numbing lips. 'While Terry drank, Jim watched me, found ways to touch me, brushing up against me when he went past.' She stopped abruptly, fought down the old panic, went back to telling Jean the story. 'If that had been as far as it went, I would have been all right. I could have put up with it, for Terry's sake. They only had two weeks, Terry couldn't seem to do without either of us.' She stumbled again, righted herself, carried on, holding onto Jean's shirt now, hands knotted in the fabric.

'One night when Terry was so drunk he couldn't stand, or even speak, Jim…'

She couldn't say it after all.

'He forced himself on you.'

She nodded, forehead against Jean's cheek.

'I'm so sorry,' Jean said, and the arms around her held her

close, the words whispered warm in her ear like a bene-
diction.

Alice felt herself relax against Jean, and she leaned closer, forgetting Jim Dempsey for a moment, concentrating instead on the way Jean felt beside her, small but so steady, rock-solid, strong enough to hold them both until the story was done.

There was only a little more.

'They left to go back to the fighting. I didn't know if Terry knew what had happened, if he'd been conscious enough to see – he certainly hadn't been in any state to stop it...' Her voice trailed off.

Jean spoke, and Alice could hear new shock in her voice. 'Jim did this to you – in front of your husband?' Her head shook in disbelief. 'Knowing he couldn't help you, that must have made it all the more terrible.' A warm hand moved to stroke the side of Alice's head. 'I'm so sorry,' Jean whispered.

'I thought maybe Terry hadn't seen it, had been passed out.' Alice stared dry-eyed into the darkness. 'But I got a letter from his Captain or someone, saying that Terry had died.' She shifted a little and looked up at Jean. 'He laid down his gun and walked out into enemy fire.'

That was it. That was the story. She closed her eyes and rested against Jean, glad it was told.

'Do you hate me now?' she asked, unable to stop herself.

The bedside lamp snapped back on and Jean twisted around to face her, hands going to hold her face, eyes fastened on hers.

'I could never hate you for that,' Jean said. 'Never.' She sucked in a breath. 'Jim Dempsey, on the other hand...'

Alice put a hand against Jean's pressing it fast against her cheek. 'He thinks he has a right to me now,' she said, and dropped her hand with a sigh. Jean took her hands, held them in her lap, and listened, eyes never straying from her face.

'I love you, Jean,' Alice said abruptly.

Jean's face crumpled into a smile. 'Oh my darling Alice,' she said. 'And I love you.'

Alice nodded. 'He waylaid us at the cemetery. I guess he knew I'd take the children there today.' She lifted her shoulders in a tired shrug. 'I want them to think good things about their father, even if I can't really forgive him for what happened at the end.' She took a hand and rubbed her face. Found her voice again. 'Anyway, long story short, Jim wouldn't take no for an answer, had the children in the car before I could do anything, and is probably organising the wedding as we speak.'

'He cannot force you into marrying him, Alice.'

She shook her head, tired. 'No. But he says if I don't go along with his plans, he will tell everyone how I've had his child, and you know everyone will believe that I was unfaithful to my husband and despise me because of it.'

Jean was shaking her head violently. 'You can't be thinking of going along with it, Alice!'

'No,' she said. 'Of course not.' Her gaze roamed around the room, looking everywhere but at Jean's beloved face. 'I'll leave town before that happens,' she said. 'I'll take the children and we'll leave town.'

She meant it too. She would never give Big Jim his way. Not while she had breath in her body. Finally she looked back at Jean. She knew what true and deep love felt like now, and she would never accept anything else. She would be on her own for the rest of her life.

Jean was still shaking her head. 'No,' she said, voice flat, emphatic. 'We will think of something else. I will not let him do this thing to you.'

Alice barked a laugh. 'Oh Jean. How would we ever stop him? Between him and my mother, they practically run the town. Nobody would believe me over him.'

Jean wasn't accepting it. 'Alice,' she said. 'Did you not see how many friends you had just the other day? How many women came around when you needed help?'

It was not the way it was however. 'He's already started getting his way, Jean,' she said, touching that precious face again, feeling the sadness moulding her own. 'He took us to the hotel for a drink this afternoon. Making sure we were seen in public, the happy little family. He told the children he would take them to the cinema on Saturday.' She dropped her hand and took Jean's in it. 'I tried to tell him we couldn't go – wouldn't go – but it was as if I never spoke.' She looked at Jean. 'I don't know what I can do, except leave town.'

Jean pulled herself from the bed, stood up and ran desperate fingers through her hair. She shook her head.

'No, Alice, it's not the answer.'

Wide, sad eyes looked up at her. 'I don't know what is then, Jean,' Alice said, and Jean wanted to scoop her up into her arms, cover her with kisses, and make everything safe for her.

'He would just follow you,' she said. 'He would just follow you and bring you back. A man like that doesn't give up.' She sniffed. 'He gets his own way, like a cheap bully.'

Alice rolled onto her side, tucking her knees up and her hands under her chin. Going to her, Jean sat back down on the bed and stroked her hair. 'Don't give up, sweetheart,' she said. 'I haven't just found you only to give you up.' Sliding down beside Alice, she wrapped herself around her in a protective shell. 'If it comes to leaving, I will go with you.'

Alice's eyes opened. 'You will?'

'Yes,' Jean whispered. 'You can count on that.' She hooked

a hand around Alice's neck and tugged her closer, kissed her lips. 'But we make no hurried decisions, okay?'

Alice's eyes glistened. 'Okay,' she said. 'Will you stay the night with me?'

Her car was parked directly outside the house. If there'd been another bedroom, or even a sitting room sofa, Jean would feel better, knowing Alice would be able to dismiss any sly suggestions about what they were doing. But Alice's house had neither, just the hard chairs in the kitchen, and one armchair to the side of the coal range, blackened with soot, tufts of stuffing popping from it as though it was trying to morph into something else altogether, something more organic.

'Yes,' she said, when she realised the silence had gone on too long after Alice's question. 'I wouldn't want to spend the night anywhere else.' She stroked Alice's face, marvelling over the truth of it. She didn't want to be anywhere else. Just here, beside Alice.

For the rest of her life.

Tamping down a sigh, she forced a smile to her lips instead. 'I need to go move my car, though.' A quick glance at the window. 'Especially if Jim is out there.' She was glad they'd left the kitchen light on, although, she realised, if anyone crept around the back of the house, they'd know straight away that neither she nor Alice was in that room.

It was no use dwelling on the difficulties they faced, however. Alice was looking at her, eyes wide, pupils large and round. Jean found herself wanting to kiss the fine, thin skin of Alice's eyelids.

'Better to be circumspect right now,' she said, and

squeezed Alice's cold hands. 'But I promise we will think of something.'

'But you will come with me and the children...?'

'I don't want it to come to that,' Jean said. 'This is your home and there has to be a better way.'

'But...'

'But if it comes to that, we will leave together.' She leaned closer. 'I couldn't bear to be without you, now that I've finally found you.'

'You promise?'

'I do.'

There was a minute's silence as that sank in for both of them, and Jean realised her life had just changed completely and forever. Months she'd spent, wanting Alice from a distance, fallen in love with her over clinking bottles of milk, watching as the glimmer of recognition in Alice's eyes grew with each meeting, telling herself to get Tim instead of her to bring the milk to Alice's door but not being able to do it, not being able to resist.

She'd loved her from almost the first time she'd pressed a cold bottle of milk into the woman's hands, and she remembered that moment as though it was forever folded between the pages of her memory. Her first day on the job, and almost exactly a year ago, but it had been colder, spring doing a poor job of things, and Alice had come to the door bundled up against the cold. Jean couldn't help the smile at the memory.

'What are you grinning about?' Alice asked, bringing her back to the present.

'The day I fell in love with you,' Jean said. 'You were wearing bright red woollen gloves.'

Alice gave a sudden, surprised laugh. 'I remember that,'

she said. 'I'd knitted the gloves myself, and even though the weather was supposed to be warming, that day was cold.' Her smile turned easy, generous. 'I was wearing a matching hat, and I hadn't meant to be at the door when you arrived.'

'You remember it too?' Jean was surprised.

'That was the day you fell in love with me?'

'It was my first day at work,' Jean said. 'You were so pretty. Your cheeks were flushed when you opened the door, and your eyes were dancing.' She shook her head. 'No, you weren't just pretty,' she decided. 'You were absolutely beautiful.'

'I opened the door and you shoved a bottle of milk in my hands,' Alice said, and she was laughing properly again now. 'I didn't even know it was going to be you! I thought it was my neighbour.'

But Jean had a question she wanted to ask. 'How come you remember it?'

Alice's expression turned thoughtful. 'I don't know exactly.' She lifted her eyes to Jean's. 'You were just suddenly there, and I've never forgotten it.' She smiled shyly. 'I started looking forward to seeing you in the mornings.' Alice touched Jean's lips, her touch sending little tremors of desire through Jean's body.

'You were always smiling,' Alice said. 'No matter what sort of morning I was having, you were always smiling.' She laughed suddenly, and Jean was amused to see a dark blush spread over Alice's face.

'Tell me,' she demanded.

'I remember one day – not which day it was – just that it happened, you gave me the milk, then went back to the truck.' A slight shrug. 'Just like every day, just like normal.'

Alice paused, but only for a moment. 'But this day I stood there on the doorstep and I watched you, and something funny was happening inside me, and I didn't know what it was to begin with, but as you let yourself out the gate and whistled on your way back to the truck, I realised what I was feeling.' The blush was still there, colouring her cheeks. Jean stroked it, feeling the skin hot under her fingers.

'Don't be embarrassed,' she said.

'I realised I was looking at you the way I would have a man.'

Jean couldn't help laughing. 'You were ogling my figure!'

Alice laughed too. 'I stood there all hot, then cold, then hot again. You were all slim and strong looking – not like me...'

'I love your curves, every single one of them.'

'And you looked so comfortable and like you'd always know what you were doing, and I discovered that I was standing there wondering what it would be like if you touched me.' She looked at Jean and Jean found herself lying still beside her, heart suddenly pounding. 'Touched me...the way...a man would.' She fell quiet.

Jean wanted to touch her right there and then. 'Not the way a man would,' she whispered, although she understood why Alice had said that. 'The way a woman like me would.'

Alice nodded. 'Yes,' she said, voice little more than a whisper.

Jean squeezed her eyes shut. 'Shit,' she said.

'What? What is it?'

The sigh was heavy. Jean opened her eyes and stared at Alice lying on the bed beside her, still dressed, the soft skin of her cleavage glowing and inviting in the lamplight. How she wanted to touch her lips to it.

'I want to make love to you,' she said. 'So very much.'

'I would like that.'

Jean found a smile. 'Then I need to go move my car.'

A hand crept forward, snatched up Jean's and placed it on a soft breast. 'Then you need to do it quickly. Move the car, that is. I want you to take your time making love to me.'

Had all the air been siphoned from the room? Light-headed, Jean decided it must have been. It took an effort to back away off the bed, and when she stood, her knees were weak. She'd thought that just something that happened in the lady's romance stories she'd glanced at, but here it was manifestly happening in the real world.

'I'll be as fast as I can,' she said, aware her voice was hoarse.

'How fast?' Alice demanded.

She tried to get her head back on straight. She could smell Alice's perfume, heated by her skin. She wanted to wallow in it.

'Ah, it would be best if I drove it all the way home, then came back,' she managed. 'If Jim is watching, we can be sure he's checking all the streets around here.'

Alice shook her head. 'He already knows about us.'

'Maybe so,' Jean said. 'But best keep a low profile until we come up with a plan.'

'But you will come back?'

'I will. Nothing could stop me.' She looked down at herself to check she hadn't accidentally got carried away except in her mind and thrown off her clothes. Her boots were in the kitchen, but otherwise she was intact.

'In the meantime,' she said. 'Lock your doors, all right? I don't want anyone to be able to get in.' She meant Jim, of course, and almost regretted mentioning it when Alice's eyes widened in shock, but no, she decided, better to be safe. There wasn't much she'd put past Jim Dempsey, and she'd never forgive herself if anything happened to Alice.

'I'll be back in an hour,' she promised.

CHAPTER 33

*B*oots on, Jean stepped out the front door, paused for a moment until she heard Alice turn the lock behind her, then nodded to herself and set off for her car. She'd locked the back door herself, giving it a good shake to see how sturdy it was. Not enough for her liking, but there was little she could do about it. It was locked, and hopefully that would be good enough. Alice was under instructions to yell the house down should Jim turn up.

She shook her head, bending down to crank the car. The man was a worse menace than she'd ever thought. How innocent she'd been, considering him just a lousy, spiteful bully.

The car engine turned over, caught, and Jean gave a sigh of relief. The last thing she needed at the moment was car trouble. But her luck was holding – the damned thing hadn't needed any babying since that day on the side of the road, coming back from the beach.

The trip back from the beach when they'd been seen by Jim Dempsey himself, slowing to a stop in his fancy new car, and she stood there beside her own car, fresh from kissing

Alice, caught like a goddamned deer in his headlights. She couldn't even remember what he'd said – probably nothing – she could only recall the wariness she'd felt, like a man faced with a wild, unpredictable animal. One with big, clawed paws, and sharp teeth.

And a mean temper.

His car wasn't on Alice's street anymore. She supposed, getting behind the wheel of her own vehicle and pulling out to head back to the boarding house, that he could be lurking on one of the surrounding streets, but if she had to guess, she thought maybe he'd got the upper hand and had gone off to amuse himself elsewhere for a while.

She pictured the insolent little salute he'd given her when he'd dropped Alice and the children off at their home. And the wink, there was no forgetting that.

'Bastard,' she said out loud, zigzagging her way down the untidy roads through town. She crashed a fist against the wheel. 'Bastard. You'll pay for this. You'll not get her.'

The boarding house loomed up from its scrubby lot at last, and Jean parked in her usual place, dragging herself from the vehicle and wondering if it was worth a quick trip inside for anything. There'd been no smokes in the car – she was doing well with quitting the smelly things, but she sure as hell could do with one now.

Stepping up onto the veranda, there was the creaking of a chair, and Jean stopped abruptly, clutching her chest where her heart beat like a baby rabbit's.

'Damn it all,' she exploded. 'Do you have to lie in wait like some sort of grim reaper in a print dress?' She bent over at the middle, trying to get her breath back.

'Guess you were just a million miles away,' Mrs B said. 'Or maybe just that you've got your head stuck up your arse.'

'Well, aren't you just the cheery one tonight,' Jean retorted.

There was a heavy sigh from the rocking chair, and Jean sank down on the wooden step. 'Got any smokes?' she asked. Another sigh, some rustling, and the landlady held out a cigarette. Jean took it, lit it gratefully.

'You never have them on you anymore.'

Jean shook out the match, breathed the smoke in, spoke. 'Alice doesn't smoke.'

She could make out the bulk of Mrs Boone sitting in her rocker now, the pale moon of her face with eyebrows raised.

'I don't want to taste of ash,' she said, the smoke streaming out through her nose.

'Well good for you,' Mrs B. said, voice dripping with sarcasm. Then she sighed again.

'What's wrong?' Jean asked, conscious of time ticking away. She went to look at her watch, but it wasn't on her wrist. Another item for her list of errands. Get a new watch.

There was a long pause before Mrs Boone spoke, and Jean was almost at the point of standing up to take her leave when the old woman finally decided to say what was on her mind.

'I'm feeling a bit stirred up,' Mrs B said.

Jean blinked at her, studying her in the dim light from the sitting room window behind her. 'What?' she said.

A grunt as the landlady shifted in the rocker, and more rustling, the scrape of a match, and she'd lit another cigarette. She made a spitting sound. 'Bah. I'm smoking too many of these things and all,' she said. 'Throat's raw like someone's taken the vegetable peeler to it.'

Jean stood. 'Let me get you a glass of water.'

Mrs Boone choked out a laugh. 'Don't be silly, girl,' she said. 'The whisky's on the sideboard. Get me a nice medicinal dose of that. And one for yourself while you're at it.' She sniffed. 'You're gonna need it.'

'I have to get back to Alice. I promised.'

The broad face turned and studied her. 'You promised, did you?'

'She's had a hard day,' Jean said. 'And yes, I did. I want to be with her.'

'Things are stirred up,' Mrs Boone repeated ominously. 'Get me that drink, and one for yourself, and then we'll talk.'

Jean stood still a moment longer, staring at the woman rocking herself and smoking on the porch, then turned without a word and went into the house, into Mrs B's private room, where the whisky bottle sat neatly beside two glasses. She poured a healthy measure in each and went back outside.

'Here,' she said, holding out one of the glasses to Mrs Boone.

The old woman took it. 'To your good health,' she said.

'Cheers,' Jean said, sitting back down on the step, feeling the evening chill as it grew later. How long had she been away now? Alice was waiting for her in bed. How long would it take her to walk all the way back?'

'I heard something concerning today,' Mrs Boone said abruptly, disrupting the run of thoughts in Jean's head.

'Concerning in what way?'

'Concerning in a way I think is going to be concerning to you.'

Jean took a moment to untangle that sentence, then stared at her whisky. 'Let me guess,' she said. 'Jim Dempsey.'

A wheezing laugh from the rocking chair. 'Got it in one, Jean. Big Jim Dempsey.' She whistled out a breath. 'But that's not all.' Jean saw her shake her head. 'Not by a long shot.'

The whisky went down in a smooth amber mouthful, then spread welcome fingers of fire through her. Jean closed her eyes and listened to the distant hooting of an owl. Somewhere behind it was the susurration of the sea, but she couldn't hear that over the rush and pull of her own blood in her ears.

'Tell me,' she said.

The chair creaked again. 'Let me tell you a story first,' Mrs Boone said. 'You got time?' There was amusement in the last question, and Jean found herself thankful for it. It made her uneasy when the landlady lost her sense of humour.

'No,' Jean replied. 'But tell me anyway.'

'I'll be quick about it, you can count on that,' Mrs Boone said. 'I've no wish to dwell on the telling of my own follies.'

Jean raised her eyebrows, but said nothing, waiting for the tale to begin.

'Once upon a time,' Mrs Boone said, and laughed, a harsh, cackling sound. 'Once upon a time, a long time ago, I was a young thing.' More creaking as she settled deeper into the chair and her story. 'And pretty to boot, though I know that's hard to believe, to look at me now.' She shot a sideways look at Jean. 'Don't you go saying any pleasantries, Jean Reardon, bless your kind heart. We both know I'm a hundred pounds overweight, and my hair's thinning where I want it, and growing where I don't.'

Jean kept her silence.

'Well,' Mrs B said and sucked long and hard on her cigarette, the whisky glass resting in her other hand, almost empty. 'Young, pretty, and in love, I was – you see, it's a story like so many others.'

Jean tried to imagine Mrs Boone young, pretty, and in love, and to her surprise, found that she could.

'He was a handsome thing too,' she continued, and did Jean imagine it or was her landlady's voice momentarily wistful? 'Handsome, a nice head of hair he had, and a slim figure that wore everything well and made you not want to keep your hands to yourself.' Jean received a sly grin. 'Oh, we were the same in those days as ever young people are.' A laugh. 'We just weren't left alone as much, for that very reason.'

'He sounds nice, Mrs B,' Jean said.

'Nice?' She laughed. 'He was handsome, smart, and the best catch in town.' Her voice softened. 'And he had his eye on me.' She sipped at her drink. 'I was besotted with him. Already planning my wedding trousseau, fixing a honeymoon destination in mind, deciding where we'd build our house, how many children the nursery would see…and walking on air every time he called for tea.'

'He, ah, returned your affections?' Jean's own drink was forgotten.

'Fetch me a refill, will you? This is a story that requires lubrication.'

Jean did as she was bidden. 'Have you ever told it before?' she asked, returning to her perch on the step, fascinated.

The landlady shook her head. 'No, though once upon a time, I suppose it used to be common enough knowledge. Now only some of us know it, and few still have cause to remember.'

'What happened to him?'

Mrs Boone's voice was bitter when she answered. 'Geraldine Thomas,' she said.

'Alice's mother?' Jean said, surprised.

'The one and only.'

Jean sat back, processing the information. 'You're not… Mrs Boone, you've not been talking about Alice's father, have you?'

'You're a smart one, Jean, I'll always give you that,' the landlady said from the depths of her rocker. She paused for a swallow of whisky. 'Avery Thomas.' A smile tweaked the edges of her lips in remembrance. 'Oh he was a sweet man, too much so for his own good, when it came down to it.' She blinked at Jean. 'His father owned the bank, and he was in line to take it over, but anyone could tell he had a real feeling for the work. There was nothing he loved more than to talk to the people of the town, divine their needs, and figure out ways to help them.' She sighed. 'His death was a tragedy, and way too early. He was still reasonably young. It was living with Geraldine that did him in, I'm convinced of it. Living with her would wear out the strongest heart.'

Jean could only agree, although she'd never had the dubious pleasure of meeting the woman.

'She took him from you?'

'She *tricked* him away from me. Managed to get him in a compromising position, and him, being the man he was, felt he had to do right by the witch. When they were married, Geraldine miscarried several times, which broke Avery's heart. When Alice finally came along, he treasured her greatly.'

Shaking her head, Jean looked at the older woman. 'I'm sorry,' she said.

A one-shouldered shrug and when the voice spoke, it was calmer. 'Ah, well, it's old news now.' Mrs Boone's eyes gleamed out at Jean. 'Or would be,' she said, voice hardening again. 'Except for your Alice.'

'I don't understand. I don't think we need to tell Alice this. She has enough issues with her mother.'

Mrs Boone inclined her head. 'I don't get out much anymore,' she said. 'But I still have friends here in town, and they keep me informed of the town's goings on.' She took a sip of her whisky, eyes not leaving Jean's face. 'And here's what I heard today – that our esteemed Geraldine Thomas had a meeting at her fancy house with a certain someone you've had the singular displeasure of knowing.' She narrowed her eyes. 'You and your Alice, both.'

'Big Jim,' Jean said, feeling her heart sink, even though she'd been sure this was coming.

'Big Jim indeed,' Mrs Boon agreed. 'Now tell me, Jean, what would Geraldine Thomas want with Big Jim?' She waved a hand before Jean could even begin to formulate and answer. 'Now before you say anything, here's two other pieces of information to chew on.' She shook her head. 'Now I'm not saying they're necessarily anything more than gossip, and when I heard them born I put my foot down and stamped them out before they could catch hold, but I heard them nonetheless and I've not forgotten them.'

Jean didn't have anything to say, she merely waited, all nerves attuned.

Mrs Boone held up a finger. 'One,' she said. 'There was talk when Avery died that he'd put money aside for his daughter.' Her eyes squinted at Jean. 'Money that Geraldine had control over, because he'd not been quick enough in the end to put it into a trust, but definitely it was intended for Alice. It was supposed to go to her when she married or reached her majority.'

Jean shook her head. 'That's impossible. Alice married when she was sixteen.'

'And she must be plenty older than twenty-one by now.'

'Twenty-five,' Jean said. 'She's just had a birthday.'

'Interesting though, wouldn't you say?' Mrs Boone asked. 'Especially, I'm inclined to think, in light of the second piece of old gossip, when combined with this secret meeting.'

'Between Geraldine and Big Jim.'

'Yes.' Mrs Boone fished in her lap and came up with two cigarettes. She pitched one at Jean, who took it and lit it without thinking. Her mind was working, and she could almost hear her own gears turning.

'What's the second piece of information?'

'That Big Jim might be the father of Alice's youngest.' Mrs Boone looked at her with a softening expression. 'Sorry to break it to you like that, kid,' she said.

Jean shook her head. 'No, no it's all right. Alice herself told me the story just tonight.'

She got a considering look. 'So it's true then?'

'Maybe,' Jean said on a sigh and looked at her glass to see if there was anything still in it. 'Jim was friends with Alice's husband and when he was home on leave Jim forced himself on her.' She sighed. 'She didn't say anything about Tilly, but the implication is there, I suppose.'

Mrs Boone leaned back in her rocker, blowing smoke up at the dark sky. 'He raped her?' she said.

'Yes.' Jean closed her eyes. 'And now, he wants her again, this time to play happy families with him.'

There was silence from the landlady. 'You two got a plan?' she asked after a long minute.

'Not as such,' Jean said. 'Alice thinks the only option is to leave town.'

That got a slow, considering nod. 'I can understand that.' She looked over at Jean. 'You'd better get back to her, girl. She's gonna need all the support you can give her over the next weeks.'

Jean nodded, stood up, passed the woman her glass. 'I have my own beef with Jim Dempsey,' she said. 'I'm not going to let him get away with this.'

'No,' Mrs Boone said. 'I'm sure you're not. And for myself, I'm no longer inclined to let Geraldine Thomas destroy any more lives.' She picked up the cigarettes in her lap and heaved herself to her feet.

'Go be with your woman, Jean,' she said. 'Things are only getting going.'

Saturday was too soon in coming for Alice's liking. She sat over a cooling cup of tea, her hands shaking.

'We need to put Jim Dempsey off for good,' Jean had said, lying awake late into the night with Alice pressed to her side, hand on Jean's ribs, feeling the steady beating of her heart and letting it calm her.

'What about the beach?' Alice asked. 'We were going to go to the beach before all this happened.' She wanted so badly to go back to the way everything had been before Big Jim decided to come back on the scene. She sighed against Jean's bare skin. Life had a funny way of not letting anything rest.

'We'll go to the beach later, if we can manage it,' Jean said, turning and kissing Alice on her forehead. Her lips were soft, gentle, comforting. 'What time is he going to try picking you up?'

'The film starts at 12.15.' Alice tucked herself closer to Jean's side. 'I don't know what is showing. I don't even want to know.' She lifted her head and gazed at Jean. 'I can't go. I can't.'

Jean smiled at her, kindly, understanding without Alice having to say anything more. 'You won't have to,' she said. 'I'll make sure of it.'

Alice wanted to ask how, but she closed her eyes instead. It had been a long day, and she was tired from all of it. The day had held the worst of things, and the best as well. Jean had been true to her word, had dropped her car off at the boarding house, then walked back through the dark town, slipping up to Alice's back door and tapping lightly on the wood. They'd greeted each other wordlessly, wanting instead the comfort of each other's embrace.

'Okay,' Alice said, content to trust that they would come up with something.

Now it was the day. Her eyes flicked a glance at the clock on the kitchen wall. The minute and hour hands were edging uncomfortably near to eleven. It was time to tell the children.

Forcing herself out of the chair, Alice went to the back door, shading her eyes to scan the yard for Jack and his sister.

They were lying on their stomachs, peering into the tiny pond with looks of intense fascination on their smooth faces. Stepping out of the house, Alice forced a deep breath and a smile.

'Now what are you two up to?' she asked, sitting down on the lawn beside them, tucking her skirt under her knees and pretending interest in the pond.

'Tapbowls, Mama,' Tilly said.

Jack groaned. 'Tilly, it's tadpoles.'

The little girl frowned at him. 'That's what I said.'

'No it isn't. You said tapbowls not tadpoles.'

Tilly shook her head. 'Did not.' She got her feet under her and plopped down in Alice's lap instead. 'We was lookin' at the tapbowls, Mama.'

'Tadpoles!'

'It's all right, Jack,' Alice said. 'She's only little.' Before he could say anything, she leaned over the pond, scanning the murky depths. 'Oh my goodness, there are a lot of them!'

Her son nodded, face serious. 'Some of them have legs already, can you see?'

She could and nodded. 'Sure can. Looks like far too many for such a tiny pond.'

Jack sat up and puzzled over what she'd just said. 'I guess a bunch of them will go looking for a bigger one when they're proper frogs,' he said, and looked satisfied with the solution.

Alice hugged Tilly on her lap and opened her mouth to speak, still not knowing exactly how to broach the subject. Nothing came out.

'What we doin' today, Mama?' Tilly said, plucking a buttercup from the grass and holding it under Alice's chin. 'Look,' she giggled. 'Mama loves butter.'

'Yes, I do,' Alice said, and tickled the child.

'We're going to the cinema,' Jack said. 'Dad's friend is taking us, remember?'

Tilly stopped squirming. 'I wanted to go to the beach.' The beach was her favourite place in the whole world.

'We're not going to the beach, Tilly,' Jack said. 'We're going to see a film.'

'We was gonna go to the beach.' Tilly twisted around in Alice's lap and stared up at her mother. 'Wasn't we, Mama? Jean was gonna take us.'

Alice nodded, reached out and touched a gentle hand to her son's arm. 'I wanted to talk to you about going to the cinema,' she said.

Jack's scowl was automatic. 'I want to go,' he said.

'Yes, I know,' Alice said, tugging him closer until he was tucked under her arm. She didn't look to see if he was happy about being there. Sometimes a mother had to use her privilege. 'I know you do, Jack, but there is something I need to tell you.'

Jack looked up at her, suspicion in his eyes. She gave his shoulders a squeeze.

'I didn't want to have to tell you these things, because you're my son, and I only want good things in your life.'

He squinted at her. 'I don't understand,' he said.

'I know, and I'm not doing a very good job of explaining.' She took a breath. 'I loved your father very much,' she said. 'But the war was very hard on him – it is on some men, some of the gentler, sweeter ones, I think.' She looked down at Jack but could only see his sandy hair so like his father's. Another breath. 'One of the things the war did to your father was make him drink too much. He started drinking so that he could cope with the dreadful things he had to see and do.' She paused and bit at her lip. Tilly stared up at her, wide-eyed and silent.

'Drinking also meant that he wasn't so good at picking his friends.' She floundered, knowing she was doing a lousy job of explaining things.

'Friends like Mr Dempsey?' Jack asked. 'That's what you mean, isn't it? You don't like him.'

'I do mean him, Jack,' Alice said, keeping her voice even but unable to stop the sadness seeping into it. 'He was around a lot when your father had his last leave home, and I got to know him very well.'

'You don't like him,' Jack repeated.

'No,' Alice said. 'No, Jack, I don't like him. He pretends to be nice, but he isn't really.'

'He told us funny stories,' Jack said. 'He bought us Coca Colas, and something to eat, and he gave me a pack of cards, so I could learn some magic tricks.' The boy looked up at her. 'And he wants to take us to the cinema. We never get to go to the cinema. He has a fancy car, he can take us.'

She hugged him. 'I know you want to go to see films and things, Jack. I know his car is terrific, but it doesn't mean that he is a nice man, it just means he has more money than us.'

'He told jokes,' Jack tried.

Alice gazed unseeingly around the yard. How to explain to a child that a man was nice to them just so he could get their mother to do the things he wanted? It was impossible to tell Jack that. She couldn't help the sigh that escaped from her.

'Was he mean to you, Mama?' Tilly asked. 'When he knew Daddy?'

Alice could have kissed the child. She stroked the little girl's creased forehead.

'Yes, sweetheart,' she said. 'I'm afraid he was. He was very mean.' She leaned her head down to touch her cheek to Jack's warm hair. 'I'm sorry, darling,' she said.

She felt the boy's struggle in the tension of his shoulders, his slight body rigid under her arm.

'I miss having a dad,' he said, voice almost a whisper.

'Jean can be our daddy,' Tilly said. 'She's not mean.'

'Jean can't be our daddy,' Jack said. 'She's not a man.'

'Well I want her to be my daddy,' Tilly said, rolling off Alice's lap. 'So there.'

'Jack,' Alice said, breaking into the escalating confrontation. 'Things are going to get better, I promise. There are lots of nice men in the world, and I'm sure we can have some of them as friends.'

He looked up at her, and she gave him a hopeful smile and after a moment, got a nod in return.

'Have you told Mr Dempsey we're not going to the cinema with him?' Jack asked next.

Alice shook her head, the nervousness back in full force again. 'No,' she said. 'I've had no way to get hold of him.'

'You're shaking,' Jack said suddenly.

'I know. I'm sorry.'

Her son's eyes, so similar to his father's, gazed at her. 'You're scared of him.'

Tilly climbed back into her lap.

'It's going to be okay,' Alice said. 'Nothing bad is going to happen.'

But Jack was sitting up, looking straight at her. She fixed a smile for him. 'It's okay, Jack, I promise. We're going to be okay.'

CHAPTER 35

Jean hesitated on the doorstep, then gathered up her courage and put her hand to the door-knocker. Barely had she lifted it when the green-painted door swung open and she was confronted with a pair of eyes the same colour as the door.

'Jean,' the woman said, the eyes staring at her with a feline pleasure. 'How interesting to see you here this morning.'

Interesting. That was an…interesting choice of words.

'Martha,' Jean said.

The mouth, painted a bright red under the green eyes, widened in a smile. 'Would you like to come in? I was just about to enjoy a pot of tea outside in the garden. I was collecting a book and thought I saw a shadow at the door.' She moved back from the doorway, letting Jean step into the fragrant dimness. 'Our milk has already been delivered, so I'm guessing that's not why you're lurking on my step.'

Jean sucked in a deep breath. 'No,' she said. 'I'm not here to deliver your milk.'

Martha laughed, a sound that had always made Jean think of a silver bell, tinkling in the morning light. She followed it through the house and outside, blinking in the light of a sun-speckled garden.

'You've been planting,' she said, looking around.

Martha followed her gaze, a proud smile on her face. 'Yes,' she said. 'The garden is still my absolute delight.'

Jean's gaze drifted around the little garden rooms designed by canny planting, then quickly averted her eyes at the memory of one particular soft patch of grass overlooked by a sprawling jasmine. Martha laughed again.

'Can I get you a cup of tea?' Martha asked.

Jean turned away from the garden and sat down at the wrought iron table on the cobbled patio. 'Please,' she said. 'That would be lovely – if I'm not intruding.'

'Oh, you're not intruding,' Martha said. 'Douglas is away in the capital at the moment.'

Clearing her throat, Jean managed a look up at those cat-green eyes. 'How is your husband?' she asked.

'Very well, thank you,' Martha said. 'I would ordinarily be with him on this trip, but we have the town fair coming up next week, and there is a lot to do.' Her smile widened. 'Oh, Jean, do relax. Douglas knows, you realise.'

Jean stared. 'What?' she squawked.

Martha poured tea into a cup and pushed it towards Jean. 'Drink some of that, you poor thing. It's hot.'

'I think I might need something stronger, actually, Martha.'

Her companion waved an airy hand. 'I told him when he came home from the war.'

Jean coughed on the liquid. 'You told him? Why would you do that?'

'I judged he could handle it, and I was right.' Martha leaned forward over the table. 'I had this inkling that such a confidence...'

'Of infidelity! With a woman!'

'Of a love affair with a woman – that it would add to our marriage, rather than take something away.' She reached over and took the tea cup from Jean and raised it to her own lips.

'I guess I don't understand,' Jean said, eyes fixed on Martha's, her reason for the visit forgotten for a moment.

The cup was replaced on the saucer. 'What you see on the surface of anything is never what's really there, Jean,' Martha said. 'To the casual gaze, this town is dull, filled with conventional people doing the conventional thing, but as with every other town, that is never the case.'

Jean simply blinked at her.

'People everywhere live secret lives, Jean,' Martha explained in a tone of indulging patience. 'Take a walk through this and every town – behind one door a man will be beating his wife, behind another he will be kissing every inch of her body. Another will be praying to a god they don't much believe in to justify their poor choices, and in the next road someone will be sitting lonely at their dinner table wishing for nothing more than someone to talk to.' She looked at Jean. And then we could take you, for instance.'

'Me?'

'Of course. You live a secret life in the undercurrents of this town's existence.' She picked up the cup again, touched a fingertip to the perfect lipstick print of her bottom lip on the rim. 'Douglas and I have an arrangement with a woman in the capital.' Her smile widened. 'He is probably with her this very moment and I am only jealous that I am not in that bed too.'

Jean held up a hand. 'Okay,' she said. 'Goodness. I get the picture.' She shook her head.

Martha laughed at her. 'Are you shocked?'

'Yes,' Jean said, and listened to Martha laugh again. 'But I'm glad for the both of you.' She sobered.

'What is it?'

'Speaking of secret lives and such, I've come to ask your help.'

'Name it,' Martha said, then got a sly look on her face. 'Is it to do with a certain Alice Holden?'

This time it was Jean who picked up the china teapot and took the cup from Martha, refilling it. 'Yes,' she said. 'And Big Jim Dempsey.'

The green eyes across the table grew serious. 'Oh,' she said. 'I think I see.'

'You do?'

'She had some trouble with him after the war ended. I remember it.' Her lips quirked. 'An impartial interest in gossip is one of my hobbies.'

'I didn't know her then,' Jean said.

'He was making a nuisance of himself, in the way he's done several times before, with various women. He does not have a good track record.' She gave Jean a considering look. 'I always thought he wasn't quite done with Alice Holden.' A painted fingernail tapped on the table. 'And then there's her mother.'

'You've heard about that?'

'I heard that she invited Big Jim to her house for a mystery interview.' The red nail scraped against the iron. 'And now he's chasing after her daughter?' A feline smile crossed her face. 'Her daughter, your lover, am I correct?'

There was no point not answering honestly. Not when it was Martha. Not when she was here to ask for help.

'Yes.'

Martha laughed. 'She's a sweetheart,' she said. 'And those kids of hers are adorable.' The eyes danced with amusement. 'I always thought you harboured a secret desire for the domestic lifestyle.'

Jean shrugged. 'Not that it's likely, when all's said and done.'

'Oh, I don't know. Women have been pretending to be roommates forever, you know. Share a house in the open, a bedroom in secret.'

Jean discovered she didn't want to talk about it. The subject touched too close to a nerve. She had always wanted to settle down, have a family, or at least be part of a family. She herself had grown up on a farm just outside of the capital city, her and half a dozen brothers and sisters running more wild than the stock. She still wrote to her mother every month.

'I'm sorry,' Jean said. 'What were you saying?'

'I was asking what you needed from me. And when?'

'Today,' Jean said. 'He's going to try to force her to go to the cinema with him for the 12.15 showing. She needs some support.' Jean choked. 'It's ah, not the first time he's forced himself on her.' She swallowed. 'So to speak.'

'Understood.' Martha stood up. 'I'd best get ready then.'

Jean stood too. 'Thank you,' she said.

'You're very welcome,' Martha told her. 'Both for your sake and Alice's, and because it's time men like Jim Dempsey learnt they can't just do as they please.' A wicked little smile appeared on her face.

'Besides,' she said. 'It will be fun.'

Alice had to force herself not to wear a track in the faded linoleum wanting to pace back and forth. She concentrated instead on making a picnic lunch.

'We're still going to the beach, children,' she said to the two earnest faces watching her from the kitchen table. 'It might not be as exciting as going to see a film, but I bet we'll have a terrific time anyway.' She cast a desperate glance at Jack.

He nodded. 'We'll build a huge sandcastle, won't we, Tilly?'

'Yeah,' squealed Tilly, and Alice gave him a grateful smile.

'It's a beautiful day for it,' she said. 'We've had the loveliest spring, it's been warm practically every day.' She was gibbering, she knew that, but the nervousness wouldn't leave the pit of her stomach where it had settled to roost.

When the knock came at the door, she jumped, heart pounding loud enough to block out almost everything else.

'I'll get it, Mum,' Jack said, looking at her.

She was frozen to the spot, trying to siphon air into lungs

that felt like they'd been filled with stuffing. Jack slid from his chair, watched by a wide-eyed Tilly, and went down the hallway to the front door, his shoulders taut and spine rigid.

'Hello there,' a woman's voice said, and Alice relaxed, the breath whooshing out of her like a deflating balloon. It wasn't Big Jim. She cast a quick glance at the clock on the wall. It wasn't him now, but it would be soon.

'It's Jack, isn't it? My, aren't you a handsome young lad. Your Daddy would be proud.'

'Did you know my Dad?' Alice heard Jack ask, and then the voices were coming closer.

'Only to say hello to on the street, I'm afraid, but you look very much like him. He was a lovely-looking man.'

Jack came back into the kitchen, a shy, pleased look on his face. 'It's some ladies,' he said. 'Not Mr Dempsey.'

For a moment, Alice couldn't find her voice, and her legs shook under her.

'Hello Martha,' she said, finding a wobbly smile.

'Hello dear,' Martha said, setting her handbag down on the table. 'I hope you don't mind, but my friends and I were desperately hoping you could help us sorting some things for the jumble sale. The town fair is only a week away, time does fly so.' She waved an airy hand, and three other women crowded in the kitchen smiling at Alice. They held washing baskets piled high with clothes. 'This is Agnes, Ruth, and Pattie.'

'Hi,' Alice said shyly. 'These are my children, Jack and Tilly.' She didn't know what else to say. 'I'd be glad to give whatever help I can.'

Martha winked at her. 'A pot of tea would be lovely, don't you think?'

'Can I put the basket down on the table, Alice?' one of the other women said. Alice thought it might be Pattie. She nodded, and all of them set down their baskets with sighs of relief.

'We have another two loads in the car, would you believe?' This time it was Agnes who spoke, bustling over the piles of clothing. 'Everyone's been very generous this year.'

'And the things are such very good quality too – a blessing after all the shortages we suffered during the war,' Ruth chipped in.

Alice wiped her hands on her apron. 'I can fetch in another basket, if you like.' She moved toward the door.

Martha intercepted her. 'No, Alice,' she said. 'It's quite all right – why don't you stay in here with us, and put the kettle on?'

Alice stared at her, understanding dawning. Martha patted her on the shoulder, emerald eyes smiling at her.

'How did…' Alice began.

'I believe I said last time I visited, that you have friends, Alice.' She slid an arm around her shoulders and moved Alice over to the range. The other women were chattering, talking to Jack and Tilly.

'But…'

Well-manicured hands patted Alice. 'Jean paid me a visit,' Martha said.

'Jean?'

'She's in love with you.' Martha tipped her head to one side, speaking low enough that only Alice could hear.

Still, it was shocking to hear someone saying so openly. Alice stared at her. 'Are you…?'

Martha laughed. 'Still in love with Jean? Oh my dear, I

never was. I am very fond of her, however, and I think I shall end up very fond of you also.'

Alice didn't know what to say. Martha smiled at her, took the kettle and went to the sink to fill it. 'Have you spoken to your mother lately?' she asked.

'My mother?' Alice winced. She was repeating just about everything the woman said. She sounded like an idiot. Drawing a deep breath, she shook her head, hoping to regain some of her senses.

Martha gave her a kind smile and popped the kettle on the stove. 'I was just wondering.'

Alice shook her head. 'No,' she said. 'I haven't spoken to my mother since that fiasco with trying to force me to move home with the children.' She glanced at Tilly and Jack, but they were happily helping to sort the jumble of clothing. Martha followed her gaze.

'They're fine,' she said. 'We all love children.' She scanned the cupboards, took down cups and saucers. Alice watched her but didn't complain. For some reason, it didn't feel like an intrusion. 'But back to your mother.'

'What about her?'

'I'm just concerned about you, is all. It worries me that your mother will go to such lengths.' A sideways look. 'She does seem to think she has a right to interfere in your life even more than most mothers.'

Alice gave a bitter laugh. 'She certainly does. It's always been like that, ever since I was a child.' She picked up the teapot and rinsed the morning's leaves out of it. 'She didn't even want me to go to my father's funeral.'

'When did your father die, if you don't mind me asking?'

Alice didn't mind at all. She looked at Martha, remembered that this was the woman Jean had had an affair with, then quickly looked away.

'Are you all right?'

She nodded. 'Yes. Of course.'

Martha wore a perfume that smelled exquisite, expensive. No wonder Jean had been attracted to her.

Martha was regarding her with laughing, feline eyes. 'You're trying to imagine Jean and I together, aren't you?'

'I'm trying not to imagine it,' Alice retorted before she thought better of it. Then she risked a curious look. 'You're very comfortable talking about these things.'

'I'm very comfortable talking about most things,' Martha said. 'It's just my nature. Now, not to be a bother, but I am very much concerned about your mother.'

'My mother?'

'Yes.' Martha looked at her with a steady green gaze. 'Jim Dempsey visited her at home recently.'

Alice gazed at her in horror. 'What?'

'It's true, I'm afraid.'

'But why?' Alice's head filled with static. 'What on earth does she think she's up to?'

There was sympathy on Martha's face. 'I imagine, knowing what I do about Geraldine Thomas – and I'm sorry to say this – that she is looking to control you in whatever way possible.'

'But...' Alice leaned against the kitchen counter and sucked in a breath. She felt like she'd been punched in the belly. 'I don't understand,' she said at last. 'Why Jim?' She could hear the anguish in her voice. 'I don't understand!'

'Nor do I, I'm afraid.'

She shook her head. 'She knows he's always been interested in me.' It was hard to get the words out and she hoped that the children couldn't see her distress. Martha moved to stand beside her, shielding their gaze, as though she'd read Alice's mind.

Alice turned slowly to stare at the other woman.

'What is it?' Martha asked.

She tried to swallow, her mouth dry. 'The other day,' she said. Cleared her throat, tried again. 'The other day my mother sent Mrs McMurtry – who's been doing her bidding since I was a child – to check up on me.' It took a minute for Alice to remember why the woman had turned up. 'She brought a message from Mother demanding my presence for lunch. I told her I would never be setting foot in that house again, and nor would my mother ever have any contact with the children again.' She turned and stared unseeing out the window. 'But that wasn't all,' she said, and now her voice was an appalled whisper.

'Mrs McMurtry arrived when the milk truck was there.' She looked back at Martha. 'I was talking to Jean.'

'Talking is no harm.'

Alice shook her head. 'My mother had already warned me against being seen with Jean.'

'She has something against Jean?' Martha looked as if she knew the answer, but Alice replied anyway.

'Jean dresses and works like a man. Which my mother thinks inappropriate. She may also not be quite ignorant of…' Alice trailed off, no idea how to say what she meant.

'Of women who love other women.' Martha sniffed. 'Well now, I think we've hit on something.'

'But what does it mean?'

Martha reached out and patted Alice's hand. 'It means we

must find a way to dissuade both Jim Dempsey, and your mother.'

It seemed an impossible task, put like that. 'You don't know my mother,' Alice said, her voice dark. 'I've been thinking I ought to leave town.' She lifted her eyes to Martha's. 'The children and I can start over.' Her gaze dropped. 'Jean said she'd come with us.'

Martha opened her mouth to speak, but there was a sharp knocking at the door instead, and a man's voice called out, followed by his footsteps in the hallway.

CHAPTER 37

Alice thought she was going to be sick, and when the kettle on the stove suddenly whistled, she gave a little scream. Martha reached for the kettle, taking it off the hotplate, giving her a reassuring smile.

'It's going to be all right,' she said.

The other women had turned to look at Jim and one of them, Ruth, had swooped Tilly up in her arms, holding her snugly against her side.

'What's going on, Alice?' Jim said. 'We had a date, remember?'

It was Martha who answered, her voice smooth and assured. 'I'm sorry,' she said, falsely bright and not sounding sorry at all. 'Urgent jumble sale business, and we absolutely needed Alice.' There were nods from around the table.

Jim sought out Alice, who was still standing beside the sink, one arm propping up her shaking body.

'I don't understand, Alice,' he said. 'We made a date.'

She shook her head. 'No,' she said, finding her voice and her courage. 'No Jim, we didn't. You tried to bully me into going out with you, and you tried to use the children so that I would have no choice but to agree, but I said I didn't want to go, and I meant it.' Her voice was strong by the end of the little speech and she stood up, drawing her shoulders back. 'I won't ever be going out with you, Jim. I'm simply not interested in any sort of relationship with you.'

His eyes narrowed, and he started forward a couple steps into the room, hands clenching into fist at his sides. 'Perhaps this would be more appropriate for a private conversation, Alice,' he growled.

She shook her head. 'I don't find there's any need. I've said all there is to say on the subject.' She paused, aware of the other women's alert attention. 'You should leave, Jim. I think that's best.'

He was shaking his head. 'I have to disagree with you, Alice. In fact, I need you to come into the other room with me, so we can discuss this like adults.'

'Are you implying I'm acting childishly?' Alice asked him, widening her eyes and realising with a shock that if she wasn't quite actually enjoying the confrontation, she was no longer frightened.

'What?' he asked, brow furrowing over his eyes. 'What are you talking about?' He took another step into the room, aiming for Alice. 'I insist we go somewhere private and speak about this.' A quick look at the other four women staring at him and his lips quirked in a twisted smile. 'After all, you wouldn't want these fine ladies to get the wrong impression about some things, would you?'

Alice cocked her head to one side. 'What sort of things, Jim?'

'You know the answer to that, Alice. We've discussed this

already.'

'Oh,' she said. 'Was that the conversation where you did all the talking? Where you made a series of threats against me and my family, and my standing in this community? Was that the one?' She shook her head and although she could barely believe it, she found a smile on her face. 'These fine women here already know what sort of a man you are, Jim Dempsey, and if you were to tell them your stories, they would know that the truth had been missed by a wide mark.' She gulped and fell silent.

He stared at her and she could see he was trying to calculate how to respond. 'You've been hanging out with the wrong sort of people, Alice Holden,' he said at last.

She made no reply.

'It won't get you anything but trouble.'

'The only trouble I'm having at the moment, is you,' Alice said. 'And now, I'd be pleased if you were to leave my house.'

His eyes, narrowed and furious, scanned the room, stopped a moment on Jack's face, but Jack, bless his heart, gave him a level stare back, face impassive.

'You'll regret this, Alice,' Jim said, but he was backing up a few steps.

It was Martha who spoke. 'No,' she said. 'I don't believe she will. We will all make sure of that.'

'Bah!' he spat. 'You are all a bunch of worthless bitches. You don't know anything.'

Alice turned away, reached for the tin of tea and measured a scoop into the pot. 'Leave, Jim, and close the door behind you. We're busy.'

The other women turned their backs on him as well, bending over the table of clothes, murmuring to each other, all except for Martha, who Alice could see out of the corner of her eye, standing her ground staring at Jim.

A moment later and he had spun on his heel and left. Alice heard the front door bang behind him. She sagged against the counter, hair falling in her eyes.

Gentle hands grasped her shoulders, steered her to a seat at the table.

'That was impressive!' Martha said, gathering up the crockery.

'You sure told him,' Pattie crowed, and squeezed Jack's shoulders. 'Aren't you proud of your mother?'

Jack nodded, and Alice looked at him with tears filming her eyes.

'He's such an awful man,' Agnes said. 'Do you know he tried to court my sister for a while this year?' She shook her head. 'Teresa went out a few times with him then swore she'd never have anything to do with him again.' Agnes sniffed. 'Got a bit fresh with her, he did.' Her eyes flickered around the table. 'A bit rough.'

There were nods all around the table although no more was said. Instead, tea was poured, someone got up and went out to the car, came back in with a cake tin, and they had thick rich slices of fruitcake with their drinks, all of them in a sudden, celebratory mood.

When Jean arrived half an hour later, Alice beamed up at her.

'He came,' she said.

Jean touched her on the shoulder. 'How did it go?'

Martha answered. 'Alice sent him away with a flea in his ear.' She looked over at Alice as though proud of her.

'I did too, Alice said, laughing up at Jean. 'Thanks to these wonderful ladies, I was brave enough.'

The women giggled. 'Think nothing of it,' Martha said. 'We were glad to be able to back you up.' She was putting clothes back in baskets. 'There's only one thing,' she said.

Alice turned to her, busy wishing she could reach out and hold Jean's hand. She could feel Jean's presence in the room next to her like they were touching. The very air in the room was different, she thought. As though it had less oxygen, making her light-headed and delighted.

'Oh nothing much,' Martha was saying. 'Only that now you really are a part of the Rural Women's Institute, and as such, we do require your assistance at our stall next Saturday.'

Alice laughed. 'I'll be there with bells on.'

Ten minutes later, the room had emptied out of women and their baskets of clothes. Jean sat down at the table next to Alice and smiled at her, helping herself to a piece of the cake that had been left on a plate.

'It really went well?' she asked.

Alice nodded. The children had slipped out the back door, and she could hear them laughing in the sunshine. She felt as though there couldn't possibly be a single cloud in the sky. 'It did. I was so scared when he turned up. But I knew he couldn't do anything to me, and then all of a sudden, I was being brave, and saying exactly what I wanted to.'

Jean wiped her mouth and reached across to take Alice's hand. 'I'm so glad,' she said.

'It's all because of you,' Alice murmured. 'You sent those lovely people around. If they hadn't been here, I don't know what would have happened.'

Jean's face turned grim. 'I don't want to imagine,' she said.

'And we don't have to, thanks to you.'

Their hands were linked together. 'I said I'd figure something out, didn't I?'

Alice laughed. 'I didn't doubt you, but still.' She turned serious. 'I like Martha,' she said. 'She's a very interesting woman.'

'Isn't she?'

'She told me that you are in love with me.'

Jean looked down at their hands. 'I am.'

A nod. 'Yes, but I thought it was nice of her to tell me. She didn't have to, you know.'

'No, I guess not. But she didn't tell you that just to be nice, you know. That's not Martha's style. She'll only say something if she thinks it's true. And relevant.'

Alice gave a little shrug. 'Nevertheless, I appreciated it.'

Jean leaned forward. 'I'm sorry I couldn't be there,' she said, and a shadow passed over her face. 'I thought it would be easier if I wasn't.' Pausing, she stroked Alice's hand. 'After all, I do have my own history with Jim Dempsey.'

Alice turned her hand over and linked her fingers with Jean's. 'You've never spoken of it,' she said. 'Not really.'

With a sigh, Jean leaned back in her chair. 'There's not all that much to tell, really – certainly nothing on the scale of your experiences with the man.'

'I want to hear anyway.'

She got a smile for that, and Jean reached over, tucked a hand behind her neck and tugged her closer. 'A kiss,' she said. 'I'd like a kiss.'

She got one, and Alice relished the touch of their lips, feeling her body swell and warm with the kiss. Unconsciously, she deepened it, sitting there leaning towards each other at the kitchen table. When they broke apart, she was panting.

Jean's eyes were shining. 'Well,' she said.

'Yes.' Alice tried to remember how to form sentences. 'You were going to tell me about your experiences with Jim,' she said.

The light in Jean's eyes dimmed. 'Seems wrong, after a kiss like that.'

Her grip tightening on Jean's hand, Alice nodded. 'But I'd still like to hear.'

'I'd like to take you to bed.' Jean's voice was little more than a growl and Alice laughed, feeling light as air again.

'It's the middle of the day!'

'What's that got to do with anything?'

'It's the middle of the day,' Alice repeated.

Jean sighed. 'Fine. Have it your way, then. I thought it was a perfectly good idea.'

Giggling, Alice gave her a smacking kiss on the cheek. 'Behave and tell me,' she said.

A bigger sigh. 'Honestly, there's not much to say. Jim's father, Will, employed me on their farm during the war.' She shrugged. 'I was a good worker, a good organiser, and before I knew it, I was pretty much running the place, me and Jamie, who must be in his sixties if he's a day, and we were all getting along well, getting everything done.'

'Until Jim came back,' Alice filled in, her fingers going back to wrap around Jean's.

'Yep. He came back but Will Dempsey wanted to keep me on – said the place was more profitable than it had ever been.' She looked at Alice, lips flattening to a straight line for a moment. 'You can imagine how that went down.'

Alice nodded. She could.

'So we went on like that for a while, only a couple months, Jim making his displeasure at a woman running things very well known, although technically he took back the running of the place, his father told him he was basically to see that whatever I said to do was done.' She shook her head. 'I'm surprised Will didn't realise how his son would take that, but I think he cares more about his land and stock than his whiny son.'

Jean stopped talking, and Alice could see her eyes far away, remembering. Then they focused on Alice and smiled.

'So one day Jim had had enough, and I'd had enough, and there was an argument, a bit of a showdown, and I quit. Walked out.' She shrugged. 'Not much of a story, although it has left Jim and I with a lasting desire never to be in each other's company. I avoid the man as often as possible.' She looked seriously at Alice. 'Although that wasn't why I stayed away today,' she said.

Alice shook her head. 'I didn't believe it was.'

'I didn't want to make things more complicated for you than they already are.'

It was Alice's turn to sigh, and she let her gaze move to the window, to the children playing outside, puttering around in the garden. There were clouds in the sky after all.

'We've not heard the last of him,' she said, looking back at Jean.

'I know.'

'He's not going to let it go that easily.' Alice shook her head sadly. 'I regret it now, saying everything I did – he left here humiliated…'

Jean ran a hand through her hair. 'He's the vindictive sort,' she said.

Getting up from the table, Alice cleared the cups and saucers, nervousness making it impossible to stay still. 'He's going to do something, I just know it.' She took the pile of crockery to the sink, sat it down, and turned to stare at Jean. 'What are we going to do?'

Jean shook her head. 'Nothing,' she said. 'There's nothing we can do except keep our wits about us.'

Another thought occurred to her. 'And my mother,' Alice said. 'What has she been doing? What's all this about Jim going around to her place and them having some sort of meeting?' Her voice was turning shrill, but she felt shrill. 'My mother is in on this somehow?'

Jean shook her head. 'I don't know what it means.'

'But it's true?'

'I think so, yes.'

Alice clenched her hands into fists. 'I will be paying my mother a visit after all,' she said.

Jean stood up, put comforting hands on her shoulders. 'Are you sure that's wise?'

She shook her head, hair in her eyes. 'Oh yes,' Alice said. 'She has finally gone too far.'

'In that case, there's something else I think you should know,' Jean said, moving her hands to rub lightly against Alice's arms.

'There could not possibly be more,' Alice said. 'Aren't things bad enough?'

Jean cleared her throat. 'It's just rumour, and old rumour at that. Mrs B told me.'

Alice looked at her, eyes wide and expectant.

CHAPTER 38

*A*lice sat on the side of her bed, the morning sun slanting in through the window, and a pair of shoes in her hand.

'Damn,' she said under her breath. 'Damn and bother.'

It was Sunday. She'd forgotten that.

Jean had slipped from between her sheets hours before morning, dressing and leaving her with kisses and a regretful expression. Alice wished she could have stayed, that they could have woken up together with the sounds of the magpies in the garden calling to each other in their wheedle-wardle voices. Instead, she'd lain in bed listening for them herself, thoughts a swirl of wishing, wanting, loving, needing.

And then hurt anger. Which was why she sat on the side of her bed, shoes dangling from one hand.

Her mother. She needed to go see her mother.

Sighing, she put on her shoes anyway, then stood, smoothing down her good dress, bottom lip caught in her teeth, mind racing. A moment later, she was at the kitchen door, calling the children.

Tilly was in the little sand box Jean had made for them. She'd carted a sack full of sand home from the beach yesterday afternoon, Tilly and Jack pestering her with questions about it all the way. Alice let herself smile at the memory. Once home, Jean and children had disappeared outside in the waning light of the evening, and when they made it inside for a bit of supper, all three were looking mighty pleased with themselves.

'I don't wanna come inside, Mama,' Tilly said, turning to pout at her from the wooden box full of her own little slice of sand. 'I playing in my beach.'

'I see that,' Alice said, stepping out into the back garden. 'Where's Jack?'

Tilly gave an elaborate shrug. 'Dunno. He was chasing foxes a minute ago.'

Alice raised her eyebrows, amused despite herself. 'Foxes?'

'Yup.' The girl's reply was matter of fact.

'I'll go look,' Alice said, and shaded her eyes, trying to catch a glimpse of Jack in the shrubbery at the back of their garden. It was wild back there, more garden than she could manage on her own, but Jack loved it.

'Jack, sweetheart? Where are you?'

There was no answer, and a tiny worm of unease woke wriggling in the pit of her stomach.

What if Jim had…

Had what? Taken Jack?

Her legs were stiff stilts as she lurched towards the back of the property, and she could hear herself shouting, but not what she was saying. She thrashed her way into the undergrowth.

'Mum!' The voice was wounded, aggrieved as only an

eight-year-old boy's can be and Alice ground to a halt in front of him, relieved. The shrieking in her head receded and words formed where it had been.

'Oh Jack, you gave me such a fright.'

He was sitting against the trunk of a stubby, drowsy tree, and glaring at her.

'Mum!' he said. 'This is my hide-out.'

'No Mama allowed,' Tilly said from behind her. Jack glared past Alice at her.

'No sisters either. How many times have I told you!'

Tilly giggled, but Alice just wiped a hand across her forehead. 'Come on, kids,' she said, her heart settling back to its normal pace. 'I need you to go next door to Mrs Jones.'

'What for?' Jack asked.

'She smells,' Tilly added.

Alice shook her head. 'That's a rude thing to say, Tilly. Mrs Jones doesn't smell. Please don't tell her that.'

Tilly scuffed a toe in the dirt. 'I not telling her,' the little girl said. 'I telling you.'

Picking her up, Alice started back to the house. 'Well thank you, sweetheart, but I know for a fact that you think Mrs Jones is very nice really, and I have to go out and I need you and Jack to be extra good for her.'

'Where are you going, Mum?' Jack asked, his face seeming too pale under his flop of hair.

'I need to talk to Grandma,' she said.

'But we don't talk to her anymore,' Tilly said. 'We don't like her.'

Patting Tilly on her back, Alice tried to smile. 'It's all right, love,' she said. 'You're going to go to Mrs Jones and I promise

I won't be long.' She put the child down. 'Now how about you get Prudence, and a book to look at?'

Mrs Jones opened the door with a smile for the children. She picked Tilly up, and Tilly sat there on the woman's ample hip, looking at her mother with a gimlet eye.

'Thank you so much, Marjorie,' Alice said, ignoring her daughter's squint. 'You're doing me a real favour.'

'Oh you know it's no problem. Me and Bob like spending time with the little ones. It's such a nice day we're going to take our tea outside. She sidled closer to Alice and spoke through the side of her mouth.

'You get things sorted with your mother, you hear? Terrible of her, it was, taking all your things like that.'

Alice smiled but she thought it might look more like a grimace. 'I got most of them back, thank goodness.' Except her sewing machine. That still hurt.

'Yes, but she had no right to take them in the first place. You're a good woman, and she should be looking after you, not making things harder.'

'I'm afraid my mother thought that was exactly what she was doing.'

'Phooey,' Mrs Jones spat. 'You can't force a grown woman to move home with you – what was she thinking?' She stepped closer still. 'You've had a lot of visitors lately, Alice. What's it all about?'

A great rushing heat blossomed under Alice's skin and she felt the blush burn her cheeks. Her neighbour wasn't talking about Jean, was she? They'd been so careful.

'A whole bunch of women over yesterday,' Mrs Jones was saying. 'And that milkman…' She frowned. 'What do you call a woman who delivers the milk? It just ain't the same, some-how. Can't go calling her a milkman.'

'Um, I don't know,' Alice said. 'But they were there because I'm helping out with the Women's Institute jumble sale next weekend at the fair. We were sorting the clothes for it.' She cleared her throat. 'And the woman who delivers our milk is called Jean.' She swallowed and took a deep breath that her neighbour didn't seem to notice. 'She's my friend.'

Mrs Jones was nodding sagely. 'Your Terry though, would he be happy with Big Jim calling on you?' She shook her grey head.

'No,' Alice said. 'And I'm not either. Please don't think there's anything going on there.' She shuddered. 'He scares me.'

Mrs Jones' eyes widened. 'Now don't go saying that in front of the little one. You'll frighten her.' But a hand patted Alice's arm. 'Looked like you sent him packing yesterday. He was out of your house looking like a nag had bit him!' She sobered. 'You mind him though, Alice. He has a temper.'

That was something Alice already knew for certain. 'If you see him hanging around, please don't let him near the children, will you promise me that, Marjorie?'

'Oh you can count on that,' she said. 'Bob and I won't let him within a hundred yards of the wee tykes.'

Relieved, Alice gave her thanks and said goodbye, drop-ping a kiss on the disgruntled Tilly and looking for Jack, but he was already gone, out the back probably, to talk to Bob Jones while the man tinkered in his shed.

Her mother's house was empty when she arrived, and Alice was glad of it. She stepped inside the cool dimness of the big villa and stood a moment staring down the passageway at the branching doorways. A grandfather clock tick-tocked solemnly at her, telling her she still had almost an hour before she could expect Sally McMurtry to pull up outside in her Austin to deliver the old dragon back to her lair.

Sniffing, Alice braced her shoulders and stepped properly into the house, pulling the front door closed behind her. The smell of furniture polish and lilies confronted her. It was the same scent she remembered from her childhood.

'Oh Daddy,' she whispered. 'How I wish you were still here.'

Her father might be gone, but his study was still intact, and that was where Alice headed, setting her hand bag down and unpinning her hat, looking around at the room with its bookshelves and heavy roll-top desk, the armchair where her father had used to sit of an evening, smoking his pipe and reading the paper. It was all still there, and Alice moved over to the desk, looking at the silver-framed wedding photo. Her father looked rather bewildered in it.

'I don't know why you're there marrying her either,' Alice whispered to the sepia picture. A sad smile lifted her lips. 'I've met someone, Daddy,' she said. 'I think you'd like her.' Her smile fell, knowing that even if her father had liked Jean, he wouldn't have liked the knowledge of them together.

On a heavy sigh, Alice rolled up the top of the desk and sat on the chair in front of it, surveying all the little drawers and compartments.

What exactly was she looking for?

Wishing Jean was with her, Alice poked a finger at one of the small drawers, opened it and looked disappointedly at the empty space. She opened another and another, and all were in the same state – empty.

The big drawers were empty too and Alice blinked down at them, confused. Surely her father had left some papers worth keeping? Where was his will? Accounts? Did you not keep that sort of thing?

She thought of Terry, who had died without a will, without anything to leave in one. He'd left nothing but a rented house and a child. Two children, she amended.

The drawer slid shut, still smooth despite its age and Alice turned in the chair, trying to find what she was looking for in the rest of the room. But it was obvious her mother had cleared everything out.

Leaving her things in her father's old study, Alice crept out of the room and into the drawing room instead. This had always been her mother's domain, with its heavy fabrics and sofa, the small tea table, and against one wall, a woman's desk and chair.

She made a beeline for the desk.

'What are you doing?'

The voice startled her, and Alice realised she'd been sunk so deeply in her thoughts she'd never heard the car pull up outside, or her mother opening the door to the house, coming down the hallway, catching her rifling through her accounts.

She turned on the chair and stared defiantly at her mother.

'I'm looking for the truth,' she said.

'And what is the truth when it's at home?' Geraldine asked, taking off her hat as though she walked in every day to someone going through her things.

Alice crossed her legs at the ankles. 'That my father left me some money.'

She watched her mother's eyebrows rise towards her hairline. 'Is that so? And where, do tell, did you hear that?'

'From someone who would have known.'

Geraldine stayed where she was, hat in hand, cold eyes on her daughter. 'And does this someone have a name, that I should know who my accuser is?'

'I am your accuser, Mother,' Alice said, shaking her head but not taking her gaze from the older woman. 'And I find several things to accuse you of.' She paused, adjusted the hands in her lap. 'But we will start with the money.'

'Will we indeed? This is no way to speak to your mother, Alice.'

Her will settled in her chest, an implacable thing that demanded answers. 'Did my father leave me a sum of money?'

Geraldine looked at her, put her hat down on the table. 'Yes, there was an amount of money meant for you.'

Alice shook her head. 'Was?'

'Was. Your father set up a savings account – not in your name, by the way, so don't go getting too excited – and from the day we knew you were on your way, he paid a monthly sum into it. When you were born a daughter rather than the son we hoped for, it was decided that the payments would still continue, for when you married.'

'I did marry!'

Her mother snorted, shook her head. 'That was no marriage – that was a farce – a spoilt child running away from home.' She straightened. 'There was no way I was going to give you a penny, not when you did nothing but show yourself incapable of sensible decisions.'

Alice was cold, as though a chill had spread upwards through the rug, into her bones. She shook her head slowly. 'But since then,' she whispered. 'You could have helped.' She spoke louder. 'I have two children, for God's sakes!'

'And I have tried to take care of both yourself and them,' her mother said.

'You tried to force us to move back in here with you!'

'Where you would have been perfectly well looked after.'

Alice couldn't believe what she was hearing. 'This is all so preposterous,' she said. 'I can't believe you would let your grandchildren live in desperate circumstances when you had the means to do something about it. You have let them go without rather than help! They have practically nothing – your handouts keep us going, nothing more, and that's the way you've always liked it, isn't it?'

'I have done my best by a stubborn daughter who chooses to defy me at every turn rather than turn to me to look after her family.' Her mother leaned forward where she stood, her face haughty, fierce. 'What am I? I am your family, but you shirk your duty towards me. I grow older, and although I have the space here, you refuse to live here, even though that would by far be the best thing for every one of us.' Her face was red, blotches of colour high in her wrinkled cheeks.

'You made it impossible for me to be in the same house as you – always controlling everything, always rules, look this way, act this way, be this way! You suffocated me!' Alice shook her head. 'I can never come back here, and I can never bring my children to live here, not when you treat them the same way you treated me when I was small.' Her hand clenched into helpless fists. 'My childhood years were miserable, Mother, and that was because of you.' She heaved a breath, spoke more calmly. 'I am grown up now, Mother. Not considering anything else, I should be supported in my desire to have my own home.'

Geraldine Thomas sat down at her table, tapping a finger against the cloth then pointing at her daughter. 'You are grown up, Alice, and if you want your own home, then by all means, have it.' She leaned back, placed her own hands in her lap and looked straight at Alice. 'But do not expect that you will have any help from me, as long as you persist in your poor choices.'

Alice didn't know what to say next. The words were backing up in her throat, too many of them to get out in any orderly manner. She settled for squeezing her eyes shut and covering her face. When she was composed enough, she looked at her mother.

'And why are you encouraging Jim Dempsey to court me?'

Geraldine blinked, expressionless. 'Because he is the father of your youngest child. Because he has a good position in this town. And because for whatever reason, he wants to marry you.'

Alice's mouth fell open.

'What?' Geraldine said. 'You don't think I didn't guess about Tilly?' She sniffed. 'I saw the state your husband was in those two weeks. Saw it and heard about it. There was hardly any other talk in the town.' Her mouth turned down in a moue of disapproval. 'There was no way he was capable of fathering a child.' She narrowed her eyes at her daughter. 'But Jim Dempsey, his constant companion, was, and obviously you have no morals, we discovered that when you were sixteen.' She lifted sharp shoulders, stared at Alice with equally sharp eyes. 'I am no innocent, Alice. You are heading for worse trouble. You have made an undesirable friend.' She blinked lizard eyes. 'Jim Dempsey is willing to marry you. I suggest you let him, before your reputation is completely ruined.'

Geraldine's lips widened into a grotesque smile as she played her trump card.

'I control the money, Alice, dear. And if you marry Jim Dempsey, there will be plenty of it to ensure a life of respectability and comfort. Jim Dempsey will at least make an obedient son in law, and ensure you do your duty by me.'

Alice looked at her mother in horror. 'And if I do not marry him?' Alice's voice was strangled.

'If you insist on ruining yourself, then there will be no money.' A short pause. 'And I will publicly disown you.'

Alice got to her feet, the floor feeling a curiously long way down. She licked her lips, waiting for the room to stop spinning.

'Mother,' she said, the word sharp enough to cut her tongue. 'How I wish you were dead.'

The old woman barked a laugh. 'That won't make any difference, I'm afraid, Alice. If you insist on continuing your unhealthy association with this Reardon woman, my death still won't bring you any wealth.' She smiled, smug. 'I have told you my conditions and those are what you must meet.'

Alice leaned forward on the balls of her feet and sucked in a deep breath. She shook her head.

'I'll see myself out, Mother.' She moved toward the door, then turned to look at the woman who had given her life. 'And in case that is too ambiguous for you, here it is in plain words: I choose love, Mother, and freedom, and I will make my own way.' She went to turn back to the door. 'And when you die, I will not miss you or your money even then.'

The room was silent behind her as she fetched her hat and hand bag. Pinning her hat back on, she looked at the photo of her father, touched a fingertip to his dusty cheek and whispered a farewell, before turning and making her way out of the house.

The sun shone on her head and she watched her feet navigate her way down the path and then further down the road. She returned a waved greeting from an old neighbour and set herself for home, thinking of her children, and thinking of Jean.

Jean. They would talk of the future, she decided, and settle it between them.

They would find a way, she thought, listening to the tap of her heels on the footpath. They would find a way to be a part of each other's life.

Who knew what was possible, when two people loved this much?

Her heart loosening, Alice lifted her head higher as she walked, feeling a free and pure joy well up inside her.

Jean, she thought.

How lucky I am.

CHAPTER 39

It couldn't go on like this, Jean decided. Leaning against a tree, she gazed out from under its spreading branches and lit a cigarette. Just the one, while she scanned the road, examined the shadows, waited for headlights to pass.

Perhaps she shouldn't be having the cigarette, after all, the glowing red tip could give away her position, could reveal that someone lurked underneath the tree on the quiet street lit only by the one streetlamp and the moon sailing overhead, a silver crescent dim upon a wave of clouds.

She breathed the smoke out her nose, thinking, knowing Alice would smell the smoke on her breath, but needing it anyway, knowing too, that Alice wasn't going to mind.

A black shape wove in and out of the trees lining the street and nosed its way up to Jean.

'Hey, boy,' she whispered, putting down a hand for the dog to sniff and getting a lick for her trouble. 'Going for a walk, are you?'

It made no reply except to mosey along on its way, nose to

the ground, following some scent only it could decipher. Jean stood upright again and was back to scanning the street, dropping the cigarette and grinding it out under her shoe. She went to check her watch, remembered again that she'd given it to Jack, and decided she'd been long enough. Alice would be waiting for her.

There was no one about anyway. Or rather, Jim Dempsey wasn't lurking in the shadows or driving the streets in his big red car, elbow out the window, eyes seeking her out, watching her make her way to Alice Holden's back door.

There was a cool breeze blowing in from the sea, and Jean sniffed the air. A change was coming, a break in the weather. She could smell rain, and when she looked up at the moon again, it was just the dimmest glow behind bunched clouds. When she looked back down, the first drops of rain fell on the dirt road beside her. She watched them, fat and heavy, kicking up dust in the streetlight, and then the rain was thundering down, a rushing, roaring tumult.

Squinting through the silver-wet night, Jean lined up her dash to Alice's door. A car drove along the road behind her, its headlights sweeping up against the rain so that it glowed like a curtain all around her.

If it was Jim, then too bad. Let him see her, she thought, wet already, her shirt sticking to her shoulders, the tree branches not enough shelter.

But she held herself still, waited for the car to pass, drive to the end of the street, make a turn like a dark, glistening leopard on the prowl. She sniffed, waiting, hair, face wet, and then it was gone, and she was out from under the tree, ducking down the side of the empty house that backed onto Alice's lot, and dodging the trees, reminding herself to steer clear in the darkness of the little pond. She did not want any of Tilly's tapbowls swimming around in her boots.

A welcome light glowed behind Alice's kitchen windows and she launched herself toward it, just as the sudden rain turned to hail. Landing against the warped wood of the back door, with its peeling paint scraping against her hands, Jean turned back to look out over the way she'd come, at the hailstones bouncing off the ground in the light.

Nope, she decided. Even if she hadn't spent the day dodging Big Jim, this wasn't the cosy situation she wanted for herself and Alice.

The doorknob was slippery, and locked, but Alice was right there on the other side and opened it for her. Jean slipped gratefully into the warmth of the kitchen.

'Oh no!' Alice said, pouncing on her straight away and drawing her closer to the warm stove. 'You look like a poor bedraggled kitten!'

Jean laughed and shook her head. 'There goes my self-image. A kitten!'

'Well,' Alice said, tipping her head to the side and considering her. 'Perhaps a tiger cub, or something?'

'Nope, not redeeming yourself,' Jean said, grinning.

Alice planted a kiss on her wet face and told her to strip her clothes off.

'What?'

She got a wide-eyed look. 'Now you're shy?' Alice asked. 'Take your clothes off. I'm getting you a towel and you can wear my dressing gown.'

Jean squinted at her. 'The pink one with the roses all over it?'

But Alice just laughed and left the room with a wave of

her hand. Jean smiled ruefully and unbuttoned her shirt, sat down in the chair that was shedding its stuffing and pulled off her boots, tucking them close to the coal range to dry. The rain was still hammering against the tin roof that sloped low over the room.

'Alice?' she said in a low voice when she'd come back in, towel in hand.

'Jean. What is it?'

She took the towel, pressed the cotton to her face, her hair. 'I've been thinking,' she said.

'So have I.' Alice's face was serious.

Jean looked at her, keeping her breathing even. 'Perhaps we ought to have a cup of tea?'

Alice nodded, moving to check the kettle, fill the teapot. Jean watched her a moment, looking at the way she moved, the curve of waist and hip, the neat, economical movements, the bounce of hair on shoulders.

'I love you,' she blurted, and Alice turned to look at her, pleasure suffusing her face.

'Oh Jean,' she said. 'I love you too.'

No, that wasn't what Jean wanted. Putting down the towel, she went to Alice and placed her hands on her shoulders. The soft hair tickled the backs of her hands in a silky sweep.

'What is it, Jean?' Alice asked, staring up at her. 'You look so serious.'

'I am feeling serious,' Jean replied, and it was true. She'd never felt this serious before.

Warm hands placed themselves on top of hers, and Alice searched her eyes. 'Tell me what's wrong.'

Jean shook her head. 'We can't go on like this, Alice,' she said.

The big green-brown eyes blinked at her, clouded over with confusion.

'What do you mean?' The words were tentative, ready to be hurt.

'No,' Jean said. 'Alice, please, that sounded wrong.'

'Then tell me what you mean.'

But Jean for once didn't know where to start. She sighed, stepped back, shaking her head. 'Listen, let me get out of these wet clothes, and then we can talk properly over a cup of tea.' She realised she was shivering.

Alice continued to stare at her for a long moment, then she nodded, trust shining from her face, the eyes clearing. She nodded. 'The tea will be ready in a moment.'

Turning away, Jean stripped the wet clothes off, edging closer to the range, her damp skin goose bumped. She tugged on Alice's dressing gown, fumbling with the buttons and pulling the sash tight around her waist.

Alice, holding the teapot, looked at her and laughed. 'Oh my goodness, I'm sorry,' she said.

'That bad, huh?' Jean surveyed the skirt of pink blooms.

'No, of course not,' Alice said, being kind. 'It's just not really...'

'Me. I can see that.'

Alice carried the teapot to the table, went back for cups. 'At least it's impossible for you to look so terribly serious now.'

'It looks a thousand times better on you,' Jean said, taking a seat at the table, and patting the chair next to her. The dressing gown might not be quite the style she was used to, but she was warming up nicely.

'So,' Alice said, sitting down. 'Tell me.' She looked seriously at Jean. 'You said we couldn't go on this way.'

A deep breath. 'I want us to live together,' Jean said all in a rush.

Alice's hand flew to her mouth. She stared at Jean for a long, silent minute before dropping her hand and speaking.

'You want us to what?'

'Live together.' There seemed to be something sharp stuck in Jean's throat and she cleared it. 'I mean, I know it's quick, that we've only been seeing each other such a short time...'

Alice was shaking her head.

'What?' Jean asked. 'I'm sorry.' She hung her head. 'It's too soon, isn't it?' She heaved a sigh, looking at her hands. 'It's just that I know I'm always going to want to be with you.' She lifted her head and looked at Alice. 'Every day I'm going to want to come home to you. Every night I'm going to want to lie next to you, every day kiss you good morning.' She shook her head. 'There's no escaping this. It's just a fact and I'm helpless in the face of it.'

'You want us to...'

'Live together, yes.' Jean cocked her head to one side and offered a crooked grin. 'I'd ask you to marry me, but I don't have a ring.' The smile widened. 'Yet.'

'What?' Alice looked even more startled. Jean saw her white throat convulse as she swallowed.

She took her hand, held the soft fingers tightly, leaned forward in the chair until their faces were close. 'I love you, Alice. Come away with me and we can find a place to call home – together.'

Alice's lips were parted, her eyes luminous in the yellow light.

'What do you say?' Jean asked, lifting a hand to push a lock of hair behind Alice's ear. She stroked the silky skin of Alice's cheek and waited for a reply.

'But...' Alice seemed to check herself, and her face blossomed into a beaming smile. 'Yes!'

'Yes?'

'Yes, oh my goodness yes!' The hazel eyes shone, and Alice leaned her head against Jean's. 'I never want to be away from you, either. I don't want to spend a single day apart.' She sat back and looked at Jean. 'I've already spent too much time without you.'

Jean felt exactly the same way. She pressed a hand to her thumping heart and laughed. 'You've just made me the happiest woman in the country, my darling Alice.'

Alice's laugh was a tinkling, joyous sound. 'Where are we going to live?' she asked, and her eyes were dazed, delirious, happy.

Shaking her head, Jean captured Alice's beloved face and kissed the shining lips. 'I don't know. Is there anything keeping you here? In this town, I mean.' She turned serious. 'What about your mother?'

Alice's smile faded, and she shook her head. 'My mother is no longer a consideration in any way.' She leaned against Jean, tucking her head onto her shoulder. 'I went to see her today – I had to, after hearing, well...'

'About the money?'

'Yes.' Alice's blue eyes gazed seriously up at her. 'There isn't any.' They blinked. 'Except that's not exactly true – there's plenty, but only if I do as my mother says.'

'What does she want you to do?' Jean asked even though she knew the answer was going to make her blood boil, and quite possibly entertain murderous thoughts. Not because she wanted any money the old woman might have, but because she simply couldn't bear the thought of anyone making Alice unhappy. That was an unforgivable sin.

'Either of two things will satisfy her,' Alice said. She held up a finger. 'One, that the children and I move back in with her, there to take care of her for the rest of her life.'

Jean forced herself to think charitably of the woman. 'She might be lonely,' she suggested.

'Oh,' snorted Alice. 'Of course she is. That's what this is all about. She's a lonely, bitter old woman. I think she's been lonely her whole life, but that doesn't make her right.'

Conceding the point, Jean asked, 'What was the second?'

Another finger was held up. 'Marrying Jim Dempsey is an acceptable alternative.' Jean could see her brow twist in a scowl. 'And now I'm going to sound bitter for a moment, so please forgive me.'

'Always,' Jean said.

'My mother told me she believes Jim to be Tilly's father.' Her voice had dropped to a whisper. 'And also that I am heading to ruination by associating with you.' The lovely eyes lifted to Jean's. 'Apparently my mother is not as innocent of such things as I'd thought.' She stared at the wall again. 'I don't understand why she would think that my being married would be so wonderful.' A pause. 'And I don't understand at all how she could stand by and see her own grandchildren going without when she not only has the means to provide for them, but indeed actually has money put aside for the express purpose!'

Jean sat up and made Alice look at her. 'What?'

Alice nodded. 'It's true. My father opened a savings account before I was even born and put money into it right up until he died. Money that was meant for me.'

'And your mother won't let you have it?'

'No. It was just a savings account, rather than a legal trust, so technically it's hers, like the rest of it. My father's intentions don't come into play on the subject.'

Leaning back in the chair, Jean gave a low whistle. 'The woman's a monster.'

Alice sat up and stared at her. 'Do you still want me? Knowing I bring nothing but hungry mouths?' She chewed her lip. 'I can get a job.'

Jean shook her head before Alice even stopped talking. 'The money makes no difference to me. Not the slightest bit.'

'But what will we do?'

Stroking Alice's hair, Jean smiled at her. 'We will figure something out. We will move to another town, maybe even the city, and I will find a job and we will find a nice little place to live, and we will be happy, that I can guarantee you.'

They made love to the sound of the rain, and the sweep of the wind that had blown up to howl around the corners of the house, seeking its way in. They made love with an urgency that matched the beat of the storm, their hands grasping, holding, seeking, their lips tasting, wanting more.

'You are so very beautiful,' Jean whispered afterwards, under the rumble of thunder, tracing a hand over the smooth length of Alice's thigh, over her gently rounded belly and up to cup the glorious weight of her breast. She could feel the dampness between her own thighs. Just the nearness of Alice was enough to make every nerve hum, even satisfied as she was.

'As are you,' Alice whispered as the lightning brightened the room for a fraction of time, capturing them in its white lens.

Jean smiled against Alice's warm skin, her hand going roaming again, admiring the way Alice stretched out beside her, comfortable, glorious in the dips and hollows of her body. 'I could lie here forever, touching you,' she said, fingers tangling themselves in damp curls.

Alice's legs shifted, and she rolled onto her side, hooking a leg over Jean's and wriggling closer so that Jean could feel the heat and tickle of her against her stomach. She closed her eyes and thanked all the saints she'd never thought to believe in until now.

'What are you doing?' Alice's voice was amused.

'Thanking God and all his saints.'

A giggle. 'For what?'

'For bringing me you.'

Alice touched a finger to Jean's lips. 'But isn't our love a sin?'

Jean shook her head. 'Not from where I'm lying. From here it feels as though there is nothing more beautiful in all the world.'

The finger was replaced by warm, soft lips. 'You say the most wonderful things,' Alice murmured.

'I'm well inspired right now,' Jean said.

It was Alice's turn to laugh, drowned out by a sudden cracking rumble of thunder. She looked at Jean with side eyes. 'I hope that doesn't wake the children,' she said. 'It's awfully loud.' She half sat and pulled the sheet up over their entwined bodies.

'I hope the lightning strikes old Jim, sitting out there in his car.

The eyes swung round and zeroed in on Jean like twin beams on full. 'What?' Alice squeaked.

Jean sighed. She hadn't meant to say that. For a moment she wished she could rewind time, go back to Alice's heavy leg over hers, the enticing tickle of her hair against Jean's stomach. But it was too late.

'He's been following me most of the day,' Jean said.

'Following you how?' Alice asked.

'In that goddamned fancy car of his. Every time I turned around, there it was lurking down a side street, grill snarling at me over the railway lines, big red flank cruising by. Wherever I was, there he was.

'But what does he want?' Alice's hands stuttered towards her mouth in the flash of lightning. 'Why is he following you?'

'Oh Alice, we did the worst thing imaginable to a man like him – you know we did.'

But Alice was shaking her head. 'I still hoped…'

'As did I,' Jean replied, sitting up as well. 'As did I, my love.'

'What do we do about it?'

'Now that I do not have an answer to.'

Alice tugged the sheet across her breasts, as if the conversation made her vulnerable. Jean watched the action and ached to be able to do something to make it better. She touched Alice on the shoulder, the warm skin unbearably intimate under her hand.

'I guess the sooner we leave town the better.' Alice was staring out into the dimness of the bedroom. She turned her eyes on Jean, looking for all the world like a frightened deer in the next burst of lightning. Overhead the storm pounded on the roof with unabating fury.

'We won't be going far in this weather,' Jean said, joking, trying to lighten the situation.

But Alice shook her head, twisting around in the bed to look seriously at Jean. 'I don't have any money,' she said. Her expression turned momentarily bitter. 'And we've already discovered I have no hope of getting any.'

Jean cupped her round shoulders in her hands, staring intently into her face. 'We don't need your mother's help to do this,' she said. 'It's people like your mother we want to get away from.'

'Get a fresh start,' Alice said.

'Exactly.'

She watched Alice draw in a deep breath. 'We can travel as cousins, or something.'

'Yes, something like that, or even just friends. We can decide that later.'

Alice was serious, looking at her. 'Can we really do this?' She squeezed her eyes shut for a moment, then they sprang open even more serious. 'I have two children, who have lived in this house their entire lives. I have no job, only a little bit of money each week from my widow's pension. Nothing that I've been able to save.'

Tugging Alice forward, Jean kissed the worrying lips. 'I have some savings,' she said. 'Enough to take us to a new town, find us somewhere to live, and we will be fine until I find a new job.'

'We can use my money for food,' Alice said, settling down a little although she winced as thunder cracked overhead.

That was the ticket. Jean watched as Alice's features smoothed out, relaxing. She stroked one hand over the soft cheek and rested her forehead against Alice's.

'You are everything to me,' she said, and felt Alice's lips curve into a smile. 'This will work out, you'll see, and all four of us will be okay.' She sat back up and looked at the lovely face in front of her, wishing she could see the colour of those eyes. 'We will be better than okay. We will be happy, we will thrive.'

Alice's eyes, though dark in the dim light, were shining, and she nodded. A hand found Jean's and squeezed it tight. 'I know,' Alice whispered. 'I know we will.'

They both jumped at another crack of thunder, and this time a wailing cry followed it, and the smack of running feet on the floor. Jean looked at Alice, wide-eyed, and scrambled from the bed, diving for her clothes, realising they weren't there, and in desperation turning to look at Alice.

Alice was slipping a night dress over her own head and trying to nudge the dressing gown toward Jean as she did so. Relived, Jean pounced upon it and tugged it on.

'Mama, the sky is cracking up.' Tilly stood in the doorway, rubbing her eyes. 'It's gonna fall on us.'

Alice held out her arms to the little girl, and Tilly scrambled up onto the bed and into her mother's lap.

'It's all right, sweetheart,' Alice said. 'It's just a thunderstorm. It can't hurt us.'

Tilly snuggled deeper into her mother's lap, and when she opened her eyes, her gaze landed straight on Jean, who had perched herself on the edge of the bed, feeling awkward.

'Hi Jean,' Tilly said. 'Are you gonna stop the thunder getting me?'

Jean glanced at Alice smiling over Tilly's head. 'Yeah,' she said. 'That's my job, all right.'

Tilly rubbed her eyes again. 'Jack told me once 'bout getting killed by 'lectrocution.'

Alice rolled her eyes and Jean couldn't help the giggle that escaped her. It was a little hysterical from almost being caught nude in the bed, but it was genuine enough. 'Big brothers say stuff like that, don't they?'

Tilly regarded her with serious eyes. 'You got brothers, Jean?'

'Sure I have. Four of them.' She grinned. 'It's why I'm so tough.'

'What you mean?'

With a glance at Alice, Jean smiled wider. 'My big brothers were wild, always fighting.' She laughed. 'I learned how to hold my own against them. And they used to tell me all sorts of awful things about thunder and lightning.'

'I only told her how getting hit by lightning could electrocute her to death,' a voice said from the door.

'I don't wanna be 'lectrocuted!'

Jack came into the room and sat himself cross-legged on the bed, leaning against his mother. Jean widened her eyes at Alice, who shook her head.

'Did the thunder wake you, Jack?' she asked. 'It's very loud.'

He scowled. 'Nah. I'm not scared of thunder.' He pointed to his sister. 'She woke me up, screaming of being electrocuted.'

Jean had to put a hand over her mouth. So this was what it was like to be a parent. She could get used to it.

'Come on you lot,' she said, getting up from the bed and tugging the dressing gown's tie tighter around her waist. 'Since we're all up, what do you say to a cup of hot cocoa?'

Jack bounced to his knees on the bed and looked at his mother. 'Can we?' he asked. 'We can have a midnight feast!'

Alice pursed her lips, pretending to think about it, then laughed. 'Sure,' she said. 'Cocoa and toast it is.'

A moment later, the children were scrambling from the bed and racing to the kitchen, leaving Jean looking at Alice.

'They didn't say anything.' She stared at the doorway, then back at Alice. 'Neither of them – not even Jack – asked what I was doing in your room.'

Alice giggled. 'Or what you were doing wearing my dressing gown.'

Jean looked down at herself. 'Well, that either.'

Alice got up and wrapped her arms around Jean. 'I think it means something,' she said.

Breathing in the warm, clean scent of Alice's hair, Jean nodded, then wondered.

'What does it mean?'

Alice looked up at her, full lips parted in a smile, eyes gleaming. 'It means, welcome to the family.'

CHAPTER 41

He knew they were in there. Hands clenching around the steering wheel, Big Jim leaned forward and peered out the windshield. He'd had to turn the engine back on and it made the car thrum under him in a way that made him think of a caged rhinoceros. That's what he felt like, sitting in the vehicle, impotent, unable to get out and do what he wanted – a caged animal.

Groping for the bottle of bourbon, he upended it, the alcohol good and strong at the back of his throat. He should never have let Alice go when he had the chance. When he'd come back from the war, bringing her husband's corpse with him, he'd come straight back to her. To be near her, supporting her, comforting her.

But she hadn't taken it like that. She'd always been a bit too independent-minded for her own good, but he'd really thought she'd come around. So much so that he'd been willing to back off a bit. Give her some space, he'd decided. That was what she needed, and goodness knows, the war had been hard on her too, bringing up young Jack all on her own.

301

The kid had been little more than a babe in arms when he and Terry had left for the Pacific Front.

Forcing his hand to relax around the bottle, Big Jim sat back in his seat, staring through the waterlogged glass, knowing he should put the engine in gear and go home.

But what waited for him at home? He had a nice place, one of two farmhouses on the property, his dad living in the other one, but there was no one there. No one to keep him warm.

Alice. He closed his eyes and imagined the pale softness of her skin. Saw her stretched out beside him, a sheer night-dress on, perhaps. Yes. He nodded. It would be something sheer and delightful, a wisp of a thing he would buy for her next time he was in the city. It would barely cover her, and he would be able to see the thatch of dark honey curls covering her pussy, and her rosy nipples, he could see those too, just a little more than shadows underneath the fabric.

It was hard to breathe in the car. All the windows were fogging up, but every time he wound down the window by his seat, the rain came pelting in cold and sharp. If he wound down the passenger's window, the leather seats would be ruined.

He should go home. Another mouthful of bourbon. He jammed the bottle between his legs so it wouldn't tip over.

His hands were fists again, blunt fingernails digging into the flesh of his palms. It took an enormous effort to relax them.

The trouble was her.

Jean.

She was in there. Jean. In there where she didn't belong.

She had a habit of getting where she didn't belong. Like

she had when he'd been away fighting, risking his life for King and Country. She'd been back home, pretending she was just as good as him, doing his job, doing it, according to his own father, just as well, if not better than him. He couldn't forget the satisfied look on the old man's face when he talked of record profits, high production yields, and damn, even happy fucking workers. Running like a well-oiled machine, his father said of the farm when he got back lucky to have life and limbs intact.

And Jean, she'd just been waltzing around the place like she owned it. She didn't own it. He did. Big Jim Dempsey. It was his place, his inheritance. And she'd just looked at him when he'd given his orders, then tried suggesting all the different ways they'd been doing things instead.

No, it hadn't been on. He ran the farm. Him. It was his job, and no uppity fucking Sheila who dressed like a man was going to tell him he wasn't doing it properly.

The memories bumped around inside his head, piling up against each other as he added to them the one burning thought that consumed him.

She was in there with Alice. Stroking that fine warm body, pushing her fingers in where only he should go.

And Alice, damn it all, was letting her, was under the perverted bitch's spell.

Well, something had to be done about that.

The car's stick was under his hand, and he shoved it into gear, the big vehicle lurching out onto the road like a hungry animal. It knew what to do, where to take him, and he drank while he drove, the bourbon the fuel that drove him.

Under his hand, the car knew the way, taking the turns,

threading through the sleeping town, thunder crackling overhead, lightning ripping open the sky in front of him.

But he was safe, the car taking him where he needed to go. It wouldn't take long to get there, and the woman wasn't going to get back before him. She would be walking, for starters.

He sniffed. Bloody bitch. Get her out of the way and Alice would turn to him, finally, realising she had no choice, that he was always her best bet anyway. And the father of her kid. That ought to count for something. He thought of the money her mother had promised him. That would be handy too. His father would be proud of him, able to buy the neighbouring block, finally.

The car, tyres purring along the wet road, turn its head-lamps on the service station at the side of the road. Fergus, the dope, never locked the doors to the garage. Or if he did, then it didn't matter, because Big Jim had long ago persuaded his good mate to give him one of the spares.

He was going to get soaked. For a moment, Big Jim stared out at the petrol pumps considering, then nosed the car forward again, toward the shed where Fergus worked on his cars. There'd be what he needed in there.

It didn't take long. He was the well-oiled machine. And what was a bit of water? Mopping the rain from his forehead he regretted the leather seats, but only for a moment because now his mind was filled with other pictures, and those ones burned hot.

First things first though – check on the whereabouts of the bitch.

Back through town, the night sky above an open sore of rain, thunder, and forking electricity. It was like driving through into some sort of hell. He thought he'd left that behind in the Pacific, but hell, it seemed, existed in lots of places.

Along with devils, he decided. The car skulked down the narrow road where Alice's house sat only a few feet back from the gravel crunching under his tyres. He eyed the dark, blinkered windows and cruised on by, turning right at the end of the street, and right again, pulling into the overgrown driveway of the house that sat abandoned directly behind Alice's. It was where the bitch Jean had lurked, waiting for him to drive on by before vaulting the fence and going to visit where she had no right.

She thought he hadn't seen her, but his eyes were sharp. He'd seen her all right, waiting under the tree. The glowing red end of her cigarette had given her away and as soon as he'd seen it, he'd known it was her. He'd driven by, but he'd known she was there.

He timed closing his car door with a great tearing rumble of thunder, peering momentarily upwards, expecting to see the very sky ripped open above him. Then he ducked forward, pulling his collar up around his neck as he headed for the back yard, confident there was no one about to see him, stumbling only a little as he walked. Everyone in the neighbourhood would be sleeping, or if the storm had woken them, then they would be huddled around their coal ranges, or Primus stoves, making cups of tea and coddling themselves, telling themselves everything was all right.

Lifting a leg over the low fence, Big Jim hoped the rain would ease soon. Surely the storm would blow itself out? He winced at another bout of thunder and wished it would move on.

Still, by the time the bitch made her way home, he'd prob-ably have his wish. And he knew how to do what he planned. He wouldn't be foiled by anything, certainly not the damned weather.

There was the house pressing up against the night, the rain clattering against its tin roof like a wild drummer. Light flickered in the kitchen, even though he knew for a fact the power was off. All the street lights had been off, and he'd had a devil of a time for a few moments at old Fergus' petrol pumps when he'd realised they wouldn't work with the power out.

But he'd sorted that one. Found a full one of what he needed right there in the garage. It had been almost too easy.

They were all up. Alice and the bitch, cosying up in the kitchen with the two kids. Big Jim turned his head and snarled into the darkness, took another drink, before looking back.

The happy little family. Couple candles burning, and the kettle on the old coal range. The bitch was making toast, concentrating hard, spreading jam on the bread. Alice was stirring cups of cocoa.

Goddamn happy little family.

Big Jim backed up, his hands all sharp knuckles again, the left gripped around the neck of the bottle.

He went back to the car and sat behind the wheel, mind a roar of rain and static that glowed white in his mind, but eventually turned red.

And when it did that, he relaxed, opened his hands, put down the bottle, turned the key in the ignition and got the car moving. Back out onto the road, wheels humming in the rain, windshield wipers swishing at him in their soft voice, urging him on.

The boarding house was in darkness too, and he nodded his head at his good luck. Maybe the weather was a boon after all. He laughed, remembering the fat old woman who ran this place. She was called Boone.

She'd be in bed. Snoring, most likely. And if she did hear him come inside, she'd just think it was one of her boarders. He laughed again. She'd just think it was goddamn Jean Reardon.

He made sure to park the car down from the house. No point giving himself away, not this close to getting the job done.

The petrol can felt good in his hand. He hefted it experimentally as he walked back to the house, listening with satisfaction to the slosh of liquid inside. Plenty in there to do the job.

He didn't even give a shit about the rain anymore. Besides, the front door was open, and he'd have time to dry off and warm up while he waited for Jean to finish up her cosy time with Alice and come home to see him.

CHAPTER 42

'You can't go home in this weather,' Alice said, eyes bright and concerned. Jean leaned over and kissed her on the tip of her nose.

'I have to,' she said. 'Uniform's at home – work day tomorrow. Car's at home too.'

'At least wear my raincoat,' Alice said, tugging Jean into an embrace which was no help whatsoever with the necessity to leave. Jean buried her face in Alice's soft hair and breathed deeply.

'I'll wear your raincoat,' she conceded. 'Can't be worse than your dressing gown.' She leaned back and peered at Alice suspiciously, the corners of her mouth tipping up in a smile. 'Can it?'

Alice giggled and shook her head. 'Perfectly respectable dark blue, no patterns whatsoever.'

'I don't want to go,' Jean said, feeling the sudden certainty of that fact despite their joking. She never did want to leave. Alice's bed was too warm, her company too precious. She closed her eyes and hugged Alice tighter. 'The children didn't mind me being here,' she said.

'Not a bit,' Alice replied. 'I thought Jack might question it, but not a peep.' She smiled at Jean. 'They enjoyed it. Us. You.'

'Our midnight feast.'

Alice's smile widened. 'Tilly wants you to be her dad.'

That made her eyebrows rise. 'She what?'

'That's what she says. She's quite set on it.'

A warmth spread through Jean's body that was quite unexpected. 'How did I get so lucky?' she asked, voice dropping to an awed whisper.

'You met us and changed our lives,' Alice said, snuggling closer, her cheek warm against Jean's jaw. 'I wish you didn't have to go.'

'I won't have to soon.'

Those big blue eyes again. 'Is it true?' Alice asked. 'Are we really going to do this?'

Jean couldn't help but kiss the soft, questioning lips. 'It's true,' she said. 'I need to be with you.'

'And we can, in a new town.' Alice's lips sought hers again, lingered there for a moment, then spoke, her breath tickling Jean. 'Can we go tomorrow?'

That made her smile. 'What about Sunday? That way I get to give notice, collect wages, and a reference as well. We'll need those things, to get ourselves set up properly.'

She watched Alice muse on the notion, then nod. 'We can take the children to the fair on Saturday then. And I can help out with the jumble sale – I'd like to do that, since those ladies were so nice to me.'

'There,' Jean said. 'It's settled.'

'And I can tell the school Jack will be moving.' Her eyes widened. 'There's so much to do!'

Her expression made Jean laugh. 'I love you to bits,' she said.

'And I love you. Where shall we go, do you think, now we have the when decided?'

Jean tightened her hold on the beautiful woman in her arms, marvelling that they were really going to do this thing. 'I don't know,' she said. 'We have a week to decide.'

'Exactly a week. We can do that.' A kiss whispered against her cheek. 'I can do anything, if we have you.'

'And I can do anything if I have you three,' Jean whispered, feeling the truth of it in her bones. It sank in and settled there, solid and real. Alice and Jack and Tilly were her family now. 'I ought to go,' she said reluctantly. 'I'm just keeping you up.'

Another kiss and Alice was fetching the rain coat, standing to watch, making sure Jean pulled it on. She did so and grinned at Alice.

'See you in the morning?' she asked.

Alice nodded. 'I'll be expecting my bottle of milk.'

'I'll make sure you get it – special delivery.' She thought better of going back for another kiss, reached for the door instead. 'See you in the morning, my love. Sleep well.'

Alice gave her a smile that melted her heart, then she stepped outside, pulling the door shut behind her, feeling the kitchen's warmth linger a moment under the raincoat, then thin and disappear as she strode down the path to the back fence, the wind searching out the skin at her neck and blowing cold upon it.

The storm had passed on out to sea, leaving behind a

damp and unruly wind, and a steady, dispirited rain that seemed almost apologetic as it dripped from Jean's rough old fedora. She should have worn her coat to come over earlier, but at least the dark blue raincoat kept the worst of the weather out.

At last, the boarding house loomed up white and ghostly against the black sky. Jean stared up at it, eyes automatically searching out the window to her room on the top floor. She was tired, she realised, her legs beginning to drag, a yawn cracking her jaw. It would be good to fall into bed for a couple of hours.

And even better from the next week not to have to get up and go home at midnight like some sort of milk-delivering Cinderella.

The door was unlocked, which was always the case. No one in town locked their doors, except, Jean thought, now Alice did – she insisted on it. She did not want Jim Dempsey breaking in unsuspected during the vulnerable night hours when she wasn't there. Alice's doors were hardly strongholds, but at least if they were locked, there'd be some warning if he tried anything.

She didn't know what he'd try, but she thought there'd be a fair chance Big Jim Dempsey would get it in his alcohol-soaked brain to do something.

Maybe they'd be able to leave town before he made a move.

The boarding house was quiet, the house sitting over her breathing softly in the dark. She crept past Mrs Boone's door, thinking for a moment of the old woman's unrequited love story. How much different would things be, she wondered, if Mrs B had got her man?

There'd be no Alice, for starters, so as much as Jean wanted her friend's happiness, she couldn't part with the thought of having Alice.

Smiling to herself at her own ridiculous ideas, she went straight to the stairs, years of practice making her unerring in her direction. The cool smooth bannister was under her hand a moment later and she looked up into the darkness, wishing not for the first time that she had a ground floor room.

But she liked her rooms in the attic. Mrs B rented out single rooms to everyone else, but Jean got two small rooms tucked up under the eaves. The staircase to those was even steeper than the main one, but she didn't care. Those two rooms were her own private haven.

There were no lights under any of the doorways, but Jean wasn't surprised. Most people she shared the house with would be up early to work – Mrs Boone didn't rent to anyone without a job – and storm or no, they'd be getting their rest.

Somewhere above her a floorboard creaked, and she stopped, one foot on the bottom step of her own staircase, head cocked, listening.

There it was again. Just the slightest sound, but she'd lived in this house since moving to town, and she knew all its night time noises.

This one didn't belong.

Quickly, Jean debated her options. How quiet had she been, climbing the stairs? Looking down towards her feet she thought she'd probably squelched rather than clomped up the stairs, but had she been heard?

The sound again, someone shifting behind her sitting

room door, shuffling, waiting, and then there was the unmistakable sound of a cough.

If he was coughing, then he likely hadn't heard her coming. There'd been no attempt to stifle it.

Bending down, Jean tugged at her wet shoelaces, undoing them and slipping off her shoes, putting them to the side of the staircase, out of her way. She turned in the darkness and went back the way she'd come, a niggling worry bursting to life.

Cleo Boone had her own suite of rooms on the ground floor, taking up one side of the house, with the kitchens at the rear. There were two doors off the hallway, one of them always locked – Mrs B used the connecting door from her sitting room to get to her bedroom, and it was that path Jean took now.

Except she didn't have to get as far as Mrs B's inner sanctum. She dropped to her knees in front of the dim figure on the floor of the sitting room.

'Cleo,' she said, touching the inert woman. 'Cleo, it's me Jean, can you hear me?'

There was a groan, low and indistinct, but a sign of life nonetheless that made Jean sag for a moment in relief. She touched her hand to her landlady's hair and her fingers came away sticky.

'Bastard,' she said to herself, knowing full well who had pushed his way in this door, breath probably reeking of cheap alcohol – bourbon, she remembered was Big Jim's poison of choice. 'If he's seriously hurt you, I'm going to kill him with my own bare hands.'

This time the groan was louder, and Mrs Boone moved on the floor, one hand groping in the air for a moment. Jean grasped it, held it in her own, feeling the chilled skin. She sucked in a deep breath and got to her feet, tucking the hand gently in to the woman's side.

'Stay right there, Cleo,' she said, and groped her way to the bedroom after all. Back a moment later, she lifted her friend's head and tucked a pillow under it, then spread a blanket over the wounded woman.

'He's waiting for you,' Mrs Boone whispered, her voice weak but surprisingly angry.

Jean nodded, even though she couldn't be seen in the dark room. 'I know,' she said. 'I already discovered that. Thinks he's going to spring a surprise on me.' She thinned her lips in a humourless smile, looking at the glowing coals of the fireplace. 'Well he's the one in for a shock.'

A hand felt for her, patted her. 'I'll wait here,' Mrs Boone said.

'Good plan,' Jean said, and leaned down to kiss the woman on the forehead. 'I'll call the constable.'

She got up and squinted into the gloom for the telephone she knew was there. Finding it, she lifted the receiver.

'Shit,' she said. 'Line's down.'

Mrs Boone didn't reply, and Jean felt the urgency surge through her body. There wasn't time to wait for the goddamned constable anyway. She had to do something and do it fast. Then one of the men could run for the doctor.

Up the stairs she went again, on stocking feet, avoiding the stairs that creaked, keeping her back to the wall, eyes lifted into the darkness above her.

She could feel the house around her. Unable to see well, she could smell instead, the scent of wood polish and aging wallpaper, of tired, hastily-washed bodies. She could hear too, the snuffling, sneezing sounds of a household asleep. Outside, an owl hooted, sounding more like the plaintive call of a child and making her shiver. Still she climbed the stairs, reached the landing, moved to her own staircase, put her foot on the lower step and started for the top.

There was no plan in her head, she'd brought the poker from Mrs B's fireplace, although in close quarters it would be a hard thing to swing. But she had the element of surprise going for her, the quiet stealth with which she reached out to touch the cold metal of the door handle, holding it steady so that it wouldn't rattle, ears straining to hear the slightest noise, trying to figure out where in the room Big Jim lurked.

She smelled something else now, but it registered too late, and she was pushing the door open and stepping into the room before the warning bells in her head began their clanging.

CHAPTER 43

There was just enough surprise on her side to give her a precious moment to realise he was right there, pressed against the wall beside the door. They stared at each other in shock, and somewhere in Jean's mind the warning bells were ringing loud enough that she barely heard his sharp intake of breath.

Because he was holding something, and it was that, the fact that she could see him perfectly well, that his face was bathed in light, the eyes wide and manic, the mouth stretched out in a yell she couldn't hear over her own shrieking warning, which told her just how much trouble she was in.

There was a candle in one hand, and his other was reaching for her before she was even in the room, latching onto Alice's blue coat, grabbing a handful of the wet fabric, pulling her into the room, swinging her around, and throwing her, his momentum taking her legs out from under her so that she went tumbling backwards...

But she'd had that short frozen moment of understanding, and she was already raising the poker when his arm shot out to grab her. Still he swung her, sending her tumbling backwards into the room, but not so quickly that she didn't have the poker already whistling through the air, some dim part of her registering even as she did it that it could be a mistake.

It hit him on the side of the head, a wild, one-armed swing, nothing more than pure instinct, the primitive need to defend herself. She heard it hit, the sickly thud of impact, and then the poker was juddering from her hand, and she was falling backwards, and he was collapsing, going to his knees, toppling forward onto the bare floorboards.

The candle though, that was what she locked her shocked gaze on, watching it spin over and over through the air as if in slow motion and she wanted to scream at it, quite possibly was screaming at it to go out, for the light to extinguish, for the flame to wink out in the wind of its own motion. Instead it flew in a wild arc, dropped to the floor, rolled.

She stared at it for just a moment, breath held tight in her chest, and then the flame dipped and wavered and just a bare second later the room was alight, and she knew she'd been right about that smell as she opened the door, knew that Big Jim had further plans than just lying in wait for her. He'd brought something with him, and there in the burning glow of the fire she saw it, a red petrol can, lying on its side, and she knew it was empty.

He'd been cunning. The flames spread in a fast line across the room, blocking off the door, sealing her escape route. He'd meant to grab her, throw her into the room, the candle after her, then slip out as the room ignited and she was trapped behind a wall of fire.

Scrabbling to her feet, lungs burning already with the

heat, Jean sucked in hot air, hearing the hungry roar of the flames in front of her, feeling their hot tongues reaching for her.

She had to move, and fast. In a moment, the one way out the door would be gone. Lifting an arm over her head, glad now of Alice's wet gabardine raincoat, she took a breath and jumped over Jim's prone figure, stumbling on his legs and skittering around like a spider until she was back on her feet and the door was right behind her.

He'd fallen in the line of fire, making a gap in the flames with his own body. They licked at his clothes, searing his flesh and in another minute, he would be engulfed. Bending down, she picked up his feet and tugged, grunting with the effort, backing up through the narrow door, taking him with her.

There was no room in the stairway to get him turned around. He'd have to go down the steep stairs feet first. Jean lifted her face, feeling the skin across her cheeks hot and tight. She coughed, smoke billowing out of the room now, following her onto the stairs as she stumbled down them.

Arms straining, squinting against the heat, the smoke, Jean struggled to turn Jim over so that he wouldn't go down the stairs on his face. He was dead weight, unconscious, and she didn't stop to assess his wounds. If she slowed at all, he wouldn't make it, would die in the fire he'd set to trap her.

But she wasn't going to let that happen. Another burst of effort and he was on his back and she was holding his feet again and backing down the steps tugging him after her, not caring one little bit that his head hit each step, only that they were moving and the great mouth of fire behind her attic door wasn't going to swallow them whole.

At the bottom of the stairs, she dropped him, and ran for the nearest door, coughing, yelling, thumping on the door.

'Get up!' she screamed. 'Fire!'

The door yanked open under her fists and she went onto the next one, still shrieking, until all the doors were open, men and women streaming out of them, their own yelling adding to the din of the fire.

It was busy in the attic still, but she knew it was only a matter of minutes and it would run out of food, the ceiling over their heads collapsing, the fire moving downwards, consuming the aged, warping timbers.

She grabbed one of the men. 'Fletcher,' she gasped, recognising him in the red light. 'Help me.' She stood over Jim Dempsey lying like a sack of potatoes at the bottom of her stairs. Everyone else had already scattered down the stairs and, she hoped, outside.

Fletcher, a big guy who ran a fishing boat off the coast, looked down at the man on the floor.

'Shit,' he said. 'It's fucking Big Jim. What's he doing here?'

He was yelling his question, but Jean could barely hear him. She shook her head, and grabbed Jim's feet again, determined to drag him down the main stairs on her own if she had to.

She didn't have to. Still shaking his head, dishevelled in nothing but a pair of underwear, Fletcher hefted the unconscious man under the arms and they stumbled down the stairs together, Jean trying to hurry. There was still Cleo to get out of the house.

The first breath of cold air outside the house was the sweetest she'd ever taken. They cleared the house by mere feet, then Jean dropped her end of Big Jim on the grass and grabbed Fletcher instead.

'Mrs Boone's still inside,' she yelled at him, pointing to Jim. 'He hit her on the head. She's hurt.'

Fletcher looked at her, wide-eyed and sooty.

'Come on,' she screamed. 'We have to get her out.'

Understanding dawned at last, and although Jean saw him give the house an uncomfortable stare, he followed her back inside willingly enough.

It was like walking into a furnace, one in which internal winds sounded hurricane-loud. She couldn't believe the noise of it. The house screamed as the fire devoured it.

'Quickly,' she yelled, ducking into the sitting room, thankful that it was right at the front of the house. They'd be able to get her out.

Mrs Boone was still where Jean had left her, swaddled in the blanket, head resting on the pillow, face pale and sweaty. Jean realised with shock that she could see her quite clearly and threw a fearful glance at the door.

Fletcher was looking at Mrs Boone in dismay. Jean punched him on the arm and took her place at one side of the hurt woman. They wouldn't get her out by lifting her like they had Big Jim. He was big, but the landlady was bigger.

'Grab her other arm,' Jean yelled, bending, getting her feet securely under her, and grasping Mrs B under the arm. Fletcher, silent, did the same, and a moment later they'd hefted her between them, Jean listing slightly as she took the weight, and Mrs Boone's head falling backwards on a rubbery neck.

There wasn't time to care, and together, they dragged her to the doorway, squeezed through first one then the other, and then they were outdoors, whooping in great lungful's of air, still dragging her, off the veranda, onto the grass, as far as the road.

They laid her down, and Jean collapsed to her knees beside her, coughing, every muscle in her body burning.

'Where's Big Jim?' she asked, throat raw, taking two goes to get the words out.

Fletcher, staring at the house, shrugged. 'They moved him.' That was good enough for him.

It was enough for Jean too. Kneeling in the wet grass, she lifted Mrs Boone's head onto her lap and stared at the burning boarding house.

Her rooms were well gone, the windows of the next floor down shattered, great eyes of flame, the walls red, more fire than wood, and as she watched, amazed at how quickly it happened, the roof collapsed, and the whole house seemed to fall in on itself until it was just nothing but fire wrapped around a ghost of a building. She wished she could get further away, and she ducked her head down over Mrs Boone's face, shielding both of them from the intense heat.

A hand touched her on the shoulder and she looked blankly into a man's face. It was creased in concern.

'Ambulance,' he said. 'Let's get the lady some help.' The gaze turned considering. 'And yourself, I think.' His eyes flickered toward the burning house then back down at Jean. 'This way. We need to get you back, get you seen to.'

She shook her head, refusing to budge until the two ambulance men, along with some recruited help from the gathered crowd, had lifted Mrs Boone onto a stretcher and only then, when it was being jolted away to the waiting vehicle, did she struggle to her feet, unsteady and exhausted. A hand took her elbow and led her to the ambulance, and she stumbled toward it with burning eyes.

There were two stretchers inside, and Jean was made to sit down at the end of one. Blinking, trying to get some moisture into her dry eyes, she stared at the other stretcher.

Then sat back and closed her eyes, coughing, letting fatigue wash over her in a wave she thought never-ending. It was Big Jim in the other stretcher.

She'd got both of them out.

Alice, she thought, balancing on the seat as the ambulance got moving, bumping down the road, siren screaming. Someone needed to tell Alice she was all right. Alice would be worried.

'What's that you're saying, love?'

She opened her eyes, saw the same face from earlier, looking at her with a kind expression.

'The telephone lines are still down,' he said to her. 'But news will be all around town. I'm sure your family will hear straight away that you're on the way to hospital.'

Her eyes sank shut again. The hospital was all the way in New Plymouth. Alice, if anyone even thought to let her know she was okay, had no way to get there.

Her thoughts bumped with the ambulance as they headed towards the hospital.

As soon as she was let go, Jean decided, she and Alice would pack up and leave town. Find a little house somewhere to share.

Somewhere nobody would even notice them.

Somewhere they could live in peace.

CHAPTER 44

$\mathcal{A}$lice stood on her doorstep, dazed and confused. She stared at the man talking to her, seeing his lips move, unable to make any sense of the words coming out of his mouth.

His eyes were a soft, sad grey above his mouth, and it was those she latched onto, not letting go of his gaze, trying desperately to fathom what he was telling her by the expression in the pained wet eyes.

'Do you hear me, Miss?' he asked, and she shook her head. The milk bottle was cold in her numb fingers and it slipped from her grip, falling to the step and shattering.

'There, there,' the milkman said. She searched for his name and came up blank. She thought he'd introduced himself, but the name was gone. 'It's all right,' he said. 'Just a broken bottle.'

What was he talking about? She looked down, saw the splash of white on the stone, the shards of glass sticking up out of it and the thought crossed her mind that she ought to sweep that up before Tilly or Jack hurt themselves on it.

Those pieces of glass could give them a nasty cut, slice into their skin, and then she would need to take them to the hospital.

The hospital.

That's what he was telling her. She blinked, swallowed, sucked in a deep breath, smelt the singe of smoke still lingering in the air, and finally it sank in what he was saying.

'Jean?' she said, her voice weak.

The man in front of her nodded. 'That's right, Miss. Mrs.' He looked confused a moment, then shook it off. 'I… ah…know you two are friends, so I thought I ought to tell you.'

She stared at him, at the crinkled lines around his eyes, and thought that he must be a nice man, to have such worried eyes.

'There was a fire?' she asked, repeating his words to her.

A nod. 'Yes.'

'At the boarding house?'

Another nod.

'Where Jean lives.'

He looked down at the broken bottle again, shifted uncomfortably on his feet, then looked back at her. 'That's right, and real sorry I am to bring you the news too.'

But Alice was shaking her head. 'I…I don't know…' she began, then trailed off. 'I need to go inside,' she said.

Someone else was walking down the path, striding towards them.

'Alice,' she said, sweeping up, her coat swinging around her legs. 'I see you've heard.'

Alice nodded, feeling like some small, dumb animal, a mouse perhaps. She wanted to scurry back inside, find somewhere dark and safe to hide while she figured out what was going on. She licked her lips but had no voice.

'Mr Fry,' the woman said. 'I'll take it from here. Would you be so kind as to fetch Mrs Holden another bottle of milk, please?'

Jean's work partner backed away, nodding. 'Take good care of her,' he said. 'Jean would want that.'

Alice watched Martha Wilson smile automatically at the man, then turn to her, examining her like she was a particularly worrisome patient.

'I'm not sure what's happened,' Alice confessed. 'He told me, but I couldn't take it in.'

Tim Fry was back with a fresh bottle of milk and Martha took it, thanked him, then stepped over the broken bottle, tucked an arm around Alice, and guided her inside.

'Where are the children?' she asked.

'In the kitchen,' Alice said. 'They're having breakfast.'

That got a nod and Martha looked around for a moment, then swept Alice into her bedroom. 'We can talk in here for a minute.'

Alice nodded mutely.

'It's all right,' Martha said. 'Everything's going to be okay.'

'But I don't know what's going on!' Alice's hands tied themselves together in an intricate knot.

'I'm going to tell you, and then I'm going to go make a cup of tea, and we'll make arrangements for the children…'

'It's a school day,' Alice interrupted.

'That's good. Jack can go off to school then, and you can decide if little Tilly is to come with us, or if there is someone who can look after her.'

'Marjorie, next door. She looks after the children for me,

if I need her to.' Alice had sunk down upon the unmade bed, the one Jean had crawled out of only a few hours ago. She wanted to spread her hand on the sheet, lie down and bury her face in the pillow, breathe in Jean's lingering scent.

'What happened?' she breathed. 'Tell me from the beginning.'

Martha glanced around, pulled the stool from the dressing table over, and sat down, leaning forward and taking Alice's hands in her own.

She had nice hands, Alice noticed. Soft and strong at the same time. Jean's hands were rough in places, hands that did heavy work, but she loved them anyway, the way they felt on her skin. She brought herself back to what Martha was telling her.

'There was a fire at the boarding house early this morning,' Martha said. 'Everyone got out okay, but Jean suffered from breathing in a lot of smoke, and she has a few burns – nothing serious, but they took her to the hospital in New Plymouth.'

'I have to go there,' Alice said.

'I know. I'm going to take you.'

Alice sighed in relief, curled over her lap for a moment, still hanging onto Martha's hands. 'Why are you helping me?' she asked.

When she looked up again, she saw the surprise on Martha's face. 'Of course I'm helping you,' the woman said. 'We're friends. Jean is my friend. You and she are close, that's important.' The eyes blinked at her, and Alice noticed how deep a green they were.

'I'm sorry,' she said to the eyes watching her. 'I shouldn't have questioned you like that.'

The hands patted hers. 'Never mind that. Let's go have that cup of tea, all right?'

Alice nodded and stood up. Her legs were still shaky but the sick feeling in her stomach had eased. 'Is Mrs Boone all right?'

'She is in the hospital as well, I'm afraid.'

Alice stared at her. 'There's a lot more to this story, isn't there?'

She got a sympathetic smile. 'Yes. There is. But let's go have that tea, get handsome young Jack off to school, and I can tell you the rest on the drive to the hospital.'

The arrangements went smoothly, Martha orchestrating everything as though she was born to it. Alice watched her come and go to the neighbours, to see Jack off at the gate, to take Tilly off to dress, while she sat at the kitchen table, hands wrapped around a cooling tea cup.

'You'd best get dressed too,' Martha said, coming into the room with a clean and neat Tilly.

'I wanna come with you, Mama,' Tilly said.

Alice shook her head. 'Not today, sweetheart.' She tried not to feel bad about not taking Tilly with her, but it would be easier without her. 'Mrs Jones will take very good care of you.'

'But when will you be back?'

'In time to make your dinner just like always,' Alice said, casting a glance at Martha, who nodded. She looked back at the child and smiled. 'You'll be fine.'

Tilly grumbled, but went next door without any more fuss, Marjorie Jones coming out onto her doorstep to gossip, her face pinched with the news of the fire.

'Isn't it terrible,' she said. 'Word is that the whole house is gone. Just a pile of cinders.' She leaned back in gruesome satisfaction. 'All those boarders – lost everything, they have.'

Martha transferred Tilly to her. 'Yes,' she said. 'They have, and it's a terrible thing.'

'Thank you for taking Tilly,' Alice added.

Marjorie sniffed. 'You know she's never a bother. Where did you say you were going again?'

'To the hospital,' Alice said, the lump forming in her throat again at the words.

'Jean's in the hospital,' Tilly whispered in Mrs Jones' ear. They'd told the children what was happening. 'She was in the fire.'

The neighbour's eyes widened dramatically, showing the whites, which were more yellow than white.

'She's okay though,' Tilly said in her little, confidential manner. 'She didn't get burnt.'

Marjorie gave Alice a questioning look, but Martha had her hand on Alice's elbow and was pulling her away.

'I'm afraid we have to get going, Marjorie,' she said. 'Visiting hours, and things – you understand.'

'Oh, of course! Do let me know how your friend is when you get back. And don't worry about little Tilly – she'll be just fine. And Jack. I'll take good care of both of them.'

Alice waved, already out on the footpath and heading for Martha's dark green Bentley. A moment later she was in the passenger's seat and her hands were tying themselves back into knots again.

CHAPTER 45

Alice couldn't speak once they parked at the hospital. Martha gave her a sympathetic smile and they walked together in through the main doors. Alice, shivering, stood waiting while Martha, competent and self-assured, discovered Jean's whereabouts.

They were directed to an empty bed, and Alice stood there blinking in the large room's wan light, staring at the crumpled sheets.

'Alice!'

She turned at the sound of the voice, recognising it straight away, even though it was several degrees rougher than usual.

'Jean?' Over by the window, rising from a chair placed beside another bed, there was Jean, and she was smiling at her, arms opening wide in greeting. In a moment, Alice was inside those arms, holding Jean tightly, and her eyes were wet with tears. 'I was so worried!' she said, standing back at last and looking Jean over.

She got a sheepish smile in return. 'I'm okay,' Jean said. 'But glad to see you.' Jean's eyes turned to Martha.

'She's been wonderful,' Alice said. 'Rescued me. The man you work with – he was trying to tell me what had happened, but I was so shocked and worried I dropped the milk bottle and I couldn't take it all in.'

Jean still had one arm around Alice, but Martha was moving away, getting them chairs, waving away Alice's words. Alice took another step back and looked more critically at Jean.

'Tell me you're really all right,' she demanded.

'I'm really all right.' A wry smile accompanied the words and Alice shook her head.

'I want the truth.'

Jean, sighing, sat down again, and Alice saw that she was pale under her tan. There were bandages around her hands and up her arms. She held it up and shrugged. 'I didn't escape completely unscathed.' A smile. 'But I'm all right, really.' She glanced down the room at the nurse standing over one of the other beds. 'They'll let me go home today.'

'Not that you have a home to go to,' Martha said, coming back with two chairs and setting them down.

'No,' Jean said with a tired grimace. 'Well, there's that, of course.'

'You have to stay with me,' Alice said. 'There's nowhere else.'

Jean's eyes turned to her with a warmth that made her want to cry out, to wrap her arms gently back around her and hold her close, just hold her close always.

'Thanks Alice, love. But you don't have a spare room.'

Alice opened her mouth to protest, then closed it again.

She glanced at Martha, then back at Jean. 'Does that matter?' she asked, defiant anyway.

'I don't know,' Jean said.

'We're leaving anyway, remember. What's a few days?'

Jean's gaze slid away from hers to look at the figure in the bed beside them, and Alice realised with a start that she hadn't even given it a glance.

'Is that Mrs Boone?' Martha asked. 'How is she?'

'In worse shape than me,' Jean said, and there was a bitterness in her voice that was hard for Alice to hear.

'What happened?' she whispered.

Jean shook her head, as though she didn't want to tell the tale.

Ice crept through Alice's veins and she reached a tentative hand to touch Jean's fingers. They were warm and held hers.

'Jim Dempsey,' Jean said, her voice rough gravel.

Now Alice's whole body was chilled, and she shivered in the warm room. When she spoke, her voice was the merest squeak, and she had to clear her throat, start again.

'He did this?'

'He really did set the fire?' Martha asked, drawing her chair closer so that they sat in a huddle.

'He was waiting for me,' Jean said. 'Just inside the doorway to my room.' She looked at Alice, squeezed the fingers in her own, then stared over at the sleeping figure of Mrs Boone. Alice followed her gaze and hoped the woman was only sleeping.

'Is she...?'

'Sleeping. Yes. She'll be all right, but they're going to keep her in for a week or two, I think. She had a nasty head wound, and her heart's not the strongest anymore.' Jean's fingers had gone limp.

'Big Jim did it?' Martha asked.

Jean nodded. 'My guess is that he needed to know which room mine was. And Cleo being Cleo, wouldn't have gone down easily.' She left Alice's hand in her lap and lowered her head into her palms, wincing as she touched the bandages. 'It's all my fault,' she said.

'No!' Alice shook her head so that her hair smacked her shoulders. 'It's my fault. He would never have gone after you if it wasn't for me.' She rocked back in her chair, the full realisation dawning on her. 'It's all because of me,' she whispered. 'If I'd…'

'What?' Martha asked, voice brisk. 'Given him what he wanted? Let him force himself on you again? Married him?' She gave Alice a piercing look. 'It is most assuredly not your fault.' Her eyes went to Jean. 'And nor is it yours either. I'm tired of us women letting bad men get away with doing bad things just because they're men.' Straightening in her chair she glowered at them.

Alice watched Jean, wishing she could sit closer. 'She's right,' she said. 'Martha is right. The only one to blame is Jim.'

'Of course I'm right,' Martha said. 'Where is the man anyway? Tell me he went down with the house.'

Jean sighed, looked at her hands, turning them over in her lap. 'I pulled him out,' she said. 'I hit him with the poker and he went down.' She gazed up at the ceiling, then smiled at Alice, softening her words. 'He was waiting for me, with a can of gasoline, which he'd spilled across the room. When I came in, he grabbed me and pushed me into the room. He was holding a candle, obviously meaning to use it to set the fire.'

'He's lucky the flame didn't ignite the fumes,' Martha said. 'What a fool.'

'I wish it had,' Jean said. 'Would have saved me the bother of hitting him. But I think there was a window open.' She paused. 'Anyway, he grabbed me, I hit him, he fell, and whoosh, everything went up.' She lifted her hands in an explosive gesture and Alice wanted to cry out. She bit her lip and kept quiet instead.

'He fell across the line of the fire,' Jean continued. 'And lucky for me he did, or I would have been trapped.' She looked at Alice and smiled. 'I have the attic rooms. It would have been a long way down.' A slight frown marred her beloved face. 'Or I had the attic rooms, I should say. There's nothing left now.' A slow blinking look and she roused herself. 'So, I hopped over him, then turned and dragged him down the stairs. Woke everyone else up and Fletcher – he's one of the men lives there – he and I got Dempsey the rest of the way out.' Another glance at the bed. 'And went back for Cleo.'

There was silence for a long minute, Alice staring at Jean in fearful admiration.

Martha broke the silence. 'I can't believe you dragged him out.' She sniffed. 'I would have left him there to roast.' A wide smile. 'You, Jean Reardon, are a better woman than I.'

Jean gave a barking laugh that degenerated into a bout of coughing, shaking her head and wheezing. 'I even turned him over onto his back,' she said, 'to go down the stairs.' She giggled and wheezed some more. 'So his face wouldn't go bounce, bounce, bounce.' She leaned forward, bandaged hands gripping her ribs, shaking with laughter.

'Should have left the miserable bastard,' a gruff voice said from the bed.

'Mrs Boone!' Alice said, getting up and going around the other side of the bed.

'Alice Holden,' the old woman said from under a strapping of blankets. 'Do you know I was once head over heels in love with your father?'

Alice stared at her blankly for a moment. Whatever she'd expected to be greeted with, it wasn't this.

'There really was never any other for me after him,' Jean's landlady said. 'Just think – you should have been my daughter.'

Alice gaped at her, then lifted her head and gaped at Jean across the stretch of starched sheets.

'Cleo, are you delirious?' Jean asked, patting the bulky body.

Mrs Boone heaved herself up from her pillow. 'Help me sit up a bit, will you? I feel like a whale been washed up on the shore.'

They helped her, squashing pillows underneath her shoulders.

'And no, I'm not delirious. I'm just getting old and senti-mental.' She looked at Alice and took her hand. 'Your mother is a terrible woman,' she said.

'I know,' Alice squeaked. 'I know she is.'

The ravaged woman smiled at her from the bed. 'But you, my dear, are not. You look after yourself, and our Jean here.' She shifted slightly in the bed, then tried on a grin. 'Because when I get out of here, I'm off to stay with my sister and live an easy life for as long as I please. I won't be about to baby the both of you.'

Alice, looking across at Jean nodded, smiling, tears in her eyes.

'Always, Mrs Boone,' she said. 'I always will.'

CHAPTER 46

Jean leaned against her as they walked to the car and Alice relished the weight of her there even as she was concerned about how tired Jean was.

'Are you sure you shouldn't be staying another night?' she asked, not for the first time.

'I don't want to,' Jean said. 'And there's nothing really wrong with me. I have to go back and have these bandages changed, but I'll be heading in every day while Cleo is there anyway.'

Alice nodded, and helped Jean slide into the back seat of the car, Martha standing there holding the door open. She climbed in beside Jean, and finally, finally, was able to hold her properly.

'I was so worried,' she whispered. 'I couldn't bear it if anything happened to you.'

Jean pressed a kiss to her damp cheek. 'Hush love. I'm okay. Everything is all right. It was a close shave, but it's over now.'

'But Jim...'

'Is in deep trouble with the police. When he gets out of hospital, I imagine he'll be going straight to spend some time in a jail cell.'

Martha, behind the wheel now, overheard her. 'I'm going to personally make it my mission to ensure that,' she said.

Alice looked askance at her and got a shrug over the seat in return. 'My husband is the local solicitor,' she said. 'I will use his connections shamelessly. A man like Jim Dempsey is a danger to himself and everyone else.'

'His father is going to be devastated,' Jean said, leaning against Alice and closing her eyes.

'That can't be helped, I'm afraid. Will Dempsey is a good man, but his son is a menace who ought to be put down like a rabid dog.'

'We don't have rabies in this country,' Jean said, but there was a smile on her lips. Alice kissed them.

'I'm just glad everyone is going to be all right,' she said.

They were back in town, and Martha twisted around in her seat for a moment. 'Do you want to see the house?' she asked.

Alice shuddered. 'No. No I don't think I could bear that.' A glance at Jean, who had her eyes closed, exhausted. 'Not yet, anyway. I just want to get Jean home.'

Martha smiled. 'Home it is, then.'

Alice found herself scanning the streets as the car cruised through the town. This was where she'd grown up, and yet she felt like a stranger in it now. Things had changed too much, and while she'd met some lovely people she knew she'd always remember, the very streets were tainted now with the sickly smell of burnt timber, and over on another street, the particular poisonous knowledge of her own mother, sitting alone and malignant in her big house, caring only for her own wants and needs.

She turned away from the view, back to Jean, startled to find Jean's rich brown eyes open and fastened on her.

'Why are you looking at me like that?' she whispered.

'You have the most expressive face,' Jean said. 'I've been watching you, and everything you feel ends up on your face.'

A deep blush welled up and Alice cursed her fair skin. 'Do you mind?' she asked.

With a wheezing laugh, Jean shook her head. 'It's incredibly refreshing.' Her look turned sly. 'But I'm never taking you to a poker game.'

Alice looked at her in astonishment, then laughed. 'No,' she said. 'I don't think I'd do well at all playing poker.'

'Hey lovebirds,' Martha said from the front seat. 'We're here, if you want to extract yourselves from each other.' She was gazing at them in the rear vision mirror, a smile on her lips.

Straightening, Alice looked out at her familiar street, and at the ramshackle little house she'd called home for the last eight years. With a sigh, she turned to Jean. 'We're here.'

Jean nodded. 'Let's get out and get the kids, shall we?'

It was the right thing to say. Alice felt the knot loosen in her stomach. But still she touched Jean's bandaged arm. 'We're still leaving though, right?'

Martha had turned around in her seat, one elbow over the back to look at them. 'Any thoughts yet where you'll go?'

They both shook their heads. 'Somewhere away from Jim Dempsey and my mother,' Alice said.

'That leaves a lot of scope.' Martha smiled.

'We'll think of something.' Jean nudged Alice and nodded toward the door. 'I think I can see a certain little girl.'

'What?' Alice turned and there was Tilly, jumping up and down in the open doorway to their house. 'What's she doing there?' Jack appeared behind her.

'Looks like we have a welcoming committee,' Jean told her. 'Thanks for the ride, Martha.'

'No problem. See you later, kids.' She grinned at them and waved them off out of her car.

Tilly squealed and ran towards them as soon as Alice put foot on the path. She was like a little rocket hurtling towards them and Alice bent down and scooped up the flying girl. Jack ran up behind her.

'Jean!' he said. 'You've got bandages on your arms.' His brow knotted. 'Did you get very hurt? Everyone is talking about how you pulled people out, walking right through the flames to do it!'

Jean laughed, then bent over coughing. 'Don't know about the flames, Jack,' she said when she could talk again. 'But there was a fair bit of smoke.'

He looked seriously at her, and Alice had to smile as he kept pace with Jean up the step and into the house. 'People are saying you're a hero.'

'Good grief,' came Jean's reply. 'That's embarrassing.'

Tilly wrapped her arms around Alice's neck and leaned her lips close to her mother's ear. 'Mrs Jones and me, we made cake.' She nodded her golden curls up and down. 'In… in…cewebwation.' She fumbled over the big word.

'Did you really?' Alice asked, hugging her. 'In celebration of what?'

'Jean saving everyone's life.' The little girl's eyes were huge, round, and a very bright blue.

'That's right,' Mrs Jones said, standing at the table and dusting her hands off on her pinny. 'Everyone's talking about it, Alice.' Her gaze slipped from Alice to Jean. 'You're the one, aren't you?' She eyed the bandages. 'They said you got hurt dragging that wastrel out of the fire.'

Jean stood awkwardly, bandaged hands at her side. She gave a one-shouldered shrug. 'I didn't do anything that anyone else wouldn't have.'

'I think there are plenty who would debate that,' Mrs Jones said, then looked at Alice. 'I'll leave you lot to get some rest.' She reached out and patted Alice on the arm. 'There are a few people homeless today. Tilly and I baked a cake for you. I think it's good that we're all looking out for each other.' She gave them all a carefully lipsticked smile, then clomped off down the hallway.

'See, Mama,' Tilly said. 'We made cake.'

'Pot is hot too,' Jean said, turning to smile at Alice. 'What's say we have ourselves a little afternoon tea?'

Alice nodded and deposited Tilly at the table. She fetched cups and plates, milk for the tea and a knife for the cake. It smelt wonderful.

She marvelled over Marjorie's words as she cut them all generous slices of fresh banana cake. Maybe something good had come out of all this after all. But when she looked up and saw Jean's drawn and tired face, she knew it didn't make any difference to them.

She still wanted a safe place for them.

CHAPTER 47

She helped Jean with the buttons on her shirt, undoing them and carefully pulling the sleeves over Jean's bandaged arms.

'Your hair's singed,' she said, feeling terribly sorry.

'It could have been a lot worse,' Jean told her, wrapping her in a hug so that Alice could feel the warmth of her skin through her own dress.

'You could have died.'

'But I didn't,' Jean whispered in her ear. 'Instead I'm just going to have to get a haircut.'

Alice stepped back and looked at Jean, shaking her head. 'You,' she said.

'Me?' Jean smiled.

'Yes you.' Alice pressed a palm against the bones of Jean's chest, feeling for her heartbeat. It was steady and deep under her hand, just like Jean herself. She listened to it echo through her own body for a moment, then looked up at Jean's face. 'I'm taking you to bed.'

She got a slow nod of agreement. 'That sounds quite all right to me.'

'You've had a long day,' Alice said. 'You must be exhausted.' In spite of her words, her hand crept to touch Jean's bare breast.

'Not that exhausted,' Jean said. 'Not really at all, as a matter of fact.'

Alice felt the smile play around her lips and she stepped closer, pressing a kiss to the corner of Jean's lips. 'Oh dear,' she said. 'Look at you – you're not going to be able to use your hands.'

She saw Jean's eyes narrow. 'I can wiggle my fingers.'

'But you can hardly bend your arms.' Her own hand moved down to press against flat stomach, fingertips dipping inside the waistband of Jean's trousers.

There was a baited pause before Jean answered, and her voice was low. 'No,' she said. 'Come to think of it, I don't believe I do have completely free movement.'

Alice shook her head. 'No, my love, I don't believe you do.' She undid buttons and slid trousers down over Jean's hips. 'I believe, actually, you need taking care of.'

The low voice was almost choked. 'I do?'

A kiss pressed to the pulse in Jean's sun-browned neck. How marvellously strong Jean's body was. Alice's hands busied themselves and clothes fell to the floor. 'You do,' Alice agreed, fingers fluttering over the hot skin.

'I think that might be okay,' Jean said. 'But you've got me at an advantage.'

'I realise that,' Alice said, and her lips parted in a smile against Jean's shoulder. 'I think you need to lie down.'

Jean opened her mouth, then simply sat down on the side of the bed.

'No, properly lie down,' Alice said, feeling the hum of desire in her blood, and the thrill of acting on it. She looked down at Jean, at the beloved face, the strong, lean body, and wanted to kiss, to touch, to taste as Jean had done to her. Suddenly, she wanted it more than anything.

'Are you sure you're not too tired?' she asked, checking herself.

Jean shook her head, tucking herself onto the bed, lying down. 'No. Funnily enough, I'm not tired at all.'

That was all she needed. Alice stood in the soft glow of the lamp and reached for her own buttons, watching Jean's eyes fasten on her hands as she slipped them undone one by one. The dress fell from her shoulders and puddled on the floor around her feet. Her slip followed it and she reached around to unclasp her brassiere, dropping it with the rest. She did it all slowly, deliberately, eyes locked on Jean's face, breathing deep and fast.

'Do you like?' she asked shyly.

'You are beautiful,' Jean said.

Her panties joined the rest of her clothes, and she knelt on the bed beside Jean. 'I want to touch you,' she said. 'I want to so very badly.'

Jean's chest rose and fell with her quick breaths, and she gazed up at Alice, nodding.

It was exquisite. Alice closed her eyes, giving herself over to sensation, to the glorious feeling of loving Jean, hot skin under her lips, secret, sweet places under her tongue. She tasted her, and pleasure flooded through her own body, rocking her where she knelt, and when she heard Jean's cry, she was suffused with happiness, emotion swirling behind her eyes in a delirious pleasure of colour. Afterwards, she wanted to do it all over again straight away, but she smiled to herself, tucking her body into Jean's side, knowing they were tired, and that there were going to be so many more days and nights to spend together.

With that thought, she fell asleep listening to the deepening breathing of Jean beside her.

When morning dawned, the first birds stretching and singing outside the window, she woke to find Jean already awake beside her, looking at her.

Sleepily, she smiled. 'What are you doing?' she asked.

'I'm busy,' Jean answered.

Alice shook her head on the pillow. 'Busy doing what?'

'Falling deeper and deeper in love with you.'

Alice looked at her.

'Every day I think I couldn't possibly love you more, and then the sun rises, and it happens anyway.'

A great light, an internal sun, flooded through Alice, and she demanded a kiss. 'I'm so glad,' she said. 'I feel the same way about you.'

The morning pressed against her consciousness, and she looked away from Jean's chocolate-coloured eyes. 'Have you been awake long?' she asked.

'A while,' Jean said. 'I've been lying here thinking.'

'What about?'

'You, us. Where to go.'

Alice propped a hand under her head, and traced Jean's collarbone with a fingertip. 'I'm listening. I'll go wherever you choose.'

Jean captured the fingers and kissed them. 'I was thinking

it needs to be a bigger town than this. So we can just blend in, so there's work to be had.'

'Maybe I can get a sewing machine. I can do alterations for people.'

'Definitely.' Jean stretched, rested a bandaged arm on Alice's hip. 'And if we do well, maybe we can save enough money to one day buy a little piece of land.' She smiled.

'Have some chickens,' Alice said.

'A garden with some good crops.'

'A house cow.' Alice prodded Jean in the shoulder. 'That you can get up and milk every day.'

That got a laugh and Alice felt her heart expand at the sound. 'And a flower garden,' Jean added.

Alice raised her eyebrows. 'A flower garden?'

'Yes,' said Jean. 'I can't help but imagine you in a flower garden. You're wearing a big floppy hat to protect that pretty pale skin from the sun, and you're picking flowers to put in a vase on the kitchen table.' She fell silent and looked at Alice.

Smoothing her hand along Jean's shoulder, Alice nodded. 'I'd love that,' she said softly, lying her head back down on Jean's shoulder, taking care not to bump against her lover's bandaged arms.

Lover, she thought. We are lovers. She listened to Jean's soft breath in her ear and thought of the life together they had ahead of them. It wouldn't matter, she knew, if they got their little bit of land or not. She would love Jean with all her heart wherever they were.

'I'll always put flowers on the table for us,' she whispered and felt Jean nod against her head.

'I know.'

Closing her eyes, Alice let herself relax, drowsing in Jean's warmth.

'Ah sweetheart?' Jean asked a minute later.

'Hmm?'

'I hear ominous sounds from the room next door.'

'Oh.' Alice looked down at herself, at Jean, stretched out together, nude and entwined under the sheet. 'I think I'd better get up.'

'We'd both better. I have nothing on.'

Alice packed a slice of cake in Jack's lunch for him to take to school, and he went off, swinging his satchel, humming to himself, pleased, Alice knew, that he had stories to tell of the hero of the day staying at his house. She hoped it wouldn't start up too much gossip, but then reminded herself that everyone who had been living in that boarding house had to be staying somewhere, probably just like Jean, with friends.

'Shall we go get your car today?' she asked. 'I can drive you in to get those bandages checked.'

'I come too!' Tilly said, standing up on her chair. Alice sat her down again.

Jean nodded. 'I'd like that. I want to see how Cleo is getting on today.'

Alice turned to her. 'I can't believe she was in love with my father.'

'Never stopped, from what I can tell.'

Alice thought about that and sighed. 'Where do you think she'll go? Since the boarding house is no longer.'

'I don't know,' Jean said. 'But knowing her, she will have some scheme in place already.'

Alice nodded, moved on. 'Jean, are you going to be all right to walk to get your car, or shall I just go and get it?'

But Jean didn't get the chance to answer because there was a knock at the front door and Tilly was scrambling down from her chair to run to see who it was. Alice hurried along beside her.

It was a man she only vaguely recognised. He took off his hat when he saw her.

'Mrs Holden,' he said and cleared his throat. 'You might not recognise me, but I'm Will Dempsey, and I heard that Jean Reardon is staying with you after the unfortunate fire of the other night.' He stood, blunt fingers gripping the brim of his hat.

Alice stared at him, realising she'd never met him before, not properly, despite knowing his son so well. She cleared her throat. 'I recognise you,' she said. He looked back at her with blue eyes sunk deep but bright in a creased and worn face. Then the eyes glanced down at Tilly clinging to Alice's skirt, and stared at her before looking up to meet Alice's again.

'Do you mind if I come in, Mrs Holden?' He looked down at Tilly again, then cleared his throat. 'I also have some business I think I need to discuss with you, actually.'

Alice felt the suspicion rise in her like hackles on a dog. His eyes were on Tilly again, and she didn't like the way he was looking at her. Not one little bit. She barked at him.

'You and I have no business to discuss, Mr Dempsey, but considering that your son tried to murder Jean in that fire you just called unfortunate, I'd say there's plenty you need to say to her.'

Even so, it took a long moment before he raised his eyes from the sight of Tilly peeping at him with her own bright blue eyes.

'You're right, of course,' he said, and Alice realised how tired the man looked. Fatigue drew down the corners of his mouth, dragged at the lines around his eyes.

'I'm sorry,' she said. 'This is probably a shock for you too.' She stepped back. 'Come in. Jean is in the kitchen.' She picked up Tilly and led the way, knowing her daughter was hanging over her shoulder looking at Big Jim's father with curious and familiar eyes.

Jean stood up as soon as she saw Alice come back in the room. There was something in those beautiful eyes that made her skin prickle. A shadow she wanted to wave away. Then she saw who it had been at the door.

'Will,' she said, unable to hide the surprise in her voice. 'What are you doing here?'

'Come to see you, Jean,' the old man said heavily. But his eyes went to Alice again, stared at her and Tilly for a moment before finally coming back to seek Jean's own. Jean glanced at Alice and saw how pale she'd gone and understanding flooded through her in a hot rush.

'Came here to talk to you,' he said, then nodded at Alice who was still standing near the doorway, Tilly in her arms. 'Both of you actually, though I don't quite know where to start.'

Jean didn't know what to say. Alice stood frozen, eyes wide and staring, like a deer caught in headlamps. She cleared her throat, nervous, and shook her head.

'I don't think there's anything you need to say, Will,' she told him. 'I've never blamed you for anything Big Jim did. Not before, when you were good enough to employ me, and certainly not now.'

Will Dempsey sighed. 'Do you mind if I sit down, Mrs Holden?' he asked, looking at Alice. 'These bones aren't near as young as they used to be.'

He was older, Jean noticed with dismay. Once a big strong man she'd had to practically trot alongside to keep up with, he was finally losing his bulk, the farm-honed muscles sagging beneath wrinkling skin. But he was obviously still fit enough for his age. Just tired. He looked tired.

'Of course,' Alice said, and Jean couldn't help admiring the way her natural sympathy overcame her fear. 'Please. I'll put Tilly down in her room and make us a pot of tea.'

Will looked about to protest, but he simply sat down at the table instead, and Jean knew he was still mostly his old self when she realised how much bigger the room looked once he'd stopped taking up so much floor space. Alice disappeared into the children's room and Jean heard Tilly protesting.

Will Dempsey cleared his throat. 'I want to apologise for what my son did to you.' He shook his head. 'It's a terrible thing, and I regret that any relative of mine could be capable of it.'

Jean was embarrassed. 'He fell a long way from the tree, Will, you needn't think I hold you in any way responsible. You've always treated me more than fairly. I appreciate the opportunities you gave me during the war and the faith you put in my abilities.'

'Faith that more than paid off,' her former employer said.

'The farm was never more well-managed than when you were in charge.' Another sigh, and a glance at the doorway. 'Which leads me to why I'm here, sort of.'

'Sort of?' Jean raised an eyebrow.

Will Dempsey leaned forward over the table and spoke in a low voice, his face reddening. 'Ah, I'm sorry to have to ask, Jean, and I know it's not really any of my business, but ah...' His voice trailed off, and he sat back, defeated, shaking his head.

'Just ask, Will,' Jean said. 'Whatever it is, can't be that bad.' She cracked a wry smile. 'And when you've asked you can tell me the why of asking.' She paused. 'Since it likely is none of your business.'

'Alice,' he said. 'You...'

'Are very protective of her, yes. She has been through a lot.'

He didn't seem satisfied but sat there tongue-tied and it was Jean's turn to sigh.

'Oh for heaven's sakes, Will, let's just get it all over with, shall we? Alice and I are close. Inseparably so. Is that what you wanted to know?' She laid her white-wrapped hands on the table and wished the conversation over with. 'You're right, it is none of your business.'

But Will Dempsey was staring at the little slice of hallway he could see from his chair. When he looked back at Jean, his brow was a deep furrow. 'It changes things,' he said.

She shook her head. 'It doesn't.' She blinked. 'Not that I even know what you're talking about, so perhaps we could start at the beginning?'

'I was going to offer you your old job back,' he said.

There was a sudden lightness behind Jean's eyes. She flattened her hands on the scuffed table. 'You were what?'

'To make up for the terrible wrong my son has done to you.'

'You were going to give me my old job back?'

'Yes. Everyone has been bothering me to get you back anyway. Reckon working under you was a far sweeter thing than dealing with Jim.' His eyes twinkled for a moment. 'Old Jamie in particular seems to think the sun rises and sets out of your arse.'

'It does,' Jean said shortly. But her mind was whirring. She looked over at Alice, back in the room minus her daughter. 'But?' she prompted.

The old man shifted in the chair and turned his attention to Alice, standing with arms folded over her breast.

He spoke to Alice. 'I received a telephone call from your mother last night.'

Alice's eyes widened, and Jean saw her turn another shade paler. 'Perhaps you ought to sit down, Alice,' Jean said softly, and Alice slid down on a chair as though her legs had given out.

Clearing his throat again, Will tapped his big fingers against his knees. 'She...she told me my son had fathered a child with you.' He blinked his blue eyes at her. 'She said I have a grandchild. A granddaughter.'

Alice's mouth was slack with shock, and her hand flew to cover it. 'She did what?' she asked and shook her head. 'She had no right!'

'Is it true, Alice? Do I have a baby granddaughter?'

But Alice was shaking her head even more wildly.

'I saw,' he said, trying again. 'I saw her when we came in.

She has my mother's eyes.' He looked at Jean, then back at herself. 'My eyes. My son's eyes.'

Alice had her face in her hands, and Jean wanted to go to her, hold her. She stayed where she was, however, wary of making things worse. She also said nothing. It wasn't her place, to stop the conversation, or to add to it.

But Alice lifted her head and looked at her with wet, red eyes. 'You tell him, Jean,' she said. 'Please? I…I can't. Tell him the truth.'

Jean stared at her for a long moment, but Alice dipped her head back into her hands, and Jean was left to look across the table at the man sitting there, hands in his lap, the look on his face a mixture of pain and hopefulness.

'Your son forced himself on Alice,' she said, and the words fell onto Will Dempsey's shoulders like heavy stones. She watched him sag under the weight of them.

'I was married!' Alice said, lifting a tear-stained face. 'I never encouraged him.'

Will shook his head, heavy, ponderous, and he rubbed a hand over his own face, scraping against the grey bristle.

'I'm so sorry,' he said. 'For what my son did. He wronged you terribly.'

Alice hugged herself for a moment, then straightened, wiping away her tears. 'I've never told the children,' she said. 'They both think Terry is Tilly's father, and that's the way it has to stay.' Jean saw her look, defiant and resolute.

Will nodded. 'I completely understand.' He looked toward the hallway, where Tilly was in her room with the door closed. 'She's beautiful,' he said. 'You must be very proud. She looks very heathy.'

'I love my children, Mr Dempsey,' Alice said with a grave

dignity that made Jean's heart melt for her. 'Both of them, no matter how they were conceived.'

'Then you are an admirable woman, Alice Holden,' Will replied. 'And I thank you for it.' But he sighed, placed a great shovel-shaped hand on the table and tapped his fingers.

Jean watched without saying anything, although in the back of her mind strings of words were trying to make themselves into some sort of order. Will Dempsey had come to offer her a job. Her old job.

She realised she wanted it with a desire that almost made her sick.

Of course, it wouldn't work, either. Old Will Dempsey was right. Her friendship with Alice changed things.

But he was talking again, looking from one of them to the other.

'I came here for two reasons,' he said. 'Besides to give you my apologies for the behaviour of my son.' His gaze settled on Jean. 'I wanted to ask if you'd come work for me again.' He looked at Alice. 'And if what your mother told me turned out to be true, I wanted to ask if you and your children would come share the farmhouse with me. It's big enough for all of us, we'd hardly ever cross paths, unless you wanted to.' Jean saw his throat move as he swallowed and felt Alice's shock from where she sat.

'I know you've not been in the most fortunate position since your husband died,' Will continued. 'And a farm's a great place to bring up children.' He looked momentarily abashed, as if realising it hadn't done anything for his own son. 'You could have said you were working for me, if you didn't want the truth of the situation known, I had nothing banked on that...'

'But now it's different,' Jean said.

The old man's face darkened, with embarrassment rather than anger.

'Because you can't have Alice and I living together under your roof.' Jean took a slow breath in, let it out. Dempsey shook his head.

'No. That would not be possible.'

'Jean and I are leaving town,' Alice said abruptly. 'We need a fresh start, somewhere we can go unnoticed.' She looked around the room. 'Why did my mother call and tell you?'

'That she did not say, I'm afraid.'

Alice shook her head. 'It makes no sense.'

'She only said I needed to do my duty where my son wouldn't.' He looked intently at Alice. 'And I intend to.'

Jean saw his shoulders relax.

'I think I have a solution,' he said, and smiled, the lines around his eyes crinkling. Nodding his head, he said slowly, as if making up his mind to something, 'yes indeed. I think I have the perfect solution. For all of us.'

Jean looked at Alice, then leaned forward and listened.

CHAPTER 49

'Whoa, little one, hold your horses!' Jean tried to get a grip on the squirming child, but Tilly had the strength – and slipperiness – of an eel.

'Don't have any horses, Jean!' yelled Tilly. 'So I can't hold 'em.'

In the face of such inescapable logic, Jean gave up trying to thread little arms into the cardigan. 'Fine,' she said. 'You win – but we're going to take this with us, okay? It might get cold later.'

Tilly scampered from the room hooting and hollering. Jean turned wide eyes to the child's brother. 'She always like this?'

He shook his head with the world-weariness of an eight-year-old who's seen it all. 'You better get used to it.' Then he tipped his chin at her and moved a little closer. 'Jean?'

'Yeah?'

'Do you really think I'll get to ride a horse?'

Jean bent to shove her feet in her boots and tie the laces. 'I don't just think it, kiddo, I know it for a fact.' She looked up and winked at him. 'That good?'

He nodded, face breaking into a beaming smile. 'Yeah! I can play cowboys and Indians!'

'Buddy, you're going to be a real cowboy by the time I've finished with you. You'll be mustering the sheep single-handed by the time you're ten years old.'

His eyes shone at her and she stood up, stretched, then ruffled his hair. 'Go see if your Mum is ready.'

He rolled his eyes. 'She's trying to decide what colour lipstick goes with her dress.'

'And whatever colour she chooses is going to be real pretty, so we'll be happy to wait.'

Jack looked dubious even so. 'You don't wear lipstick,' he said.

'I'm not pretty like your Mum.' She grinned and looked around for her hat. It was sitting on her old pal the chair losing its stuffing. She jammed it on her head. 'This is far more my style.'

Jack grinned at her. 'I want a hat just like yours.'

'Well maybe they sell them at the fair. We'll have a look. Every lad needs a hat like this, don't you say?'

He nodded. 'And sometimes ladies too.'

'Yeah,' she agreed, herding him towards the door. 'Some of us ladies too. Now let's get us to that fair.'

With a whoop just as loud as the one his sister had done, Jack raced down the hallway and out to the car. Jean stuck her head in the bedroom and whistled.

'You are the most beautiful woman I've ever seen, Alice Holden,' she said.

With a bright red smile, Alice twirled around for her. 'You

think so? You don't think this is too much?' Her face fell. 'It's too much, isn't it? I should never have let you buy it for me.'

Jean stepped into the room, snatched Alice up by the waist and planted a kiss on her cheek so that she didn't smear the lipstick.

'You are absolutely gorgeous,' she said. 'There's no denying it – and the dress is a real treat. I'm going to spend today sneaking looks at you and thanking my lucky stars.'

Alice leaned back in her arms and beamed. 'You're a complete charmer, Jean Reardon.'

Letting go of Alice, Jean shrugged modestly. 'I do my best.' She moved to the doorway. 'Kids are in the car already. Jack wants a hat like mine, and Tilly wants me to win her a teddy bear bigger than her.' She smiled at the children pressing themselves against the window of the car waiting for them. 'I'd say I have my work cut out for me, wouldn't you?'

Alice, purse in hand, sashayed past, giving her an arch look. 'And what about me?' she teased. 'What are you going to win for me at the fair?'

Jean watched the swaying hips with a great deal of appreciation and pulled the front door closed behind them. They were all set, a picnic lunch packed in the car, drinks and food for everyone, and the sun was shining down on them like it meant to stay all day. She couldn't have asked for better.

'I'm going to win you the world, Alice Holden,' she said. 'The whole damned world.'

Everybody was at the fair, or so it seemed to Jean. They made their way into the middle of things, Jean walking with her hands shoved deep in her pockets so that she wouldn't reach out and take Alice's hand. Jack waved frantically at a bunch of his school friends, and she gave him a handful of pennies then grinned at Alice when he bolted like a rabbit with the farmer's dog after him.

'Marvellous day for it, isn't it?' she said.

Alice nodded, then spoke out of the corner of her mouth. 'People are looking at us. Do you think they can tell?'

Jean put on her most innocent look. 'Tell what?'

With a glance down at Tilly walking beside her looking in amazement at all the people, Alice edged a little closer, a mischievous smile twitching her lips. 'That last night you teased me with your tongue until I was almost screaming.'

'Almost? I seem to remember having to put the pillow over your face.' Jean grinned at Alice beside her. 'But to answer your question, they'll be able to tell something is up, considering you've gone beet red.'

Alice rolled her eyes, then stared at her for a lingering moment that said she wanted to lean over and press those red lips of hers to Jean's, to whisper words of love in her ear. Then she scooped up Tilly.

'Can you do without us for a while? I'm going to go do my stint with Martha and the girls at the jumble table.'

Jean waved a hand. 'Be my guest.' She smiled widely, and Alice narrowed her eyes at her.

'What will you be doing?'

'I'm thinking there's a cold beer in the tent over there that has my name on it.'

Alice laughed. 'I'm so happy,' she said suddenly, her face glowing. 'Tell me it's all true, Jean.'

'It's all true, Alice. I promise.'

'We're really going?'

'Really truly.'

'We're going to have chickens?'

'And a garden, and a house cow.'

Alice beamed. 'And you're going to have a tractor.'

'Sure am. Will Dempsey said he was getting a brand-new Fergusson delivered.'

'I want to kiss you.'

'And I you.' She slipped her hands deliberately back into her pockets. 'Away with you now. Those ladies will be waiting.'

Alice nodded, and moved off into the crowd, Tilly on her hip, little hand pointing out all the sights. Jean turned with a sigh of satisfaction and set her feet in the direction of the refreshments tent. And not the one serving tea and crumpets.

'Jean. Bit of a turnout, wouldn't you say?'

She turned at the sound of the voice and a smile spread from ear to ear. 'Jamie, you old sod, how the hell are you?'

'Never better, Jean.' He stuck out his hand and Jean shook it happily. 'I heard the news.'

'Excellent. What do you reckon? You game to come?'

The old man nodded. 'Bit of a change at my time of life, but I got nothing holding me here anyway, and I hear the farming is good down south.'

They walked side by side, heading for the tent. 'Be a fair bit colder down there,' Jean said.

Jamie shrugged. 'I'm so old my skin's turned to cowhide anyway. Don't make any difference to me.'

She laughed at that and held the tent flap open for both of them to duck through into the dimness. 'Let me buy you a drink, Jamie – in celebration. We're going to make a grand team.'

With an appreciative sniff, Will's old farmhand made his

way to a vacant table, while Jean went in the opposite direction to the makeshift bar.

'Hey Jean,' the young man behind the counter said. 'What'll it be?'

She widened her eyes. 'Boyd? That you?'

'Sure as shit,' he said. 'We've got beer and that's about all.'

'Two pints, for Jamie and me, and one for your own good self.' She leaned against the planking. 'How's life treating you?'

He shrugged. 'Can't complain. Sandra's going to have another baby.'

'Congratulations! That's your second, isn't it?'

He shook his head, siphoning the beer from keg to glass with the finesse of someone born to the task. 'Nope. You been gone too long, Jean. This one will be number three.'

'Shit.'

He slid the two glasses across in front of her, took her money, and poured himself one. 'Cheers.'

She held hers up. 'Cheers yourself.'

Boyd drank, then gave her a considering look. 'Mr Dempsey said you were looking for a crew to take down South with you.'

She nodded. 'Yeah. Interested?'

He shook his head. 'Nah, Sandra would skin me alive if I took her away from her family and everything. Besides, I'm making good at the farm now you're not there.' He gave her a wink. 'Young Eddie might be a good pick for you though.'

'Eddie?' She screwed up her face, trying to place the name.

'Didn't think he'd amount to much when he came back from the war, but he's coming along nicely. Has a real way with horses. All the animals, come to think of it.'

Jean shook her head. 'Why don't you want him then?'

'I got my cousin coming up from the Manawatu district. Promised him a job.' He leaned forward over the bar and spoke confidentially. 'Honestly though, Eddie will do you fine.'

'No attitude I could do without?'

Boyd laughed and stood up again, picked up his glass. 'Nope. That boy lives for the animals. Taking orders from a Sheila wouldn't bother him a bit.'

'Excellent.' Jean said. 'I'll drive up and have a word with him. Cheers, Boyd.'

'No worries, Jean. Good idea of yours – moving south.' He paused. 'Leaving town.'

Jean felt the familiar wariness creep through her veins. 'What makes you say so?'

Behind the bar, Boyd flexed his muscular shoulders in a shrug. 'What happened at the boarding house.'

She narrowed her eyes at him. 'That a question or a statement.'

'Statement.' He leaned forward, propping himself against the plank counter. 'People calling you a hero for dragging that sorry sack of shit outta there, and Mrs Boone, of course.'

'But?'

'But there's also a lotta talk about why Big Jim was lurking there with a can of gasoline in the first place, if you get my drift.'

Jean sighed. 'I get your drift.'

'Not that it's anyone's business, but you know how people are.' He straightened and picked up a glass, started cleaning it.

With a nod, Jean glanced around the rest of the room. 'No,' she said. 'It's not anyone's business. Alice and I are friends. It happens. It's certainly not my fault Big Jim got some imaginary bee in his bonnet.'

'The man's a lunatic. Always has been.' Boyd put the glass back with the others. 'Most everyone thinks that's the relevant fact, but you know how it is. Once the shock wears off, there might be more chatter.' He looked at her. 'Going to work out every way you look at it, really. That's a sweet offer Old Dempsey gave you.'

'Yeah, he was feeling pretty bad about Jim.' She shrugged. 'Plus, you know – I'm the best.' With a wink, she picked up the two drinks and turned.

Threading her way through the tables, she nodded greetings at the men there. Most tipped their glasses to her but a few, she noticed, already had a speculative gleam to their eyes. She pretended not to notice. Most of the men in the tent – and it was all men – were people she knew, and most of those ones were people she liked. She could count on that for a while longer at least.

But Jamie was looking towards the entrance when she got to their table, consternation on his face. 'Uh oh, Jean,' he said. 'Here comes trouble.'

She put the glasses down and turned to see what the fuss was. 'Oh God, where did he come from?'

'Dunno, lass, but if I were you, I'd be ducking out the back.'

'It's a tent, Jamie. There is no back.'

He shrugged and picked up his glass, draining half of it. 'You know who he's looking for.' It was said as a statement.

Jean knew just fine. All around her, the men had fallen silent, and Boyd was stepping out from behind his bar, flexing the big muscles in his shoulders, ready for trouble. She watched him start talking, his voice just a low murmur.

Big Jim was shaking his head, and Jean could still see the white of bandages sticking out under his clothes. Her own arms were still bandaged, but she'd been downgraded just the day before to gauze plasters under her shirt.

He pointed suddenly at her. 'Jean, you bitch. I got things to say to you!' There was no trouble hearing him across the room.

She sighed, looked at Jamie with her eyebrows raised. He shrugged, tipped his glass to her, then drained it. She looked regretfully at her own, then turned and made her way between the tables toward Big Jim. Behind her, men got up from their own tables and crowded at her back.

'Jim,' she said. 'I don't want any trouble.'

'Fuck you,' he spat. 'I should have killed you while I had the chance.'

'I believe you tried,' Jean said, folding her arms over her chest. Then she sighed. 'Let's take this outside, shall we? These good people are trying to enjoy their beer.'

Boyd grabbed him by the forearm and attempted to hustle him out through the flap. Big Jim yelped at the touch, then went with him, calling back at her.

'Outside,' he ordered her. 'I got things to say.'

How glad she was that Alice wasn't with her. With a little bit of luck, Alice wouldn't even hear Big Jim was here. She stepped out into the sunlight, blinking. Jim was waiting for her, fists clenched at his sides.

'All right, you pervert bitch, tell me what the fuck you think you're doing?'

She crossed her arms again, squinting at him in the sun.

'Well, Big Jim, I was trying to enjoy a quiet drink with the fellas here.'

There was a titter of laughter behind her.

'Jim,' someone yelled from the crowd. 'What you doing out of jail anyway, you sonofabitch?'

She watched him glower at the men she knew stood behind her. 'I didn't come from jail. I've been in hospital.'

'Where you been drinking the floor polish, from the stink of ya,' another someone yelled.

He stood there and shook a fist. 'This woman has stolen everything of mine,' he said. 'And now I hear she's taken my job!' He looked straight at Jean.

'That was supposed to be my job,' he said, voice a growling howl of fury. 'And my father goes and gives it to you!'

She shook her head. 'You don't want to move to the South Island, Jim. You never did. And your father was never going to give you that job. You'd already messed up the one you had here working right under his nose.'

Someone laughed. 'What you talking about anyway, Jim? Only place you're going is to jail. Arson and attempted murder, remember? For having a go at killing Jean here.'

Another man spoke up. 'Even that you fucked up though. Wasn't for her, you'd be crispy in your own fire.'

From the back of the crowd. 'Thanks to you I've lost everything. Have to stay with my goddamned sister.' The crowd grumbled.

Big Jim ignored them all, eyes staring straight at Jean instead. She held her ground under their gaze, aware of the weight of men at her back. None of them were happy with Big Jim Dempsey, and for now they were pleased to place all the blame on him. She only had to keep him ranting for a little longer until the constable turned up.

There was a crowd gathering behind Jim too now, and Jean scanned it rapidly, not seeing Alice there, but catching a glimpse of several young boys, one of them with suspiciously sandy hair. She winced, then focused again on the man waving a meaty fist at her.

'That was my job whether I wanted to take it or not!' he yelled at her. 'I'm sick to death of you.'

She prayed he wasn't going to bring up Alice. Not in front of the whole town.

'You have no right taking good work from a man.' Jim staggered slightly, and she realised the earlier comment was right – the man was drunk on his feet. 'You took my job, my own father thinks the sun shines out of your arse, and you took my goddamned wo...'

'Make way, folks, gotta get this old gal in place.'

Jean blinked, not quite believing what she was seeing when the crowd parted to let Jamie through.

He was towing a large black and white cow, a wicked grin on his face.

'Come on folks, Daisy ain't gonna hang onto her load much longer. Woulda bin here sooner but had to make sure she was fed up full with the good stuff.'

Jean gaped at him, along with the rest of the crowd. She risked a glance at Big Jim, but he was standing in his spot, swaying slightly, lips still parted on the last word he'd been about to say. Jean could have kissed old Jamie. Just when Jim had been about to publicly proclaim her relationship with Alice, along he'd come.

With a cow. She frowned. 'What the hell are you doing, Jamie?' she asked. The crowd whooped behind her.

He cocked his head at her and scratched his ear as though confused about her question.

'Why, Jean, don't you remember?' he asked. 'The last time you and Big Jim here got into it? The day he fired you from working his old man's farm?'

A smile tweaked her lips. Yeah. She remembered. But she shook her head and Jamie rolled his bloodshot old eyes.

'Let me get Buttercup here into position,' he said. 'We can discuss the particulars of your faulty memory later.' He dragged the cow forward a few steps, made a pantomime of looking from cow to Big Jim and back again. He tugged her a few more paces and scratched his head again.

'There,' he sniffed. 'Reckon that's about right.'

Big Jim bellowed at him. 'What are you doing, old man? Get the fuck out of the way. I'm talking to her.'

Jamie nodded, face solemn. The crowd was silent, holding itself still for the punchline it sensed was coming.

'Why Jim, keep your hair on,' Jamie said, and swung an arm to slap the cow on the side of her rump. She turned a startled head toward him and gave a long, plaintive moo, and then she lifted her tail and dropped a fresh, steaming cow pat onto the grass.

'There,' Jamie said with a satisfied nod of the head. 'Perfect, wouldn't you say, Big Jim? Just the right place, I'm thinking.'

'What the fuck are you on about?'

'Well now,' Jamie said, and now Jean struggled to keep the smile from her lips, listening to him, knowing what was coming next. The old man had always enjoyed a good practical joke.

'Thing is,' he said. 'The last time you lost your temper with Jean here, you took a mighty big swing at her.' He paused, giving his audience a chance for that to sink in.

'Only Jean here might be smaller and lighter than you, but she's a lot smarter, and a lot quicker on her feet.' He sniffed, drawing the moment out, then spat on the grass and grinned.

'Oh she sidestepped you neatly as anything! And did you go flying? Yes, you did – and did you land face down in a big ol' pile of shit? Why yes you did!'

He tugged on the cow's rope halter and led her out of the way. 'So you see, I'm just lining everything up, since it was such a fine show last time.'

The crowd erupted in laughter around her, hooting and whistling while Jim Dempsey stood in the middle of the ring, hands fisted, face red.

'I'd pay my good beer money to see that,' someone called. 'Come on Big Jim, take a swing, I dare ya!'

'That's enough, everyone,' a man said, stepping up to Jim and clamping a hand on his shoulder. It was the constable, and Jean saw he was trying very hard not to laugh with everyone else. 'Back to the hospital with you, Jim, and this time I'm going to recommend the crazy ward.'

Jim's face was contorted into a look of pure hatred, but he went along with the constable, only peering back over his shoulder at Jean once, before dropping his gaze to the ground and being led off, the sound of laughter echoing after him.

Jean closed her eyes and felt the sun on her face, breathed in the sweet stench of beer, spring grass, and fresh cow dung.

It was a blessed mix.

CHAPTER 50

*A*lice was a bundle of nerves. She looked across the room, where Jean, her bandages completely gone now, skin pink and shiny where the burns had healed, was brushing her hair back from her face before bending to pick up the last suitcase.

Maybe she felt Alice's gaze, because she looked up and smiled, eyes crinkling, lips widening in a smile that made Alice feel better there and then.

'Are you ready?' Jean asked, and for a moment Alice couldn't bring herself to reply. Her mouth was too dry. She nodded, and Jean put the suitcase back down, came over to where Alice stood by the old coal range, out now, the ash cleared out, every surface scoured clean. A moment later, Jean's arms were around her, and Alice felt her warm hair against her cheek.

'It's okay to be a little sad,' she said.

Alice's nod was muffled. 'I'm not sad,' she said. 'Not really.' She stood up and looked at Jean's dark eyes. 'It's just that this was home for so long.' A glance around the room. 'So many memories. The children…'

'Grew up here. That's precious.'

'Yes,' Alice agreed, and smiled. 'It is precious.' She took a deep breath and nodded, firmly this time. 'I'm ready.'

'We'll make new memories.'

'Better ones,' Alice said. 'Wonderful ones.' She stepped out of Jean's embrace and leaned over for one last look out the window. 'I still can't believe it, you know.'

'I know.'

'A whole high-country station to run?' She shook her head, seeing the sun catch the water in the pond, but thinking of the photographs of the lake Will Dempsey had shown them, mountains at its rim, everything so glorious, and in their new back yard. She turned to face Jean. 'It's the perfect solution.'

Jean nodded. 'Will was very generous.'

'Oh, but it will pay off for him – you'll run the place perfectly.' She giggled. 'And with me there as cook and house-keeper, everything will run smoothly.'

'And we can be together.'

'Yes,' Alice said, stepping back into Jean's arms. 'And we can be together.'

Jack clattered into the kitchen. He stood there wide-eyed, staring at his mother.

'Jack, what is it?' Alice was already moving towards him.

'It's Grandma,' he said, and pointed back the way he'd come. 'She's outside.'

A sudden chill wound its way under Alice's skin and she glanced back at Jean, then, pressing a hand to her chest, walked down the hallway and out onto the front path.

'Mother,' she said. 'What are you doing here?'

Her mother stood in her best coat and hat, Tilly in her arms looking like she was about to resort to biting and scratching to get down. Alice reached over and plucked the child from her mother, set her on the ground.

'Jack,' she said. 'Can you take Tilly inside, please?'

He did as she asked, and she turned to her mother. 'What do you want, Mother?'

'I'd prefer to have this conversation inside, Alice,' her mother said.

She shook her head. 'No. Just say whatever it is you came to and then go.'

Her mother frowned at her for a moment, and Alice simply looked away. Sally and Mrs McMurtry looked back at her from the car parked on side of the road.

'Will Dempsey told me what he'd done for you.'

She shifted her gaze back to the woman in front of her and said nothing.

'I telephoned him, you know.'

She did know. Will Dempsey had recalled the conversation for her. The only thing he'd been unable to tell her was why her mother had done it.

'He told me,' she conceded. 'But I don't understand why you did it, Mother.'

'If I'd known he was going to send you away to the other end of the country, I wouldn't have.'

'I'm glad to go.' Alice was cold, despite the sun on her head. She should have been warm, but touching her fingers to each other, they were icy, bloodless.

But her mother was talking, as though Alice hadn't said anything. 'I told him about his granddaughter so that he would do his duty by you. I knew he would take you in, give you a respectable home.'

'His son forced himself on me, Mother, how would that have made anything respectable?'

'You would have been better off than living here.'

Alice had had just about enough. 'I could have lived somewhere better than here, with some real help from you.'

But her mother was shaking her head. 'I've been trying to help you. But you – you never would do anything the right way. Always had to follow a whim.'

Alice closed her eyes. 'Did you come here for any particular reason, Mother, or just to remind me why I'm so happy to leave this town?' She looked at her mother.

For a moment, her mother's face crumpled, and Alice saw the age and pain in it. The stubborn dissatisfaction with the world that had only succeeded in pushing everyone away.

'I came to tell you that I would miss you,' Geraldine said, her voice wooden.

It was hard to believe she'd heard her properly. 'You'll what?' asked Alice.

'Miss you. And the children.' Her mother met her eyes. 'I always tried to do right by you, you know.'

Alice sighed, putting her hands on her hips. She felt rather than saw movement in the doorway, and twisting slightly, she saw Jean there, checking on her. She turned back to her mother.

'Why couldn't you have accepted me as I was?' she asked, for one last, desperate time.

Her mother shook her head. 'Because I am as stubborn as you are, my dear.' She took a step forward. 'May I at least say good bye properly?'

'Since all your dreadful schemes have backfired and now you're losing me and your grandchildren all together?'

Geraldine stared at her. 'Quite,' she said. 'I tried, and I lost.'

Alice looked at her, holding her breath. This was going to be the last time she saw her mother. Biting her lip, she stepped forward and put her arms around the woman standing stiff and straight on the broken path.

'Perhaps you should just have tried love, Mother,' she whispered in the woman's ear. 'It's the simplest thing.'

She stepped back and her mother looked at her. 'Goodbye Mother.'

Geraldine met her eyes, then nodded, turned around and walked away. Mrs McMurtry, averting her eyes from Alice, opened the car door and helped her mother in. Sally gave her a sad smile, and a little later, the car was gone.

'That was odd,' Jean said, coming up behind Alice where she stood still gazing off down the street. 'What do you think that was about?'

It took a while for Alice to decide. 'I think she came to say sorry,' she said.

'I wish she didn't have so much to be sorry for.' Jean touched a hand to her arm, and Alice covered it with her own and nodded.

'Still,' Alice said. 'I think I'll write to her when we're settled. Keep in touch a little.' She gazed at Jean whose face dissolved in a smile.

'You have the kindest heart, Alice,' Jean said.

CHAPTER 51

Alice sighed and smoothed down her wrinkled dress. They'd been travelling for so many hours she'd lost count.

'Where are we now?' she asked, blinking out of the train window at the station.

'Mama? We there now?' Tilly, curled up in the nest Alice had made of her coat for her, peered up at her, rubbing her eyes.

Alice looked to Jean. 'This is it?'

'This is it. Come on, Jack lad, let's start unloading our bags.' She turned and lifted their things down from the shelf above their heads.

'How long is it from here, Jean?' Jack asked, picking up a bag and lugging it to the door.

'I'm not sure,' Jean said. 'Maybe two hours?'

Two hours. Alice would be the gladdest she'd ever been when they finally arrived. She wanted a long, hot bath, a strong, hot cup of tea, and she wanted both of them at the same time. Then she wanted a soft bed and she wanted to stay in it at least a week.

Outside, standing on the platform, Alice hefted Tilly in her arms, and looked with tired interest at Jean speaking earnestly to a young man. A smile plied her lips as she watched. Jean was tireless, she decided. The whole trip, she'd kept calm, dealing with everything with good-natured humour.

They would have separate bedrooms in their new house, Alice knew that, but she was looking forward to sharing a bed again with Jean. They'd had to stay in separate rooms in the couple hotels on the way down, and she found herself looking at Jean now, longing to stretch out against that lean, warm body, basking in simply being close.

Jean turned, saw her looking, and gave her a tired grin, walking over to where Alice stood with the children.

'Another boat ride,' she said.

'What?'

'Yep. We're taking a steamer from here, going up the lake. Glenorchy is right at the tip of the lake, so everything goes by boat.' Her smile widened. 'The guys from the farm – station – are here, and guess what for?'

'Us?' Alice said.

'Besides us.' Jean was as excited as a kid, rubbing her hands together in glee.

Alice laughed, despite her fatigue. 'You'd better tell.'

'My tractor!' Jean's eyes were wide with delight.

'Where is it?' Jack said, frowning and looking around as if it was right there.

'It's being loaded onto the steamer right now,' Jean said.

'On the boat?'

'Yes, along with 200 sheep.'

'Good grief.' Alice felt a stirring of her own excitement. 'This really is happening, isn't it?'

'It really is.' Jean stared at her, smiling widely and Alice could feel her desire to wrap her arms around her in an exuberant hug. Coming here, she thought, had been exactly the right decision. And she sent a little prayer of thanks to Will Dempsey, who was determined to do what he could to support the granddaughter he hadn't even known about.

'Where's the boat, Jean?' Tilly asked. 'I wanna go to our new home.'

'We're going there now,' Jean said, and she practically danced a jig before looking at Alice. 'Okay,' she said. 'I can't keep the secret any longer.'

'What secret?' Alice was instantly alarmed, despite the grin on Jean's face.

Jean ticked off a list of items on her fingers. 'Tractor, sheep, household goods, sewing machine...'

'Sewing machine!' Alice was suddenly giddy. 'What?'

Jean slipped an arm under her elbow and tugged her along the platform. 'These guys are going to bring our bags. I'll introduce you when we're on the boat.'

'Hang on, Jean Reardon,' Alice said. 'What's this about a sewing machine?'

There was a happy flush on Jean's cheeks. 'Well, I know you don't need a job anymore, but since you like to sew, I had a word with Dempsey when we were going over the list of things we'd need at the new place...'

'And you convinced him to include a sewing machine?'

'Well, he didn't take much in the way of convincing.'

Alice's mind was racing. 'What about fabric?'

'Our good steamship here, the SS Earnslaw, tootles up and down the lake every week. You can buy everything you need here in Queenstown.' She got them moving again. 'But right now, let's get on board and go home, what do you reckon?'

Alice was practically walking on air. Her tiredness forgotten, she herded Jack onto the ship and stood there on the deck gazing around at the mountains rising up from the lake.

'I've never really seen anything like it,' Jean said, coming back to stand next to her so that Alice could feel her warmth beside her.

She shook her head. 'I thought I'd miss the beach, but this…I think this might just more than make up for it.' She turned a full circle. 'It's like being in a painting. There's still snow on some of them.'

'They're beauties, all right.'

'I feel like I've landed in some magical world.'

It was a feeling that stayed with her the whole trip up the lake, the ship's big paddle wheel turning, the boat surging forward towards the hidden head of the lake. Still dazed when they off-loaded, she found herself clinging to the children's hands, surrounded by sheep, dogs, men on horses, and there somewhere in the midst of it, Jean's new tractor. She didn't know which way to turn.

'This way,' Jean said. 'The guys are going to drive the sheep to the station.'

'Drive?'

'Not in cars, Mum,' Jack piped up. 'Right, Jean? They're going to ride the horses, and the dogs will herd the sheep.'

Jean ruffled his hair. 'Got it in one, kid.'

Jack looked around, impressed. 'So you really weren't kidding when you said about the horses.'

That made Jean laugh. 'I really wasn't kidding. You'll be riding a horse within a week.'

'What about me?' Tilly said, peeping out at all the sheep streaming off the boat.

'A nice little pony for you.'

'I want a donkey.' Tilly blinked. 'And a goat. A baby goat.'

'You got it.' Jean turned them away from the boat and over to a car. 'This is our ride,' she said.

'Who's driving us?' Jack asked.

'Me,' said Jean.

Alice allowed herself to be ushered into the front seat. Tilly went in the back next to her brother. 'How do you know the way?'

Jean laughed. 'I'm good at asking for directions.'

Twisting around in her seat, Alice looked back at the milling men on horses and getting into trucks. 'Do they all work at the station?' she asked, thinking of the meals she'd have to cook.

'Nope,' Jean said. 'Two of them do, but the rest are our neighbours, come to help the big move.'

'That's nice of them,' Jack said.

'Sure is. Now, are we ready?'

Alice was more than ready. Sliding a hand across the seat, she placed it on Jean's warm thigh, relishing the heat and nearness of it. Jean looked at her and smiled.

I love you, she mouthed.

The road wound up and around the lake, took off cross-country and Alice could hardly catch her breath.

'It's stunning here,' she gasped. 'All these mountains, and the forest…'

Jean sighed happily beside her. 'They don't call it the Gateway to Paradise, for nothing.' She smiled. 'In fact, our little place is right next to a big station called Arcadia Station, in an area that actually is called Paradise.'

'That is absolutely perfect,' Alice said, and wanted to scoot over to rest her head on Jean's shoulder. Instead, she turned around and smiled at the children. They were on their knees, each looking out a window, eyes wide and excited.

'Here we are,' Jean said, turning onto a bumping road and putting the car in a lower gear. 'This is our new home.' She pulled to a stop and switched the motor off.

For a moment, there was only the sound of the engine ticking as it cooled in the high-country air. Then every car door opened at once, and Alice scrambled out after the others to stand in awe.

'This is our place?' she asked, shaking her head. 'Surely not!'

Jean came around and put an arm around her shoulder, hugging her against her as they stared up at the house.

'Welcome home,' she said in a low, choking voice.

Alice couldn't stop shaking her head. 'This can't be it.'

'It is.'

'Mama, can we go inside?' Tilly was bouncing up and down.

There were tears in Alice's eyes. She left them there, nodding at her daughter. 'Yes,' she said, and both children took off at a run for the front door.

'It's the size of my mother's house,' she said.

'Might be,' Jean agreed. 'Plenty of room for everyone.' She

swept a hand at the trees at the end of the lawn. 'Behind there should be the worker's huts, and a couple barns, but there's another road that goes to them, so we have complete privacy.'

Alice turned around. 'You can see the lake from here.'

'And there's another one not far from here.'

'Another what?'

'Lake.' Jean tugged on Alice until she was looking at her. 'What do you think?'

It took a moment for Alice to decide what she wanted to say first. Joy bubbled up inside her, an irrepressible spring.

'I think, Jean,' she said, 'that this is the best day of my life.' She paused. 'Or I would think that if I weren't completely sure that tomorrow will be even better – and the day after and the day after that!'

Tilly came tumbling out of the house. 'Mama! Jean!' she yelled from the porch. 'I chosen my room!'

Alice smiled at the sight of her daughter, her blonde curls bouncing as the child jumped up and down, blue eyes shining, before she twirled about and vanished back into the house again. She turned to Jean.

'I love you more than anything,' she said, cupping her hands around Jean's face and looking into the cocoa-coloured eyes she'd first fallen in love with when the woman they belonged to delivered her milk every morning. 'I love you so much and so well, you make me happier than anything.'

Jean closed her dark eyes for a moment, and when she opened them, her arms slid around Alice's waist.

'Oh Alice,' she said. 'You are a dream come true.'

Alice kissed her then, and it was long and sweet, and she didn't want it to ever end. But when it did, everything was okay, because there were plenty more where it had come from.

There was also a house, and a farm. Chickens and a garden, a house cow and a tractor. Just as they'd dreamed.

There were the children, with enough to eat, and with people who would take care of them. Security, just as she'd needed so badly.

And there was Jean.

Alice looked at her, at the face she loved so much, the lips always so ready to curve into a smile or a kiss, the eyes that seemed to warm and glow just looking at her.

There was Jean, and they were home.

* * *

The End.

Lily Hammond is the historical romance penname of Kate Genet, a New Zealand writer passionate about immersive and authentic stories of strong women who love other women. She lives in Dunedin, New Zealand with her American wife Valerie. Kate also writes contemporary romances under the name Ana McKenzie. If you enjoyed this book, please look for other titles by Ana McKenzie, Lily Hammond and Kate Genet (some of them are listed on the next page), and subscribe to the Sapphica Books mailing list for poetry, short stories, Lily Hammond postcards, and to hear about new releases, sales, and monthly giveaways of books and swag.